COLD BLOOD

COLD BLOOD

EDITED BY

RICHARD T. CHIZMAR

MARK V. ZIESING
SHINGLETOWN, CA
1991

Dustjacket design by Arnie Fenner.
Dustjacket painting by and © 1991 Nancy Niles.
Frontispiece and endpaper artwork and interior
hand lettering by and © 1991 Arnie Fenner.
All other interior typography produced at
Watson Creative Solutions, P.O. Box 4674, Englewood, Colorado 80155.
Interior book design by Andy Watson and Arnie Fenner.

Trade Edition ISBN 0-929480-57-0
Signed & Limited Edition ISBN 0-929480-58-9
Library of Congress No. 90-072038

FIRST EDITION
10 9 8 7 6 5 4 3 2 1

Published by
MARK V. ZIESING, P.O. BOX 76, SHINGLETOWN, CA 96088

For my parents,
William and Olga Chizmar,
For turning the pages and lighting the way.

ACKNOWLEDGMENTS

Sincere and heartfelt thanks to:

A wonderful "family" of supporters: Mary, Glenn, and Andrea Wilson; Nancy, John, Kim, Richard, and Jessica Chizmar; Laura Hammel, and all of the Tiptons.

To all the *COLD BLOOD* contributors; for trusting enough to offer their very best.

Mark Ziesing; for being everything a good publisher and a good friend is supposed to be—and much more.

Dave Hinchberger and *The Overlook Connection*; for his friendship and enthusiasm.

Richard Gallagher; for his guidance and his books—both of which meant so very much to me.

Frank Mezzanotte; for sharing his wisdom.

Brian Anderson, Bill Caughron, Bob Crawford, Bob Eiring, and Steve Sines; for years of friendship.

Jimmy Cavanaugh; for making my childhood an endless summer afternoon, full of fun and adventure . . . a special time I'll never forget.

Max; for making me smile.

And, of course, to Kara—for knowing me better than I know myself.

TABLE OF CONTENTS

FOREWORD
RICHARD T. CHIZMAR

COLD BLOOD: New Tales of Mystery & Horror is—by title and content—a cross-genre anthology. Read just a few of the following stories and you'll discover this fact quickly enough for yourself. The short stories and novelettes found within this volume are, what I prefer to call, tales of "dark mystery"—a powerful blend of horror, mystery, and/or suspense fiction.

The tales are a varied lot. Psychological and supernatural; graphic and subtle; mysterious and horrific—it's all here. Admittedly, some of the tales are much darker and disturbing than others. A few manage to read outrageously humorous as well as frightening, while others are as dark and grim as cold-blooded murder. The final decision on all the stories is, of course, your own.

Before Douglas E. Winter, a gentleman commonly referred to as "the conscience of horror" takes center stage and properly introduces this book, allow me to add that this is Volume One in a proposed series of *Cold Blood* anthologies. So perhaps, in time, we will meet again. . . .

Richard T. Chizmar
Edgewood, Maryland
October 1990

INTRODUCTION
DOUGLAS E. WINTER

COLD BLOOD: "Used in common parlance to designate
a willful, deliberate, and premeditated homicide."
—Black's Law Dictionary

Tonight I am going to kill someone.

    I wrote those words not so very long ago, while sitting
in my room at the Stanley Hotel, high in the Rocky Mountains. The sun was setting on a day that was grey and wet with
rain. My wife, well aware of my intent, napped peacefully in
the bed behind me. The Stanley had inspired Steve King to
write *The Shining*, and though now only creaky floorboards
and motes of dust haunted its corridors, it seemed an appropriate place to ponder the prospect of murder.

In less than an hour, I would be reading a new short story, "Less Than Zombie," to a conference of readers and writers of horror fiction. I wanted to say something before-hand—words of explanation . . . and expiation. My story was constructed entirely around its nasty climax: the slow and brutal murder of a young woman on the streets of Los Angeles. I had planned her death with loving care, and in a matter of minutes, I was going to kill her before an audience of two hundred people, then fold up my manuscript, smile and walk away. Free. But not innocent.

The story had started off as a lark: Asked by John Skipp and Craig Spector to contribute to their ultraviolent "living dead" anthology, *The Book of the Dead*, I thought almost immediately of satirizing Bret Easton Ellis, whose *Less Than Zero* I'd often called, with tongue firmly in cheek, the best zombie novel of the Eighties. Why not take that book to its inevitable conclusion, while indulging in the pleasures of Ellis's deadpan, flood-of-consciousness style?

Writing the story proved unnervingly easy; once I had moved Ellis's disaffected teens into the world of *Night of the Living Dead*, they seemed to know exactly where to go, what to do and say. The words came so quickly that I felt like a helpless confessor for the darker inhabitants of my subcon-scious, spilling a nihilistic blur of sex and death onto the page without pause. Certainly I was not comfortable with what I found typed beneath my name: A grim fairy tale about murderous indifference, in which the zombies who inhabit the films of George A. Romero and Lucio Fulci were more alive, more sympathetic, than my lost and empty souls, whose cups had run over with blood.

The æsthetic had been suggested by a book about a new and controversial form of psychotherapy in which sexual deviants were overexposed to the imagery of their deviance. Thus erstwhile therapists would plunge pedophiles into a nirvana of child pornography until they were presumably bored into submission. Whether they were "cured" is of course open to question; but the parallels to our couch potato culture of one-way information overload seemed inescapable: In a world increasingly lacking for dialogue, is it not possible that, sitting mesmerized by the latest music video or sitcom or splatter film, we are, in Neil Postman's words, amusing ourselves to death? Being stimulated into zombiedom?

Sam Peckinpah's *The Wild Bunch* is one of my favorite films. Although an elegiac masterpiece about the death of the West—and the death of the Western film—what is most striking, and most remembered, about *The Wild Bunch* is its sense for the fearsome beauty of violence. Particularly in its final setpiece, Peckinpah choreographed what was at once a beautiful and brutal ballet, whose images of death literally were transcendent. I've seen *The Wild Bunch* countless times, but I've never shaken the experience of once having a filmgoer in front of me begin suddenly to shudder with joy in the film's closing minutes, gasping at each bullet impact and each exploding wound in murmurs of nearly sexual frenzy. I wanted the readers of "Less Than Zombie" to share in that experience—to see themselves, as consumers of the violence of horror, in the worst possible light—and to begin to question themselves and their motives in pursuing this kind of entertainment, even as they questioned those of its creators.

In "Less Than Zombie" my characters visit a peculiar sort of after hours club, pursuing visual horrors beyond those available on video. I pushed the imagery into a realm of violence that I had never before explored in my fiction: The narrator of my story was a watcher, a voyeur, and I wanted the reader to be there with him, behind his eyes, watching, feeling, enjoying . . .

That night in Colorado, some people left in the middle of the reading; others were visibly upset. I was, too. When I was finished, there was applause, but that only made me wonder.

I changed nothing. When the story later appeared in *The Book of the Dead*, and then was reprinted in Paul

Sammon's pæan to the Literature of Assault, *Splatterpunks*, there were reviews—a rare treat for a short story. The *Village Voice*, delighted with the prospect of an Ellis sendup, embraced "Less Than Zombie" as an antic jest while vilifying most other writers of the "splatter" æsthetic. The *Washington Post* lauded me, in typically backhanded fashion, as "not especially misogynistic." Tyson Blue, who was there on the night of the reading, wrote that the story was "repulsively brilliant."

I find cold comfort in these reviews, or in the words of those friends and readers who say that they like the story. I didn't much like "Less Than Zombie" when it was written, and I can't say that I like it now. Technically, it's fine. Thematically, it hurts . . . even now, nearly two years after it was written.

For the first time in my writing, I truly felt that I had killed. That it was justifiable homicide—intended to make a point—did not obliterate the fact that it was willful, deliberate, premeditated.

In cold blood.

Let's not mince words: What you are holding is a book about violence and death. As Joe Bob Briggs has been known to say: Heads will roll. It's not going to be pretty. But if you've come this far along on the ride, you should know better. The title and the cover and the table of contents and even this introduction are fair warning. No one is forcing you to be here. Reading fiction is an act of complicity. If I am to be indicted for committing murder, dear reader, then you too are going to take the fall.

So: Why *are* you here? Chance, perhaps . . . or what Madison Avenue types like to call an "impulse purchase": This is the book that happened to catch your eye while you were standing in the checkout line or waiting at the airport terminal. Not likely. Even if that *is* what happened, you are here by choice. You selected this book—or at least this *kind* of book—for a reason, if only because it seemed to speak to you in a certain way, to fill some kind of need. Perhaps it was simply the need to pass some time, to be distracted, to be entertained. Perhaps it's something else . . . something you'd rather not talk about. Or even think about. Perhaps it's because you *like* these kinds of stories.

Does that bother you? It should. The taking of life is probably the paramount dramatic image of our time. Certainly it is the fulcrum of our entertainment: from the sublime of David Lynch's "Twin Peaks" to the most ridiculous of cop-show formulas, murder sets the scene and closes the final curtain. Media watchdogs claim that an average American, sitting in gape-mouthed worship before the altar of television, will witness more than one million mock murders before reaching the age of 25. Our movie screens likewise have become an abattoir of the imagination: The past summer's crop of films—*Total Recall* and the sequels to *Robocop*, *Predator*, and *Die Hard*, among many others—were littered with body counts so high as to make Peckinpah look like a minimalist. Add in the daily news footage, and then the dementia of tabloid TV and "America's Most Wanted," which twist true crime into entertainment. In the age of CNN, even war is packaged like a media event, with its own logos and sound bites and personality parades—now even our bombs have video cameras.

The violence in what is fast becoming our only window onto reality—the electronic screen—is not so much gratuitous or pointless as it is inevitable. Popular entertainment is nothing less than a mirror of society . . . and with each passing day, it looks increasingly like Nietzche's abyss. These are, after all, the 1990s: The decade when Charlie Manson is eligible for parole, while the Supreme Court ponders such weighty questions as whether nude dancing is protected by the First Amendment. I live in a state where it is easier to purchase firearms than to rent X-rated videos; I work in our nation's capital—of politics and of crime, a city whose murder rate has doubled within three years and shows no sign of relenting.

The cracks in our society are showing. Like Humpty Dumpty, somewhere, sometime, perhaps not so very long ago, we fell off the wall. And we can't seem to put our world back together, reassemble the Fifties or some other placid Golden Age.

It is ironic, then, that most arguments against horror as entertainment concern its imagery, not its ideas: The problem with "splatter" film and fiction is not the message (which is often quite conservative, if not reactionary) but the insistent messiness: They are pursued by self-styled moralists with all the ardor of a mother fussing over a impulsive child, insisting that she grow up.

Let's put aside the fact that those who criticize the imagery of horror willingly embrace that imagery when presented in other contexts: when the network interrupts its program for a special news report or the traffic slows at the sight of an automobile crash, or when the reader turns the pages of *Guns & Ammo* or the Bible. The imagery, we are told, is immature; foulmouthed; irreverent; immoral; sexist; not politically correct. That this opposition is often well-intentioned makes it all the more beguiling. Take Donald Wildmon, that champion of "family values" whose perverted concept of Christianity justifies economic boycotts against corporations that choose to advertise in *Playboy*. Or the women's movement, whose quest for "equal rights" has triggered occasional witch hunts and repression unknown since the glory days of Senator McCarthy.

If horror is not the most mature or moral or well-mannered of fictions, certainly it is the most truthful. Horror *is* in bad taste. It is not politically correct, or morally correct, because that is the *point* of this literature: To attempt to come to grips with the things that are wrong about our world and about ourselves.

The world is a messy place. Corpses are not squeaky

clean. Bullets tear and explode flesh and bone. Parents abuse their children. Sex can kill. Yet in pursuit of morality, too often we have argued for dishonesty: that there are certain things that we or our children should not see. Our morality (including, not the least, our attitude toward women) thus is powered by that most simplistic of taboos—the puritan notion that what we can't see won't hurt us.

There is of course some logic to this stance: Sometimes images are so overpowering that all hope is lost; the reader or viewer can react only with a single emotion—revulsion or disgust. But sometimes images are so powerful that they are liberating, a tearing away of the veil. There is no bright line of the sort that the Motion Picture Association of America would dictate through its ratings system: We constantly redefine the limits of our art and entertainment. Hitchcock's *Psycho* was groundbreaking because it showed a toilet; Bergman's *Scenes from a Marriage* because it depicted a woman using one; Pynchon's *Gravity's Rainbow* because of its descent into one; King's *IT* because a monster exploded out of one.

The maxim that a picture may be worth a thousand words presumes a society that not simply can see, but also can understand, the picture. I fear that ours is quickly losing its ability to understand—that, lost in the glow of the electronic screen, we are becoming people who are unable to distinguish words from ideas, ideas from actions, actions from causes, causes from symptoms, symptoms from solutions. We are becoming a society of surfaces, where a picture is worth only a picture, and words, whether one or a thousand, are obsolete. These are not the impulses of an Orwellian world, but a Falwellian one, urging us ever on toward a brain-dead, common denominator, white bread society: zombiedom.

Too often horror—particularly in its more violent incarnations—has joined in this parade, its stories succumbing to the temptations of surface: thus we have film and fiction that is nothing but a show of force, an exercise at creating a bigger and better fireworks display until there is nothing to celebrate but the fireworks themselves.

Pornography is not pernicious for the usual, and obvious, reasons espoused by self-styled moralists—its depiction of nudity and that most natural of human endeavors, sex. The problem with pornography is its insistent reduction of human sexuality to impersonal machine-like patterns. It is an art of the forbidden that has become so focused on the forbidden that it shows that one thing, to the exclusion of all else . . .

Is this the fate of horror?

There is no murder.
We make murder, and it matters only to us.

In the closing pages of Thomas Harris's brilliant *Red Dragon*, his scarred sleuth, Will Graham, contemplates the loveliness and terror that is Shiloh, its modern greens and golds belying the blood red battlefield where in April 1862 so many tens of thousands died in a matter of hours. Graham is supremely capable of solving crime, just as Harris is capable of writing about it, because each is capable of killing. They make murder, and it matters to them.

As writers and readers of horror fiction, we likewise are not innocent. We do what we do for a reason. If that reason is merely to find entertainment, then surely we are lost. "We make murder, and it matters only to us." When it does not matter, when we no longer care, then we are no longer humans. We are not even zombies . . . but something less.

When we care, this fiction of fear and death is our way of exercising darker emotions, of knowing the capability of the human animal to do evil things. Unlike the wayward evangelist, we should not deny these emotions; nor should we condemn them. We need to embrace them if we are to understand. In their truths shall we find our answers . . . or at least new questions to ask.

Thus when Will Graham looks out over the beauty and brutality of Shiloh, he sees there the healing potential that is horror:

"He wondered if, in the great body of humankind, in the minds of men set on civilization, the vicious urges we control in ourselves and the dark instinctive knowledge of those urges function like the crippled virus the body arms against.

"He wondered if old, awful urges are the virus that makes vaccine."

Like Will Graham, I wonder. But I also believe.

Our obsession with murder as entertainment is nothing new. We can trace the idea of it, at least in its contemporary form, to that most tragic and tortured of American literary talents, Edgar Allan Poe, who fathered both the modern horror story and the modern mystery. Most standard editions of Poe are entitled *Tales of Mystery and Imagination*, and rightly so: There is little of the supernatural in his writing. Poe's horrors were very personal and intensely human, his fiction driven by the pathology of guilt. "The Tell-Tale Heart," for example, is as double-edged as its title. Most readers understand, if only instinctively, that it is less a story about supernatural revenge than one of the triumph of the conscience of the heart over the cunning of the head. Even that most baroque of Poe's fictions, "The Masque of the Red Death," speaks of death by bureaucratic neglect, and remains as powerful a commentary today as when it was first published nearly 150 years ago: Indeed, George A. Romero once proposed to film the story, using AIDS as the plague from which the powerful strive so futilely to hide.

The most influential of Poe's tales deserves special note, for it is the story in which horror and mystery were wed. "The Murders in the Rue Morgue" first appeared in the April 1841 issue of *Graham's Magazine* of Philadelphia. This tale of "ratiocination" introduced the world's first fictional detective, C. Auguste Dupin, and, in the words of no less an authority than Dorothy L. Sayers, "constitutes in itself almost a complete manual of detective theory . . . " The elements of

Poe's story, then unique, are now utterly familiar: the eccentric amateur criminologist and his worshipful assistant; the crime that baffles the police; the innocent suspect; the locked room; and, of course, the surprise solution. Although Sir Arthur Conan Doyle, creator of the indomitable Sherlock Holmes, contended that Poe had left detective story writers "with no fresh ground they can confidently call their own," he was uncommonly generous in his remarks. Certainly Doyle, and others since, have made that ground their own.

Perhaps the only surprise is that the paths of mystery and horror should diverge so quickly in the years that followed. Today these books are shelved on different racks, and each, it would seem, has its own set of conventions and formulas, images and ideas. Yet when the twain do meet, the results are often memorable. Consider, for example, that the true crimes of Edward Gein spawned *Psycho* in book and film; that Fredric Brown's *The Screaming Mimi* inspired *L'uccello dalle piume di cristallo (The Bird with the Crystal Plumage)* and thus the career of Dario Argento; that John Franklin Barden and Jim Thompson and Robert Bloch begat Thomas Harris; and that, as if reaching full circle, Clive Barker would choose to write of "New Murders in the Rue Morgue."

And now, we have the stories of *Cold Blood*.

Richard T. Chizmar is the editor of the quarterly magazine *Cemetery Dance*. In its pages, he has championed the fiction of fear in its myriad incarnations, from monsters and mayhem to more subtle, shadowed screams. Now, in his first book, *Cold Blood*, he has assembled some of the best writers in the field and tried to focus them on the issue of murder. The result is a collection of what Richard calls "dark mystery," in which supernatural elements are downplayed, and often dispensed with entirely, in favor of the more personal horrors of which Poe spoke so profoundly.

In a time when the "horror" story is too often characterized by its icons—creatures and crucifixes, small towns and sinister scientists—this anthology is a welcome change of pace. At its best moments, it rejects some of the more recent notions of horror as a *genre* of the fantastic and revisits its more worldly antecedents. Among its wonderful curiosities are "Home Repairs," in which F. Paul Wilson continues the adventures of his anti-detective, Repairman Jack; John Shirley's delirious "Jody and Annie On TV"; the stageplay version of Joe R. Lansdale's cut-throat brilliant "By Bizarre Hands"; Nancy A. Collins's unearthing of the dark damp dirt of Southern decadence, "How It Was with the Kraits"; Tom Monteleone's truly twisted "Love Letters"; and an excerpt from Ramsey Campbell's novel-in-progress, *The Count of Eleven*. Along the way you will find contributions from other veterans and newcomers alike, all gathered together for a single, time-honored cause.

Tonight it is their turn to kill.

—Douglas E. Winter
Alexandria, VA
March 1991

COLD BLOOD

F. PAUL WILSON *crosses genres with his fiction as well as anyone. Read* The Keep, The Tomb, *and* Black Wind *and see if you don't agree. Wilson returns to a favorite character, Repairman Jack, in the following tale of domestic terror, an exceptionally "dark" example of dark mystery.*

HOME REPAIRS
F. PAUL WILSON

The developer didn't look like Donald Trump.

He was older, for one thing—mid-fifties, at least—and fat and balding to boot. And nowhere near as rich. One of the biggest land developers on Long Island, as he was overly fond of saying. Rich, but not Trump-rich.

And he was sweating. Jack wondered if Donald Trump sweated. The Donald might perspire, but Jack couldn't imagine him sweating.

This guy's name was Oscar Schaffer and he was upset about the meeting place.

"I expected we'd hold this conversation in a more private venue," he said.

Jack watched him pull a white handkerchief from

his pocket and blot the moisture from a forehead that went on almost forever. Supposedly Schaffer had started out as a construction worker who'd got into contracting and then had gone on to make a mint in custom homes. Despite occasional words like venue, his speech still carried echoes of the streets. He carried a handkerchief too. Jack couldn't think of anyone he knew who carried a handkerchief—who *owned* a handkerchief.

"This is private," Jack said, glancing at the empty booths and tables around them. "Julio's isn't a breakfast place." Voices drifted over from the bar area on the far side of the six-foot divider topped with dead plants. "Unless you drink your breakfast."

Julio came strutting around the partition carrying a coffee pot. His short, forty-year-old frame was grotesquely muscled under his tight, sleeveless shirt. He was freshly shaven, his mustache trimmed to a line, drafting-pencil thin; his wavy hair was slicked back. He reeked of some new brand of cologne, more cloying than usual.

Jack coughed as the little man refilled his cup and poured one for Schaffer without asking.

"God, Julio. What *is* that?"

"The smell? It's brand new. Called Midnight."

"Maybe that's when you're supposed to wear it."

He grinned. "Naw. Chicks love it, man."

Only if they've spent the day in a chicken coop, Jack thought but kept it to himself.

"Is that decaf?" Schaffer asked. "I only drink decaf."

"Don't have any," Julio said as he finished pouring. He strutted back to the bar.

"I can see why the place is deserted," Schaffer said, glancing at Julio's retreating form. "That guy's downright rude."

"It doesn't come naturally to him. He's been practicing lately."

"Yeah? Well somebody ought to see that the owner gets wise to him."

"He is the owner."

"Really?" Schaffer mopped his brow again. "I tell you, if I owned this place, I'd—"

"But you don't. And we're not here to talk about the tavern business. Or are we?"

"No." Schaffer suddenly became fidgety. "I'm not so sure about this anymore."

"It's okay. You can change your mind. No hard feelings."

A certain small percentage of customers who got this far developed cold feet when the moment came to tell Repairman Jack exactly what they wanted him to fix for them. Jack didn't think Schaffer would back out now. He wasn't the type. But he'd probably want to dance a little first.

"You're not exactly what I expected," Schaffer said.

"I never am."

Usually they expected either a glowering Charles Bronson-type character or a real sleazo. And usually someone bigger. No one found Jack's wiry medium frame, longish brown hair, and mild brown eyes particularly threatening. It used to depress him.

"But you look like a . . . yuppie."

Jack glanced down at his dark blue Izod sports shirt, beige slacks, brown loafers, sockless feet.

"We're on the Upper West Side, Mr. Schaffer. Yuppie Rome. And when in Rome . . . "

Schaffer nodded grimly.

"It's my brother-in-law. He's beating up on my sister."

"Seems like there's a lot of that going around."

People rarely sought out Jack for domestic problems, but this wouldn't be the first wife-beater he'd been asked to handle. He thought of Julio's sister. Her husband had been pounding on her. That was how Jack had met Julio. They'd been friends ever since.

"Maybe so. But I never thought it would happen to Ceilia. She's so . . . " His voice trailed off.

Jack said nothing. This was the time to keep quiet and listen. This was when he got a real feel for the customer.

"I just don't understand it. Gus seemed like such a good guy when they were dating and engaged. I liked him. An accountant, white collar, good job, clean hands, everything I wanted for Ceil. I helped him get his job. He's done well. But he beats her." Schaffer's lips thinned as they drew back over his teeth. "Dammit, he beats the shit out of her. And you know what's worse? She takes it! She's put up with it for ten years!"

"There are laws," Jack said.

"Right. Sure there are. But you've got to sign a complaint. Ceil won't do that. She defends him, says he's under a lot of pressure and sometimes he just loses control. She says most of the time it's her fault because she gets him mad, and she shouldn't get him mad. Can you *believe* that shit? She came over my place one night, two black eyes, a swollen jaw, red marks around her throat from where he was choking her. I lost it. I charged over their place ready to kill him with my bare hands. He's a big guy, but I'm tough. And I'm sure he's never been in a fight with someone who punches back. When I arrived screaming like a madman, he was ready for me. He had a couple of neighbors there and he was standing inside his front door with a baseball bat. Told me if I tried anything he'd defend himself, then call the cops and press charges for assault and battery. I told him if he came anywhere near my sister again, he wouldn't have an unbroken bone left in his body to dial the phone with!"

"Sounds like he knew you were coming."

"He did! That's the really crazy part! He knew because Ceil had called from my place to warn him! And the next day he sends her roses, says how much he loves her, swears it'll never happen again, and she rushes back to him like he's done her a big favor. Can you beat that?"

"Nothing to keep you from getting a bat of your own and waiting in an alley or a parking lot."

"Don't think I haven't thought of it. But I've already threatened him—in front of witnesses. Anything happens to him, I'll be number one suspect. And I can't get involved in anything like that, in a felony. I mean I've got my own family to consider, my business. I want to leave something for my kids. I do Gus, I'll end up in jail, Gus'll sue me for everything I'm worth, my wife and kids will wind up in a shelter somewhere while Gus moves into my house. Some legal system!"

Jack waited through a long pause. It was a familiar Catch-22—one that kept him in business.

Schaffer finally said, "I guess that's where you come in."

Jack took a sip of his coffee.

"I don't know how I can help you. Busting him up isn't going to change things. It sounds like your sister's got as big a problem as he does."

"She does. I've talked to a couple of doctors about it. It's called co-dependency or something like that. I don't pretend to understand it. I guess the best thing that could happen to Ceil is Gus meeting with some sort of fatal accident."

"You're probably right," Jack said.

Schaffer stared at him. "You mean you'll . . . ?"

Jack shook his head. "No."

"But I thought—"

"Look. Sometimes I make a mistake. If that happens, I like to be able to go back and fix it."

Schaffer's expression flickered between disappointment and relief, finally settling on relief.

"You know," he said with a small smile, "as much as I'd like Gus dead, I'm glad you said that. I mean, if you'd said okay, I think I'd have set you to it." He shook his head and looked away. "Kind of scary what you can come to."

"She's your sister. Someone's hurting her. You want him stopped but you can't do it yourself. Not hard to understand how you feel."

"Can you help?"

Jack drained his coffee and leaned back. Past the pots of dead brown plants hanging in the smudged front window he could see smartly dressed women wheeling their children, or white-uniformed nannies wheeling other people's children in the bright morning sunlight.

"I don't think so. Domestic stuff is too complicated to begin with, and this situation sounds like it's gone way past complicated into the twilight zone. Not my thing. Not the situation my kind of services can help."

"I know what you're saying. I know they need shrinks— at least Ceil does. Gus . . . I don't know. I think he's beyond therapy. I got the feeling Gus *likes* beating up on Ceil. Likes it too much to quit, no matter what. But I want to give it a try."

"Doesn't strike me as the type who'll go see a shrink because you or anyone else says so."

"Yeah. But if he was hospitalized . . . " Schaffer raised his eyebrows, inviting Jack to finish the thought.

Jack was thinking it was a pretty dumb thought as Julio returned with the coffee pot. He refilled Jack's but Schaffer held a hand over his.

"Say," Schaffer said, pointing to all the dead vegetation around the room, "did you ever think of watering your plants?"

"Wha' for?" Julio said. "They're all dead."

The developer's eyes widened. "Oh. Right. Of course." As Julio left, he leaned over the table toward Jack. "Is there some significance to all these dead plants?"

"Nothing religious. It's just that Julio isn't happy with the caliber of his clientele lately."

"Well he's not going to raise it with these dead plants."

"No. You don't understand. He wants to lower it. The yuppies have discovered this place and they've been swarming here. He's been trying to get rid of them. This has

always been a working man's bar and eatery. The Beamer
crowd is scaring off the old regulars. Julio and his help are
rude as hell to them but they just lap it up. He let all the
window plants die, and they think it's great. It's driving the
poor guy nuts."

"He doesn't seem to mind you."

"We go back a long way."

"Really? How—"

"Let's get back to your brother-in-law. You really
think if he was laid up in a hospital bed for a while, a victim
of violence himself, he'd have a burst of insight and ask for
help?"

"It's worth a try."

"No, it isn't. Save your money."

"Well, then, if he doesn't see the light, I could clue
his doctor in and maybe arrange to have one of the hospital
shrinks see him while he's in traction."

"You really think that'll change anything?"

"I don't know. I've got to try something short of
killing him."

"And what if those somethings don't work?"

His face went slack, his eyes bleak.

"Then I'll have to find a way to take him out of the
picture. Permanently. Even if I have to do it myself."

"I thought you were worried about your family and
your business."

"She's my sister, dammit!"

Jack thought about his own sister, the pediatrician.
He couldn't imagine anyone beating up on her. At least not
more than once. She had a brown belt in karate and didn't
take guff from anyone. She'd either kick the crap out of you
herself or call their brother, the judge, and submerge you to
your lower lip in an endless stream of legal hot water. Or both.

But if she were a different sort, and somebody was
beating up on her, repeatedly . . .

"All right," Jack said. "I know I'll regret this, but I'll

look into it. I'm not promising anything, but I'll see if there's anything I can do."

"Hey, thanks. Thanks a—"

"It's half down and half when I've done the job."

Schaffer paused, his expression troubled.

"But you haven't agreed to take the job yet."

"It might take me weeks to learn what I need to know to make that decision."

"What do you need to know? How about—?"

"We're not practicing the Art of the Deal here. Those are the terms. Take it or leave it."

Jack was hoping he'd leave it. And for a moment it looked as if he might.

"You're asking me to bet on a crapshoot—blind-folded. You hold all the aces."

"You're mixing metaphors, but you've got the picture."

Schaffer sighed. "What the hell." He reached into his breast pocket, then slapped an envelope down on the table. "Okay! Here it is."

Without hiding his reluctance, Jack tucked the envelope inside his shirt without opening it. He removed a notepad and pencil from his hip pocket.

"All right. Let's get down to the who and where."

Jack rubbed his eyes as he sat on the lawn chair and waited for the Castlemans to come home. His third night here and so far he hadn't seen a hint of anything even remotely violent. Or remotely interesting. These were not exciting people. On the plus side, they had no kids, no dog, and their yard was rimmed with trees and high shrubs. Perfect for surveillance.

On Monday, Ceil had come home from teaching fifth grade at the local suburban Long Island elementary school. She entered their two-story, center-hall colonial, turned the TV on, and poured herself a stiff vodka. A thin, mousy, brittle-looking woman whose hair was a few shades too blonde to be anyone's natural color. She watched a soap for an hour, during which she smoked three cigarettes and downed another vodka. Then she started slicing and dicing for dinner. Around five-thirty, Gus Castleman came in from a hard day of accounting at Borland Industries. A big guy, easily six-four, two-fifty; crew-cut red hair, round face, and narrow blue eyes. A bulging gut rode side-saddle on his belt buckle. He peeled off his suit coat and grunted hello to Ceil as he went straight to the refridge. He pulled out two Bud Lights and sat down before Eyewitness News. When dinner was ready he came to the kitchen table and they ate watching the TV. After dinner there was more TV. Gus fell asleep around ten. Ceil woke him up after the 11:00 news and they both went to bed.

Tuesday was the same.

On Wednesday, Ceil came home and had her vodkas in front of *Santa Barbara* but didn't slice and dice. Instead she changed into a dress and drove off. When Gus didn't show up, Jack assumed she was meeting him for dinner. Almost eleven o'clock now and they weren't back yet. Jack hung on and waited.

Waiting. That was always the lousy part. But Jack made a point of being sure about anyone before he did a fix. After all, people lied. Jack lied to most people every day. Schaffer could be lying about Gus, might want him laid up for something that had nothing to do with his sister. Or Ceil might be lying to her brother, might be telling him it was Gus who gave her those bruises when all along it was some guy she'd been seeing on the side. Jack needed to be sure Gus was the bad guy before he made a move on him.

So far Gus was just boring. That didn't rate hospital-level injuries.

At the sound of a car in the driveway, Jack slipped out of the lawn chair and eased into the foundation shrubbery around the garage. The car parked on the driveway. He recognized Gus's voice as they got out of the car.

"... just wish you hadn't said that, Ceil. It made me feel real bad in front of Dave and Nancy."

"But no one took it the way you did," Ceil said.

Jack thought he detected a slight quaver in her voice. Too many vodkas? Or fear?

"Don't be so sure about that. I think they're just too good-mannered to show it, but I saw the shock in Nancy's eyes. Didn't you see the way she looked at me when you said that?"

"No. I didn't see anything of the sort. You're imagining things again."

"Oh, am I?"

"Y-yes. And besides, I've already apologized a dozen times since we left. What more do you want from me?"

Jack heard the front storm door open.

"What I want, Ceil, is that it not keep happening like it does. Is that too much to ask?"

Ceil's reply was cut off as the door closed behind them. Jack returned to the rear of the house where he could get a view of most of the first floor. Their voices leaked out through an open casement window over the kitchen sink as Gus strode into the kitchen.

"... don't know why you keep doing this to me, Ceil. I try to be good, try to keep calm, but you keep testing me, pushing me to the limit again and again."

Ceil's voice came from the hall, overtly anxious now.

"But I told you, Gus. You're the only one who took it that way."

Jack watched Gus pull an insulated pot-holder mitten over his left hand, then wrap a dish towel around his right.

"Fine, Ceil. If that's what you want to believe, I guess you'll go on believing it. But unfortunately, that won't change what happened tonight."

Ceil came into the kitchen.

"But Gus—"

Her voice choked off as he turned toward her and she saw his hands.

"Why'd you do it, Ceil?"

"Oh, Gus, no! Please! I didn't mean it!"

She turned to run but he caught her upper arm and pulled her toward him.

"You should have kept your mouth shut, Ceil. I try so hard and then you go and get me mad."

He saw Gus take Ceil's wrist in his mittened hand and twist her arm behind her back, twist it up hard and high. She cried out in pain.

"Gus, please don't!"

Jack didn't want to see this, but he had to watch. Had to be sure. Gus pressed her flat chest up against the side of the refrigerator. Her face was toward Jack. There was fear there, terror, dread, but overriding it all was a sort of dull acceptance of the inevitable that reached into Jack's center and twisted.

Gus began ramming his padded fist into Ceil's back, right below the bottom ribs, left side and right, pummeling her kidneys. Her eyes squeezed shut and she grunted in pain with each impact.

"I hate you for making me do this," Gus said.

Sure you do, you son of a bitch.

Jack gripped the window sill and closed his eyes. He heard Ceil's repeated grunts and moans and felt her pain. He'd been kidney punched before. He knew her agony. But this had to end soon. Gus would vent his rage and it would all be over. For the next few days Ceil would have stabbing back pains every time she took a deep breath or coughed, and would urinate bright red blood, but there'd be hardly a mark on her, thanks to the mitten and the towel-wrapped fist.

It *had* to end soon.

But it didn't. Jack looked again and saw that Ceil's knees had gone rubbery but Gus was supporting her with the arm lock, still methodically pummeling her.

Jack growled under his breath. All he'd wanted was to witness enough to confirm Schaffer's story. That done, he'd deal with dear sweet Gus outside the home. Maybe in a dark parking lot while Schaffer made sure he had an air-tight alibi. He hadn't counted on a scene like this, but he'd known it was a possibility. The smart thing to do in this case would be to walk away, but he'd been pretty sure he wouldn't be able to do that. So he'd come prepared.

Jack hurried across the back patio and grabbed his duffel bag. As he moved around to the far side of the house, he pulled out a nylon stocking and a pair of rubber surgical gloves; he slipped the first over his head and the second over his fingers. Then he removed a .45 automatic, a pair of wire cutters, and a heavy-duty screwdriver. He stuck the pistol in his belt, then used the cutters on the telephone lead, and the screwdriver to pop the latch on one of the living room windows.

As soon as he was in the darkened room, he looked around for something to break. The first thing to catch his eye was the set of brass fire irons by the brick hearth. He kicked the stand over. The clang and clatter echoed through the house.

Gus's voice floated in from the kitchen.

"What the hell was that?"

When Gus arrived and flipped on the lights, Jack was waiting by the window. He almost smiled at the shock on Gus's face.

"Take it easy, man," Jack said. He knew his face couldn't show much anxiety through the stocking mask so he put it all in his voice. "This is all a mistake."

"Who the hell are you? And what're you doing in my house?"

"Listen, man. I didn't think anybody was home. Let's just forget this ever happened."

Gus bent and snatched the poker from the spilled fire irons. He pointed it at Jack's duffel.

"What's in there? What'd you take?"

"Nothing, man. I just got here. And I'm outta here."

"*OhmyGod!*" Ceil's voice, muffled. She stood at the edge of the living room, both hands over her mouth.

"Call the police, Ceil. But tell them not to hurry. I want to teach this punk a lesson before they get here."

As Ceil limped back toward the kitchen, Gus shook off the mitten and the towel and raised the poker in a two-handed grip. His eyes glittered with anticipation. His tight, hard grin told it all. Pounding on his wife had got him up, but he could go only so far with her. Now he had a prowler at his mercy. He could beat the living shit out of this guy with impunity. In fact, he'd be a hero for doing it. His gaze settled on Jack's head like Babe Ruth eyeing a high-outside pitch.

Talking to a psychiatrist was going to turn this guy into a loving husband. Sure.

He took two quick steps toward Jack and swung. No subtlety, not even a feint. Jack ducked and let it whistle over his head. He could have put a wicked chop into Gus's exposed flank then, but he wasn't ready yet. Gus swung the poker back the other way, lower this time. Jack jumped back and resisted planting a foot in the big man's reddening face. Gus's third swing was vertical, from ceiling to floor. Jack was long gone when it arrived.

Gus's teeth were bared now; his breath hissed through them. His eyes were mad with rage and frustration. Jack decided to goose that rage a little. He grinned.

"You swing like a pussy, man."

With a guttural scream, Gus charged, wielding the poker like a scythe. Jack ducked the first swing, then grabbed the poker and rammed his forearm into Gus's face with a satisfying crunch. Gus staggered back, eyes squeezed shut in agony, holding his nose. Blood began to leak between his fingers.

Never failed. No matter how big you were, a broken nose stopped you cold.

Ceil hobbled back to the threshold. Her voice skirted the edge of hysteria.

"The phone's dead!"

"Don't worry, lady," Jack said. "I didn't come here to hurt nobody. And I won't hurt you. But this guy—he's a different story. He tried to kill me."

As Jack dropped the poker and stepped toward him, Gus's eyes bulged with terror. He put out a bloody hand to fend him off. Jack grabbed the wrist and twisted. Gus wailed as he was turned and forced into an arm lock. Jack shoved him against the wall and began a bare-knuckled work-out against his kidneys, wondering if the big man's brain would make a connection between what he'd been dishing out in the kitchen and what he was receiving in the living room. Jack didn't hold back. He put plenty of body behind the punches, and Gus shouted in pain with each one.

How's it feel, tough guy? Like it?

Jack pounded him until he felt some of his own anger dissipate. He was about to let him go and move into the next stage of his plan when he caught a hint of motion behind him. As he turned his head he had a glimpse of Ceil. She had the poker, and she was swinging it toward his head. He started to duck but too late. The room exploded into bright lights, then went dark gray.

An instant of blackness and then Jack found himself on the floor, pain exploding in his gut. He focused above him and saw Gus readying another kick at his midsection. He rolled away toward the corner. Something heavy thunked on the carpet as he moved.

"Christ, he's got a gun!" Gus shouted.

Jack had risen to a crouch by then. He searched for the fallen .45 but Gus was ahead of him, snatching it from the floor before Jack could reach it. Gus stepped back, worked the slide to chamber a round, and pointed the pistol at Jack's face.

"Stay right where you are, you bastard! Don't you move a muscle!"

Jack sat back on the floor in the corner and stared

up at the big man.

"All right!" Gus said with a bloody grin. "All *right!*"

"I got him for you, didn't I, Gus?" Ceil said, still holding the poker. She was bent forward in pain. That swing had cost her. "I got him off you. I saved you, didn't I?"

"Shut up, Ceil."

"But he was hurting you. I made him stop. I—"

"I said *shut up!*"

Her lower lip trembled. "I . . . I thought you'd be glad."

"Why should I be glad? If you hadn't got me so mad tonight I might've noticed he was here when we came in. Then he wouldn't have took me by surprise." He pointed to his swelling nose. "This is your fault, Ceil."

Ceil's shoulders slumped; she stared dully at the floor.

Jack didn't know what to make of Ceil. He'd interrupted a brutal beating at the hands of her husband, yet she'd come to her husband's aid. And valiantly, at that. The gutsy little scrapper who'd wielded that poker seemed miles away from the cowed, beaten creature standing in the middle of the room.

I don't get it.

Which was why he had a policy of refusing home repairs. Except this time.

"I'll go over to the Ferrises'," she said.

"What for?"

"To call the police."

"Hold on a minute."

"Why?"

Jack glanced at Gus and saw how his eyes were flicking back and forth between Ceil and him.

"Because I'm thinking, that's why!"

"Yeah," Jack said. "I can smell the wood burning."

"Hey!" Gus stepped toward Jack and raised the pistol as if to club him. "Another word out of you and—"

"You don't really want to get that close to me, do you?" Jack said softly.

Gus stepped back.

"Gus, I've got to call the police!" Ceil said as she replaced the poker by the fireplace, far out of Jack's reach.

"You're not going anywhere," Gus said. "Get over here."

Ceil meekly moved to his side.

"Not here!" he said, grabbing her shoulder and shoving her toward Jack. "Over there!"

She cried with the pain in her back as she stumbled forward.

"Gus! What are you doing?"

Jack decided to play the game. He grabbed Ceil and turned her around. She struggled but he held her between Gus and himself.

Gus laughed. "You'd better think of something else, fella. That skinny little broad won't protect you from a forty-five."

"Gus!"

"Shut *up!* God, I'm sick of your voice! I'm sick of your face, I'm sick of—God, I'm sick of everything about you!"

Under his hands, Jack could feel Ceil jerk with the impact of the words as if they were blows from a fist. A fist probably would have hurt less.

"But—but Gus, I thought you loved me."

He sneered. "Are you kidding? I hate you, Ceil! It drives me up a wall just to be in the same room with you! Why the hell do you think I beat the shit out of you every chance I get? It's all I can do to keep myself from killing you!"

"But all those times you said—"

"Lies, Ceil. Nothing but lies. And you're such a pathetic wimp you fell for them every time."

"But why?" She was sobbing now. "*Why?*"

"Why not dump you and find a real woman? One

who's got tits and can have kids? The answer should be pretty clear: your brother. He got me into Borland 'cause he's one of their biggest customers. And if you and me go kaput, he'll see that I'm out of there before the ink's dry on our divorce papers. I've put too many years into that job to blow it because of a sack of shit like you."

Ceil almost seemed to shrivel under Jack's hands. He glared at Gus.

"Big man."

"Yeah. I'm the big man. I've got the gun. And I want to thank you for it, fella, whoever you are. Because it's going to solve all my problems."

"What? My gun?"

"Yep. I've got a shitload of insurance on my dear wife here. I bought loads of term on her years ago and kept praying she'd have an accident. I was never so stupid as to try and set her up for something fatal—I know what happened to that Marshall guy in Jersey—but I figured, what the hell, with all the road fatalities around here, the odds of collection on old Ceil were better than Lotto."

"Oh, Gus," she sobbed. An utterly miserable sound.

Her head had sunk until her chin touched her chest. She would have fan-folded to the floor if Jack hadn't been holding her up. He knew this was killing her, but he wanted her to hear it. Maybe it was the alarm she needed to wake her up.

Gus mimicked her. "'Oh, Gus!' Do you have any idea how many rainy nights you got my hopes up when you were late coming home from your card group? How I prayed— actually *prayed*—that you'd skidded off the road and wrapped your car around a utility pole, or that a big semi had run a light and plowed you under? Do you have any *idea?* But no. You'd come bouncing in as carefree as you please, and I'd be so disappointed I'd almost cry. That was when I really wanted to wring your scrawny neck!"

"That's about enough, don't you think?" Jack said.

Gus sighed. "Yeah. I guess it is. But at least all those premiums weren't wasted. Tonight I collect."

Ceil's head lifted.

"What?"

"That's right. An armed robber broke in. During the struggle, I managed to get the gun away from him but he pulled you between us as I fired. You took the first bullet— right in the heart. In a berserk rage, I emptied the rest of the clip into his head. Such a tragedy." He raised the pistol and sighted it on Ceil's chest. "Good-bye, my dear sweet wife."

The metallic click of the hammer was barely audible over Ceil's scream.

Her voice cut off as both she and Gus stared at the pistol. Quickly Gus worked the slide, ejecting the unspent round, and pointed it again at Ceil. This time there was no scream from Ceil. She only flinched at the sound of the falling hammer. Jack allowed two more misfires, then he stepped around Ceil and approached Gus.

Frantically Gus worked the slide and pulled the trigger again, aiming for Jack's face. Another impotent click. He began backing away when he saw Jack's smile.

His dummy pistol. Actually, a genuine government-issue Mark IV, but the bullets were dummy—and so was the guy he usually let get hold of it. Jack brought it along when he wanted to see what somebody was really made of. It rarely failed to draw the worst to the surface.

He bent and picked up the ejected rounds. He held one up for Gus to see.

"The slug is real," Jack said, "but there's no powder in the shell. It's an old rule: Never let an asshole near a loaded gun."

Gus charged, swinging the .45 at Jack's head. Jack caught his wrist and twisted the weapon free of his grasp. Then he slammed it hard against the side of Gus's face, opening a gash. Gus tried to turn and run but Jack still had his arm. He hit him again, on the back of the head this time.

Gus sagged to his knees and Jack put a lot of upper body behind the pistol as he brought it down once more on the top of his head. Gus stiffened, then toppled face first onto the floor.

Only seconds had passed. Jack spun to check on Ceil's whereabouts. She wasn't going to catch him twice. But no worry. She was right where he'd left her, standing in the corner, eyes closed, tears leaking out between the lids.

Nothing Jack wanted more than to be out of this crazy house. He'd been here too long already, but he had to finish this job now, get it done and over with.

He took Ceil's arm and gently led her from the living room.

"Nothing personal, lady, but I've got to put you in a safe place, okay? Someplace where you can't get near a fire poker. Understand?"

"He didn't love me," she said to no one in particular. "He stayed with me because of his job. He was lying all those times he said he loved me."

"I guess he was."

"Lying . . ."

He guided her to a closet in the hall and stood her inside among the winter coats.

"I'm just going to leave you here for a few minutes, okay?"

She was staring straight ahead. "All those years . . . lying . . ."

Jack closed her in the closet and wedged a ladder-back chair between the door and the wall on the other side of the hall. No way she could get out until he removed the chair.

Back in the living room, Gus was still out cold. Jack turned him over and tied his wrists to opposite ends of the coffee table. He took two four-by-four wooden blocks from his duffel and placed them under Gus's left lower leg, one just below the knee and the other just above the ankle. Then he removed a short-handled five-pound iron maul from the duffel. He hesitated as he lifted the hammer, then recalled Ceil's eyes as Gus methodically battered her kidneys—the pain, the resignation, the despair. Jack broke Gus's left shin with one sharp blow. Gus groaned and writhed on the floor, but didn't regain consciousness. Jack repeated the process on the right leg. Then he packed up all his gear and returned to the hall.

He pulled the chair from where it was wedged against the closet door. He opened the door a crack.

"I'm leaving now, lady. When I'm gone you can go across the street and call the police. Better call an ambulance too."

A single sob answered him.

Jack left by the back door. It felt good to get the stocking off his head.

When Jack dialed his answering machine the next morning there was only one message. It was from Oscar Schaffer. He sounded out of breath. And upset.

"You bastard! You sick, perverted bastard! I'm dropping the rest of your money off at that bar this morning and then I don't want to see or hear or even think of you again!"

Jack was on his second coffee in Julio's when he spotted Schaffer through the front window. He was moving fast, no doubt as close to a run as his portly frame would allow, clutching a white envelope in his hand. Perspiration gleamed on his pale forehead. His expression was strained. He looked like one frightened man.

Jack had told Julio he was coming so Julio intercepted him at the door as he did all Jack's customers. But instead of leading him back to the Jack's table, Julio returned alone. Jack spotted Schaffer hurrying back the way he had come.

Julio smiled as he handed Jack the envelope.

"What did you do to spook him like that?"

Jack grabbed the envelope and hurried after Schaffer. He caught the developer as he was opening the door to a dark green Jaguar XJ-12.

"What's going on?" Jack said.

Schaffer jumped at the sound of Jack's voice. His already white face went two shades paler.

"Get away from me!"

He jumped into the car but Jack caught the door before he could slam it. He pulled the keys from Schaffer's trembling fingers.

"I think we'd better talk. Unlock the doors."

Jack went around to the other side and slipped into the passenger seat. He tossed the keys back to Schaffer.

"All right. What's going on? The job's done. The guy's fixed. You didn't need an alibi because it was done by a prowler. What's the problem?"

Schaffer stared straight ahead through the windshield.

"How *could* you? I was so impressed with you the other day. The rogue with a code: 'Sometimes I make a mistake. If that happens, I like to be able to go back and fix it.' I really thought you were something else. I actually envied you. I never dreamed you could do what you did. Gus was a rotten son of a bitch, but you didn't have to . . . " His voice trailed off.

Jack was baffled.

"You were the one who wanted him killed. I only broke his legs."

Schaffer turned to him, the fear in his eyes giving way to fury.

"Don't give me that shit! Who do you think you're dealing with? I practically built that town! I've got connections!" He pulled a sheaf of papers from his pocket and threw it at Jack. "I've read the medical examiner's report!"

"Medical examiner? He's dead?" *Shit!* Jack had

heard of people with broken legs throwing a clot to the heart. "How?"

"Aw, don't play cute! Gus was a scumbag and yes I wanted him dead, but I didn't want him tortured! I didn't want him . . . *mutilated!*"

It was time for Jack's fingers to do a little trembling as he scanned the report. It described a man who'd been pistol-whipped, bound by the hands, and had both tibias broken; then he'd been castrated with a Ginsu knife from his own kitchen and gagged with his testicles in his mouth. After that he'd undergone at least two hours of torture before he died of shock due to blood loss from a severed artery in his neck.

"It'll be in all the afternoon papers," Schaffer was saying. "You can add the clippings to your collection. I'm sure you've got a big one."

"Where was Ceil supposed to be during all this?"

"Locked in the hall closet. She got out after you left. And she had to find Gus like that. No one should have to see something like that. If I could make you pay—"

"When did she phone the cops?"

"Right before calling me—around three a.m."

Jack shook his head. "Wow. Three hours . . . she spent three hours on him."

"'She?' Who?"

"Ceil."

"What the hell are you talking about?"

"Gus was trussed up and out cold with two broken legs but very much alive on the living room floor when I left. I opened the door to the closet where I'd put your sister, and took off. That was around midnight."

"No. You're lying. You're saying Ceil—" He swallowed. "She wouldn't. She couldn't. Besides, she called me at three, from a neighbor's house, she'd only gotten free—"

"Three hours. Three hours between the time I opened the closet door and the time she called you."

"No! Not Ceil! She . . . " Schaffer stared at Jack, and Jack met his gaze evenly. Slowly, like a dark stain seeping through heavy fabric, the truth took hold in his eyes. "Oh . . . my . . . God!"

He leaned back in the seat and closed his eyes. He looked like he was going to be sick. Jack gave him a few minutes.

"The other day you said she needed help. Now she really needs it."

"Poor Ceil!"

"Yeah. I don't pretend to understand it, but I guess she was willing to put up with anything from a man who said he loved her. But when she found out he didn't—and believe me, he let her know in no uncertain terms before he pulled the trigger on her."

"Trigger? What—?"

"A long story. Ceil can tell you about it. But I guess when she found out how much he hated her, how he'd wanted her dead all these years, when she saw him ready to murder her, something must have snapped inside. When she came out of the closet and found him helpless on the living room floor, she must have gone a little crazy."

"A *little* crazy? You call what she did a *little* crazy?"

Jack shrugged. He handed back the ME's report and opened the car door.

"Your sister crammed ten years of pay-back into three hours. She's going to need a lot of help to recover from those ten years. *And* those three hours."

Schaffer pounded his mahogany steering wheel.

"Shit! It wasn't supposed to turn out like this!" Then he sighed and turned to Jack. "But I guess things don't always go according to plan in your business."

"Hardly ever."

Jack got out of the car, closed the door, and listened to the Jag roar to life. As it screeched away, he headed back to Julio's. A new customer was due at noon.

CHET WILLIAMSON *lives in small-town Pennsylvania with his wife and son. He loves jazz and old movies, plays the saxophone in his basement, and writes wonderful novels about very real people. Although he is best known for such acclaimed novels as* Ash Wednesday, Reign, Dreamthorp, *and* McKain's Dilemma, *Williamson has sold over 50 short stories to such diverse markets as* Playboy, The New Yorker, The Magazine of Fantasy and Science Fiction, Twilight Zone, *and* Alfred Hitchcock's Mystery Magazine.

THE BEST PART
CHET WILLIAMSON

The world seemed suddenly hushed. After the futile scream of tires, the crunch and rip of metal, the rattle of glass skittering across the street, and a final thud like a bass drum almost too low to hear, there was a deep, primal silence as nearly as brief as it was complete. It lasted less than a second, but while it held, before the city began to speak again, Del Rivers saw the black face glow.

The boy (or man—he had one of those ageless faces) was standing only a few yards from where the truck had skidded into the car, standing as if nothing out of the ordinary had occurred, standing as if all his life he had seen this kind of thing happen on this street, and now it had simply happened again. Del could swear he saw a smile cross the boy's face before he faded into the gathering crowd.

A sudden impulse came over him to follow the boy, but instead he did what everyone else did, edged closer to the site, watched the trucker slam a beefy shoulder against the jammed door until it popped open and he fell onto the sidewalk.

The woman behind the wheel of the car looked dazed, oblivious to the blood running from her nose, or the cries of the infant strapped into the car seat beside her. No one helped. They only watched, Del among them, thinking that he *should* do something, he would *like* to do something. But he didn't know what. There was no fire, no explosion to drag anyone from. And after all, he was a short order cook, not a doctor. What could he do?

He had read about accidents before, of people standing by, and had thought that it sounded cruel and heartless. But now he understood. What *could* you do? You could wait. That was all.

So they waited, and soon an ambulance came, and everyone was taken care of—the trucker, the mother, the child, all driven away somewhere to be bandaged and healed.

As the red lights winked around the corner, Del continued his walk home from the diner. He wondered again why the boy, who had seemed so intent the moment the accident took place, had disappeared, had chosen to leave the crowd just as it was gathering, when the best part was starting.

The best part.

He heard the words coming into his head and tried to pull them back, but it was too late.

The best part.

The part, he thought, where you see other people hurting, and it's good because it's not you, because when you see somebody bleeding or somebody in pain, then your own hurts don't seem quite as bad, and you can forget how much it aches to see your kid only twice a year, or to have your boss call you a dumb fuck when you drop a skillet of home fries on the floor, or have your landlord tell you the apartment you've lived in for four years is going co-op in a few months. All that stuff isn't important any more, because *this* is what suffering is all about.

So why did the kid leave? Before the best part?

It was a summer Sunday four months later when he saw the boy again. Del was walking down Eighth Avenue between 42nd and 43rd on his way to Ernie's apartment. Ernie was the dishwasher on the evening shift, and he had just bought himself a VCR and joined a video rental club.

"Good deal," he had told Del. "Three bucks to rent a film for two days. Besides, the grind houses been closin' down—you wanta see pussy films, you gotta see 'em at home now. Come on over Sunday afternoon, we'll have some beers, and I'll get a coupla movies. A porno and maybe a Schwarzenegger or something."

It sounded good to Del, who, six-pack under his arm, was looking forward to an afternoon of Budweiser, Arnold punching badasses, and smut. He was even able to ignore the hookers and the homeboys chilling or rapping on the sidewalks, making him step out into the street to get around them.

As he stopped at the corner, he noticed a window washer on a scaffolding eight stories up on a building across the street. *Poor shit. Sunday yet*, he thought. Then he figured that the man was probably drawing double time, and decided he wasn't worth the pity. The light changed, and Del was just about to step off the curb when he saw, diagonally across the intersection, the same boy he had seen at the site of the traffic accident months before.

The boy's hair was cut shorter now, and he wore a plain white t-shirt that displayed a tight if not overly muscular frame. He leaned casually against a shop window, ankles crossed, hands in jean pockets, and slowly let his glaze slide upward to the window washer eight floors above.

Suddenly there was a cry, and when Del swung his head around, he saw a gray streak flash past and turn to red as it struck the pavement. He looked up in disbelief and saw that the scaffold was empty.

The black hush, came, settled, left in the space of a heartbeat, and now people were shouting, some turning around, some looking, coming closer. The boy only cocked his head, uncrossed his ankles, straightened, and started walking east. Del wasn't sure, but he thought he was smiling.

Something in him wanted Del to stay for the best part, to watch until the ambulance came, be there as the man was picked up and loaded into the back. Something else, a soft, small, and unheeded voice, wanted him to walk on to Ernie's place and get drunk and watch strangers have sex. But what he did, what he had to do, was follow the black boy as he sauntered down 42nd toward Broadway, crossing it and moving steadily east.

Del stayed fifty yards behind at all times, ready to enter a store or look in a window if the boy should turn his head. But he didn't, not once. He walked along with the cockiness of youth and the self-assurance that came, Del sensed, from something deeper.

At Fifth Avenue Del thought that maybe he was being foolish, that the feeling he had that the boy was in some way responsible for the two accidents was just stupid. It could have been coincidence, couldn't it? After all, *Del* had been there both times as well. But still, when the boy moved on, Del followed.

The boy turned south on Madison, walked down to 38th, and stopped in the doorway of a travel agency, from where he watched the intersection. Del stepped into a doorway as well. Through a pane of recessed glass he could see down the street far enough to know if the boy left his haven.

He didn't have long to wait. In a few minutes a cab entered the intersection as the light turned red, just in time to meet a Ford Escort whose driver had anticipated his green.

Right fender met left fender at a perfect right angle, bouncing the cars off one another like a billiard shot, and slewing the lighter Escort up onto the sidewalk and into a bus stop sign, which snapped off neatly at its base and toppled like an aluminum sapling onto the car's roof.

As the echoes of metal battling metal faded up and away to become lost in Manhattan's towers, each driver, uninjured, left his vehicle and began to berate the other, but the boy didn't stop to watch. He walked on, Del behind him, sure now, but wanting to see just one more time, to be positive beyond the shadow of any wild and unimaginable series of coincidences.

The boy started moving north again, then west, leisurely strolling the few blocks to Bryant Park. Instead of standing, he sat on a bench near the playground equipment, watching children anywhere from three up to youths nearly his own apparent age swinging, riding seesaws, running, grabbing hold of merry-go-rounds and leaping onto them with the wildness of Apaches vaulting onto saddleless horses. The boy was whistling something, but Del couldn't hear it from behind the fence.

It was nearly a half hour before something happened. If a child had fallen off a sliding board, or lost his grip and dropped into the open maw of the merry-go-round, Del might still have had a doubt. But to see the boy look at the swings, and then to see one of the chains break, throwing its sailor-suited occupant to the ground where she wailed until her mother came scurrying, sweeping her up and away to some overcrowded emergency ward...to see *that* was to *know*.

He followed the boy as he left the park and headed toward the garment district. *Don't get involved*, he had told himself a thousand times in his life. But this was different. Uncanny, impossible, and true. At 35th Street he caught up to the boy, who was obeying the *"Don't Walk"* sign. Del stood beside him, looked directly at him. The boy returned the gaze long enough for Del to see that up close it was a very normal face. There was no expected intensity around the eyes, no stern set of jaw. The boy looked once at Del, then across the street, as if Del were not worthy of further study.

"I've been watching you," said Del in a steady voice.

The boy turned toward him with that sour look with which New Yorkers regard weirdos. But the expression of mild annoyance shifted to one of concern, as if he realized that Del was not a typical street crazy. Then his eyes flicked back to the sign, still commanding, *"Don't Walk."*

"You understand?" Del said, tense, ready to spring back should the boy do something unpredictable. "I've seen what you do. Today. And before. The window washer. The cars. The kid on the swing."

The boy was shaking now, his whole body jittering with nervous tension. Del saw a black pearl of sweat slip down his temple. "Hey man . . . " he said with a half laugh, as if trying to pretend Del was jiving.

"What the hell are you?" Del said, not angry, not vengeful, only very curious, more so than he had ever been in his life. He put a beefy hand on the boy's arm to make him stay. But at the touch the boy panicked, pulled away, and stepped into the street directly in front of a crosstown bus traveling thirty miles an hour.

There was a loud slap when the bus and the boy connected. The pressure kept the boy against the grille as the bus entered the intersection, but when the shocked driver braked and the bus stopped, twenty yards past the point where it had hit him, the boy slid wetly down the front, slipped off and disappeared beneath.

"Oh Christ," Del muttered. "Oh Christ Jesus." He took a few steps toward the bus and the boy lying unseen beneath it, then stopped, sure that the boy was dead. At the moment of impact, he had seen the head break open like a soft cantaloupe.

So he turned and walked the other way, fairly certain that no one had seen him and the boy together, or noticed the boy pulling away from him. He kept walking, trying not to think about it, yet telling himself over and over that it wasn't his fault, that he hadn't pushed the boy, that it was the kid's own foolish actions that had taken him into the crushing path of the bus.

At the same time came a triumphant feeling of having been *right* in his suppositions. The boy *had* been the one. Somehow or other he had *directed* those accidents. Whether it was subconscious or willing Del wasn't sure, but there was no doubt the boy had been the source.

And along with the guilt and the triumph was an overwhelming sense of loss. He didn't know why he felt grief, other than that something was gone of whose existence he had only learned, as an illiterate who learns to read is immediately blinded before even starting to climb the magic mountain of books that awaits him.

Del bought a hot dog from a street vendor and paused to eat it, thinking that he really should start back to Ernie's. The six-pack was warm under his arm, and when he looked at his watch he was amazed to see how much time had passed—nearly two hours since he began to follow the boy. Clutching the half-eaten hot dog, he stepped into a phone booth and dialed Ernie's number.

"Yell-o," Ernie barked over the line.

"Ernie, Del, I—"

"Where the hell are you? I was gonna start watchin' by myself."

"I got hung up. Sorry."

"Well, hop on it, bud. I go on shift at seven, y'know."

Del promised to come right over and hung up. He remained in the booth for a moment, took another bite of hot dog, munched thoughtfully, and wondered where and how the kid had ever learned to do it.

He was just leaving the booth when he heard the crash, felt the moment of stillness that hung in the street, broken by a harshly screamed, "Son of a *bitch!*" that seemed even louder than the sound of the collision.

A string bean of a driver clad in gray coveralls was climbing out of a banana truck down whose yellow side ran a long gash of silvery black. A creased chauffeur got shakily out of a Caddy stretch limo. The Caddy's front fender was crumpled so that it resembled a giant corn flake more than anything made of metal.

"You *asshole!*" the skinny trucker shrieked, shaking a bony fist and whipping off his baseball cap to reveal a shock of steel gray hair cropped close. Veins bulged through the narrow, corded neck. "You didn't *see* me? You didn't see a goddam bright yellow fucking *banana truck?*"

The chauffeur, without speaking a word, reached inside his coat pocket. "Hold it!" the trucker yelled. "What are you doin'?"

The chauffeur spoke too softly for Del to hear, and slowly drew a long billfold from his jacket.

"You ain't bribin' *me*, man! No sir! I want a cop, goddam it, there's never a cop when you want one!"

The chauffeur shook his head, said something else, held up a New York state driver's license.

"Oh *sure*," the trucker said. "Just a license, oh *sure!*"

Del kept watching the pair, fascinated by the contrast between the little man's enormous amount of energy and the chauffeur's unruffled calm. The trucker stalked and preened, shrieked and cursed. The chauffeur stood there, saying something quietly every now and then. At last a policeman arrived, quieted the trucker, took command. The best part was over.

Del was so pumped up from having watched the confrontation that he walked a whole block before he thought about the remarkable coincidence of having seen another accident that same day. But what the hell, he reasoned, accidents were always happening in New York City. Soon he'd be thinking that the black boy was back, making them happen.

Funny, though. Everywhere the boy had gone today, Del had been there, and everywhere he stopped, Del had stopped.

And now . . .

Del stopped again, looked at the street, saw a bicyclist with a tank top and safety helmet flying down the bike lane, saw a small gas line cap suddenly throw him off balance, wrench the handlebars from his grip, twist the wheel. The man hit the street rolling, elbows in, knees tucked. There were, luckily for him, no cars in his path.

He lay still for a moment as if testing his muscles and joints, then slowly got up, picked up his bike, cursed sharply at its twisted frame, and began to walk it down the street.

Jesus.

What had he thought when he first tried to talk himself out of believing in what the black boy had done? *After all, I was there too.*

I was there too.

Del caught a crosstown bus at the next corner, got off at Riverside Park, and went down to the water's edge. There were dozens of small craft sailors out on the Hudson, their red and white and blue and yellow sails ballooned with the warm, humid, slightly sour air of the river. No one would be hurt here, Del thought, though he had always imagined that if you stuck a hand in the Hudson, the chemicals would strip it cleaner than a school of piranha.

Still, they'd have to take their chances.

He eyed a slick green catamaran knifing through the water, and, so quickly that it startled him, the wind shifted. The sailor was unprepared and the boat tilted precariously, then fell over on its side, hurling its occupant into the river. The man, a deeply tanned blond, came up spitting, and righted his craft with no trouble.

Del looked at another boat, and over it went.

And another.

And another.

He watched the weekend sailors get their dunkings, straighten their boats, and climb on board again. After the sixth tipping, he turned laughing and walked away from the river, thinking how foolish the boy had been to walk away from the best parts. He dimly remembered from years ago a comic strip character—from *Lil' Abner*, he believed—named Joe something, a mass of unpronounceable letters, who created havoc everywhere he went, a true jinx seemingly in despair over his strange power.

But what, Del conjectured, if Joe had really enjoyed it? What if Joe, like Del, was a fan of the best parts?

He dumped the warm six-pack in a trash can. He didn't need to worry about the $4.50 he had spent on it. There could be plenty of money for someone who had the talent he had, plenty of favorites who could trip on race tracks so that other horses could win at higher odds. He didn't bother to call Ernie either. He simply walked to Times Square and had fun for an hour, each time watching the best part, and looking somewhere else when it was over.

Then he flagged a cab and told the driver where he wanted to go. He was excited, expectant, and, in a way, apprehensive, hoping he could yet hoping he couldn't, already dimly aware of the responsibility that had fallen on him.

Then the cab arrived at Kennedy Airport, and he got out and headed toward the observation area, his eyes already on the darkening sky.

RONALD KELLY *is one of the genre's brightest new stars. Once a small-press regular, Kelly made the transition to the mass-market with relative ease and much fanfare. His novels include* Hindsight, Pit Fall, *and* Something Out There. *Kelly is versatile—he has also written mystery and western novels—and is one of several* Cold Blood *authors with a unique southern voice.*

YEA, THOUGH I DRIVE
RONALD KELLY

There was a massacre in progress on I-53.

The interstate system stretched from Atlanta, Georgia, across Tennessee and Kentucky, clear to Cincinnati, Ohio. Until the autumn of that year, it was known mainly for its scenic beauty and the Southern hospitality exhibited at the restaurants and motels that served as overnight havens between the long miles of rural solitude. Then the killings began.

In three short months, the "Roadside Butcher" had murdered seventeen travelers along Interstate 53, each one varying in degree of brutality and mutilation. Some drivers were found sitting in their cars or eighteen wheelers with their throats neatly slashed from ear to ear. Others were found lying at the side of the road, sliced open from gullet to groin, gutted like a deer at hunting season. And then there were the more grisly of the Butcher's victims . . . those who had been hacked to death, dismembered, or decapitated. The strange thing about the whole ordeal was that there was no definite pattern. The victims had been hitchhikers and drifters, as well as vacationing travelers and burly truckers who regularly frequented the five hundred mile stretch of southern interstate.

The Highway Patrol was out in full force, as were the State Troopers and the FBI, but the increase in law enforcement did not seem to deter the Butcher from performing his fiendish whims. It got so that veteran travelers of the road began to carry pistols and sawed-off shotguns, secretly stashed in glove compartments and sleeper cabs. Most of the truckstops began to sell a rather popular bumper sticker which read, "YEA, THOUGH I DRIVE ALONG THE HIGHWAY OF THE SHADOW OF DEATH, I WILL FEAR NO EVIL, FOR I AM THE MEANEST S.O.B. ON I-53." However, at least a couple of those fearless motorists were found lying across their front seats with their throats cut down to the neckbone or their entrails dangling from the rear view mirror like strands of Christmas garland.

The sudden increase in freeway paranoia did not help Mark Casey's situation any. He had been a drifter for years, possessing a nagging need for wandering and the freedom of the open road. Before the chaos on I-53, the long hair and beard had not hampered his ability to catch a ride, either from one exit to the next or straight through to his intended destination. But these days, hitchhiking was becoming one big pain in the ass. Whenever he hung out at a truckstop or stood at the roadside with his thumb in the air, he felt the eyes of potential rides appraising him negatively and noticing his uncanny resemblance to Charles Manson. Never mind that the wild eyes and swastika carved on the forehead were absent; the motorist would still see all that hair and the baggy field jacket that could easily conceal any number of sharp implements. They would see all that in one fleeting glance, shake their heads "no chance," and drive on, leaving Mark frustrated, sorefooted, and cold.

If it hadn't been for his sudden pairing with Clifford Lee Gates, Mark was sure he would have ended up walking clear from Florida to Ohio that week in mid-December. Clifford Lee was a lanky boy of eighteen from Cloverfield, Georgia, a farming community that boasted a gas station, a general store, and a whopping census of one hundred and eighty-two citizens. Clifford Lee had high aspirations of becoming a country music singer. His constantly good-natured grin and overabundance of optimism were signs that he actually believed that he would make it big in Nashville, armed only with a beat-up Fender acoustic and his rural charm, despite his obvious lack of money and connections. Mark knew at once, upon meeting him at a greasy spoon called Lou's Place, that he should watch out for this wide-eyed innocent. The boy would be easy pickings with a psychopath like the Butcher on the loose.

Anyway, it was Clifford Lee's infectious charm that netted them a ride north with an overweight copier salesman by the name of A.J. Rudman. Rudman was returning home to Louisville from a Xerox convention held in Daytona Beach the previous week. They had overheard him talking to the truckstop waitress and, when he was paying his check at the register, Clifford Lee approached him with a big ole country-bumpkin grin. The middle-aged salesman was apprehensive at first, eyeing the young man's bearded friend with immediate suspicion. But, soon, the boy's benevolence won over the man's worries and he told them he would give them a lift that stormy autumn night.

The long drive started out in silence, a silence born of tension and uneasiness. Mark sat in the front, while Clifford Lee took the backseat, upon Rudman's firm insistence. Obviously, the Kentucky salesman wanted the more suspicious of the two where he could keep an eye on him.

Mark suffered the blatant mistrust quietly, just thankful that he and the Georgia farmboy were inside a warm, dry car and not humping the dark countryside in the pouring rain.

By the time they crossed the Tennessee state line, the mood had lightened somewhat. Idle conversation had echoed between the three and Clifford had even picked some country tunes on his guitar. The hillbilly twang in Gates's voice grated on Mark's nerves, but he settled into the Lincoln's plush velour seat and tried to enjoy it anyway. A.J. Rudman seemed to be having digestive problems. He drove with one hand on the wheel and the other tucked into the mid-section of his tan raincoat over his prominent beer belly. *Probably has a bad peptic ulcer,* thought Mark, not without a flare of mean-spirited satisfaction. *I guess that's what you get when you're a part of the corporate rat-race these days, right, Pops?*

"Where are you boys bound for?" Rudman asked out of pure boredom. His nervousness seemed to be gradually increasing for some reason. He was popping Rolaids like they were jelly beans.

"Well, I'm heading for Dayton," Mark replied, trying to inject a friendly tone in hopes of dispelling the man's distrust in him. "I'm going home to my parents' place for Christmas. Mom always has a big spread laid out; turkey, candied yams, the works."

"How about you, son?" the salesman asked over his shoulder.

Clifford Lee had been softly singing a medley of Dwight Yokum songs. He looked up and grinned sheepishly. "I'm off to Nashville, Tennessee, to be a big country star. I grew up on country and western music. Me and my pa, we'd listen to the Grand Old Opry every Saturday night. I got to singing and picking on the guitar here and the folks said 'Why, you're as good as any of 'em, Clifford Lee! You oughta head on up to Music City and try your luck.' So that's what I aim to do."

During the farmboy's longwinded explanation, Mark

noticed his hand squeeze past the guitar strings and disappear into the hole of the Fender's hourglass body. He grinned. Surely Clifford Lee didn't have a secret stash hidden inside his guitar. Mark had been around enough potheads to know a few who hid their grass in strange places, including musical instruments. But, no, Clifford Lee Gates was no more a smoker of marijuana than Jesse Jackson was the Imperial Wizard of the Ku Klux Klan.

Still, the thought of a good smoke, straight or otherwise, brought out that craving for nicotine in Mark Casey and he absently reached into an inside pocket of his olive drab coat for a pack of Marlboros. Suddenly, the big Lincoln Continental was whipping back and forth across the double lanes of the northbound stretch of I-53, shooting onto the paved shoulder on the far side and braking to such a sharp and screeching halt that the bearded hitchhiker would have butted his head against the windshield if his seatbelt hadn't been buckled.

A breathless silence hung within the car for a long moment. The pattering of steady rainfall on the roof was the only sound to be heard. Then Mark turned and regarded the pale-faced salesman. "What the hell did you do that for?" he yelled. "Are you trying to kill us or something?"

A.J. Rudman swallowed dryly, his right hand still pressed against his gastric woes. "What were *you* doing?" he croaked back. "What were you reaching for . . . inside your coat?"

"My smokes, man, that's all!" Mark pulled the cigarettes from his pocket and slammed them down on the dashboard. He stared at the businessman incredulously. "You thought I was going for a knife, didn't you? You thought that I was the freaking Roadside Butcher, didn't you? That I was gonna pull a big knife outta my coat and carve your sonofabitching head clean off. That's exactly what you thought, wasn't it?" He snorted and shook his head in disgust. "Well, I ain't the damned butcher . . . you got that? I may look like some drug-crazed devil worshiper to you, but I'm just a regular guy trying to get from point A to point B and, believe it or not, I'm just as jumpy as you are where that butchering crazy is concerned."

"Well, I thought . . ." began Rudman in embarrassment. "It's just that you reached into your pocket without any warning and . . ."

"Yeah . . . yeah, I know, man. Just a big misunderstanding. Why don't you just loosen up and put us back on the road again, okay?"

The salesman nodded. He was about to shift back into drive, when Clifford Lee chuckled from the backseat. "Shucks, Mr. Rudman, old Mark ain't the killer. Shoot fire, he's one of the nicest fellas I've ever met," he grinned. "Heck, naw, he ain't the Roadside Butcher. But, you know something kinda funny? I *am!*" And, with that, the farmboy reached around the padded headrest and laid a pearl-handled straight razor against A.J. Rudman's flabby throat.

"What are you doing, man?" Mark asked. He looked at the goofy Georgian with the cowlicked crop of reddish-blond hair and the slightly bucked teeth. Suddenly, as he stared into that freckled face, he realized that what he had initially interpreted as down-home naïveté had actually been a dark, underlying madness all along.

"What do you think I'm a-doing?" giggled Clifford Lee. The honed edge of the shaving razor glinted sinisterly in the pale glow of the dashboard light. "I'm fixing to kill this nice gentleman. Now, don't go looking so danged surprised, Mark. And don't worry . . . I ain't gonna hurt you none. You're my friend."

Mark Casey watched in numb disbelief as Clifford Lee made his victim shut off the engine, unbuckle his seat belt, and, ever so carefully, climb out into the stormy night. As if in a trance, Mark left the car also, walking around the rear bumper to watch the inevitable bloodletting. Clifford had Rudman's head pulled back by the hair, the straight razor positioned at a deadly angle above the man's carotid artery.

"But *why*, man?" Mark asked, his stomach sinking at the dread of having to stand there and watch a crimson gorge open beneath Rudman's double chin. "Why are you doing this?"

Clifford Lee Gates gave his roadmate a toothy grin and shrugged. "Why not?"

Then something very strange happened, something that neither Mark or Clifford anticipated. A.J. Rudman still had his hand tucked inside his raincoat. It had been there all during the tedious transition from dry car to wet pavement. Mark had just figured the poor guy's ulcer was about to explode. But he saw now that hadn't been the case.

Rudman slowly withdrew his hand and . . . clutched in his pudgy fingers . . . was the biggest damned bowie knife that Mark Casey had ever seen in his life.

He didn't know exactly why he did it, but he yelled "Look out, Clifford!" The razor-wielding musician leaped back just as Rudman turned and slashed in a broad arch that would have taken out most of the boy's abdomen if he had been standing in the same spot. The twelve-inch blade sliced through cold, misty air with a loud *swoosh*.

Rudman laughed. "The Butcher, like hell! You're nothing but a damned copy-cat . . . and not a very good one at that. Oh, slitting throats is just fine and dandy, but it shows a great lack of creativity." The middle-aged salesman passed the heavy knife teasingly from one hand to the other. "Come on, farmboy, let me show you how I express myself."

Mark could only stand and watch as the two men squared off in the twin beams of the Lincoln's headlights. The guitar-picker stood poised and ready, the joint of the razor's blade and handle gripped between thumb and forefinger. The salesman crouched in a classic fighter's stance, the big bowie held, long and perfectly balanced, in one chubby hand. Like a couple of duelists, they circled one another, appraising strengths and weaknesses, then came together in a violent fury of flashing steelwork and spurting blood.

Mark knew he should have run for his life, but he was transfixed. Grunts of pain and the ripping of clothing and flesh echoed across the empty lanes of Interstate 53. The frightened hitchhiker witnessed the awful bloodfeud, torn between revulsion and fascination. He rooted for neither man, although one had been a newfound friend until only a few moments ago.

The fight ended abruptly when the two men struggled to the pavement and rolled toward the front of the car, away from Mark's view. A torturous scream split the air, followed by a wet gurgle. For a moment, the headlights revealed only the glistening pavement ahead and the driving rainfall. Then a single form stood up.

"I won," grinned Clifford Lee.

Mark backed away as the young man started around the car for him. Clifford's denim jacket was in bloody tatters, his face criss-crossed with deep gashes. He had traded his razor in for the broad-bladed bowie. "You know when I said I wouldn't hurt you, Mark?" asked Clifford Lee brushing aside a flap of loose skin that hung below his left eye. "Well, hell, I lied. I'm sorry, buddy, but I'm gonna have to kill you, too. Can't leave no loose ends, you know. Hope you understand."

But Mark didn't understand. He leaped off the road and into the darkness. With a maniacal cackle, Clifford Lee was in hot pursuit. Unfortunately, there was no solid ground beyond the glow of the car's high beams, only a steep dropoff into a wooded hollow below. The two tumbled head over heels, landing at the bottom of the grassy incline. Mark was the first one up and that was to his advantage. Clifford Lee was groggy from bashing his head against a rock on the way down. He crawled toward his lost blade, but didn't quite make it. Mark reached the big knife first and, without a second's hesitation, drove it between his traveling buddy's heaving shoulder blades.

"What'd you do that for?" croaked Clifford Lee, blood spraying from his mouth and nostrils. "I thought we were pals."

"I thought so, too," replied Mark. "God help me, I really did." He withdrew the knife and buried it to the hilt one more time, just to be on the safe side.

Moments later, Mark was climbing back up the grassy face of the hollow for the interstate. His wild high of exhilaration and relief faded into confusion when he reached the lip of the thoroughfare. A dark form crouched beside the body of A.J. Rudman, then stood and shucked a revolver from a side holster when he saw Mark stumble out of the darkness.

"Killed him . . . " Mark managed, trying to explain, pointing back into the hollow. "I killed him . . . stabbed him . . . "

The state trooper lifted his .357 magnum in a two-handed hold. "You just stop right there," he barked. "Drop it and don't move a muscle."

Mark couldn't understand why the lawman refused to listen. "The Butcher . . . " he gasped. "Dead . . . I killed the . . . "

"I said, *drop the knife!* This is my last warning!"

"But you don't understand . . . " Mark sputtered. He lifted his hands to reason with the man and there it was, the knife, completely forgotten until it flashed electric blue in the patrol car's cascading lights.

Three shots rang out. Three hollowpoint slugs obliterated the top of Mark Casey's skull and sent his body sprawling across the white borderline of the medium. Clumps of brain and splinters of skull littered the dark pavement, but they were soon washed away as the black rains of the storm soaked Interstate 53 and scrubbed it clean.

Officer Hal Olsen holstered his revolver and walked back to the patrol car. He sat down heavily and picked up the mike of his radio. "Unit H-108 to headquarters. Send me additional back-up, will you? I've got one hell of a mess out here on I-53, two miles north of the Monteagle exit. I've just shot the Roadside Butcher, but not before he killed two others." When he was assured that help was on its way, the officer replaced the mike and turned his radio off.

He sat there and stared at the body lying there in Army fatigue jacket and faded jeans. Shaking his head, he withdrew an object wrapped in canvas from beneath his car seat and walked over to where Mark Casey laid.

"I don't know who you were, fella, but you just got me off the hook."

Officer Olsen withdrew a long-bladed machete from the wrapping and hefted its comforting weight in his hand one last time, before tossing it as far as he could into the wet darkness of the backwoods hollow. Then he returned to the car and waited for his fellow officers to arrive.

JOE R. LANSDALE *is one
of the most talented and
original writers working today.
And he's not picky. He blasts
all genres—horror, suspense,
mystery, crime, western, science
fiction—with both barrels and
always hits the mark. Read a
Lansdale novel or short story
and be prepared to be completely mesmerized. Start with*
The Magic Wagon, Cold In July,
and Savage Season, *then read*
By Bizarre Hands, *a short story
collection unlike anything
you've ever read. The following
piece is a rare treat—an
original Lansdale play.*

BY BIZARRE HANDS

PLAY VERSION
JOE R. LANSDALE

This stage version of "By Bizarre Hands," though spiritually the same as the short story, is different enough that I feel no compunctions about it being presented here, not only because the play form is interesting and a different reading experience, but because the ending of the story varies, as do a number of small details. The bit with the dog, for instance.

Why the changes?

Simple. I liked the story and felt it had the potential for a dynamite play, but found the ending, though fine in short story form, to be too anti-climactic for the stage. Also, the original version required two scenes and a different set, and I wanted it to be a one scene, one set affair. This made it necessary to change the interior of the story somewhat, as well as the ending. It worked better than I could have imagined.

Hope you enjoy it. Both versions are personal favorites of mine, and supposedly the play version of this, along with another play of mine, based on "Drive-In Date", will appear October 1990 Off-Broadway along with a number of other one-acts written by horror writers under the title *Screamplay*.

Read the story, and break a leg.

Joe R. Lansdale (Nacogdoches, Texas)

◊

Lights up on a rural scene. East Texas. Fall. Late afternoon. A ramshackle house with a sagging front porch. Living room, except for an open window on the side opposite the porch, is a cut away and it's furnished simply. Couch. Coffee table. End-table with a wooden hula-girl lamp on it. An old Sylvania TV set with foil-covered rabbit ears on top. A faded, framed embroidery on the wall that reads: GOD WATCHES OVER THIS HOUSE. Outside, in the yard, is an old fashioned rock well with a roof over it and a pulley with a rope and bucket. A woman, THE WIDOW CASE, is at the well. She's in her forties, whipped by sun, wind and ignorance, wearing a colorless sundress and a man's shoes without socks. She's slowly and painfully cranking the heavy well bucket up. CINDERELLA is nearby on her knees in the dirt, one eye close to the ground. She has a little stick in one hand and is using it to work something on the ground not quite visible to the audience. Cinderella is about twenty, but has the mind of a not too bright three year old. She's twenty pounds overweight, barefooted, dressed in a short, little-girl dress with white panties stained by dirt. The panties are visible to the audience as she wiggles on her knees and cocks her butt up and makes grunting sounds and moves the stick; now and then she lifts the stick up, picks something from it with her free hand and puts it in her mouth.

CINDERELLA: (To herself.) Ant.

SOUND OF A CAR stopping nearby. The Widow Case takes notice. Cinderella doesn't, continues to twist the stick.

CAR DOOR SLAMS. Enter PREACHER JUDD. He's decked out in black suit, white shirt, string tie and black loafers. Has on a short-brimmed black hat. Wears an alligator smile. As he enters he takes off his hat. He glances now and then in Cinderella's direction. Cinderella still has not taken notice. She is back at work with her stick.

WIDOW CASE: (Placing the bucket of drawn water on the well-curbing.) Reckon you've come far enough. You look like one of them Jehovah Witnesses or such.

PREACHER JUDD: No, I ain't, ma'am.

WIDOW CASE: If you're here to take up money for them starving African niggers, I can tell you now, I don't give to the niggers around here, and I sure ain't giving to no hungry foreign niggers can't even speak English.

PREACHER JUDD: Ain't collecting money for nobody. Not even myself.

WIDOW CASE: Well, I ain't seen you around here before, and don't know you from white rice. You might be one of them *mash* murderers for all I know.

PREACHER JUDD: No ma'am. I ain't a *mash* murderer, and I ain't from around here. I'm from East Texas. I'm traveling through here, so I can talk to white folks about God.

Preacher Judd puts on his hat and stares at Cinderella who is still twisting her stick, starting to move to the side on her knees. As she does, we see that what she's been playing with is a small dead dog and she has the stick stuck into one of its eye sockets, twirling it as though mixing a recipe. There is the SOUND OF FLIES BUZZING. Widow Case notes Preacher Judd's interest in Cinderella's activities.

WIDOW CASE: I don't normally let her play with no dead dog like that, but way she is, I can't hardly watch her all the time and get things done. She'll drag dead stuff off the road if she sees it. It's the ants interest her the most. She eats 'em.

Preacher Judd watches as Cinderella deftly uses her free hand to snag something off her arm and deliver the prize to her mouth.

CINDERELLA: Ant.

PREACHER JUDD: I think that there was a fly.

WIDOW CASE: She'll eat them too. She calls all bugs ants.

They stare at Cinderella. She pulls the stick from the dog's eye socket and watches intently as the messy remains of the stirred eyeball, like thick semi-hard snot, drip to the ground.

CINDERELLA: Eye.

PREACHER JUDD: It sure ain't sanitary. That dog could have some germs.

Cinderella uses the stick to push the eyeball goop around on the ground.

WIDOW CASE: She don't know no better. Ain't got no sense at all. All she does is play around all day, eat bugs and drool. Finds something dead, she'll mess with it for hours. Kind of keeps her out of my hair, though . . . Case you ain't noticed, she's simple.

PREACHER JUDD: Yes ma'am, I noticed. In fact, that's one of the reasons I'm here. I heard about her in town.

WIDOW CASE: There's people talking about her in town? (Sharply to Cinderella as the girl re-snags the eyeball on her stick and moves it toward her mouth.) DON'T EAT THAT!

Cinderella turns, looks at the Widow Case as if the old woman has wounded her. She reluctantly pops the goopy eye off the stick and onto the ground.

WIDOW CASE: Now, you said they was talking about Cinderella?

PREACHER JUDD: It was friendly talk. I did a little preaching outside a honky tonk there, trying to save a few sinners, and this one fella, he prayed with me and told me he has a simple headed little boy and how bad he used to hate going home on account of it. Said he thought about trying to run over the boy with his car. Had all kinds of bad thoughts. Finally he and his wife had to put the boy in a home. Said they go to see him Christmases. Anyway, we talked on and he mentioned you having a daughter same way as his boy.

WIDOW CASE: That has to be Old Man Favor. I don't reckon he came to Jesus.

PREACHER JUDD: I think maybe he did. He said he did.

WIDOW CASE: Go back by that honky tonk on your way out, and see if he ain't back in there on a stool. Come tomorrow, he won't remember you or Jesus.

PREACHER JUDD: That just might be. . . . But the thing got me interested in your daughter here is the fact that they don't usually get God training. Retards, I mean. They get looked over. You see, I had a sister same way. Retarded, like your girl. She got killed on Halloween, ten years ago to this night. She was raped and murdered and had her trick-or-treat candy stolen, and it was done, the sheriff said, by bizarre hands.

WIDOW CASE: No kiddin'?

PREACHER JUDD: No kiddin'. Figure she went on to hell cause she didn't have any God talk in her. And retard or not, she deserved some so she wouldn't have to cook for eternity. I mean, think on it. How hot it must be down there. Her boiling in her own sweat, and she didn't do nothing, and it's mostly my fault she's down there 'cause I didn't teach her a thing about the Lord Jesus and his daddy, God.

WIDOW CASE: Took her Halloween candy too, huh?

PREACHER JUDD: Whole kitandkaboodle. Rape, murder and candy theft, one fatal swoop. That's why I hate to see a young'n like yours who might not have no word of God in her. And come Halloween, I think on it more than ever. (Looking at Cinderella.) Is she without training?

WIDOW CASE: She ain't even toilet trained. You couldn't perch her on the outdoor convenience if she was sick and her manage to hit the hole. Old man Favor's boy can at least do that. He can talk about the weather some. Cinderella, she can't talk much or do nothing that don't make a mess. Can't teach her a thing. Just runs them ants with that stick all day. Half the time she don't even know her name. You don't yell at her, she don't pay you any mind at all. (To Cinderella in a normal tone of voice.) Cindereller.

Cinderella pays no attention. She continues to rock and twirl her stick. Suddenly she raises up and thrashes her stick in the air as if striking an invisible opponent or conducting an important musical movement, then she begins to run around in a circle, her knuckles practically dragging. She makes little hooting sounds. She resumes her former position, starts twirling her stick in the hollow of the dog's eye.

WIDOW CASE: See? She's worse than any little ole baby, and it ain't no easy row to hoe with her here and me not having a man around to do the heavy work.

PREACHER JUDD: I can see that. Woman like you has got her work cut out for her. It takes some real courage and dedication to do what you have to do. . . . By the way, call me Preacher Judd. . . . And can I help you tote that bucket up to the house there?

WIDOW CASE: Well now, I'd appreciate that kindly.

Preacher Judd goes to the well smiling, takes the bucket.

WIDOW CASE: Come on into the house. (She starts toward the house, pauses.) You got to watch the porch and walk on the far side. It's starting to rot through in the middle. You don't want to fall through there cause there's a big hole where a old well used to be underneath.

PREACHER JUDD: You don't mind me saying so, you ought to get that fixed.

WIDOW CASE: I get the time and money and a man willing to swing a hammer, I will. (She bends and picks up a little rock, chunks it softly at Cinderella, hits her in the head. Cinderella looks up.) Leave that ole mutt alone! Get on in the house! And mind that porch! (To Preacher Judd) Only thing I've taught that she knows good, and that's to watch for them rotten boards. Good thing too, big as she is she'd drop through there like a stone. They'd find her in China.

Cinderella drops her stick, jumps up and runs in circles with her back bent and her knuckles dragging, hooting as she goes.

PREACHER JUDD: Now ain't that cute.

WIDOW CASE: When you're trying to get her to do something, it gets a mite less cute. (To Cinderella) Come on here, now. Get on up to the house!

Preacher Judd follows the Widow Case onto the porch. He observes how carefully she mounts the porch. He follows her lead through the front door. Cinderella, like a little duck following bigger ducks, comes in after them, carefully staying away from the rotted lumber. Once in the living room, she forgets about them. She sits in the middle of the floor and rocks and looks up and about, as if observing the stars.

WIDOW CASE: (As she takes the bucket from Preacher

Judd.) Thank you. I'll take it now. Good to see the world ain't empty of gentlemen yet.

Cinderella is now pulling her dress up. Picking something off her knee. She puts it in her mouth.

WIDOW CASE: (Glaring at Cinderella.) Pull your dress down, girl. And don't eat them ants. They ain't good for you.

Cinderella pays absolutely no attention, continues to search for ants on her person.

PREACHER JUDD: Figure them ants will make her sick.

WIDOW CASE: Figure not. You took all the ants she's et, there'd be enough to tote off a good sized cow. I'm gonna pour this water up.

PREACHER JUDD: (Takes a Bible from his coat pocket.) You don't mind if I try and read a verse or two to Cindy, do you?

WIDOW CASE: You make an effort on that while I fix us some tea. You're hungry, I'll bring some things for ham sandwiches.

PREACHER JUDD: Now that's right nice of you. I could use a bite.

Widow Case smiles, exits with her bucket. Cinderella has pulled her dress up to expose her panties. Preacher Judd studies Cinderella for a long moment, watching her look for more ants.

PREACHER JUDD: (Softly to Cinderella.) You know

tonight's Halloween, Cindy?

Cinderella pays no attention. She'd found another ant and she darts her fingers to her mouth to dispose of it.

PREACHER JUDD: (As much to himself as to Cinderella.) Halloween is my favorite time of the year. That may be strange for a preacher to say, considering it's a devil thing, but I've always loved it. It just does something to my blood. It's like a tonic for me, you know?

Cinderella gets up, wanders over to the TV and turns it on, sits on the floor in front of it. Banal TV prattle is heard.

PREACHER JUDD: Let's don't run the TV just now, sugar baby. Let's you and me talk about God.

Preacher Judd goes over and turns the set off. Cinderella continues to stare at it. Preacher Judd opens his Bible and lets it lie open in one hand while he raises the other as if pointing to God. He reads.

PREACHER JUDD: "For God so loved the world, he gave his only begotten son." (Lowers his hand and uses a finger to find the next verse he wants.) Let's see, blah, blah, blah, "I have need to be baptized of thee, and comest thou to me?" Amen.

CINDERELLA: Uhman.

Preacher Judd jumps with happy surprise, slams the Bible shut and dunks it in his pocket.

PREACHER JUDD: Well, well, now, that does it. You got some Bible training.

Widow Case enters with a tray of sandwich fixings: a small
ham on the bone, tomatoes, a huge butcher knife, a mustard jar and two glasses of iced tea.

WIDOW CASE: What's that you're saying?

PREACHER JUDD: (Happy as if he'd just been jacked
off.) She said some of a prayer. God don't expect much
from retards, and that ought to do for keeping her from
burning in hell. (Practically skips over to the Widow Case
and dunks two fingers into a glass of tea, whirls and flicks
the drops on Cinderella's confused, upturned face.) I
pronounce you seriously baptized. In the name of God,
The Son, and the Holy Ghost. Amen.

WIDOW CASE: Well, I'll swan. That there tea works for
baptizing? (She sits the tray on the coffee table.)

PREACHER JUDD: It ain't the tea water. It's what's said
and who says it makes it take. Consider that gal legal
baptized. . . . Now, she ought to have some fun too, don't
you think? Since she's baptized, she ought to celebrate a
little. Not having a full head of brains don't mean she
shouldn't have some fun.

WIDOW CASE: (Defensively) She likes what she does
with them ants. (She sits on the couch, begins to cut slices
of ham.)

PREACHER JUDD: I know, but I'm talking about something special. It's Halloween. Time for young folks to have
fun, even if they are retards. In fact, retards like it better
than anyone. They *love* this stuff. . . . A thing my sister
enjoyed was dressing up like a ghost.

WIDOW CASE: (Preparing the sandwiches.) Ghost?

PREACHER JUDD: (Excited) We took this sheet, you see, cut some mouth and eye holes in it, then we wore them and went trick-or-treatin'.

WIDOW CASE: I don't know I got an old sheet. And there ain't a house close enough for trick-or-treatin' at.

PREACHER JUDD: I could take her around in my car. That would be fun, I think. I'd like to see her have fun, wouldn't you? She'd be real scary too under that sheet, big as she is and liking to run stooped down with her knuckles dragging.

Preacher Judd makes his point by hunching over and running around in a circle, knuckles dragging, making hooting noises as he goes.

WIDOW CASE: (Laughs) She would be scary, I admit. . . . Though that sheet over her head would take away from it some. Sometimes she scares me when I don't got my mind on her, you know? Like if I'm napping in there on the bed, and I sorta open my eyes, *and there she is*, looking at me like she does them ants. I declare, she looks like she'd like to take a stick and whirl it around on me.

PREACHER JUDD: Whatd'ya say?

WIDOW CASE: I don't know. . . .

PREACHER JUDD: She'd get so much candy you and her could eat on it for a week.

WIDOW CASE: Well now, I like candy. . . . Maybe it would be nice for Cindereller to go out and have some fun.

PREACHER JUDD: Good. It's decided. You need a sheet.

A white one, for a ghost suit.

WIDOW CASE: (Slightly hesitant.) I'll see what I can find.

PREACHER JUDD: (Rubbing his hands together as
Widow Case rises.) Good, good. You can let me make the
outfit. I'm real good at it.

Widow Case exits into a "bedroom". Preacher Judd picks
up one of the sandwiches and takes a bite out of it. He
looks at Cinderella. She's staring at him as if she just now
discovered him. He hands the sandwich to her. She
promptly takes the bread off, lays the mustard-swathed
bread on her knees and eats the meat by tilting her head
and lowering it into her mouth. She smacks and gobbles
loudly, starts in on the bread.

PREACHER JUDD: That good, sugar?

Cinderella smiles mustard bread as Widow Case enters
carrying a sheet and a pair of scissors.

WIDOW CASE: This do?

PREACHER JUDD: (Taking the sheet and scissors.) Just
the thing! (To Cinderella) Come on, sugar. Let's you and
me go in the back room there and get you fixed up and
surprise your mama.

WIDOW CASE: You got to take her by the arm. Lead her
around like a dog.

PREACHER JUDD: (Taking Cinderella's arm) Come on,
Cindy. (As he walks her to the bedroom, calls to the Widow
Case.) You're gonna like this. This'll be fun.

Preacher Judd exits into the bedroom. Widow Case sits down on the couch and goes back to making sandwiches, casting an eye now and then toward the bedroom. From in there WE HEAR CINDERELLA GRUNTING, SCISSORS SNIPPING and the MUMBLE of PREACHER JUDD'S VOICE, but we can't make out what he's saying. A few moments of silence, and—

—the bedroom door flies open and out darts Cinderella wearing the sheet with mouth and eye-holes cut in it. She has her arms out in front of her and she runs around the room in circles yelling.

CINDERELLA: Wooo, wooo, goats! Wooo, wooo, goats!

Cinderella hits the coffee table, sends it and the sandwich makings flying, trips, goes tumbling across the floor. Widow Case pulls herself into a defensive position. Preacher Judd enters and he goes over and helps Cinderella up. He has something white draped in the crook of an arm.

PREACHER JUDD: That's ghosts, Cindy. Not goats.

CINDERELLA: Goats! Goats!

PREACHER JUDD: We'll work on that.

WIDOW CASE: (Recovering from Cinderella's entrance.) Damn you, Cinderella . . . (Noticing what Preacher Judd has on his arm.) What's that you got there?

PREACHER JUDD: One of your piller cases. For a trick-or-treat sack.

WIDOW CASE: (Stiffly.) Oh.

Widow Case eases off the couch and rights the coffee table. She's reaching for the ham on the floor when—

PREACHER JUDD: I think we've got to go now.

WIDOW CASE: (Surprised. Straightening up.) But you ain't et yet.

PREACHER JUDD: I can eat some trick-or-treat candy.

WIDOW CASE: A sandwich will do you a mite better for supper. I can wipe this ham off with a rag and it'll be good as new.

PREACHER JUDD: It'll be ambrosia, I'm sure. But we ought to run on and get started good. Get to the houses late they quit giving you candy and start sticking apples and bananas and stuff like that in your bag. We'll be back in a few hours, just long enough to run the houses around here.

WIDOW CASE: Whoa, whoa! Trick-or-treatin' I can go for, but I can't let my daughter go off with no strange man.

PREACHER JUDD: I ain't strange. I'm a preacher.

WIDOW CASE: You strike me as an all right fella that wants to do things right, but I can't let you take my daughter off without me going. People will talk. You can understand that.

PREACHER JUDD: I'll pay you some money to let me take her.

WIDOW CASE: I don't like the sound of that none, you offering me money.

PREACHER JUDD: I just want her for the night. (He puts his arm around Cinderella and pulls her close.) She'd have fun.

WIDOW CASE: I don't like the sound of that no better. Maybe you ain't as right thinking as I thought. (She grabs the butcher knife off the floor and points it at Preacher Judd.) I reckon you better just let go of her and run on out to that car of yours and take your ownself trick-or-treatin'. And without my piller case.

PREACHER JUDD: No ma'am can't do that. I've come for Cindy and that's the thing God expects of me, and I'm gonna do it. I got to do it. I didn't do my sister right and she's burning in hell. I'm doing Cindy right. She said some of a prayer and she's baptized. Anything happened to her, wouldn't be on my conscience.

Cinderella lifts up her ghost suit and looks at herself. She's naked underneath. The Widow Case's mouth falls open.

WIDOW CASE: You pervert! Let go of her right now! And drop that piller case. Toss it on the couch would be better. It's clean.

Preacher Judd doesn't move. Beat.

PREACHER JUDD: I won't do that. I'm taking her.

WIDOW CASE: (Gritting her teeth.) Hell you are!

Widow Case slashes at Preacher Judd with the knife. He dodges, drops the pillow case. Cinderella breaks away, runs about the room, yelling, "Wooo, wooo, goats", in nervous agitation.

Another slash from the Widow Case. Preacher Judd isn't fast enough. It cuts his coat sleeve.

PREACHER JUDD: (Leaping back.) You Jezebel! You just ruined a J.C. Penney's suit.

They start to circle, like wrestlers preparing for the run together. Preacher Judd stops abruptly. Holds out his left hand and sticks up two fingers and wiggles them like rabbit ears.

PREACHER JUDD: Lookee here!

Widow Case is snookered. She looks. Preacher Judd grabs her wrist and tries to wrestle the knife away. They fall over the coffee table and roll around on the floor, grunting. Cinderella is still zipping about, yelling, "Wooo, wooo, goats!" She hits one of the rabbit ears on the television set, knocks it winding.

Preacher Judd gets hold of the ham with his free hand and strikes Widow Case a couple of greasy blows in the head with it. He loses the ham, applies both of his hands to her knife hand, twists the knife away. Widow Case screams and tries to roll out from under him and crawl away on her hands and knees. Preacher Judd grabs the knife and leaps at her and puts an arm around her neck and brings the knife high up and down into the center of her back.

Cinderella has stopped whipping about the room and is standing in one place bobbing up and down and waving her arms as if preparing to fly. Widow Case has gone down on her belly and is moaning and crawling. Preacher Judd still has hold of the hilt of the knife, and as Widow Case crawls, he is pulled after her. He's working frantically to free the knife, wiggling it up and down, but it won't come

free. He turns his attention to the frantic, moaning
Cinderella.

PREACHER JUDD: (To Cinderella) It's okay, sugar.
Everything's gonna be all right, now.

WIDOW CASE: Help! Help! Bloody murder!

PREACHER JUDD: (To Widow Case.) Shut up, goddamn
it! (Jerking his face heavenward, he speaks calmly.) Forgive
me my language, oh Lord. (To Cinderella.) Ain't nothing
wrong, baby chile. Not a thing.

WIDOW CASE: Oh Lordy Mercy! Mercy! I'm being kilt.

PREACHER JUDD: Die you stupid cow!

Cinderella is in a blind panic. She has started stepping
from side to side and is going "Uhuhuhuhuhuh." Widow
Case struggles to rise, dragging Preacher Judd, who is still
clinging to the knife, up with her. As she struggles up, she
whips an elbow around and hits Preacher Judd in the ribs.
He is knocked back. Knife remains in her back. She
stumbles forward and falls against the wall, slides into the
end-table and knocks over the hula-girl lamp, popping the
shade free. She falls to the floor on her stomach, lies there
panting like a dog.

Preacher Judd leaps forward and grabs the hula-girl lamp
and hits Widow Case in the head with it. She tries to get up
and he pops her again. She falls out flat. He hits her again.
Then again.

Cinderella has begun climbing out the window.
Preacher Judd turns from beaning the Widow Case just as
Cinderella makes it "outside", and exits the stage running.

PREACHER JUDD: Cindy! Wait! (Still carrying the hula-girl lamp, he moves weak and wobbily to the window and looks in the direction of her exit.) Don't run off. Come on back. Preacher Judd'll be nice to you. I promise. (Hand cupped to his mouth.) Cinderella! Come on back, honey! I got something for you. I ain't gonna hurt you. . . . *You little bitch! Come here!*

He starts to climb out the window, but goes limp. He takes in several deep breaths. Deflated, he leans on the window. After a moment, he looks at the heavens and drops to his knees and lays the hula-girl aside and pushes his hands together, props his elbows on the window sill, closes his eyes and prays.

PREACHER JUDD: God. All the talking I do in your name, you're supposed to make things work out better for me. But you don't. Why's that? (He opens his eyes as if watching for God, waiting for an answer. No sign from the heavens. He closes his eyes and continues.) Night I took my sister trick-er-treatin', that didn't work out. It could have, but you didn't let it. . . . Her naked under that sheet, it got to me, God. I had to have her, but you let her scream and . . . (He lets it hang.) I had to eat her trick-or-treat candy so it'd look like theft. Can't touch a Tootsie Roll to this day. . . . It was a kind of a relief, her being dead. She was lots of trouble. Messed the bed. Embarrassed us around sensible people. Drank straight out of the water jar in the 'frigerator. . . . Her dying was no real crime. 'Cept she wasn't baptized. (Long beat.) This here girl, Cindy. She's been baptized, so it don't matter she lives or not. What's she gonna accomplish? Brain surgery? She couldn't sort rocks from peas. So, God, can't you show love to your humble servant, this once. I got some needs to satisfy. . . . Won't you help me, God? Won't you—

CINDERELLA: (OS) Wooooo, woooo, goats! Wooooo, wooooo, goats!

Preacher Judd looks and sees Cinderella run by the window still wearing the ghost suit.

CINDERELLA: (As she runs by.) Woooo, wooo, goats! (She goes around the front of the house and disappears behind it. But she can still be heard OS.) Woooooo, woooo, goats! Wooooo, woooo, goats!

Preacher Judd lifts his face to the heavens again and mouths AMEN. He pops up with the hula-girl in hand and darts for the front door, tugs it open. Cinderella has reversed and is coming around front of the porch again.

CINDERELLA: (As she passes, not noting Preacher Judd.) Woooo, woooo, goats!

PREACHER JUDD: (Stepping forward enthusiastically with his club cocked.) Cindy, baby! Wait up!

Cinderella is halfway around the house now.

Preacher Judd, in his haste to catch her, steps in the wrong spot and boards shatter beneath him and he goes through the flooring, drops the hula girl lamp and catches himself at arm-pit level. He screams and writhes, trying to pull himself up.

PREACHER JUDD: Oh, God, you're doing it again! You're starting on me! I'm hurt here, Ol' Man. You hear me, hurt? Something's sticking in me. . . . God, for the love of mercy, help me!

Cinderella comes around the edge of the house again. She's

strolling now. She finally takes note of Preacher Judd. She watches him in a curious dog way, turning her sheet-covered head from side to side.

PREACHER JUDD: (Spots her, turns friendly, but it's obvious he's in serious pain.) Cindy! Oh, girl, am I glad you came back. Old Preacher Judd, he's hurt here. I got something stuck in me, sugar. Hurts awful bad. Give me a hand, will you, honey?

CINDERELLA: (Staring at Preacher Judd, speaking softly) Woooo, woooo, goats.

PREACHER JUDD: (Smiling) That's right, you little fool. Woooo, wooo, goats. Now get Ol' Preacher Judd out, will you?

Cinderella has already lost interest. She stops looking at Preacher Judd, spots the dead dog and starts for it.

PREACHER JUDD: Cindy! Cindy! You brainless bitch! Come back here! Come here!

She reaches the dog, squats down by the corpse and recovers her stick. She begins working the stick against the corpse.

PREACHER JUDD: Now you come here! You mind your elders, you hear me!

CINDERELLA: (Holding up her stick, examining it.) Ant. (Her tongue snakes out of the mouth hole in the sheet and licks the ant off the stick, then she goes back to work on the dog.) Puppy.

Preacher Judd struggles painfully, and after some major

effort, manages himself out of the hole and onto the solid remains of the porch. He lays panting with his legs toward us, and we see that a long sliver of board has broken off and gone straight into his crotch. It is long enough and wide enough to look like a small, bloody, beaver tail.

PREACHER JUDD: (Looking down at his injury.) Oh, sweet Jesus, I'm ruined! . . . Ruined!

Cinderella continues to capture ants onto her stick and lick it clean.

Preacher Judd takes hold of the broken board and yanks and screams. Cinderella lifts her head at the sound of the scream, but seems unable to locate its source. She goes back to her ants. Preacher Judd falls back in agony on the porch and lays there for a long moment, puffing like a busted steam engine. Finally, he comes up on one elbow and looks at Cindy. There is no love in his eyes.

He looks about, locates the hula-girl lamp, grabs it, tries to stand and can't. He begins crawling off the porch, toward Cinderella.

PREACHER JUDD: (As he crawls.) Then don't come. I'll come to you. I got a little present for you, retard. Something nice. Something solid.

Cinderella pays no attention to Preacher Judd. She might as well be on the moon. She's totally absorbed in her play and ant eating.

Preacher Judd draws closer, pauses with pain, begins to crawl again, blood trailing behind him like slug slime.

Closer.

Closer.

Closer.

And now he's right behind her. He rises painfully to his knees, cocks the lamp and swings—

—and about that time Cinderella sees an ant to her left and—

CINDERELLA: (Leaning to the left, almost touching her head to the ground.) Ooooooh, big ant.

Preacher Judd's swing is brutal and it carries him forward, hard, and with his victim moving at just the wrong moment, his blow strikes the dead dog with a sound like a bag of mud being thumped, and he falls forward on top of the dog with a cry of pain.

Cinderella, unaware, licks the ant off the ground, sits up and sees Preacher Judd beside her. His hat has finally fallen off, and that catches her eye. As Preacher Judd struggles unsuccessfully to get up, Cinderella picks up his hat and puts it on over her sheeted head. She rises, runs in a circle around him and the dog, spanking her butt with the stick.

CINDERELLA: Wooooo, wooooo, goats!

Preacher Judd can't get up. He's spent. He twists instead and rolls onto his back, the dead dog for a pillow. He puts a hand between his legs and holds himself. He lifts the hand and looks at it. It's covered in blood.

PREACHER JUDD: Insult to injury, God. Insult to injury.

CINDERELLA: (Still circling.) Wooooo, woooo, goats!

PREACHER JUDD: (Angrily to Cinderella.) *It's ghosts! Ghosts! You imbecile!*

Preacher Judd's head nods to the side and the hand holding the hula-girl lamp fans out and strikes the ground with a thump and the lamp rolls away. That's all for Preacher Judd, but the rolling lamp attracts Cinderella, and she looks first at it, then at Preacher Judd. She turns her head from side to side. She goes cautiously to her knees and bends over Preacher Judd, the brim of the hat almost touching his face. She watches him for a time, scanning from one ear to the next, her eyes following something.

CINDERELLA: (Casually poking his face with the stick.) Ant . . . Ant. (She pokes into his eye and tries to pull the stick back, but it doesn't come. She tugs harder, begins to stir it around and around, grunting as she does. She finally draws the stick out, and as we see what is now on the end of it, she says . . .) Eye. Eye. (And as the lights dim around her, she puts the tip of the stick and her morsel into her mouth, and at that moment she says—) Eye. Eye. (—and the lights go down and we have—)

CURTAIN

JOHN SHIRLEY *is the author of* In Darkness Waiting, Cellars, *and* Dracula In Love. *Shirley's prose is fast and daring and all his own; some of his best short work can be found in his Scream Press short story collection,* Heatseeker. *The following tale is outrageous and violent and sadly enough, also very timely.*

JODY AND ANNIE ON TV

JOHN SHIRLEY

First time he has the feeling, he's doing 75 on the 134. Sun glaring the color off the cars, smog filming the North Hollywood hills. Just past the place where the 134 snakes into the Ventura freeway, he's driving Annie's dad's fucked-up '78 Buick Skylark convertible, one hand on the wheel the other on the radio dial, trying to find a tune, and nothing sounds good. But *nothing*. Everything sounds stupid, even metal. You think it's the music but it's not, you know? It's you.

Usually, it's just a weird mood. But this time it shifts a gear. He looks up from the radio and realizes: You're not driving this car. It's automatic in traffic like this: only moderately heavy traffic, moving fluidly, sweeping around the curves like they're all part of one long thing. Most of your mind is thinking about what's on TV tonight and if you could stand working at that telephone sales place again . . .

It hits him that he is two people, the programmed-Jody who drives and fiddles with the radio and the real Jody who thinks about getting work. . . . Makes him feel funny, detached.

The feeling closes in on him like a jar coming down over a wasp. Glassy like that. He's pressed between the back window and the windshield, the two sheets of glass coming together, compressing him like something under one of those biology-class microscope slides. Everything goes two-dimensional. The cars look like the ones in that Roadmaster videogame, animated cars made out of pixels.

A buzz of panic, a roaring, and then someone laughs as he jams the Buick's steering wheel over hard to the right, jumps into the VW Bug's lane, forcing it out; the Bug reacts, jerks away from him, sudden and scared, like it's going, "Shit!" Cutting off a Toyota four-by-four with tractor-sized tires, lot of good those big fucking tires do the Toyota, because it spins out and smacks sideways into the grill of a rusty old semitruck pulling an open trailer full of palm trees. . . .

They get all tangled up back there. He glances back and thinks, *I did that*. He's grinning and shaking his head and laughing. He's not sorry and he likes the fact that he's not sorry. *I did that*. It's so amazing, so totally rad.

Jody has to pull off at the next exit. His heart is banging like a fire alarm as he pulls into a Texaco. Goes to get a Coke.

It comes to him on the way to the Coke machine that he's stoked. He feels connected and in control and pumped up. The gas fumes smell good; the asphalt under the thin rubber of his sneakers feels good. *Huh*. The Coke tastes good. He thinks he can taste the cola berries. He should call Annie. She should be in the car, next to him.

He goes back to the car, heads down the boulevard a mile past the accident, swings onto the freeway, gets up to speed—which is only about thirty miles an hour because the accident's crammed everyone into the left three lanes. Sipping Coca-Cola, he looks the accident over. Highway cops aren't there yet, just the Toyota four-by-four, the rusty semi with its hood wired down, and a Yugo. The VW got away, but the little caramel-colored Yugo is like an accordion against the back of the truck. The Toyota is bent into a short boomerang shape around the snout of the semi, which is jackknifed onto the road shoulder. The Mexican driver is nowhere around. Probably didn't have a green card, ducked out before the cops show up. The palm trees kinked up in the back of the semi are whole, grown-up palm trees, with the roots and some soil tied up in big plastic bags, going to some rebuilt place in Bel Air. One of the palm trees droops almost completely off the back of the trailer.

Jody checks out the dude sitting on the Toyota's hood. The guy's sitting there, rocking with pain, waiting. A kind of ski mask of blood on his face.

I did that, three of 'em, bingo, just like that. Maybe it'll get on TV news.

Jody cruised on by and went to find Annie.

It's on TV because of the palm trees. Jody and Annie, at home, drink Coronas, watch the crane lifting the palm trees off the freeway. The TV anchordude is saying someone is in stable condition, nobody killed; so that's why, Jody figures, it is, like, okay for the newsmen to joke about the palm trees on the freeway. Annie has the little Toshiba portable with the 12" screen, on three long extension cords, up in the kitchen window so they can see it on the back porch, because it is too hot to watch it in the living room. If Jody leans forward a little he can see the sun between the houses off to the west. In the smog the sun is a smooth red ball just easing to the horizon; you can look right at it.

Jody glances at Annie, wondering if he made a mistake, telling her what he did.

He can feel her watching him as he opens the third Corona. Pretty soon she'll say, "You going to drink more than three you better pay for the next round." Something she'd never say if he had a job, even if she'd paid for it then too. It's a way to get at the job thing.

She's looking at him, but she doesn't say anything. Maybe it's the wreck on TV. "Guy's not dead," he says, "too fucking bad." Making a macho thing about it.

"You're an asshole." But the tone of her voice says something else. What, exactly? Not admiration. Enjoyment, maybe.

Annie has her hair teased out; the red parts of her hair look redder in this light; the blond parts look almost real. Her eyes are the glassy greenblue the waves get to be in the afternoon up at Point Mugu, with the light coming through the water. Deep tan, white lipstick. He'd never liked that white lipstick look, white eyeliner and the pale-pink fingernail polish that went with it, but he never told her. "Girls who wear that shit are usually airheads," he'd have to say. And she wouldn't believe him when he told her he didn't mean her. She's sitting on the edge of her rickety kitchen chair in that old white shirt of his she wears for a shorty dress, leaning forward so he can see her cleavage, the arcs of her tan lines, her small feet flat on the stucco backporch, her feet planted wide apart but with her knees together, like the feet are saying one thing and the knees another.

His segment is gone from TV but he gets that *right there* feeling again as he takes her by the wrist and she says, "*Guy*, Jody, what do you think I *am?*" But joking.

He leads her to the bedroom and, standing beside the bed, puts his hand between her legs and he can feel he doesn't have to get her readier, he can get right to the good part. Everything just sort of slips right into place. She locks her legs around his back and they're still standing up, but it's like she hardly weighs anything at all. She tilts her head back, opens her mouth; he can see her broken front tooth, a guillotine shape.

They're doing 45 on the 101. It's a hot, windy night.
They're listening to *Motley Crue* on the Sony ghetto blaster
that stands on end between Annie's feet. The music makes him
feel good but it hurts too because now he's thinking about
Iron Dream. The band kicking him out because he couldn't
get the solo parts to go fast enough. And because he missed
some rehearsals. They should have let him play rhythm and
sing backup, but the fuckers kicked him out. That's something he and Annie have. Both feeling like they were shoved
out of line somewhere. Annie wants to be an actress, but she
can't get a part, except once she was an extra for a TV show
with a bogus rock club scene. Didn't even get her Guild card
from that.

Annie is going on about something, always talking,
it's like she can't stand the air to be empty. He doesn't really
mind it. She's saying, "So I go, 'I'm *sure* I'm gonna fill in for
that bitch when she accuses me of stealing her tips.' And he
goes, 'Oh you know how Felicia is, she doesn't mean anything.' I mean—*guy*—he's always saying poor Felicia, you
know how Felicia is, cutting her slack, but he, like, *never* cuts
me any slack, and I've got two more tables to wait, so I'm all,
'Oh right poor Felicia—' and he goes—" Jody nods every so
often, and even listens closely for a minute when she talks
about the customers who treat her like a waitress. "I mean,
what do they think, I'll always be a waitress? I'm *sure* I'm,
like, totally a Felicia who's always, you know, going to be a
wait-ress—" He knows what she means. You're pumping gas
and people treat you like you're a born pump jockey and
you'll never do anything else. He feels like he's really *with* her,
then. It's things like that, and things they don't say; it's like
they're looking out the same window together all the time.
She sees things the way he does: how people don't understand. Maybe he'll write a song about it. Record it, hit big,
Iron Dream'll shit their pants. Wouldn't they, though?

"My Dad wants this car back, for his girlfriend," Annie says.

"Oh fuck her," Jody says. "She's too fucking drunk to drive, *any*time."

Almost eleven-thirty but she isn't saying anything about having to work tomorrow, she's jacked up same as he is. They haven't taken anything, but they both feel like they have. Maybe it's the Santa Anas blowing weird shit into the valley.

"This car's a piece of junk anyway," Annie says. "It knocks, radiator boils over. Linkage is going out."

"It's better than no car."

"You had it together, you wouldn't have to settle for this car."

She means getting a job, but he still feels like she's saying, "If you were a better guitar player . . . " Someone's taking a turn on a big fucking screw that goes through his chest. That's the second time the feeling comes. Everything going all flat again, and he can't tell his hands from the steering wheel.

There is a rush of panic, almost like when Annie's dad took him up in the Piper to go skydiving; like the moment when he pulled the cord and nothing happened. He had to pull it twice. Before the parachute opened he was spinning around like a dust mote. What difference would it make if he *did* hit the ground?

It's like that now, he's just hurtling along, sitting back and watching himself, that weird detachment thing . . . Not sure he is in control of the car. What difference would it make if he *wasn't* in control?

And then he pulls off the freeway, and picks up a wrench from the backseat.

"You're really good at getting it on TV," she says. "It's a talent, like being a director." They are indoors this time, sitting up in bed, watching it in the bedroom, with the fan on. It was too risky talking out on the back porch.

"Maybe I should be a director. Make *Nightmare On Elm Street* better than that last one. That last one sucked."

They are watching the news coverage for the third time on the VCR. You could get these hot VCRs for like sixty bucks from a guy on Hollywood Boulevard, if you saw him walking around at the right time. They'd gotten a couple of discount tapes at Federated and they'd recorded the newscast.

" . . . we're not sure it's a gang-related incident," the detective on TV was saying. "The use of a wrench—throwing a wrench from the car at someone—uh, that's not the usual gang methodology."

"Methodology," Jody says. "Christ."

There's a clumsy camera zoom on a puddle of blood on the ground. Not very good color on this TV, Jody thinks; the blood is more purple than red.

The camera lingers on the blood as the cop says, "They usually use guns. Uzis, weapons along those lines. Of course, the victim was killed just the same. At those speeds a wrench thrown from a car is a deadly weapon. We have no definite leads. . . . "

" 'They usually use guns,' " Jody says. "I'll use a gun on your balls, shit-head."

Annie snorts happily, and playfully kicks him in the side with her bare foot. "You're such an asshole. You're gonna get in trouble. Shouldn't be using my dad's car, for one thing." But saying it teasingly, chewing her lip to keep from smiling too much.

"You fucking love it," he says, rolling onto her.

"Wait." She wriggles free, rewinds the tape, starts it over. It plays in the background. "Come here, asshole."

Jody's brother Cal says, "What's going on with you, huh? How come everything I say pisses you off? It's like, *any*thing. I mean, you're only two years younger than me but you act like you're fourteen sometimes."

"Oh hey Cal," Jody says, snorting, "you're, like, Mr. Mature."

They're in the parking lot of the mall, way off in the corner. Cal in his Pasadena School of Art & Design t-shirt, his yuppie haircut, yellow-tinted John Lennon sunglasses. They're standing by Cal's '81 Subaru, that Mom bought him "because he went to school." They're blinking in the metallic sunlight, at the corner of the parking lot by the boulevard. The only place there's any parking. A couple of acres of cars between them and the main structure of the mall. They're supposed to have lunch with Mom, who keeps busy with her gift shop in the mall, with coffee grinders and dried eucalyptus and silk flowers. But Jody's decided he doesn't want to go.

"I just don't want you to say anymore of this shit to me, Cal," Jody says. "Telling me about *being* somebody." Jody's slouching against the car, his hand slashing the air like a karate move as he talks. He keeps his face down, half hidden by his long, purple streaked hair, because he's too mad at Cal to look right at him: Cal hassled and wheedled him into coming here. Jody is kicking Cal's tires with the back of a lizardskin boot and every so often he kicks the hubcap, trying to dent it. "I don't need the same from you I get from Mom."

"Just because she's a bitch doesn't mean she's wrong all the time," Cal says. "Anyway what's the big deal? You used to go along peacefully and listen to Mom's one-way heart-to-hearts and say what she expects and—" He shrugs.

Jody knows what he means: The forty bucks or so she'd hand him afterward "to get him started."

"It's not worth it anymore," Jody says.

"You don't have any other source of money but Annie and she won't put up with it much longer. It's time to get real, Jody, to get a job and—"

"Don't tell me I need a job to get real." Jody slashes the air with the edge of his hand. "Real is where your ass is when you shit," he adds savagely. "Now fucking shut up about it."

Jody looks at the mall, trying to picture meeting Mom in there. It makes him feel heavy and tired. Except for the fiberglass letters—*Northridge Galleria*—styled to imitate handwriting across its offwhite, pebbly surface, the outside of the mall could be a military building, an enormous bunker. Just a great windowless . . . *block.* "I hate that place, Cal. That mall and that busywork shop. Dad gave her the shop to keep her off valium. Fuck. Like fingerpainting for retards."

He stares at the mall, thinking: That cutesy sign, I hate that. Cutesy handwriting but the sign is big enough to crush you dead if it fell on you. *Northridge Galleria.* You could almost hear a radio ad voice saying it over and over again, "Northridge Galleria! . . . Northridge Galleria! . . . Northridge Galleria! . . . "

To their right is a Jack-in-the-Box order-taking intercom. Jody smells the hot plastic of the sun-baked clown-face and the dogfoody hamburger smell of the drive-through mixed in. To their left is a Pioneer Chicken with its cartoon covered-wagon sign.

Cal sees him looking at it. Maybe trying to pry Jody loose from obsessing about Mom, Cal says, "You know how many Pioneer Chicken places there are in L.A.? You think you're driving in circles because every few blocks one comes up. . . . It's like the ugliest fucking wallpaper pattern in the world."

"Shut up about that shit too."

"What put you in this mood? You break up with Annie?"

"No. We're fine. I just don't want to have lunch with Mom."

"Well goddamn Jody, you shouldn't have said you would, then."

Jody shrugs. He's trapped in the reflective oven of the parking lot, sun blazing from countless windshields and shiny metalflake hoods and from the plastic clownface. Eyes burning from the lancing reflections. Never forget your sunglasses. But no way is he going in.

Cal says, "Look, Jody, I'm dehydrating out here. I mean, fuck this parking lot. There's a couple of palm trees around the edges but look at this place—it's the surface of the moon."

"Stop being so fucking arty," Jody says. "You're going to art and design school, oh wow awesome I'm impressed."

"I'm just—" Cal shakes his head. "How come you're mad at Mom?"

"She wants me to come over, it's just so she can tell me her latest scam for getting me to do some shit, go to community college, study haircutting or something. Like she's really on top of my life. Fuck, I was a teenager I told her I was going to hitchhike to New York she didn't even look up from her card game."

"What'd you expect her to do?"

"I don't know."

"Hey that was when she was on her Self-Dependence kick. She was into Lifespring and Est and Amway and all that. They keep telling her she's not responsible for other people, not responsible, not responsible—"

"She went for it like a fucking fish to water, man." He gives Cal a look that means, *no bullshit*. "What is it she wants *now?*"

"Um—I think she wants you to go to some vocational school."

Jody makes a snorting sound up in his sinuses. "Fuck that. Open up your car, Cal, I ain't going."

"Look, she's just trying to help. What the hell's wrong with having a skill? It doesn't mean you can't do something else too—"

"Cal. She gave you the Subaru, it ain't mine. But you're gonna open the fucking thing up." He hopes Cal knows how serious he is. Because that two-dimensional feeling might come on him, if he doesn't get out of here. Words just spill out of him. "Cal, look at this fucking place. Look at this place and tell me about vocational skills. It's shit, Cal. There's two things in the world, dude. There's making it like *Bon Jovi*, like Eddie Murphy—that's one thing. You're on a screen, you're on videos and CDs. Or there's *shit*. That's the other thing. There's *no fucking thing in between*. There's being *Huge*— and there's being nothing." His voice breaking. "We're shit, Cal. Open up the fucking car or I'll kick your headlights in."

Cal stares at him. Then he unlocks the car, his movements short and angry. Jody gets in, looking at a sign on the other side of the parking lot, one of those electronic signs with the lights spelling things out with moving words. The sign says, *You want it, we got it . . . you want it, we got it . . . you want it, we got it . . .*

He wanted a Luger. They look rad in war movies. Jody said it was James Coburn, Annie said it was Lee Marvin, but whoever it was, he was using a Luger in that Peckinpah movie *Iron Cross*.

But what Jody ends up with is a Smith-Wesson .32, the magazine carrying eight rounds. It's smaller than he'd thought it would be, a scratched gray-metal weight in his palm. They buy four boxes of bullets, drive out to the country, out past Topanga Canyon. They find a fire road of rutted salmon-colored dirt, lined with pine trees on one side; the other side has a margin of grass that looks like soggy Shredded Wheat, and a barbed wire fence edging an empty horse pasture.

They take turns with the gun, Annie and Jody, shooting Bud-Light bottles from a splintery gray fence post. A lot of the time they miss the bottles. Jody said, "This piece's pulling to the left." He isn't sure if it really is, but Annie seems to like when he talks as if he knows about it.

It's nice out there, he likes the scent of gunsmoke mixed with the pine tree smell. Birds were singing for awhile, too, but they stopped after the shooting, scared off. His hand hurts from the gun's recoil, but he doesn't say anything about that to Annie.

"What we got to do," she says, taking a pot-shot at a squirrel, "is try shooting from the car."

He shakes his head. "You think you'll aim better from in a car?"

"I mean from a *moving* car, stupid." She gives him a look of exasperation. "To get used to it."

"Hey yeah."

They get the old Buick bouncing down the rutted fire road, about thirty feet from the fence post when they pass it, and Annie fires twice, and misses. "The stupid car bounces too much on this road," she says.

"Let me try it."

"No wait—make it more like a city street, drive in the grass off the road. No ruts."

"Uh . . . Okay." So he backs up, they try it again from the grass verge. She misses again, but they keep on because she insists, and about the fourth time she starts hitting the post, and the sixth time she hits the bottle.

"Well why *not?*" she asks again.

Jody doesn't like backing off from this in front of Annie, but it feels like it is too soon or something. "Because now we're just gone and nobody knows who it is. If we hold up a store it'll take time, they might have silent alarms, we might get caught." They are driving with the top up, to give them some cover in case they decide to try the gun here, but the windows are rolled down because the old Buick's air conditioning is busted.

"Oh right I'm *sure* some *7-11* store is going to have a silent alarm."

"Just wait, that's all. Let's do this first. We got to get more used to the gun."

"And get another one. So we can both have one."

For some reason that scares him. But he says: "Yeah. Okay."

It is late afternoon. They are doing 60 on the 405. Jody not wanting to get stopped by the CHP when he has a gun in his car. Besides, they are a little drunk because shooting out at Topanga Canyon in the sun made them thirsty, and this hippie on this gnarly old *tractor* had come along, some pot farmer maybe, telling them to get off his land, and that pissed them off. So they drank too much beer.

They get off the 405 at Burbank Boulevard, looking at the other cars, the people on the sidewalk, trying to pick someone out. Some asshole.

But no one looks right. Or maybe it doesn't feel right. He doesn't have that feeling on him.

"Let's wait," he suggests.

"Why?"

"Because it just seems like we oughta, that's why."

She makes a clucking sound but doesn't say anything else for awhile. They drive past a patch of adult bookstores and a video arcade and a liquor store. They come to a park. The trash cans in the park have overflowed; wasps are haunting some melon rinds on the ground. In the basketball court four Chicanos are playing two-on-two, wearing those shiny, pointy black shoes they wear. "You ever notice how Mexican guys, they play basketball and football in dress shoes?" Jody asks. "It's like they never heard of sneakers—"

He hears a *crack* and a thudding echo and a greasy chill goes through him as he realizes that she's fired the gun. He glimpses a Chicano falling, shouting in pain, the others flattening on the tennis court, looking around for the shooter as he stomps the accelerator, lays rubber, squealing through a red light, cars bitching their horns at him, his heart going in time with the pistons, fear vising his stomach. He's weaving through the cars, looking for the freeway entrance. Listening for sirens.

They are on the freeway, before he can talk. The rush hour traffic only doing about 45, but he feels better here. Hidden.

"What the *fuck* you doing?!" he yells at her.

She gives him a look accusing him of something. He isn't sure what. Betrayal maybe. Betraying the thing they had made between them.

"Look—" he says, softer, "it was a *red light*. People almost hit me coming down the cross street. You know? You got to think a little first. And don't do it when I don't *know*."

She looks at him like she is going to spit. Then she laughs, and he has to laugh too. She says, "Did you see those dweebs *dive?*"

Mouths dry, palms damp, they watch the five o'clock news and the six o'clock news. Nothing. Not a word about it. They sit up in the bed, drinking Coronas. Not believing it. "I mean, what kind of fucking society *is* this?" Jody says. Like something Cal would say. "When you shoot somebody and they don't even say a damn word about it on TV?"

"It's sick," Annie says.

They try to make love but it just isn't there. It's like trying to start a gas stove when the pilot light is out.

So they watch *Hunter* on TV. Hunter is after a psychokiller. The psycho guy is a real creep. Set a house on fire with some kids in it, they almost got burnt up, except Hunter gets there in time. Finally Hunter corners the psychokiller and shoots him. Annie says, "I like TV better than movies because you know how it's gonna turn out. But in movies it might have a happy ending or it might not."

"It usually does," Jody points out.

"Oh yeah? Did you see *Terms of Endearment*? And they got *Bambi* out again now. When I was a kid I cried for two days when his Mom got shot. They should always have happy endings in a little kidlet movie."

"That part, that wasn't the end of that movie. It was happy in the end."

"It was still a sad movie."

Finally at eleven o'clock they're on. About thirty

seconds worth. A man "shot in the leg on Burbank Boulevard today in a drive-by shooting believed to be gang related." On to the next story. No pictures, nothing. That was it.

What a rip off. "It's racist, is what it is," he says. "Just because they were Mexicans no one gives a shit."

"You know what it is, it's because of all the gang stuff. Gang drive-bys happen every day, everybody's used to it."

He nods. She's right. She has a real feel for these things. He puts his arm around her; she nestles against him. "Okay. We're gonna do it right, so they really pay attention."

"What if we get caught?"

Something in him freezes when she says that. She isn't supposed to talk like that. Because of the *thing* they have together. It isn't something they ever talk about, but they know its rules.

When he withdraws a little, she says, "But we'll never get caught because we just *do it* and cruise before anyone gets together."

He relaxes, and pulls her closer. It feels good just to lay there and hug her.

The next day he's in line for his unemployment insurance check. They have stopped his checks, temporarily, and he'd had to hassle them. They said he could pick this one up. He had maybe two more coming.

Thinking about that, he feels a bad mood coming on him. There's no air conditioning in this place and the fat guy in front of him smells like he's fermenting and the room's so hot and close Jody can hardly breathe.

He looks around and can almost *see* the feeling— like an effect of a camera lens, a zoom or maybe a fish eye lens: Things going two dimensional, flattening out. Annie says something and he just shrugs. She doesn't say anything else till after he's got his check and he's practically running for the door.

"Where you going?"

He shakes his head, standing outside, looking around. It's not much better outside. It's overcast but still hot. "Sucks in there."

"Yeah," she says. "For sure. Oh shit."

"What?"

She points at the car. Someone has slashed the canvas top of the Buick. "My dad is going to kill us."

He looks at the canvas and can't believe it. "Mu-ther-*fuck!*-er!"

"Fucking assholes," she says, nodding gravely. "I mean, you know how much that costs to fix? You wouldn't believe it."

"Maybe we can find him."

"How?"

"I don't know."

He still feels bad but there's a hum of anticipation too. They get in the car, he tears out of the parking lot, making gravel spray, whips onto the street.

They drive around the block, just checking people out, the feeling in him spiraling up and up. Then he sees a guy in front of a Carl's Jr., the guy grinning at him, nudging his friend. Couple of jock college students, looks like, in tank tops. Maybe the guy who did the roof of the car, maybe not.

They pull around the corner, coming back around for another look. Jody can feel the good part of the feeling coming on now but there's something bothering him too: the jocks in tank tops looked right at him.

"You see those two guys?" he hears himself ask, as he pulls around the corner, cruises up next to the Carl's Jr. "The ones—"

"Those jock guys, I know, I picked them out too."

He glances at her, feeling close to her then. They are one person in two parts. The right and the left hand. It feels like music.

He makes sure there's a green light ahead of him,

then says, "Get 'em both," he hears himself say. "Don't miss or—"

By then she's aiming the .32, both hands wrapped around it. The jock guys, one of them with a huge coke and the other with a milkshake, are standing by the driveway to the restaurant's parking lot, talking, one of them playing with his car keys. Laughing. The bigger one with the dark hair looks up and sees Annie and the laughing fades from his face. Seeing that, Jody feels better than he ever felt before. *Crack, crack.* She fires twice, the guys go down. *Crack, crack, crack.* Three times more, making sure it gets on the news: shooting into the windows of the Carl's Jr., webs instantly snapping into the window glass, some fat lady goes spinning, her tray of burgers tilting, flying. Jody's already laying rubber, fishtailing around the corner, heading for the freeway.

They don't make it home, they're so excited. She tells him to stop at a gas station on the other side of the hills, in Hollywood. The Men's is unlocked, he feels really right *there* as she looks around then leads him into the bathroom, locks the door from the inside. Bathroom's an almost clean one, he notices, as she hikes up her skirt and he undoes his pants, both of them with shaking fingers, in a real hurry, and she pulls him into her with no preliminaries, right there with her sitting on the edge of the sink. There's no mirror but he sees a cloudy reflection in the shiny chrome side of the towel dispenser; the two of them blurred into one thing sort of pulsing . . .

He looks straight at her, then; she's staring past him, not at anything in particular, just at the sensation, the good sensation they are grinding out between them, like it's something she can see on the dust-streaked wall. He can almost see it in her eyes. And in the way she traps the end of her tongue between her front teeth. Now he can see it himself, in his mind's eye, the sensation flashing like sun in a mirror; ringing like a power chord through a fuzz box. . . .

When he comes he doesn't hold anything back, he can't, and it escapes from him with a sob. She holds him tight and he says, "Wow you are just so awesome you make me feel so *good . . .*"

He's never said anything like that to her before, and they know they've arrived somewhere special. "I love you, Jody," she says.

"I love you."

"It's just us, Jody. Just us. Just us."

He knows what she means. And they feel like little kids cuddling together, even though they're fucking standing up in a *Union 76* Men's restroom, in the smell of pee and disinfectant.

Afterwards they're really hungry so they go to a Jack-in-the-Box, get drive-through food, ordering a whole big shitload. They eat it on the way home, Jody trying not to speed, trying to be careful again about being stopped, but hurrying in case they have a special news flash on TV about the Carl's Jr. Not wanting to miss it.

The Fajita Pita from Jack-in-the-Box tastes really great.

While he's eating, Jody scribbles some song lyrics into his song notebook with one hand. "The Ballad of Jody and Annie."

They came smokin' down the road
like a bat out of hell
they hardly even slowed
or they'd choke from the smell

Chorus:
Holdin' hands in the Valley of Death
(repeat 3X)

Jody and Annie bustin' out of bullshit
Bustin' onto TV
better hope you aren't the one hit
killed disonnerably

Nobody understands em
nobody ever will
but Jody knows she loves 'im
They never get their fill

They will love forever
in history
and they'll live together
in femmy

Holdin' hands in the Valley of Death

He runs out of inspiration there. He hints heavily to
Annie about the lyrics and pretends he doesn't want her to
read them, makes her ask three times. With tears in her eyes,
she asks, as she reads the lyrics, "What's a femmy?"

"You know, like 'Living In femmy.'"

"Oh, infamy. It's so beautiful. . . . You got guacamole
on it, you asshole." She's crying with happiness and using a
napkin to reverently wipe the guacamole from the notebook
paper.

There's no special news flash but since three people
died and two are in intensive care, they are the top story on
the five o'clock news. And at seven o'clock they get mentioned
on CNN, which is *national*. Another one, and they'll be on the
NBC Nightly News, Jody says.

"I'd rather be on *World News Tonight*," Annie says.
"I like that Peter Jennings dude. He's cute."

About ten, they watch the videotapes of the news
stories again. Jody guesses he should be bothered that the

cops have descriptions of them but somehow it just makes him feel more psyched, and he gets down with Annie again. They almost never do it twice in one day, but this makes three times. "I'm getting sore," she says, when he enters her. But she gets off.

They're just finishing, he's coming, vaguely aware he sees lights flashing at the windows, when he hears Cal's voice coming out of the walls. He thinks he's gone schizophrenic or something, he's hearing voices, booming like the voice of God. *"Jody, come on outside and talk to us. This is Cal, you guys. Come on out."*

Then Jody understands, when Cal says, *"They want you to throw the gun out first."*

Jody pulls out of her, puts his hand over her mouth, and shakes his head. He pulls his pants on, then goes into the front room, looks through a corner of the window. There's Cal, and a lot of cops.

Cal's standing behind the police barrier, the cruiser lights flashing around him; beside him is a heavyset Chicano cop who's watching the S.W.A.T. team gearing up behind the big gray van. They're scary-looking in all that armor and with those helmets and shotguns and sniper rifles.

Jody spots Annie's Dad. He's tubby, with a droopy mustache, long hair going bald at the crown, some old hippie, sitting in the back of a cruiser. Jody figures someone got their license number. He can picture the whole thing: The cops had the license number, took them awhile to locate Annie's Dad. He wasn't home at first. They waited till he came home, since he owns the car, and after they talked to him they decided it was his daughter and her boyfriend they were looking for. Got the address from him. Drag Cal over here to talk to Jody because Mom wouldn't come. Yeah.

Cal speaks into the bullhorn again, same crap, sounding like someone else echoing off the houses. Jody sees people looking out their windows. Some being evacuated from the nearest houses. Now an *Action News* truck pulls up, cameramen pile out, set up incredibly fast, get right to work with the newscaster. Lots of activity just for Jody and Annie. Jody has to grin, seeing the news cameras, the guy he recognizes from TV waiting for his cue. He feels high, looking at all this. Cal says something else, but Jody isn't listening. He goes to get the gun.

"It's just us, Jody," Annie says, her face flushed, her eyes dilated as she helps him push the sofa in front of the door. "We can do anything together."

She is there, not scared at all, her voice all around him soft and warm. "It's just us," she says again, as he runs to get another piece of furniture.

He is running around like a speedfreak, pushing the desk, leaning bookshelves to block off the tear gas. Leaving enough room for him to shoot through. He sees the guys start to come up the walk with the tear gas and the shotguns. Guys in helmets and some kind of bulky bulletproof shit. But maybe he can hit their necks, or their knees. He aims carefully and fires again. Someone stumbles and the others carry the wounded dude back behind the cars.

Five minutes after Jody starts shooting, he notices that Annie isn't there. At almost the same moment a couple of rifle rounds knock the bookshelves down, and something smashes through a window. In the middle of the floor, white mist gushes out of a teargas shell.

Jody runs from the tear gas, into the kitchen, coughing. "Annie!" His voice sounding like a kid's.

He looks through the kitchen window. Has she gone outside, turned traitor?

But then she appears at his elbow, like somebody switched on a screen and Annie is what's on it.

"Hey," she says, her eyes really bright and beautiful. "Guess what." She has the little TV by the handle; it's plugged in on the extension cord. In the next room, someone is breaking through the front door.

"I give up," he says, eyes tearing. "What?"

She sits the TV on the counter for him to see. "We're on TV. Right now. We're on TV. . . . "

BENTLEY LITTLE *is the type of writer who makes other writers green-eyed with jealousy. His work is swift and lean, and he writes quicker than should be allowed. Case in point: When I asked for a* Cold Blood *story, the following supernatural gem arrived in my mailbox less than a week later with the attached message: "I wrote this the other afternoon. I hope you like it." Little's work has appeared in virtually all the genre and men's magazines. His debut novel,* The Revelation, *was published in hardcover by St. Martins, and* The Mailman *was recently released by NAL.*

BUMBLEBEE
BENTLEY LITTLE

Trinidad was still alive when I found him. Barely. Julio had called and told me that he'd seen the redneck's pickup heading through the desert north of Cave Creek, hellbent for leather on the old dirt road that led to Bloody Basin, and while Julio wasn't exactly the world's most reliable songbird, I believed him this time, and I decided to follow up on it.

I found Trinidad lying face down in a low drainage ditch. He was easy to spot. The ditch ran right next to the road, and the coyote's red flannel shirt stood out like a beacon against the pale desert sand. I jumped out of the Jeep without bothering to turn off the ignition and slid down the side of the ditch. The redneck hadn't made much of an effort to either cover his tracks or hide the body, which made me think he hadn't intended to kill the coyote, only scare him, but Trinidad was still badly hurt. His face was a swollen demonstration of various bruise types, blood leaked from his nose, mouth and both ears, and it was clear from the awkward angles at which he held his arms and legs that there'd been a lot of bones broken.

I knelt down next to the coyote. His eyes were closed, and he did not open them even when I called his name. I touched my hand to his bloody cheek, and he moaned, trying to pull away. "You okay?" I asked.

"Bumblebee," he whispered, eyes still closed.

He was obviously far gone, delirious, and I cursed myself for not having fixed the CB in the Jeep. It was a ten minute drive back to Cave Creek, and nearly an hour's drive back to the nearest hospital in Scottsdale. Phoenix Memorial had a chopper and theoretically could fly over and pick him up, but there was no way to get ahold of them.

I was afraid to move Trinidad, but more afraid to leave him, so I quickly ran up the side of the ditch, opened the Jeep's back gate, spread out a blanket and slid back down to where the coyote lay. Trinidad was heavier than I thought— it's never as easy to carry a man in real life as it seems in the movies—but adrenalin strength let me lift him up the incline. I placed him carefully down on the blankets, my arms soaked with the warm wetness of his blood. I closed the gate. "Don't worry," I told him. "I'll get you home safely."

He moaned in agony. "Bumblebee," he repeated.

By the time we reached Cave Creek he was dead.

The sun rose precisely at five forty-five. By six-thirty, the temperature was already well into the nineties. The television weatherman on the morning news told me while I was drinking my wakeup coffee that it was going to be "another gorgeous day," and I flipped him off. To him it might be "another gorgeous day," but to those of us with no air conditioners in our cars, who had to work outside of climate controlled offices, it was going to be another sentence in hell.

I finished my coffee and quickly scanned the news-paper to see if Trinidad's death had made the back pages or the obituary column. Nothing. Nada. Zip. I wasn't surprised. Print space in Arizona newspapers was generally reserved for those with Anglo ancestry. Even Latinos who had crossed over into mainstream success got short shrift, and the passing of people like Trinidad, who were successful only in the immigrant underground, weren't acknowledged at all.

Some days I was ashamed to be white.

Last night, I'd told everything I knew to the police. They dutifully took it down, but the case against the redneck was weak at best, the evidence based solely on hearsay accounts by notoriously unreliable witnesses, and I knew the investigation into Trinidad's death would get the Phoenix Special—a two day open file with no accompanying legwork, and an "UNSOLVED" stamp on top of the folder. The situation might have been different if Trinidad had been white, if he'd been respectable, but then again it might not. Heat seemed to make a lot of people lazy, especially cops.

Bumblebee.

I'd been puzzling over that all night, unsure if it was supposed to mean something or if it was merely a word dragged from the depths of Trinidad's dying hallucinating brain. I was going to assume that it was meaningful, that the coyote was trying to tell me something. I owed him at least that much. Besides, death lent weight to mysteriously muttered phrases whether they deserved it or not.

I finished my coffee, finished my paper.

Just before eight, I called up Hog Santucci, a friend of mine who worked downtown in Records, and ran the name by him. It didn't seem to ring any bells, but then it had been a shot in the dark anyway. Even if Trinidad had been trying to tell me something, I still didn't know whether "Bumblebee" was the name of a man, the codeword for a booked passage, or the identification of an item or process known only to him.

I figured I'd check with Julio next, see if he knew what the name meant, see if he knew any more about Trinidad's rendezvous with the redneck at the same time.

The redneck.

That son of a bitch was really starting to get to me. Usually, when I take a case or get involved in an investigation, it's easy for me to keep my distance, to maintain my professionalism. I don't make moral judgements, I simply do what I am hired to do, and I only take a job if its parameters are well within the boundaries of legality. This Raymond Chandler crap about straddling-the-line, or those Bogart and Mitchum movies where the detective always falls for a pretty face and battles for her honor with the villain, that's all bullshit. Pure fiction. But the redneck really was like one of those movie villains, and I hated the son of a bitch. Especially since I couldn't seem to get a single scrap of evidence on him.

What made it even worse was that the redneck seemed to be almost a folk hero to some of those pin-striped pinheads who passed for human in the downtown offices of the INS. It was well-known in certain circles that he'd had a hand in the fire that had destroyed one of the big Sanctuary safehouses down in Casa Grande, and that he'd had something to do with those fourteen illegals who'd roasted to death in that abandoned semi outside of Tucson. But while the feds and the locals were making a big show out of fighting it out over jurisdictional rights, both were making only token efforts to drudge up evidence. As they saw it, the redneck was doing their work for them, in his own crudely violent way. As a criminal, he was not subject to the same restrictions they were, and in a warped and twisted way they seemed to admire his racist ingenuity.

Strangely enough, I'd been hired by Father Lopez, a priest involved in the Sanctuary movement, to look into the matter. Tired of dealing with the intransigence of the blue uniforms, the grey suits and the red tape, afraid for the safety of the dozen or so Salvadoran refugees he was hiding in the basement of his church, he'd asked me to see if I could dig up anything on the redneck which could put him away for good. Father Lopez had been threatened more than once, and he knew it was only a matter of time before those threats were carried through.

So far, I'd come up snake eyes, but I was getting close and the redneck knew it. That's why he'd roughed up Trinidad. And that's why the deal had gone wrong. I don't think he'd intended to kill the coyote, but he had. He'd panicked, gone too far, and now the noose was starting to tighten. It was only a matter of time before he slipped up, made a mistake, and I pulled that sucker taut. The law might not be willing to work to bring down the redneck, but they couldn't and wouldn't turn him out if he was dropped, case closed, into their fat blue laps.

Julio was gone when I stopped by his apartment, and his old lady didn't seem to know where he'd gone to. Or at least wasn't willing to inform a cowboy-booted gringo of his where-abouts, so I decided to drop by and see Father Lopez.

At the church it was pandemonium. Father Lopez had made the mistake of telling his guests that Trinidad was walking with God, hoping they'd help him pray for the coyote, but the result had been to panic the refugees. Trinidad had brought most of them over, was their sole symbol of strength and stability in this country, and his killing frightened them badly. They naturally thought that his murder was the result of a death squad bent on tracking them down. When I arrived, Father Lopez was trying to explain that the coyote had been killed by an American, an American acting on his own and not in the employ of their government, but it was clear even to me that few if any of them were buying it. They seemed to want to leave the church now, strike out on their own and take their chances scattered on the street.

"Father," I said. "I need to talk to you for a minute."

"Hold on." He spoke rapidly in Spanish to the agitated people in the basement, trying to assuage their fears.

My Spanish was nowhere near fluent, but I moved next to the priest, motioned for him to be quiet, and gave the refugees my own version of the story. Since I was white and obviously American, my words carried a little more weight than those of the priest, though they were spoken haltingly. I guess to them I represented some sort of authority.

Father Lopez looked at me gratefully, then expanded on what I'd said, speaking quickly and reassuringly. It seemed to work. I went back upstairs to wait.

After the situation had settled down and Father Lopez had emerged from the basement, I spoke to the priest alone. We were in his office off the vestibule, and I was seated in a low comfortable chair. I leaned forward. "Does the name Bumblebee mean anything to you?" I asked.

He had been casually leaning back in his chair, and suddenly he sat up very straight. His face was pale. "Who told you about Bumblebee?"

"Trinidad," I said. "Although he didn't really tell me. It was the last thing he said before he died."

The priest crossed himself. "No," he said.

"Yes." I stood up. I put my hands in my back pockets and began pacing. "Look," I said. "If there's something I should know, you'd better tell me. When I work for a client, I expect that client to be straight with me, to lay all of his cards on the table. I don't care if you are a priest, I expect you to tell me everything. I'm on your side. And I can't look out for your interests if I don't have all the facts."

Father Lopez seemed to have regained his composure. He nodded slowly. "All right," he said.

"Good." I sat down again. "So what exactly is Bumblebee?"

"It's a town. An old ghost town in the Sonora Desert past Tucson. I'm surprised you haven't heard of it. There was a big battle there in the late 1800s between United States troops and a small group of Mexican renegades. The renegades weren't affiliated with the Mexican government, but they were basically fighting the same fight. Only the men at Bumblebee didn't lose their battle, although Mexico eventually lost the war. Seventeen untrained fighters successfully held off and killed over a hundred American troops. The Americans just kept coming, and they just kept getting killed. Finally they gave up, decided to avoid the town and fought elsewhere. I guess they wrote it off as a loss. When the fighting was over and the boundaries were redrawn, however, Bumblebee became part of Arizona. Politics destroyed what war couldn't."

"That's a nice story," I said. "But what does it have to do with Trinidad?"

"I don't know," the priest told me, meeting my gaze.

He was lying. I knew he was lying, and he knew I knew he was lying. I sat unmoving. Father Lopez was neither a stupid nor cowardly man, and he wouldn't have played albino and crossed himself if there hadn't been something heavy on his mind. Bumblebee and whatever that implied had scared the holy shit out of him, but I knew if I pressed him any further he was going to Pismo up on me, so I decided to drop back. I felt I had enough to work with.

It was time to take a trip.

Bookbinder Baker lived in the desert outside Tonopah amidst the bones and bodies of the cars he'd bought and scavenged over the past forty years. Traded Torinos, abandoned Audis and roadkilled Ramblers lay bleached and rusted, sinking into the sand surrounding his three-room shack. His property covered nearly twenty acres of the most godawful terrain known to man. Tonopah itself was a town in name only, an all-night gas station and burger stand halfway between Phoenix and the California border which catered almost exclusively to long-distance truckers, and Baker's place was some fifteen miles down a dirt road beyond that, flat in the middle of the sagebrush infested flatlands. He liked it there, though. Always had.

Baker didn't appear to be around when I arrived, didn't answer either my honks or my call, but I knew he'd be back eventually, and I went inside to make myself at home. As always, his front door was open, screen unlocked, and I simply walked into his living room and sat down on the sagging couch. He'd put a few new hubcaps up on the wall since the last time I'd seen him, and I examined those while I waited.

At one time in the dim and distant past, Baker'd been a teacher of some sort, a historian. He still knew more about the history of the Southwest, major and minute, than anyone I'd ever met. One whole wall of his bedroom was lined with books and magazines on various historical subjects. It was just that now his job and his hobby had been switched. Instead of being a teacher who tinkered with cars on the weekend, he owned an auto yard and studied history on the side, although where he got customers for his auto salvaging service I never could figure out.

I heard the sputtering cough of Baker's engine about five minutes later, and I walked outside to meet him. The tow truck pulled up, empty, in front of the shack. "Hey!" he said. "Long time no care!"

I held up my middle finger, and he laughed.

After the pleasantries, after he'd broken out the beer, we got down to business. I asked him if he'd ever heard of a town called Bumblebee. I repeated Father Lopez's story.

He chuckled. "Hell yes, I remember Bumblebee. That's not its real name, though. That's the American name, given 'cause that's where we got stung. The Spanish name is longer. It means 'magic sands' or something like that." He took a swig of his beer. "Yeah, I been down there many times, taking pictures, checking the place out. It's kind of like our Alamo, you know? Only it never got as much publicity because there weren't nobody famous died there, and because, well, I guess Texans are just better at talking themselves up than we are."

"But why do you think the priest was so scared?"

"Well, Bumblebee was some type of, I don't know, not sacred land exactly, but something like that. I wish I had it documented so I could look it up, but it's not anything that's been written about. I just know that the area was supposed to have some sort of significance for the Mexicans, was supposed to have some sort of magic powers. In the treaty, you know, the original boundaries of our state were different. Mexico wanted to keep Bumblebee, give us Nogales. But we wanted a nice square border, and of course they were in no position to argue." He chuckled. "The legend is that it was the magic which let the Mexicans hold off the troops, that even though they got shot they didn't die."

I looked at him, and I suddenly felt cold.

They didn't die.

"Like I said, I been there before," Baker said. "And I'm not saying I believe all that hocus pocus. But I sure as hell don't disbelieve it either."

When I got back to Phoenix it was nearly dark, and I decided to go straight home.

The police were waiting for me when I arrived.

Lieutenant Armstrong was leaning against the hood of a patrol car, and he stood straight as I got out of the Jeep. He had a wad of chaw in his mouth, and he spit at the ground before me as I walked toward him.

"How long've you been here?" I asked.

"Not long. Five, ten minutes." He smiled at me with his mouth, but his piggy eyes remained hard.

"What do you want me for?"

"Want you to take a little ride." He nodded his head, and a uniformed officer opened the car door. He spit.

I stepped over the brown spot on the sidewalk and got into the back seat.

I stood at the edge of the county cemetery and

looked where Armstrong pointed. Ten or fifteen graves scattered throughout the cemetery had been dug up, caskets and all, leaving only holes and piles of dirt. One of the graves, he had told me in the car, was that of Trinidad.

They waste no time burying "indigents" in Arizona.

"You know anything about this?" the lieutenant asked.

I shook my head.

"Come on, they're your people."

"My people?"

He spit. "You know. Chili eaters. Mesikens. Gonzalez and all them other boys. I know you know what's going on."

"I don't," I said. "I really don't."

Armstrong looked at me. I saw the hate in his eyes. "You want to play it that way?"

"I'm not playing."

He poked me in the chest with a strong fat finger. "You know what you are? You're a traitor. You're . . . " He trailed off, glared at me, unable to think of the word. "What's white on the outside, brown on the inside? The opposite of a coconut?"

"I don't know," I told him. "But I know that you're round on the outside, brown on the inside."

"What?"

"You're an asshole."

He hit me then, and I went down. The punch had not been that hard, but I was unprepared for it, and it went straight to the stomach. I tried to breathe, tried to gulp air, but my lungs seemed to have atrophied.

Armstrong stared at me, watched me clutching my gut on the ground. His face was impassive, but inside I knew he was smiling. "You walk home," he said, turning away.

After I stood, after I caught my breath, after I called him a crooked sack of rancid racist pigshit, I did walk home.

The lieutenant spit at me as, halfway down the block, his car drove past.

◊

I woke up the next morning sweating. The fan had crapped out on me sometime during the night, depriving my bedroom of what little air circulation I could afford, and the sheet I'd used to cover myself was sticking to my soaked skin. I was still tired, but not tired enough to remain in bed and brave the heat. I got up and walked to the bathroom to take a cool shower.

Father Lopez's murder was the top story on the morning's newscast.

I stood in the kitchen, still dripping from the shower, the empty coffeepot in my hand, staring dumbly into the living room at the TV. The scene was live. A blonde female reporter was standing in the midst of a group of people in front of the church, while in the background, clearly framed by the cameraman, Father Lopez's body lay face down on the wide front stairs. Even on television, I could see dark blood trickling down the steps in tiny waterfalls.

I heard the name "Lopez," the words "murdered" and "Sanctuary movement," but I was not listening to the reporter. I was already moving, throwing the metal coffeepot into the sink, grabbing my keys and running out the door.

White-uniformed flunkies from the coroner's office were loading the priest's bagged body into the back of an ambulance when I arrived. Armstrong and another officer were talking closely in hushed tones to a police photographer. The television news crew was packing up and readying to go.

I hadn't known Father Lopez well enough to really feel sad, that deep emotion reserved for people whose loss will affect the rest of our lives, but I felt hurt, disgusted and deeply angry. I strode up to Armstrong. "What happened?" I asked.

He looked at me, said nothing, turned away, and continued his conversation with the photographer.

"Who did it?" I demanded.

The lieutenant did not even glance in my direction.

"Drive by," he said.

I started up the church steps. I knew the refugees were long gone, had probably fled at the first sound of gunfire, but I wanted to see for myself.

"Get out of there!" Armstrong said. He was looking at me now. His voice was as loud and ugly as his expression. His pointing finger punctuated each word. "This is a crime scene, and you are not allowed on it. I want no evidence disturbed."

I could have fought him on that, should have fought him—I was a licensed detective whose client had just been murdered—but I didn't feel up to it. Besides, I knew there was probably nothing I could find that the police hadn't already noted. I scanned the crowd, looking for familiar faces. I saw Julio and walked up to him.

The songbird looked sick to me, but when I got closer I saw that it was anger which had distorted his features. Anger mixed with a trace of fear. I stepped up to him. "What happened?" I asked.

He looked up at me, and for a second it was as though he didn't know who I was, then his vision focused. He saw me, recognized me. "It was the redneck," he said.

I nodded. I'd guessed as much.

Julio glanced around, to make sure others in the crowd weren't listening to our conversation. "We got him," he said.

"What?"

He stepped closer to me, until his mouth was next to my ear. I could smell his stale breath. "He's in a safehouse."

"What are you talking about? The redneck?"

Julio nodded. "They caught him at a stoplight, called in reinforcements, surrounded him."

"And you didn't—?"

"No cops," he said, answering my unfinished question.

"You know I can't—"

"We're taking him to Bumblebee."

I stood there, staring at him, my next words, my next thought stuck in my throat. Bumblebee. I didn't know why the songbird was telling me this. I didn't know how he knew about my knowledge of Bumblebee. I suddenly felt cold, chilled, though the morning sun was fiery.

"I'll pick you up," he said. "Tonight."

I wasn't sure I wanted to be picked up. I wasn't sure I was willing to keep this from the police. I wasn't sure about anything.

But then I thought of Trinidad, thought of Father Lopez, thought of those illegals in the semi, thought of the refugees.

"Okay," I agreed.

Julio nodded, moving, and was gone, losing himself in the crowd.

I saw Armstrong staring at me, and I turned away.

The songbird didn't show up at my apartment until after eight, almost dark. He pulled next to the curb, honked, and I stepped up to the open passenger window. Julio grinned. There was something about that grin which I didn't like. "Going stag," he said motioning his head toward the back seat. "Got some extra baggage."

I peered through the back window.

Father Lopez was lying across the rear cushion in his body bag.

"Time's wasting," Julio said, chuckling. "You follow me."

I don't know why I didn't argue, why I didn't say anything, why I didn't ask anything, but I didn't. I simply nodded dumbly, went down to the carport, got in the Jeep and followed Julio's car down the street toward the freeway. I don't remember what I felt, what I was thinking.

The trip was long. There were a lot of cars on the highway at first, but the further we drove from the valley, the less crowded the road became, until soon Julio's Chevy tail-lights were the only ones before me on the road.

It was nearly midnight and we were well past Tucson when I saw Julio pull off the highway onto an unmarked dirt road. For the first time in a long while, I thought of Father Lopez's body lying across the back seat of the car. I thought of the redneck. *We got him.* The words seemed so much more sinister in the darkened moonlit desert. I realized I had no idea what was going on, what had been planned by Julio and his friends, whoever they were. I could have turned back then; I thought about it, but I did not. I had gone too far already. I had to see this through.

The road twisted and turned, snaking down unseen ravines, crossing dry washes and gulches, until my sense of direction was thoroughly confused.

And then we were there.

Bumblebee was not as big as I'd thought it would be, and did not look nearly so much like a fort. I'd imagined something like the Alamo, I suppose because of Baker's story, but the sight that greeted me was far different. Twin rows of parallel buildings ran along both sides of the dirt road, ending at what looked like a church at the far end. The buildings were old, abandoned, like those of any ghost town, but they were primarily adobe. Although there were a few delapidated wooden structures—a one-room barbershop with a painted pole faded in front of it, a long-porched saloon with a collapsed roof—most of the buildings were a pale weathered extract of hardened mortared desert sand.

It was then that I noticed that the town wasn't empty. In front of the church at the far end, I saw a large crowd of people, maybe sixty or seventy of them. Looking around, I saw the shadows of their vehicle blending with the surrounding saguaro and cottonwood.

Julio got out of his car.

Father Lopez emerged from the back seat.

I can't say I was surprised. It was something I'd been

half expecting ever since Julio had told me this morning that they were taking the redneck to Bumblebee. But I was frightened. Far more frightened than I would have expected. I had dealt with death before, had seen more than my share of bodies, and no amount of blood or gore had ever really bothered me. But the unnaturalness of this, seeing the priest's body lurch out of the back of the car, peeling off the open plastic body bag, scared me. It seemed to me fundamentally wrong, almost evil.

I got out of my own car. The town was dark, there were no lights, but the moon was bright enough to see by. Father Lopez walked slowly, awkwardly, like Frankenstein, but his steps grew quicker, stronger, more assured, as he followed Julio down the empty dirt street toward the church. The songbird seemed to have forgotten me, or else he had more important things on his mind than guest etiquette, so I invited myself to pursue the two of them, instinct overriding fear.

We moved down the dirt street. The buildings to my left and right loomed in my peripheral vision like hulking creatures, but I concentrated on the creature before me, the reanimated corpse of Father Lopez. *Magic powers.* Baker had said that he'd felt something here, something supernatural. Maybe it was my imagination, but I seemed to feel something too. A kind of tingling in the air, a vibration which spread upward through the soles of my shoes as I walked and which grew stronger as I approached the crowd in front of the church. This close, I could see that most of the gathered people were women, Mexican women dressed in traditional funereal peasant garb, black dresses and lacy mantillas.

With them, held by two or three women at a time, were dead men, men who had obviously died violently. Dead men whose eyes were blinking, limbs were moving, mouths were working. I saw bloodless bullet holes, cleaned knife wounds in pasty flesh.

They all turned to look at us as we approached. I saw

similarities in the features of the dead and the living.

Now Julio acknowledged my presence. As Father Lopez continued on and two older women moved forward to take the dead priest's arms, the songbird backed up and turned to me. "Don't say anything," he warned. "No matter what happens, just watch."

"But—"

"It's up to the women," he said. "They have the faith. They make the rules."

I may not be the smartest guy in the world, but I know when to shut my trap and roll with the flow. And standing in a ghost town in the middle of the desert at midnight, surrounded by walking dead guys and their wives and mothers and daughters, I figured this was one of those times.

Led by the women, the crowd moved into the doorless church.

I followed.

The inside of the building was lit by a double row of candles which lined indented shelves along both side walls. The trappings of Catholicism which I'd expected to see were absent. Indeed, aside from the candles, the church was devoid of any sort of adornment or religious decoration. The crumbling mud walls were bare. There were no pews. I looked toward the front of the elongated room. On the raised dais, where a pulpit would ordinarily be, the redneck stood naked, tied to a post.

I wish I could say that I felt justice was being served, that in some mysteriously primitive way the natural order of things was being put to right, but, God help me, I felt sorry for the redneck. He was crying, tears of terror rolling down his blubbery face, urine drying on his legs. I knew he was crying only for himself, was sorry for his actions only because of the circumstances surrounding his capture, but I suddenly wished that I had told everything to that fat bastard Armstrong and that the redneck was sitting safely in a cell in South Phoenix. He deserved to be punished, but he did not deserve this.

No one deserved this.

But a wish and a nickel will get you a piece of gum. The redneck was not in jail in South Phoenix. He was tied to a porch at the front of this empty church.

And the dead men and their women advanced on him.

The redneck screamed, a high womanly sound which should have been gratifying but somehow was not. At the front of the room the living and the dead separated, women filing to the left, dead men moving to the right. As I watched, the women fell to their knees and began praying. The sound of their mumbling filled the room. I was chilled, but I was sweating. I stood unmoving next to Julio.

The women sang a hymn, a minor key hymn I did not recognize in a dialect of Spanish which was unfamiliar to me.

In single file, as if part of a ritual, they left the church through a side door in back of the dais.

As one, the dead men stood.

The church was silent now save for the pitiful whimpering of the bound murderer and the amplified beating of my terrified heart. One of the dead men stood apart from the crowd, stepped out of the line, moved forward. I recognized the familiar profile of Trinidad. The blood on the coyote's head had been cleaned off, but his skin was grey, his body anorexically thin. He moved easily, normally, as though still alive, and stepped up to the redneck.

He unfastened the ropes tying the murderer's hands and feet to the post.

Another dead man moved forward, handed Trinidad a pistol, and the coyote put the gun into the redneck's hand.

There was not even a pause. "Die fuckers!" The redneck began shooting the second his fingers touched the trigger, arms twitching in panicked terror, laughing hysterically. Bullets hit the walls, slammed into the dead men. But the reanimated corpses did not fall. The pistol ran out of bullets almost immediately, and the redneck jumped off the dais, trying to escape, using the gun like a blackjack and beating on the heads of the men he had killed. They did not die again, however, and the murderer found himself unable to penetrate the corpses' defensive line.

I heard a scream, the bullwhip sound of a bone cracking. I heard the wet sickening sound of flesh being ripped.

The dead men were tearing their killer apart.

I left the building. The sight was too much for me, I could not watch. Julio, and two other men I did not know who were standing at the rear of the church, remained watching, not flinching.

I caught my breath outside. I could still hear the screams, but the other, more gruesome and personal sounds of death were mercifully inaudible. The warm night air felt fresh and good after the dank closeness inside the church.

The women waited in front of the building with me. We did not speak. There was nothing to say.

Julio and the two other men emerged ten minutes later. Ten minutes after that, the dead men filed silently out. I had no desire to peek inside the church and see what was left of the redneck.

Julio stepped next to me. The songbird seemed happier than he had earlier, less tense, more confident. "It is done," he said. "We can go."

I looked at him. "That's it?"

He grinned. "What more did you want?"

I turned toward the dead men, now reunited with their loved ones. Women were hugging their departed husbands, kissing their late lovers, taking the corpses into their arms. I saw Trinidad, saw Father Lopez. The priest looked at me, nodded. A young woman I did not know grasped his hand, held it tightly.

I turned away.

What would happen now? I wondered. Where would

they go? What would they do? The redneck's victims were still alive, even after their murderer's death, so they had not been resurrected merely for revenge. Would they wander off into the desert, eventually die? Or would they live here—no, exist here—in Bumblebee, set up some sort of dead community, pretend as though nothing had happened, as though they had not kicked the bucket, as though they were still alive?

I was going to ask Julio, see if he could tell me, but I suddenly realized that I didn't really want to know.

"Let's go," the songbird said. The other two men were already walking back toward the cars. "This part is for the women."

I didn't know what he meant. I didn't ask.

I followed Julio down the empty dirt street. I would talk this over later with Baker. We would sit around his shack, down some beers, and I would tell him what went down. We would get drunker, he would explain to me what this all meant, why the women ran this show, what parallels there were with the past, we would talk it all out, and everything wouldn't seem so goddamn scary, so evil and fucking horrifying as it did right now. Distance would soften this. Time would turn this into history.

I hoped.

I prayed.

I got into my car, started the ignition, looked out the window. I saw the women take the hands of their husbands, lovers, sons, lead them across the street away from the church. Through a crack between the two adobe buildings between which they were walking, I thought I could see a monstrous pile of dried manzanita and sagebrush.

I started my car, passed Julio without waving, and drove back the way I had come.

I turned on the radio. I could get nothing but a Mexican station, but I didn't care. I just wanted to hear voices. Living voices. I floored the gas pedal.

It was a half hour later when I reached the highway.

I looked once in my rearview mirror, and in the middle of the vast black expanse behind me, in the approximate spot where Bumblebee was located, I thought I saw the low glow of a far away fire.

I turned onto the pavement. I didn't want to think about it. I turned up the radio.

The next glow I saw was the light from Phoenix as I approached the city perpendicular to the dawn.

BRIAN HODGE *has
the most entertaining
stationery in the business,
complete with cartoons
and witty sayings.
His novels include
Dark Advent and* Oasis
*and the recent Dell
release,* Nightlife,
*a cross-genre book
about organized crime
and voodoo. Hodge's
short fiction has appeared
in* The Horror Show,
Book of the Dead, *and
several other publications.*

CANCER CAUSES RATS
BRIAN HODGE

ready, sandra? roll tape. three

She would be here today, no matter what, even if it weren't all in a day's work.

two

Just to make sure he was actually put away for good, he who had vowed to do no hard time. Not unlike the old joke: We'll go to his funeral to make sure he's dead.

one

Static for the lens, she is framed off-center so that her backdrop is clearly seen: a building of vast graystone tonnage and Corinthian columns, too stately for anything so gauche as a statue of Blind Justice. She is young, the low side of thirty. Trim, the consummate professional, dark hair conservatively stylish; one of the city's favorite daughters, albeit adopted. She has no need of introduction of self and place, for time must not be wasted. The more stories per thirty-minute newscast—minus commercials, sports, and weather—the more exciting the flow. The more excitement, the more viewers and the higher the Arbitrons. Self and place will be added in-studio, superimposed text from the Chyron machine. *Sandra Riley, ActioNews 8 Reporter. Municipal Court Building.*

Microphone in hand, she dives in:

"The reign of terror that began eighteen months ago has finally reached its fitting end this afternoon at the sentencing hearing for Darryl Hiller. The twenty-six year old Hiller—the so-called Tapeworm—was convicted five weeks ago on sixteen counts of rape and murder. This afternoon, Judge Thornton Steckler passed down the expected maximum sentence of life imprisonment without parole."

She is coolly steady, forever striving for the perfect blend of authority and compassionate story involvement. That intangible quality which will later, on playback after editing and splicing with other footage, reach out through the tube to seize viewer attention. Telling one and all, *I speak the truth, and it's something you want to hear, and no one can tell it quite like I can.*

Sandra's trick: She focuses not on the camera lens, as do so many lesser-talented competitors in the broadcast journalism wolfpack. She focuses, instead, two feet *beyond* the lens, a starmaking quality that plunks her firmly inside the living room of an entire city.

In truth, Darryl Hiller has yet to be sentenced. Sandra and her crew—cameraman, sound recordist, and film editor—have taped the segment in advance. If they're wrong, they'll reshoot later. But no one in his right mind expects the Tapeworm to get slammed with anything less than the max. Pre-hearing is simply less congested outside the Municipal Court; less background clutter to detract attention from Sandra Riley. And it will give them more time post-hearing to scrounge reaction footage of the principle players in the Tapeworm's final day as a newsmaker: attorneys, police officers, victims' families.

As well, she has her own private press conference to give, and the anticipation is obscenely delicious. Her contemporaries and competitors citywide—from network affiliates, network O&Os, local indies—have already accused her of grandstanding. Such accusations she can afford to laugh off, knowing full well they are born of professional jealousy. All of them report the news; only Sandra is an insider on this, *making* the news as well as distilling it for public consumption. She had no say in the manner by which it plummeted into her lap.

"But even as the city breathes a collective sigh of relief," she continues, "this day of justice cannot be considered a total victory. Police have no leads in the copycat killings patterned after the Tapeworm's methods of rape and murder, which began two months ago . . . "

Sandra wraps it, packages it, and Kevin the cameraman bags it. She reaches around her back and unclips the Sony from her skirt's belt, draws the earphone line from beneath her jacket. Every word was taped informally from a written script so she could listen and repeat verbatim—no TelePrompTers on site—and be free to concentrate on projecting through the lens. That's show biz.

"Let's get set up outside Courtroom C," she tells her crew as they pack it up. No cameras allowed *inside* the courtroom.

Sandra lights a nervous cigarette and the nicotine rush calms her empty stomach. She's eaten nothing today but a handful of peanuts gulped for breakfast, and the cigarette helps her forget.

Kevin straightens from his camera, a tall and handsome black man with a moustache and squaretop haircut. "You oughta give those up. They'll give you those pucker lines around your mouth, look like hell on camera someday."

She smiles, considers grinding the cigarette with a shoetip but doesn't. "By the time I get the lines, my airtime days will be over." She's on a fast-track rise, gunning for network anchor by thirty-five. Only the youthful need apply; there are no female equivalents of wise old Walter Cronkite and Harry Reasoner. Her biological clock is ticking, and it has nothing to do with childbirth.

Gear is packed for mobility and Sandra pitches in to help lug it along. No off-camera star demeanor for her, and the crew loves her for it. *She's one of us.* But in her heart she questions the purity of her own motives. Even altruism can be self-serving.

As they reach the court steps they realize something is unequivocally wrong. Pandemonium and harsh voices rebound along marble corridors. Sandra and her crew break into doubletime and gear is readied on the run, and they find themselves in a swarm of confusion. Civilians are herded away by cops. Courthouse deputies speak frantically into walkie-talkies. A custodial type flanked by two cops aims a fingertip along a ceiling path, as if following ductwork. A pudgy, weeping, red-haired man in rumpled jailhouse clothes is gently escorted from a men's bathroom, wearing handcuffs, but these are quickly removed. Moments later a uniformed deputy is stretchered out of the bathroom, a bloody mask for a face, and a police sergeant is screaming for everyone to get back, back—

"Are you getting this?" she snaps to Kevin.

His camera is balanced on one broad shoulder. "Every bit."

The sound tech feeds her impatient hand a microphone, and they wade into the fray. Sandra digs in for internal focus, that center of calm, grace under pressure. They battle chaos to find someone who can tell them what's going on, but deep within she knows it's all about this man who vowed he would do no hard time.

Thrusting the microphone into official faces in reverse phallic violation, she is rebuffed time and again, until at last she shanghais a young uniformed cop trying gamely at crowd control.

"Can you tell us what's happened?" she asks again.

He whirls, irritable, ready to tell her to get lost. But the recognition is instantaneous—*it's her*—and his will dissolves in a giddy rush of celebrity proximity. Putty in her hands. He will later be severely reprimanded for his poor judgment and big mouth.

"He got away! Darryl Hiller got away!" he says breathlessly.

Sandra doesn't let the hammerblow of distress register one flicker across her face. "How did this happen, do you know?"

"He . . . he told his guard he wanted to go to the crapper, and . . . and I don't know *what* happened! He slipped his cuffs and beat the hell out of his guard and handcuffed that poor guy—" a quick point toward the plump red-haired man—"and stole his clothes. And then he . . . he disappeared!"

"By disappeared, you mean—"

"He's gone, but there was no place for him to go." The young cop is white-faced. "Miz Riley . . . that bathroom doesn't even have a *window!*"

Seven months earlier, November:

She came home, near midnight, and the day had been typically long and exhausting. She sorted mail in the sixteen-story elevator ride up to her floor, some addressed to Sandra Riley, the rest to Shanna Riley. The latter was technically correct. Some long-ago news consultant down in Dallas had suggested a change in pro name. Shanna sounded too close to Sheena, as in Queen of the Jungle, which some female viewership might find threatening. Management backed him, but at least she got to pick her own replacement monicker.

Her feet ached, and she wore L.A. Gear tennies instead of heels toward the day's end, when spit and polish were less crucial. She closed her apartment door, triple-locked it. Shed her overcoat and collapsed onto the sofa, a single lamp on for company. Home was a jumbled contrast to her immaculate video image, stacks everywhere of current magazines and non-fiction books, a hamster-in-wheel race to keep abreast of all matters financial and political, scientific and cultural.

A few tears, then, and cramps. *ActioNews 8* was a battleground of mammoth egos and hesitant managerial shufflings. In "The Waste Land" T.S. Eliot had deemed April the cruelest month, but she knew better. It was November. November saw the year's most crucial Arbitron sweep, and *ActioNews 8* was currently ranked fourth in a nine-station market. Unacceptable. As reporter and weekend co-anchor, she didn't have the most to lose . . . but enough.

The whole city was, of course, abuzz over the murders. Some whackout who assaulted women in their homes, bound them with vinyl tape so they couldn't flee, taped over their mouths so they couldn't scream . . . then taped over their noses so they couldn't breathe. He raped them as they convulsed into suffocation, then left them for someone else to come home to.

After victim number three, when a police captain was quoted as saying, "We'll catch this worm," media pundits were quick to christen the killer the Tapeworm, for a populace preferring its more murderous aberrations to be packaged with readily-identifiable labels. Sandra hated the name, had no choice but to use it. Over drinks, the more battle-hardened reporters even hoped that the Tapeworm would send the police taunting notes. Given the vinyl and the rape, the notes could then—in a morbid nod to C.S. Lewis—be called *The Screwtape Letters.*

A little requisite tube-time before bed. Sandra reached for the remote control for the TV and VCR, always stationed on the coffee table, and only then realized something was amiss.

It wasn't there.

The TV winked on as if by magic, and she whirled in sudden panic. Saw him strolling out of hallway shadows, remote in one hand and cutlery in the other. There was never any doubt as to who he was. The roll of tape braceleted over one wrist was mere confirmation.

Sandra scrambled for the door, but he was quicker, lithe as a gymnast, and blocked her way. *Back to the sofa*, he motioned with the knife, and she obeyed against her own will. Ridiculous; compliance hadn't saved sixteen priors. The sense of invasion was horridly sickening.

"I'm not here for that," he said. "Please don't be afraid."

She poised on the sofa like high-tension wire while he took the nearest chair. She looked for weapons, escapes. Nothing in this room, at least, looked as formidable as the blade. The bedroom, however . . .

He pointed at the TV console and its outboard gear. "You tape the competition's newscasts and watch them later, don't you." He appeared pleased with this deduction.

She nodded, studied him, fighting for control. He was remarkable only in his complete ordinariness. The Tapeworm's identity and appearance had been a matter of great speculation, as he had left no one behind to provide a description. He was young, mid-twenties, with limp blond hair and the pale pallor of someone who holed up with too much late-night TV. His eyes were devoid of feverish madness, touched instead by an intelligent gaze of intense curiosity.

Stronger than he looks, though, she had to reason. He could not have broken in through her front door. Which meant this bland lunatic had scaled sixteen floors of balconies to meet her.

"That's smart, taping the others' news. I'm sorry, I had to take your tape out, but I rewound it for you. It'll be okay. You have to know your competition." He nodded, toyed with the knife.

"What do you want, then?" Her voice, so tight, so wired, was not at all what she heard when reviewing her own newscasts.

"I brought my own tape. I edited it myself. It's called *Sex, Death, and Videotape.* Let's watch." He hit the remote again and the VCR kicked in. She felt his eyes never leave her, couldn't trust her, no, couldn't trust her yet.

She watched a moment of snow, then

herself Sandra Riley rapidfire edited images of her at scene after scene after scene of the crime change of seasons noted by change of wardrobe her professional sympathetic concern always the same "This is Sandra Riley" crying families frustrated cops whirling red lights and yellowtape crime scene cordons "We'll catch this worm" victim profiles black and white color photos of young women who breathed no more "This is Sandra Riley" academic neo-Freudian graybeard spouting psychological murderer's profile then footage of older murders older crime scenes shootings knifings bludgeonings strangulations never connected never related because of wildly varying MOs frightening cavalcade jumpcut montage "This is Sandra Riley" herself at weekend anchor desk "For ActioNews 8, this is Sandra Riley" same closing image on flashcut repeat Sandra Riley/Sandra Riley/Sandra Riley/Sandra Riley/Sandra Riley/Sandra Riley—

Snow, and white noise.

"What . . . what is this?" she managed to choke out.

"Don't you get it?" He looked at her earnestly. "It's my résumé."

Sandra Riley, numb and blank. A media first.

"Don't you see?" he asked. "I want to *work* with you!"

She staggered inside, trying to convince herself. This is not personal, this is nothing personal. Survival depended on divorcing personal from professional. Professionally she was unflappable. Last fall she'd done a live Special Olympics report while covering a softball game, wearing a jersey. Of numerous airtime mandates, there was but one unforgivable sin: Thou shalt not lose control on the air. She had done two minutes of live feed with calm, warm, caring composure with these handicapped children. After returning it to the studio, she had astonished her crew by shrieking and twisting until she dislodged two locusts from inside her jersey.

"Work together," she repeated evenly. "How so?"

"Ooooh, I could feed you so much information. So everyone could know me. They've barely scratched the surface. It's like . . . admiring the painting without knowing the artist." He rose, grew much more animated, excited windmill arms waving the knife. "I mean, look what I've done for your career, already! And look what you've done for me!"

She met him eye to eye. "I'm not the only one, by any mean. Everyone's covered you."

He dismissed them all with an irritated flip of the blade. "Hacks, they're all doing hackwork, assembly line journalism." He lowered to his knees, imploring her as if proposing marriage. "You're the best. I watch my coverage every night—*every night*—and you're the only one who can take me back there. I watch you standing there where I've been and I can smell it, I can taste it, I can feel myself right back there . . . 'cause you step right out and take me by the hand and pull me back through that screen with you."

A moment's flash: *What have I created . . . ?*

"*You* understand, I can see it in your eyes on that screen. *You* know what it takes to get noticed, you've got the formula down. See, see, I was too smart for my own good at first, I never killed quite the same way twice . . . and nobody thought to connect them. But then I wised up." He winked, sagely tapped his temple. "I developed a trademark. And now the whole city knows me. Just like they know you."

"So, this work arrangement." Keep him talking,

keep him on his own twisted agenda. "What's in it for me?"

He wet his lips, excited as a child at Christmas. "I can call you, tell you where I've just been. You'll get the jump on everyone else. You understand, you know what it takes."

She kept him talking about particulars: timetables she kept, ethics of cooperation, randomly touching on anything she could think of to make him believe he was being taken seriously. At last, when fantasies of lasting stardom had gotten the better of him, she sunk the vital hook:

"Why don't we do a background piece. Right now." Shaking inside the professional shell, Sandra pointed to her videocamera in the jumble of electronics beside the TV. "Tell me more about yourself."

"Yeah. Hey. Good idea." He then grew rigid, as if scenting an ulterior motive. "But keep me in shadow. I don't want anyone else knowing what I look like. That's how they do it on TV."

She crossed the room and knelt beside her camera, went through the motions of loading a cartridge and checking the battery pack. She breathed a quick prayer, then hurled the camera at the Tapeworm's head. Plastic cracked, and he roared in surprise and rage.

She was running then, full-tilt toward the bedroom, thanking the gods of aching feet for her L.A. Gear shoes, then falling to the bedroom floor by the night stand, opening the drawer and pulling out the .32-caliber Colt, aiming back down the hallway as he bled and raged a blade-slashing path of shrieking torment after her.

Aiming for his head . . .

Not believing herself when the professional shell refused to submit to the personal core. Kill him now and here's where the story ends. Let him live, and the arrest, the trial, the sentencing . . . the publicity would go on, and on, and on. Play it right, parlay it into a week-night anchor slot, then maybe a ticket out of bush league local and into a network correspondent's position. She saw it all.

And aimed for his leg.

Twice.

Sandra Riley and her crew and all her other peers hover around the Municipal Court for hours upon end, like buzzards, until every last scrap of news is devoured and there is no more. Of Darryl Hiller there is no trace. The only reasonable theory—that somehow he got into the building ductwork from within the bathroom—is proved invalid. Darryl Hiller has pulled a Houdini of stupefying proportions.

The day's best footage is of a man who gives his name as Reggie Blaine—the stout redhead who was assaulted in the bathroom after Hiller freed himself and smashed his guard's face into the porcelain sink. Blaine tells an upsetting tale of being forced to trade clothes with the madman, then submit to the indignity of his handcuffs inside a stall so he cannot see where Hiller goes next.

That evening, as soon as possible, Sandra and her crew go for badly-craved drinks at a favored watering hole called Turnstiles. The mellow wood and brass are comforting, but tonight there is no quick wit and cynical banter. Tonight there is morose reflection.

"Why don't you let *us* take you home tonight?" Kevin suggests. His dark face, usually amiable, is pinched with worry.

Sandra shakes her head. "Thanks. But that's okay."

"Supposing he shows up again at your place. Babe, *you* got to be number one on his list."

She steadies her hands around a margarita. "The police called me at the station this evening. I'll be safe. They'll have people all over my building."

Kevin shrugs. "Still might need someone to talk to. Come on. You got a comfortable couch, I don't mind sleeping a night there."

She touches the back of his hand across the table, tenderly, thankfully. He is probably the best friend she has in the world, and all she can professionally aspire to is to give him cause to watch her dust while she heads to New York. Sometimes she has to wonder who the true worm in all of this really is.

"He won't be back," she says with certainty. "He won't."

"How do you know? Sick twistoid like that, you can never tell."

"He won't." The margarita is cold, salty, anesthetizing. "I already gave him what he wanted all along. He got what he wanted."

"What's that, Sandy?"

She bows her head with the shame of a fool fallen prey to an elaborate con game of heart and soul. And she sighs.

"A public forum."

Four weeks earlier, May:

Darryl Hiller was as anxious to break the silence of his jail cell as the city was to learn what made him tick. One catch: He would talk only with Sandra Riley; his mentor. The gears of *ActioNews 8* ground quickly, getting clearance from the police and the prosecutor's office, whose primary stipulation was that the interview be conducted after the trial, so as to keep further publicity from jeopardizing his rights to an impartial jury. Post-trauma stress behind her, Sandra set about the task of producing a week-long series of special reports on the mind of the Tapeworm.

The interview was conducted in a sterile room in the county jail, sparsely furnished beyond a scarred table. Kevin set up two cameras and lights and reflectors; sound levels were monitored. Darryl Hiller was the last to arrive, manacles on his wrists and ankles, with a pair of Rushmore-faced deputies standing guard a few feet away in case he got frisky.

roll tape. three, two, one

"I forgive you," was the first thing he said to her.

"I don't hold it against you that you turned me in. I was disappointed at first, sure. But now I understand it had to be this way."

"Did you *want* to get caught six months ago?" she asked.

He shook his head, eyes full of visions no one else in the room could perceive. "No." A smile. "But it had to be that way. I'd gone as far as I could remaining anonymous. I had to go to the next level. Beyond. And now?" He beamed. "Everybody knows Darryl."

Sandra thought he looked exceedingly average in that chair, across that table. Still pale. His hair had been trimmed and looked oddly boyish. His face still plain. Only a small scar marked his forehead to commemorate contact with her videocam. His hands fidgeted on the table, more out of idleness, she thought, than nerves. She decided it wiser to let him ramble and free-associate rather than try to direct him in an orderly flow of Q & A. They had plenty of tape to roll.

He told stories of childhood. What went wrong? Everything. Nothing. He said he'd been a sometimes bedwetter in gradeschool and that his mother used to tape his prepubescent penis to his lower belly every night as punishment, and whip him in the morning if he had freed it. Then he laughed and said he'd made it all up. The truth could have been anything.

"Sixteen young women raped and suffocated," Sandra interjected at one point. Properly outraged, under control. Professional. "*Why* did you do it? Your very core reason."

He tilted his head back, let his eyes rove over the ceiling. He had a habit of avoiding eye contact when answering.

"The worst crime a person can inflict on himself is anonymity. It eats people alive inside if they go on too long with their grubby little lives, not counting for anything, good or bad. They just exist. No one should have to live an anonymous life. Me? I just had the courage to become known. That's all. I mean . . . how else could I do it? I don't have a cure for cancer or zits. I can't balance the federal budget. I'm not Tom Cruise in some new movie. So I had to use my imagination. And the tools at my disposal." Now, finally, eye contact. "And *you*. You inspired me. Because you've got it down to an art. You know what it's like to be public property."

"Did you believe you had some sort of moral superiority?"

He looked irritated, as if she'd missed the point entirely. "It doesn't have anything to do with morality. Or superiority. It's a question of economics. Supply and demand."

"Economics," she repeated.

"Right," he said. Most natural thing in the world. "When does newspaper circulation rise? When does everyone tune in TV and radio news? Not when the doctor with the cure is on. Not when a budget analyst is on. Not when Tom Cruise is on. *No*. It's when there's a killer on the loose. You know ... we're not so different, you and me. There's a symbiosis. You need me as much as I need you."

She was about to formulate a rebuttal, but he broke in: "Do you believe in cancer?"

She sputtered, flustered. Have to edit that out later. "Of course. Everyone knows someone touched by cancer."

He nodded. "And do you believe in rats?"

She didn't like this track of inquiry. "Yes."

"And do you believe in the cause-and-effect relationship between them?"

"Rats cause cancer?" Her voice was incredulous.

"No, that's backwards. Cancer causes rats."

"You've lost me with this line of reasoning."

He hunched forward toward Sandra and camera one. "Cancer's out there, oh, it's out there. Feeding on people. All these food additives and chemicals and all this crap in the environment? Cancer has a field day with that stuff. Now. You got all these labs everywhere, scientists looking for new drugs to fight cancer, right? Places breed all these lab rats just for experiments. That's all the rats are good for. They would *not* exist if it wasn't for cancer." A deep breath; reloading. "That's the way it is between you and me. All this crap wrong with cities today, and small towns, and society? You guys are like cancer, feeding on it with your cameras, poking your microphones into it. Pretty soon . . . you just have to expect rats like me popping up to give you more to work with."

"You're making something perverse out of something inherently noble. There's nothing cancerous about keeping the public informed."

"Keep thinking that, if it helps." He chuckled merrily. "Do you think doctors want to cure cancer? No way. Not in a million years. They don't want to wipe it out *because of economics*. It's a multibillion dollar a year industry. All they want is to cure some individual patients . . . and keep the hope alive with everyone else." He settled back in his chair with a grin. "So don't get so self-righteous on *me*. I may disgust you, and you may hate me. But your job would never ever be the same without me."

"And how do you feel about the continuing cycle of murder? By now you surely know about the copycat killer who started imitating your methods last month."

Darryl's forehead creased thoughtfully. "I feel honored," he said slowly. "I influenced someone's life." A broad, dawning grin. "For once, *I* was the inspiration."

Fifty minutes later, once the interview was concluded, Sandra hurried to the nearest bathroom and hung over the toilet in dry heaves. She'd eaten nothing all day, but the rejection reaction was the same.

The following week—after drastic editing, rearranging, splicing, and redubbing—the five-part series on Darryl Hiller was shown on the eleven o'clock news.

And drew the largest audience in *ActioNews 8*'s history.

◊

November is the cruelest month, but *ActioNews 8* weathers it well. They are top of the heap in a nine-station market, no small thanks due to Sandra Riley and her considerable drawing power. She is now a weeknight anchor with a hefty salary kicked up into six figures, and management's only cause for fretting is that she has contracted her new position with them for no more than a year at a time. She wants to be reasonably free to jump when those inevitable network offers start to materialize.

The copycat Tapeworm gives them a body every few weeks. It's not the original rapist-murderer; genetic analysis of the semen he leaves behind proves that. Of the original, no one knows. But Tapeworm is as Tapeworm does, and the public fearfully tunes in, dreading another dose of grisly reality, enthralled when they get it. Sandra anchors the footage shot in the field by a younger protege who idolizes her, and every time, Sandra dies a little more inside. Remembering her role. But her makeup does not run.

The package arrives by UPS courier one afternoon, brown paper wrapper, neatly handlettered and marked to her attention at *ActioNews 8* studios. No return address, but the postmark is across the country in Seattle.

She pops it into the VCR in her office—a larger one befitting her status, with windows this time—when she gets a free moment on this blustery November afternoon. She presses PLAY and sits down.

The amateur filmmaker has rigged up a cheerful title card, reading *Sex, Death, and Videotape 2*. Sandra sits straighter, electric in her chair, and painfully bites down on a knuckle as her eyes widen

and there he is, Darryl Hiller, seated on a stool with nothing in the background but stark white. Medium close-up, chest and head and shoulders. The camera does not move, as if tripod-mounted.

"There was so much I wanted to tell you before I left

last June." He gazes directly at her without blinking. "But you understand the situation. I know you do. You always do.

"There was a lot I didn't understand when we did our interview. Not that I was wrong, I'm never wrong, I was just . . . incomplete. When I told you I had to go beyond to the next level, I had no idea. No idea. Remember how you asked me how I felt about inspiring someone to follow in my footsteps and I said it felt good? I found out it meant more than that. It meant there'd been a change in me. I wasn't just a rat anymore, because I'd created something in my own image. He wouldn't have existed without me. And that meant I had just upgraded to cancer." He begins to chuckle, the only one who gets the joke. "That's how I got away at the hearing. They escorted me right out of that bathroom and took the cuffs off me themselves. Poor, poor Reggie Blaine. Innocent bystander. All I had to do was break one guy's face and tell one lie."

Sandra forgets to breathe, begins to comprehend. Recalling that footage of Reggie Blaine, Victim, forced to wear jailhouse blues. Except there was only one set of clothes all along, she knows this now. Knows it as surely as she knows she was, at the very least, a midwife for an entirely new aberration. She dies inside all the more for it. But her blank-faced shell sits, watching

as Darryl Hiller's face contorts ripples rearranges. Pudgy cheeks, red hair, she has seen it all before, weeping for the cameras along marble corridors. And then it is gone, replaced by a new face which could easily belong to the boy next door. But the voice continues.

"See, I became the cancer—"
new faces, leering at the lens
"—and I'll be back to see you very very soon—"
a rogue's gallery of pure anonymity
"—but you won't see me—"
lifting a roll of vinyl tape to the camera eye and peeling a strip free to lick its sticky underside

"—because I've learned the one fundamental trick of cancer:"

his last word, rapidfire flashcut repeat, a different face speaking with every flick of the editing block

"Mutation/Mutation/Mutation/Mutation/Mutation."

Fade to black.

BARRY HOFFMAN *is
a Pennsylvania school
teacher with several
anthology and magazine
sales. Although Hoffman
is one of the field's most
promising new authors,
he spends most of his
energy at the helm of*
Gauntlet, *an annual
trade paperback
devoted entirely to the
subject of censorship.
Hoffman has a very
bright future ahead of
him; read the following
story and see if you
don't agree.*

ASHES TO ASHES
BARRY HOFFMAN

Cal and Bobby were on a routine stakeout of a liquor store when the call came. Not over the radio, but in Cal's mind.

Bobby had been telling Cal about his most recent spat with his wife of twelve years when the words suddenly turned to screams . . . the screams of a child calling to Cal deep within his mind. Cal saw the scene unfold before him. The scream as the youth retreated upstairs while flames clawed at her from behind. She closed her door and made for the window—her escape blocked by security bars. Smoke snaked its way beneath the door and the room appeared bathed in a morning fog. Terror-stricken, the girl crouched in a corner and screamed again.

Cal tried to calm her. "Where child?" his mind called out. "The address. Tell me where you live." He waited, turned to his partner and said, "Bobby, there's a fire at 5th and Luzerne. Call it in."

His partner, interrupted in mid-sentence, merely nodded and radioed the message as Cal steered into traffic— siren cutting through the early-afternoon silence like a scissor through paper. Cal knew his partner had long ceased questioning his uncanny forewarnings when it came to fires . . . and children trapped in the infernos. He had sounded the alarm seven times in their three years together.

Though skeptical, the first time, Bobby had indulged him. Two children had been saved minutes before the roof of their three story tenement caved in—carried out by Cal before the first of the fire trucks arrived.

That first time had been the worst, Cal remembered. His partner had peppered him with questions while he tried to soothe the terrified children.

His friend was silent now. Despite the air conditioning Cal was gushing sweat as he felt the heat from the conflagration. He smelled gasoline and almost gagged as he turned onto Luzerne.

"Arson," he said aloud as the blazing rowhouse came into view.

Cal bolted up the stairs while his partner waited for help to arrive. That first time, he recalled, Bobby had wanted to go with him.

"You'll only get in the way."

He'd protested, tried to restrain Cal and had been knocked on his ass.

Now, like a meticulously choreographed dance, Cal made his way inside alone with Bobby left behind to cordon off the area and look for anyone suspicious—the arsonist who'd started the fire.

The flames held no terror for Cal. Never had. As a child he'd been entranced by the fingers of flame that clawed at him now. He'd played with fire, invited its warmth, yet had never been scalded by its heat. Over the years, like evenly matched warriors, they'd come to an understanding. He'd let his adversary take the house as long as it relinquished its claim to the child.

On the second floor he kicked in the door and called out to the girl.

"Speak to me, Tiffany. Tell me where you are."

"Over here," shrill, nearly overcome with terror.

"No, over here," barely audible, but there nevertheless.

Two voices. One real. One a phantom.

He made his way towards the window and saw a child, no more than seven, hunkered against the wall. Her face was white as coals left to simmer for a barbecue. Her hair was orange like the fire that fought him, with the child its prize. He lifted her and strode to the door, safety within his grasp.

"Don't leave me."

The phantom voice again. He ignored it and passed by the bed. A hand reached out and gripped his ankle; the fingers searing his flesh. Cal glanced down, sickened, at the burned-scarred hand. Even as he looked the flesh peeled off like a snake shedding its skin. The noxious odor of rotten eggs assaulted his nose.

"Free me, Cal. Come back to me."

He stepped on the hand, bones crunching like dry cereal under his weight and it released him.

"You're not real! You're dead. I can't save you, Trish," he said, tears welling in his eyes.

Outside paramedics relieved him of his burden and he sought out his partner.

"Anyone familiar?" Cal asked. His eyes, like those of a hawk scouring the landscape for prey, darted through the crowd of onlookers.

"Just your sister. She got here a minute or two after

we did. Took up her vigil, as usual, willing you to safety. I envy you two, your gift."

"Poetic today, aren't we?" he said with no attempt to hide his irritation. "I'm getting sick of this 'gift' crap. Next you'll be putting me up for Sainthood."

"There are twelve kids alive today who wouldn't have had a chance without your ESP, second sight or whatever the fuck you want to call it. I'd call that a gift."

"Most would call it a gift, granted. If that's the case, though, I'd just as soon wrap it and give it away. Give it to you, maybe. It's a curse . . . my curse, plain and simple; my cross to bear for my failure."

"You can't blame yourself for your sister."

"I can and I do." He said it without rancor, however, his tone softening. He went through sudden mood changes after each fire. He'd come to live with them, as had his partner. "Look, I'd better see how Terri's holding up. It's worse for her. She's out here waiting, never knowing if this is the time the fire gets the upper hand and claims me for itself."

"Now look who's waxing poetic."

"Go fuck yourself." He was smiling, though, and laughed when his friend shot him the finger. A dynamo, he was on the move looking for his sister. He was consumed by a high, soon after each rescue, not much different than the rush coke provided an addict. The depression and anxiety that inevitably came as the drug wore off was not far away. That's why he needed Terri. She was his safety-net, his shield. She'd be his cocoon for the night, protecting him from the devils of his past; protecting him from Trish, her twin, who he'd once again allowed to perish.

She ran to him now and hugged him; less like a brother than a lover returned from war. She absorbed his torment like a sponge. What would he do without her? he thought.

◊

There was no escaping the past. Since being visited by the "gift" they'd learned that reliving the past was the only way to exorcise Trish . . . until the next fire. Cal's memory of that night fifteen years ago was fuzzy, at best, and only Terri could provide the missing pieces and get him through the night.

"You were twelve," she said and the ritual began. "Gangly and awkward. What a temper you had. Irish to the core."

"You and Trish were thirteen," Cal answered. "The two of you the same yet so different." Though twins, Cal recalled, even strangers could tell them apart in an instant. Terri, subdued, could never maintain eye contact for more than a moment—staring at her shoes as if they'd come to her rescue. She was uncomfortable with her changing body and draped herself with loose fitting clothes as a shield from prying eyes. Trish, on the other hand wore her emotions on her sleeve, defying anyone to contradict her in any way, shape, or form. "I was in love with you both. My fantasies would have made you blush."

"No, it was Trish you fantasized. You were so much alike. It was always a test of wills between. I was shy, cautious and self-conscious. She was like you—impulsive, a daredevil and a tease. The battles you had. How I envied the two of you. You loved her, but not just as a sister. You wanted her. You tolerated me."

"You were overly sensitive. Still are. We fenced with each other, nothing more. You were into your books, into yourself and saw things that just weren't there. We wanted you to join in our banter, but you were always the observer."

"The outsider."

"Only in your mind."

She told him again about the events leading up to the fire fifteen years before. He remembered an argument with Trish, though the details escaped him. Terri could shed no

light on the matter as she'd been downstairs doing her chores
. . . and Trish's.

"I walked into our room and you held Ted in one
hand, a match in the other. 'Dare me!' You told her. 'You're
bluffing,' Trish answered. 'Then dare me, Miss-know-it-all,
or are you chickenshit?' "

Ted, Trish's stuffed bear, had been her faithful
companion since she was an infant, Cal remembered. Even at
thirteen she took him to bed with her, told him her innermost
secrets and fears and patched the patches that held him
together. No matter how angry he'd been at his sister he
wouldn't have hurt Ted. But he had. There was no disputing
the facts.

"You stood there, your face set hard, red with fury.
Your freckles were like stars glistening in the light of the
match. 'You're so big and bad, burn him. . . . I dare you,'
Trish said.

"I saw you hesitate. Then she laughed at you. And
that had been too much. I knew you couldn't back down. You
refused to lose face. So you lit his arm. I don't know who was
more surprised—you or Trish. She always knew just how far
she could go and couldn't believe she'd gone over the edge. She
grabbed for Ted, cursing you all the while, and you held him
over your head, just beyond her grasp. The flames spread
quickly and I saw panic creep into your face. You shook him
to put the fire out, but he burned even more. Trish lunged and
knocked him from your grasp—onto the curtains which burst
into flame."

They sat quietly, each wrapped in their own thoughts.
No matter how many times she'd told the story Cal found it
difficult to believe. Yes, he'd been intrigued by fire, he
admitted to himself. Just the day before he'd set a roll of
flypaper ablaze and watched the flames race to the top
incinerating the insects held fast by the sticky goo. But burn
Ted on a dare? Why couldn't he remember? He'd hit his head,
he knew, but he remembered the details of the fire, once it

started, like it was yesterday.

He and Terri had used a bedspread to beat the flames, but it too caught fire—then the carpet. All the while Trish strained to reach Ted, lodged behind the bureau next to the window. She was oblivious to the blanket of flame that made its way to cover her.

"I remember falling," Terri continued, "over a chair and hitting my head on the floor. It's all I remember until I got outside."

Cal took up the story—the part that burned all too vividly in his mind.

"Until you fell I had no doubt I'd prevail. I'd played with fire, toyed with it, but I'd always been in control. Now, though, with you and Trish in danger I wasn't so sure of myself. I began to drag you out of the room. I wasn't strong enough to carry you. 'Trish, get out! The fire's spreading.' She looked at me for an instant, like awakening from a dream. 'As soon as I get Ted.' Calm as could be, like she had everything in hand. 'Forget about fucking Ted! Get out now!' She ignored me. I dragged you to the stairs. You were coming to and you leaned on my shoulder while I led you downstairs, then outside. I went back for Trish.

"The room was ablaze. Trish was in the corner, Ted, still smoldering, clutched to her chest. A wall of fire separated us. A tongue of flame licked at me from behind, scalding my leg.

'Come to me, Trish.'

"She didn't move. Knew it was hopeless. She just rocked back and forth humming to Ted. The floor beneath her buckled, splintered and gave. For a second the flames parted. I grabbed hold of her hand as she dangled in the air.

"'Help me, Trish. Pull yourself up.'

"I stared into her face and knew she was no longer aware of what was happening around her. Her skirt caught fire, the flames caressing her body like a lover. Her hand was slick, the skin blistered and peeling. It slipped from my grasp and I saw her plunge. She looked up at me, without reproach, as she fell. Then her face melted like wax and she was gone.

"Somehow I struggled out of the room and I remember falling down the stairs. A pair of hands dragged me out of the house. I opened my eyes and was next to you."

"It was Dad," Terri said. "He was in the basement, smelled smoke and found you at the foot of the stairs. He returned for Trish, but was driven back. You were in a fog . . . "

"A fog that's never lifted."

"You asked me what happened. At first you remembered nothing. You had a lump the size of a grapefruit on the back of your head. When Chief Dougherty came over I told him I didn't know how the fire started."

"You protected me."

"What was I to do? I'd lost my sister. Was I to lose you too?"

They lapsed into silence and Cal recalled receiving the gift. Ten years to the day Trish died Cal was a rookie cop walking the beat on Market Street. He'd smelled smoke, his guts aflame and began to sweat like a pig. He thought it was a heart attack. Then he'd heard the voice of a boy calling for help. He'd answered. Told a street vendor to call for help and ran the five blocks to an abandoned Chinese restaurant at 8th and Arch. Smoke billowing from the door had attracted a few onlookers, but the flames had been confined to the interior. He'd found the boy and gotten him out as the fire trucks arrived. He'd seen Terri, ashen-faced, in the crowd. She'd sensed the fire, too, and knew Cal was in the building. He told her he'd heard Trish. Told her he'd almost gone back until he realized it must have been his imagination.

There had been three more fires before he'd been teamed up with Bobby. Each time Trish beseeched him and each time he'd ignored her pleas. Terri had always been summoned, but only to observe—her presence penance for protecting her brother; for living at her sister's expense.

"When will it end?" Cal finally said. "How do we earn her forgiveness?"

"She's not really there. Our foreknowledge of the fires is real. The children's voices are real. I hear them, too. But Trish's presence is your guilt gnawing at you. I've never heard her, never seen her. She'll leave when you want her to."

"You're wrong. She grabbed me tonight. She's never done that before. She means to pull me down, take me with her, or maybe this time she wants to be saved. I don't know."

"She's gone, Cal. Let her be. Accept our gift . . . our curse for what it is—something unexplainable. Maybe it's your penalty for Trish's death; mine for surviving when you could have saved her. Don't read anything sinister or heinous into it."

Terri dozed. Cal usually did too. Reliving the past, accepting their responsibility was akin to confession. It had always had a cleansing effect and left them drained. A dreamless slumber beckoned. Not this time. Not for him.

His ankle throbbed where Trish had grabbed him. Taking off his socks he saw the imprint of her fingers. Fading, now, but still visible. He hadn't shown Terri. He didn't want to upset her, true, he thought to himself, but that wasn't all. Trish *was* reaching out to him. Whether she meant to harm him or forgive him he didn't know. But in his heart he knew this was between he and his sister. Intertwined and dependent on one another as they were this didn't involve Terri.

Over the next three weeks Cal was a tightly wound spring. Over a year had separated the first and second fires and nearly a year before the third. Over the years their frequency had increased steadily. At first Cal hadn't been aware. As Terri suggested, he didn't dwell on the power that had been bestowed upon him. But, in the past nine months he'd been warned of three fires. Cal sensed an urgency in Trish's pleas; a strength that hadn't been there before. Like a novel he was reaching the end. But unlike any novel the terror was real. He expected to be summoned at any moment and his heightened awareness took its toll. He was irritable and unresponsive. All but Bobby steered a wide berth of him.

"Why don't you take a vacation?" Bobby suggested, finally. "You look like shit."

"Thanks for the compliment." He spoke in a monotone with none of the feistiness that characterized him. He managed a wan smile—like those clowns painted on.

"I'm serious. You lost, what ten, maybe fifteen pounds the past three weeks. You were thin as a rail to begin with. All you do is nibble on your food."

"Yes, mother."

"Don't patronize me, dammit. You're stressed out. Maybe . . . maybe you should seek, you know, professional help."

A flicker of life gleamed in Cal's eyes. "See a shrink? Cute. If anyone but you and Terri finds out about my so-called 'gift' I'll be a guinea pig—to be probed, studied and dissected. Then it's a desk job or disability. And, it won't make a fucking bit of difference. Look, I'm on edge because there's going to be another fire soon. There's a pattern—not totally predictable, but not random either. So, yeah, I'm a bit stressed out, but it's not something some shrink can handle."

"What if you got your mind on something else?"

"Like what?"

"Like who's starting the fires."

Cal was silent for a good five minutes. Successful partners, like good wives, know when to prod, when to badger and when to shut up. Cal considered Bobby's suggestion and welcomed his friend's patience. There would be a fire—soon, but he couldn't do anything about it. Routine patrols and stakeouts, though, couldn't keep him from dwelling on the time bomb waiting to explode. He had no appetite and hadn't gotten a full nights sleep since the last fire. His mind and body were on constant alert for the call. Maybe Bobby was right. Coming to grips with the arson angle might be just the ticket to keep his mind occupied. He couldn't put off the inevitable, but maybe he'd be better prepared for the confrontation with Trish if he were healthy.

"Okay," he said—all that was needed. With the decision made a great weight was lifted. As mundane as police work was solving the puzzles that sometimes presented themselves kept the job from becoming tedious. During his infrequent investigations he became totally immersed in the riddle. The joy was in the journey, seeing the puzzle unfold. Oddly enough he was often depressed when the mystery was solved as it could be months before another presented itself.

At lunch the two men outlined what course to follow. Halfway through Bobby burst out laughing.

"What's so damn funny?"

"You. You're eating like a horse."

He was. He hadn't realized it, but he felt like a man ending a fast. "Maybe you're in the wrong field, shithead."

"Oh?"

"You'd make a good shrink." They both laughed raucously, oblivious of the stares of the other diners.

The work was painstaking . . . invigorating. The fires were not confined to any one part of the city, though always close enough for Cal to arrive to avert loss of life. They were not confined to any one racial or ethnic group. The only common denominator was the children. Time of day? Nothing concrete either—whenever Cal happened to be on patrol.

Even before he'd teamed up with Bobby, Cal knew the fires had been the work of arsonists. This had been confirmed by the fire department. But working alone he'd been hamstrung—couldn't be in two places at once; couldn't observe the crowd that gathered to gawk. With Bobby's help, though, they'd photographed the curious onlookers at the last six crime scenes. Arsonists, any layman could tell, got more of a high viewing their work and the reaction it provoked than starting the fire itself. For the umpteenth time they scrutinized the pictures for familiar faces.

Another dead end. Except for Terri only one other person appeared at more than one fire—Benny Salese, a pickpocket known as Benny the Sleaze. He'd been in prison during all but the first and last blazes they'd photographed.

"So what do we have?" Bobby asked looking at the board that summarized their findings. Bobby, Cal knew, was a stickler for detail and organization. Every shred of evidence was categorized, labeled and color-coded. Even his tiny pocket-sized notebook was divided into sections. Cal, for his part, wrote random thoughts on napkins, often finding them in his pockets two weeks later. All his notes were stuck haphazardly in a huge manila folder, now bursting at the seams. It wasn't that Cal didn't do his share of the work or was slothful. He just stored a huge amount of information in his head—the written data needed only for verification. And it was Cal's hunches, based on Bobby's thoroughness, that invariably led to a break in the case. That's why they'd been a successful team. Each had his own strengths. They fed off one another.

They'd gathered their information and for the third day were trying to make some sense of it. Today Bobby would ask the questions and Cal would respond. Tomorrow they'd reverse roles.

"One arsonist?" Bobby asked.

"It looks like it. Gasoline with a simple time-delayed fuse at each fire."

"Motive?"

"Kicks, plain and simple. There's no connection— no one landlord; no one insurance company targeted; none of the victims knew one another."

"Random?"

"No. There's always children involved and never adults in the dwelling. Our arsonist isn't out to hurt a lot of people—no apartment buildings or high-rise offices. Yet, he . . . "

"Or she."

"Right, he or she hasn't targeted vacant buildings either."

"Suspects?"

Cal was silent for a minute as he grappled with the question that still eluded them. "Suspects . . . Me, Terri or Trish." He shrugged, as if to apologize.

"Dead end," Bobby said, sitting down. He'd been pacing as if movement would keep them going forward. When he sat, Cal knew, he was deflated . . . defeated.

"No. We've stopped here everyday. For once let's take a look at the suspects. It could be me. I target a location, set a time-delayed fuse, pretend to hear voices and drive to the location just as the fire erupts. No loss of life and I come out a hero. Any loopholes?"

"One. Aside from the fact I know you too well to accept your scenario, how could you be sure there'd be a kid in the dwelling when it went up—and no one else in the building? How do you know where the child is? How come they never escape without your help? Sorry, pal, but it doesn't wash."

"Thanks. Maybe you should become a lawyer?"

"Maybe you should kiss my ass."

"All right," Cal continued after they'd stopped laughing. "What about Terri? She had the opportunity. She's been at all the crime scenes, knows what shift I'm on and generally where I'll be."

"Aside from lack of motive how does she get you to the fires? The kids call for you, she doesn't. It's too full of holes."

"That leaves Trish," Cal said and could feel his friend tensing.

"Which leaves us nothing because we can't arrest a ghost."

"We're not out to arrest anyone. We're trying to figure out who is setting the fires. She's a suspect, let's deal with her."

"Your dead sister, a suspect? Isn't that stretching it a bit?"

"Okay, then answer this. Is she a figment of my imagination or do you believe me?"

It was Bobby's turn to be silent; to ponder this most important of questions. Cal had come to respect this man. More important, he loved him—in the way close brothers felt for one another. Bobby was the older brother he'd never had—at thirty-three, six years his senior. They were both average height, both lean, due more to metabolism than exercise. An Italian, Robert Santini had the hard edges and gruff exterior more commonly associated with thugs than cops. But beneath his thinning black hair were compassionate eyes that could have belonged to a priest. Cal had only to look at his partner's eyes to gauge his emotions. They contained no guile, but were a direct link to the man's soul. These eyes now showed concern.

"I've never experienced anything supernatural," he said, picking at his thin mustache; a nervous tic Cal unmercifully teased him about. Now, though, he remained silent. "The only thing that goes bump in the night in my house is me trying to get to the john without waking Sally. But I believe in you and this foreknowledge you have of fires isn't luck and isn't coincidence. If your 'gift' is real maybe your ghost is, too. But tell me this: why would she start the fires?"

"To get close to me. To punish me for killing her. To give me a chance to atone by saving her. To . . . "

"Then why the kids?"

"What do you mean?"

"If she wants *you*, whatever the motive, the children are, how do you put it . . . interlopers—yeah, you know they don't belong. They're in the way. If she wants you she'd want you alone."

"So, we've reached a dead end," Cal said, a note of

desperation in his voice.

"A crossroads, not a dead end. We either drop the case or attack it from a different angle tomorrow."

"What angle haven't we covered?" Bobby had pushed, prodded and goaded him and where had it got them—no place. He made no attempt to hide his exasperation. "What the fuck is there left to unearth?"

"How the fuck should I know?" He was silent for a moment and Cal could see the germ of an idea taking shape. "Maybe we *can* find out if Trish exists anyplace other than in your head."

"This sounds good. Pray tell—a seance? A Ouija board? A . . . "

"It's a longshot," Bobby said ignoring the sarcasm. "And it can be painful if we come up blank."

"Cut the crap and cut to the chase. I'll deal with the possibility I'm hallucinating without going off the deep end."

"Fine. We talk to the kids. Trish spoke to you at each of the fires. One of them must have heard her *if* she exists. Worth a try?"

"Why the fuck not," Cal said and shrugged.

"Because you're scared shit at what we'll learn."

"Yeah, but I won't be able to live with myself if we don't. Tomorrow, then?"

"Tomorrow."

They spent the next morning visiting four children from the most recent fires with the logic they'd have the clearest memory of the events. In each case it was the same.

"All I heard was you telling me not to move, to be calm; that you were on your way."

Cal didn't know whether to be relieved or upset. Bobby seemed to read his mind.

"Look we haven't proven she *doesn't* exist, just that the kids were tuned into you at the exclusion of everything else. Jesus, I can't believe I'm trying to convince you a ghost might exist." He looked at Cal and stopped—noting all the tell-tale signs—the sweat oozing, the brows furrowed in concentration, hands gripping the wheel so tightly they were white as snow. "A fire?"

"It's started. 11th and Juniper. Two kids, I think."

Flames were sprouting out of the second floor window when they arrived. Cal stared at the house and hesitated.

"What's wrong? Are we too late?"

"It's the house I grew up in."

"You told me it was leveled."

"This could be its double. See the flames from the second floor window? The twin's room—same location, anyway." Cal shook off his fears and made for the front door.

The room on the second floor was identical to his sister's in layout.

Crouched beneath the window was a black girl of nine or ten. He lifted her and was about to flee. Between coughs she shook her head "no."

"There's another . . . a girl . . . there." She pointed to the corner. Hunkered by the bureau was a figure obscured by clouds of smoke. "Stay put. I'll be right back," he called. He didn't know if the child heard him. He only hoped there was time.

Outside he gave the choking child to Bobby and was about to return when his partner grabbed his arm.

"There's no one else."

"Yes there is. I saw another child."

"I spoke to the mother. Lorraine, her daughter, was alone. You can't go back in—the ceiling could collapse any minute."

"She saw her," Cal said pointing at the youth in Bobby's arms. "I've got to go back."

The smoke had thickened like a blanket of fog in an effort to stymie his return. Teary-eyed he made out a blurry image next to the bureau. It was Trish, as she'd been at thirteen. Long brown hair, with a trace of red; eyes the blue of the sky on a cloudless day; the lithe figure of a natural athlete; breasts that had blossomed with the coming of Spring. In her arms was Ted. He was relieved at the sight. Whatever the outcome he knew he was nearing the end of his journey.

"What do you want from me, Trish?" An impenetrable wall of flame separated them. He wanted to go through, to hold his sister, but knew it was hopeless. "I'm sorry I killed you . . . sorry I can't save you now."

"You didn't kill me, Cal."

"I know, but I was responsible."

"You weren't. Terri started the fire. I've been trying to tell you, but there's never enough time. She was jealous. Jealous that I was extroverted and she was shy. Jealous of all the attention I received. Jealous you and I shared so much in common. In a fit of anger she set fire to Ted. Flung him across the room when I tried to grab him. The rest you know."

The fire raged around them, but he was unaware—his attention riveted on his sister; a fury mounting within him.

"So you started these fires to reach me. Damn you to hell! You played with the lives of these children . . . "

"I didn't start the fires. I summoned you to save the children. Yes, and summoned you to free you from your guilt. Called you, too, to free myself by telling you the truth."

"But why summon Terri? You want her to suffer, don't you? You want her helpless out there, never sure if I'll come out."

"I spoke only to *you*, Cal."

The floor beneath her buckled and splintered, just as it had in the fire that took her life. He reached out to her, oblivious of the fire searing his arm. She swatted it away.

"You can't save me. Not now and not then. You've mourned me long enough. Remember what we shared and what we meant to each other. Carry that in your heart and I'll never die. I don't need your guilt or your self-pity."

The floor collapsed beneath her. She hovered for an

instant, the flames eager to devour her, then turned to ash. The window imploded and her ashes, like snowflakes, drifted gently onto him—a shield from the inferno that threatened to engulf him.

Arms grabbed him from behind and wrestled him out of the room. He looked at Bobby and allowed his friend to lead him to safety.

"She spoke to me, Cal. Told me to come get you."

"Terri?"

"No, Trish. It was like a radio in my head; the station all fuzzy, the words barely discernible . . ."

"Where's Terri?" He scanned the crowd of on-lookers.

"She was here a minute ago. I told her you went back in. Told her there was no one else inside, but you insisted there was. She was shaken. I don't know where she went off to."

"I do. Come on."

"Don't you want to be alone with her?"

"This is a family affair and you're part of this family."

Terri lived in a renovated townhouse on 23rd and Lombard. She'd rented the place five years before with an option to buy. She'd never been able to sock enough away for a down payment and the owner could never get his asking price. It was spacious enough so she could set aside a number of rooms for the sculptures she made for a living.

Cal saw the strain on her face when she opened the door. She looked through Bobby as if he didn't exist. He followed her upstairs to her studio. Cal's anger had mounted as they'd driven in silence to Terri's. She'd put him through torment and he wasn't about to fence with her.

"I saw Trish—spoke to her. She told me *every-thing*."

Terri averted his stare, just as when they were young. "I don't know what you're talking about," she said, but

Cal could discern the fear behind the denial. The little girl caught with her hand in the cookie jar.

"Lies. From the beginning you lied to me. *You* set the fire that killed Trish. Why didn't you tell me?"

"I was scared. You and Trish were the adventurous ones. You two were always up to your eyeballs in trouble, yet you always managed to wrangle your way out with nothing more than a slap on the wrist. I couldn't deal with what I'd done. I knew you could. I carried the guilt around . . . "

"Bullshit! You felt no guilt—no remorse. You got rid of the competition. You had me to yourself. We shared a common bond. Our secret. You wanted it that way—admit it!"

"Can't you forgive me?"

"I could forgive the lie you wove in panic. I can't forgive the deception all these years, when you knew my guilt was tearing me apart. And I can't forgive the hell you've put me through with the fires." The last had been like a slap in the face and Cal pressed his advantage. "You started *all* the fires."

"NO!"

"Trish told me. She never spoke to you—only to me after you'd started a fire."

"That's crazy."

"We have all the evidence. You were at each fire, yet Trish never summoned you. Don't deny it. Tell me why?"

"You know damned well why! After I got over the shock of what I'd done I felt . . . powerful. I'd manipulated you and you fell for it hook, line, and sinker. But more than that there was the thrill of the fire itself. You've told me how intrigued you were with fire. I felt a high—a feeling I had to recapture. I didn't do it often; once a year at first, and always an abandoned building. Then there was the abandoned restaurant with the boy. I swear I didn't know he was there. You appeared with your cock-and-bull story of being summoned. I followed your lead. I'd been called, too. The thrill was heightened with the child in the house and you going to save him. It became an itch that demanded to be scratched. I could relive the experience, in my head, for a year, then nine months. Lately I've felt the urge after only a few weeks." For the first time she met his eyes in defiance, waiting for his response.

Cal's rage was deflated. This wasn't his sister talking, but some junkie; an addict—someone who needed help, not scorn. His face betrayed his thoughts and further fueled Terri's anger.

"I don't want your pity. I knew Trish betrayed me when she spoke to Bobby. I knew you'd come. You're going to help me, right? Put me away where I can't hurt anyone. The fuck you are!"

She'd been moving the entire time. They were backed into a corner. Cal smelled gasoline—too late. Terri struck a match and tossed it at his feet. The room was instantly ablaze. He felt a gentle breeze and a residue of ash blew off him. Terri was at the foot of the stairs. She stared down and screamed.

"Stay away from me!" she called to something neither Cal nor Bobby could see amidst the flames.

She retreated, ran to her room, shut and bolted the door.

Cal and Bobby fought their way to the stairs, out of the house and breathed the crisp fresh air.

"I'm going back," Cal said. He looked at his friend's incredulous stare. "I've got to. She's my sister."

Before he had a chance to act the glass from Terri's room shattered and she plunged to the pavement—arms flailing like a bird with its wings clipped. She hit the ground, spread-eagled, with the sound of a tomato falling from a table. The two men rushed to her; felt for a pulse; found none. Cal saw a handprint on the back of Terri's blouse. He looked up and saw Trish at the window. Saw her turn to ash, this time to be scattered by the wind. He glanced back at his sister's blouse and the handprint was gone. He looked at Bobby who nodded. He'd seen it all.

He saw Bobby following the dissipating ash; saw him pick at his mustache.

"Partner, you look like you've just seen a ghost."

THOMAS F. MONTELEONE *is
a brash, outspoken author
from Baltimore, Maryland.
Highly-respected as a prose
stylist, Monteleone's non-fiction
Mafia columns—which have
appeared in* Horrorstruck,
The Horror Show, *and*
Mystery Scene—*have
attracted almost as much
attention as his fine novels
and short stories. Monteleone
claims he "experimented"
with the following tale.*

LOVE LETTERS
THOMAS F. MONTELEONE

June 19

LetterBoxes
P.O. Box 69
Intercourse PA 17534

Dear LetterBoxes Ladies:
    Okay, I'm sending you my money order for
$19.95. You can write me at the address on the envelope.
I'm already excited.

Yours Truly,
Wayne Gundersen

◊

July 8

Wayne Gundersen
RFD 12 - Route 43
Ingram WI 54535

My Dearest Wayne:
        I was so glad to get your letter. I've been waiting
to find a pen-pal for so long now, and now that I know
you'll be writing to me, it just makes my whole body tingle,
especially my "pussy" (if you know what I mean!).
I thought you might want to see what I'm talking about, so
I sent you a picture. (smile)
        I didn't think you'd mind. . . .
        Well, I'd better be getting back to work at the shoe
store. I'm the Assistant Manager. Write soon!

                                        Yours,
                                        Candy

◊

July 8

Candy
c/o LetterBoxes
P.O. Box 69
Intercourse PA 17534

My Dearest Candy:
        I was real glad to get your letter but I thought it
would be maybe a little longer. Good to know you got a job
though. Assistant Manager sounds good to me. I never had
a job. Just work on this farm with my Dad now that my
stepmother left us (okay with me cause I kind of hated her).
I got 2 sisters (I kind of hate them too, but at least I can
peek at them when they are in the bathroom). I'm going to
be a senior in high school this Fall, but I can't wait to get

out of that place. Bunch of rich snots and grits and uppity girls (not like you). I've never had a girlfriend, and only once I had sex with somebody else (do you have sex?), but I can't ever tell about that. But I might tell you someday if we stay real close like I think we will. Why don't you write and tell me more about yourself, and I'll tell you more about me and my dog Bowser. Oh yeah and thanks *loads* for the great picture! I keep it in my socks drawer and I'm putting a Polaroid of me and Bowser in the envelope. He likes to take showers with me.

> Yours Truly,
> Wayne

◊

August 23

Wayne Gundersen
RFD 12 - Route 43
Ingram WI 54535

Wonderful Wayne:

The weather is so hot this time of year I just hate to wear clothes—know what I mean? In my apartment, after work, I just walk around naked all the time, only it can be such a bother to remember to keep my shades down. Sometimes I forget, and I guess I give my neighbors a thrill. I'm sending you a picture of what you might see if you were standing outside my window.

I love to get your letters, so write soon!

> Your Girlfriend,
> Candy

◊

◊

August 23

Candy
c/o LetterBoxes
P.O. Box 69
Intercourse PA 17534

Sweet Candy:
 Your last letter was great even though it was
short. I was wondering though how you got that picture
of yourself through your bedroom window? And speaking
of pictures, how come you didn't say nothing about the
picture I sent *you*? It must be nice to have a typewriter to
write your letters on. I'm thinking of buying one at the
Sears in town so my letters will look as good as yours.
School starts soon and I can't wait to show the kids my
letters from you. Maybe now they'll understand how
important I am to have a great girlfriend like you. My
stepmother always told me I'm a loser just like my father,
but she never really knew me like you do. I feel like I could
tell you anything Candy. And maybe I will someday. Well I
got to go to work for Dad. Write soon.

Lots of Love,
Wayne

◊

October 10

Wayne Gundersen
RFD 12 - Route 43
Ingram WI 54535

Big-Wad Wayne:
 I have decided to take up camping this Fall.
There's something about being outside, close to nature,
that makes me hot (if you know what I mean)—no matter

what the temperature! The last time I camped in my tent,
I crawled into my sleeping bag without a stitch on, and I
felt so lonely without you and your big piece of manhood to
keep me company.

Just to show you what it was like, I'm sending you
a picture of me just before I zipped up my bag. Please
write soon, I think I'd just *die* if I didn't get your letters!

Love Forever,
Candy

P.S. I'm supposed to remind you—this is your third letter
from me and the people here who run LetterBoxes wanted
me to remind you to send in another $19.95 for three new
ones! We've started such a great relationship, I know you
won't forget. Thanks, Sweetie!

◊

October 10

Candy
c/o LetterBoxes
P.O. Box 69
Intercourse PA 17534

Sexy Candy:

Okay, here's another money order. I sure do like
your letters and the picture of you in your sleeping bag. I
like to camp too, but mostly I like walking in the woods
north of our farm. I found an old well there and the wood
cover had rotted through. The kids always said that a bum
had fell in the well a long time ago and when he started to
rot, he poisoned the water. I used a boat anchor to fish up
some pieces, and I'm not sure it was a bum and I heard the
voice of the thing that lives down there and feeds off the
parts. It wanted me to bring it food so I started catching
little animals and throwing them down there, and the thing

really liked that. It really liked the kittens and the baby pigs. I still go there sometimes, but not as often since you and me fell in love. I'm planning a surprise for you soon!

> I Love You,
> Wayne

◊

November 24

Wayne Gundersen
RFD 12 - Route 43
Ingram WI 54535

Wild-Man Wayne:
     Thanks for sending in another $19.95. I'll make sure your next three letters are worth every penny! Old Man Winter is here and that means it's time for me to curl up on my bearskin rug by the fireplace. I love to feel all that heat on my naked skin! (I hope you like the picture of me in front of the fire . . .). I get lonely, and I wish you were here during these long winter nights.

> Your Hot Woman,
> Candy

◊

December 15

Candy
c/o LetterBoxes
P.O. Box 69
Intercourse PA 17534

Hey Listen Candy:
     Sorry it took me so long to write back but I had this surprise for you. When I got your last letter and picture I told my father I needed some money to buy a table saw

for the shop in the garage and I used the money to take a
Greyhound bus to Intercourse Pennsylvania. But the lady
at the post office counter there had never heard of you. She
didn't want to tell me anything but I waited in the parking
lot till she got off work that night and I told her about the
well and the animals and then she told me that all the mail
to LetterBoxes got forwarded to Denver Colorado. How
come you never told me you lived in Denver? I love you and
I can't keep living like this. We need to be together Candy.
So don't worry. I'll find a way to get out to Denver so we
can be together.

I Love You,
Wayne

◊

United States Postal Service
Official Business

Hiram Gundersen   December 18
RFD 12 – Route 43
Ingram WI 54535

Mr. Gundersen:
        I would like to speak to you in person at your
earliest convenience. Please call me at (717)555-2300 so
that we may arrange an appointment.
        Thank you very much.

Sincerely,

Albert Moler
Postal Inspector
Mid-Atlantic District 4

◊

U.S. POSTAL SERVICE INTER-OFFICE MEMO

TO: District Supervisor
FROM: A. Moler

January 10

   Here's something else on Case #66782-4. I thought it might be a good idea to have some on file ahead of time just in case there's any funny business later.
   When I received no response from Wayne Gundersen's father, and had no luck in reaching him by telephone, I had the investigation transferred to Mid-West District 3. Inspector Hans Juernburgh conducted a personal interview with Hiram Gundersen.
   Just to make sure nothing's out of order on this one, I thought it might be a good idea to attach a xerox of Inspector Juernburgh's report.

enc. Inspector's Report, Mid-West District 3

◊

U.S. POSTAL SERVICE INTER-OFFICE MEMO

TO: District Supervisor
FROM: H. Juernburgh

January 26

   Case #66782-4.
   I visited the farm of Hiram Gundersen on January 25. It is a run-down operation. If I had to describe the place in one word, "grim" would be my first choice. "Scary" my second. Mr. Gundersen is a small acreage farmer near Ingram, Wisconsin. He denies allega-

tions that his son, Wayne, had ever been to the Intercourse
Post Office, and stated that he would swear in a court of
law that the boy was working on the farm on the day in
question (November 27). He would not allow me to speak
to his son, and when I asked for permission to look around
the property, he threatened me with a post-hole digger.
Mr. Gundersen's exact words were "Get out of here before I
open you up for a piece of snow-fence."

I left the property immediately. FYI: unofficially
and off the record, it's my personal opinion Hiram
Gundersen is only half-wrapped. There's no doubt in my
mind the son scared the pee out of our District 4 employee,
but we would have a difficult time proving it. I don't see
any choice but to drop the matter, but I think we should
alert the local authorities to the situation out at the
Gundersen farm. If the son's anything like the father, I'd
say we have a couple of weirdos on our hands.

◊

February 3

Candy
c/o LetterBoxes
P.O. Box 69
Intercourse PA 17534

My Candy:
It's been a long time I've been waiting to get
another letter from you. I figured something must be wrong
when I got a check from LetterBoxes. I couldn't understand it because I never asked for a refund. Please write
me Candy. I will die if I don't get some kind of proof that
our love is still the best. I got a visit from a postal inspector
awhile back, but my Dad talked to the guy. You didn't tell
anybody I was looking for you did you? Lately I been
spending more time with Bowser. He likes the showers
more and more. I don't want to sound like I'm getting

angry or making any threats, but if I don't get a letter from you soon, I might have to start writing to some of the other women who really like me and would love to be my girl-friends. Like maybe Madonna and Paula Abdul (even though I think she might be a nigger) and Tiffany. When I go out to the woods, the voice in the well tells me things about you that maybe you don't love me anymore and maybe I'll just start listening. Think about it.

Still Yours,
Wayne

◊

February 5

Paula Abdul
Apex Records
Box 13788
Northridge CA 91324

Dear Paula:

I had to tell Candy it was over. You are the only woman in my life now, and I promise to make you happy forever. When I see you at your concert, I'll show you my love-meat. I'd do anything for you. Even kill or die for you. I like to watch you dance and can imagine you doing it with no clothes—definitely not for MTV. Bowser likes you too even though he's only a dog and won't be allowed in the shower with us. Write soon.

Love Always,
Big-Wad Wayne Gundersen

◊

April 21

Darin McDowell
Los Angeles Security Services
23444 Melrose Ave, Suite 655
Los Angeles CA 90069

Mr. McDowell:

Enclosed please find this month's batch of letters. Things are getting pretty hectic as we prepare for Ms. Abdul's first concert tour of the year. As usual, thank you very much.

Sincerely,
Jamie Lerner
Personal Secretary
to Ms. Abdul

◊

MEMORANDUM

Date: May 3
From: Darin McDowell, Director
To: Joseph D'Agostino
Re: Priority Ones

Enclosed please find NA's of all the Priority One letters. We have a Red Flag on Subject #1 (Wayne Gundersen). Be aware that Subject #1's letters rang up the highest scores ever recorded on all three Test Indices. Subject #1 is considered to be extremely unstable and dangerous. I want you on location in Wisconsin for a complete dossier work-up. The Abdul tour starts next week—with a stop in Madison, so we will want to be ready for anything.

◊

MEMORANDUM
CONFIDENTIAL

Date: May 19
From: J. D'Agostino
To: Mr. McDowell
Re: Wayne Gundersen

Everything I've been able to uncover about the subject indicates we have a real dough-nut on our hands.

No known friends, bad relationships with his teachers, parents, and the local authorities. School records show below-average Stanford-Binet intelligence scores, unsubstantiated claims of sexual abuse while still in elementary grades, poor classroom attendance, and non-existent parental involvement with the education process. A series of misdemeanors on the county docket ranging from Malicious Destruction of Property to Animal Cruelty to Voyeurism.

I've been able to observe the subject at fairly close range. He spends most of his time just meandering around the family farm or in the nearby woods. Once in the woods, he either stands over the opening of an abandoned well talking to himself, or committing acts of sodomy with his dog. We are talking about a very sick boy out here in cheese country.

◊

June 12

Paula Abdul
Apex Records
Box 13788
Northridge CA 91324

My Paula:

I don't understand what is going on here. Why did you let those men jump on me at your concert? I tried to tell them you said it was okay to come up and sing and dance with you. They took me to a trailer and used Bruce Lee stuff on me. The police were just as bad, and I kept waiting for you to come and save me and you never did. Don't you still love me? And when are you going to buy my Dad's farm so we can get rid of him and my two (brat) sisters? The thing in the well told me I should be mad about all this, but I love you so much I just can't. But write soon or I will be upset.

Your Wayne Gundersen

◊

MEMORANDUM

Date: July 15
From: Darin McDowell
To: Joseph D'Agostino
Re: W. Gundersen

Sorry to keep you twisting in the wind so long, but it looks like you're going to have to stay on this one. We've faxed copies of all our documentation to the Portage County D.A. The ball's in their court now. Till then, I want you so close to Gundersen he'll have to goose you to get into his pajamas at night. Talking to the kid's father is a waste of time. Talk about chips off the old block. Continue to fax me weekly report memo. I want our documentation to be air-tight in case we run into trouble down the line. And Joe—thanks for going the extra mile on this one.

◊

◊

July 31

Paula Abdul
Apex Records
Box 13788
Northridge CA 91324

My Naked Dancer, Paula:
Okay, everything is ready for you out here. You can buy everything and nobody will say anything about it. Bowser says he will like you too. I'll teach him to lick you in the shower like he licks me. The only problem we're going to have is keep the thing in the well happy. The more I give it to eat the more it wants and it says it will make me do what it wants. You have to come out here and help me.

I Love You Paula,
Wayne The G-Man

◊

FROM THE DESK OF
HUGHES STURDEVANT, ESQ.
PORTAGE COUNTY DISTRICT ATTORNEY'S OFFICE

August 15

Judge Hartkey:
After reviewing the material on the case against Wayne Gundersen (case #33467), I've decided not to pursue charges. The State's evidence is mostly based on what even a public defender is going to have thrown out as hearsay or innuendo. Admittedly, we have a kid who *appears* to be potentially dangerous, but, at least up until now, hasn't actually committed any crimes.
Give me a call if you have any comments, sugges-

tions, etc. By the way, I saw Leo in the cafeteria yesterday, and he is itching for a rematch on the links this Sunday. Interested?

Hugh

◊

PRIVATE INVESTIGATOR MISSING

Ingram, Wisconsin - Portage County Sheriff Stanley Houseman confirmed claims made by the Los Angeles Security Services that Joseph D'Agostino, an employee of LASS, has been missing without a trace for twenty-one days. Mr. D'Agostino works for a private agency which provides maximum security for public figures such as singers and actors. When President of LASS, Darin McDowell, was questioned about the presence of Mr. D'Agostino in Portage County, McDowell said his employee was working on a confidential assignment. Sheriff Houseman said the search for Mr. D'Agostino has already commenced.

◊

MEMORANDUM
CONFIDENTIAL

Date: August 22
From: M. Lonnigan
To: Darin McDowell
Re: Ingram WI

Hard to believe it took that asshole Sheriff this long to listen to us. They just dragged the abandoned well at the Gundersen farm and found what we figured—plus a lot more. Looks like Joe's been in there at least two weeks. The rest of the family's been there maybe a week longer. They also found some bones of another body—probably the stepmother. But here's the weird part: they found the Gundersen kid in there too. There were parts of his fingernails on the edge of the well, like he was trying to hold on and something was trying to pull him in. The local John Laws were so glad to wrap this up, they just glossed over that little oddity. I might go back tonight and check out the scene after the County ME pulls out. I'll call you later.

◊

SECOND INVESTIGATOR MISSING

Ingram, Wisconsin – Sheriff Stanley Houseman refused to confirm or deny claims that a second investigator from the Los Angeles Security Services, a Mr. Mickey Lonnigan, may be missing in Ingram, Wisconsin. The President of the California-based company, Darin McDowell has announced plans to personally investigate the matter.

ARDATH MAYHAR *writes in several genres and succeeds with them all. Perhaps best known for her fantasy work, Mayhar has published horror, mystery and suspense, crime, science fiction and western fiction—novels and short stories. Mayhar, a resident of Texas, exhibits a strong sense of locality in the following short-short.*

THE CREEK, IT DONE RIZ
ARDATH MAYHAR

Only the Lord knows why I ever took the old road that day, particularly since the water was out all over the map from the big rains. I could have stuck a dozen times, coming across the bottom lands. It's a wonder in this world that none of the rickety little bridges were washed out—or that one of them didn't go out with me halfway across. Still, Pa's old 1939 Plymouth could mighty nearly swim, and we always took it out when we were going way down into the boondocks.

The whole thing was a lot of foolishness, anyway. I didn't get a degree from Texas A&M in order to go paddling around in the river-bottom in the middle of a flood to count hogs. But try telling the boss that. He sits in his air-conditioned office, thinking up dumb schemes, and never knows if it rains or shines. And he can come up with some of the gosh-awfulest ideas. A hog census! Now I ask you. How he thought that knowing where every hog in the county was located would help him sell his damn feed, I don't know.

Anyway, there I was in the river bottom in a car twice as old as I was, sloshing down a road that wasn't much more than a lane, when I could see it, which wasn't often. The wet sweetgum saplings were bent way down and slapping across the windshield. I was crawling along, cussing some, when I saw something out in the woods.

I crept on until I could feel gravel under the wheels; then I stopped. I could have sworn I saw an old man sitting on a stump. I stuck my feet into the rubber boots I had learned to take along with me, being as most hog-pens can't be said to do shoes any good at all. Then I got out and started off into a thicket. And sure enough, there was a grizzly-headed old cuss, soaked to the bone, dripping water off his nose and his eyebrows. He never acted as if he saw me, just muttered to himself as if that's what he'd been doing for quite a while.

When I got close enough to hear, I stood there for a minute, admiring his style. You don't hear cussing like that anymore, with real feeling and meaning to it. And he was cussing the weather, which deserved everything he gave it and then some. But it was wet as all get-out, and finally I went up and touched him on the shoulder.

"Sir, I beg your pardon," I said, "but would you like a ride someplace? Out of the wet?"

He gave a jerk and looked up at me for a minute, sizing me up. Then he gave me a couple of cusses, too.

I shook my head admiringly. "It's a privilege to listen to a man who can handle the language the way you do," I said. "Even my Pa, and he's no slouch, can't touch you. But it does look like you're set to catch your death of cold, if you sit out here much longer."

Then he squinched up his eyes and looked me over, real carefully. "You look to be a Jenkins," he said, when he had gone from top to bottom. "Got that Jenkins jaw. Any kin to Ralph Jenkins?"

"That's my Pa," I said. It's the darndest thing . . . anyplace I go, people spot me for Pa's son right off. Even if they never laid eyes on me before.

He grunted and shifted on the stump. "Tell you, Son," he said, "I ain't got no place to go that you can take me to in no car. But bein' as you're Ralph's boy, why you might help me out a little bit."

Now that's where I should've said goodbye and been off to count hogs. But Pa raised us all to be polite and helpful to old folks, and I can't seem to break the habit. When an old geezer looks at you kind of slant-eyed, with his head cocked on one side like he's figuring out how far he can con you, it's time to take off. Not me, though. No brains, that's me.

So pretty soon I found myself slogging down a pig-trail through the woods, looking sharp for cotton-mouth moccasins and stump-holes. He kept talking all the time, as if he was scared I'd change my mind and leave him. Nothing he said made me anxious to keep on.

"I've got a kind of boat a little piece further on, tied up along Eel Creek. If it's still there, we can take it and get up to my house. The house ain't washed away; it's just the damn creek's done riz so I can't get to the yard. With a strong young fellow like you to help me with the boat, I kin make it." He paused, and panted a while. I could see that he wasn't in too good shape.

I turned around and said, "Why Pa could put you up until the water goes down. He'd be glad to. Why don't you just go back to the car with me, and I'll take you straight on in and have you dry in no time at all."

He started shaking his head before I was done. Then he looked all around, really careful, as if anybody but a couple of fools would have been out in the woods with the river out of its banks.

"I guess I ought to tell you, Son, seein' as how you're

helpin' me and all. I've got my life's savings buried in that yard. If the river backs the creek up too high, it'll likely wash it right away. It's all I've got to stand me through my old age. I just got to get back there and get it out before the water comes up any more."

Well, he did sound pitiful. I couldn't help but wonder why he didn't dig up his money before he left, but I guessed that you might be forgetful at his age. So we went on, and the water was mighty near the tops of my boots before we came to his boat. Then I saw why he called it a kind of a boat. The bailing bucket was the only thing that didn't have a hole in it. A good, sound log would have been a lot safer to try to travel on.

"You sure you want to risk that thing?" I asked him.

"It's a sight better than it looks," he answered. "I been fishing in that boat for twenty years and never drowned yet."

I never was one to believe in miracles, but maybe such things happen, or else he was an uncommonly solid ghost. But I was pledged to help him, so I bailed out the water that was sloshing around in the bottom of the thing and heaved it out into the creek. I stood there and watched the little wiggles of water come through the holes and start moving down the sides.

He got right in and started bailing. "Reason I had to have help," he said, "is somebody has to bail while the other one rows. I always borrow one of Rupe Miller's kids to do the bailing, when I go fishing, but they left when the water got high. Get in, Boy. Let's get moving. That water's not going to wait on us."

So I said a prayer, which would have pleased Ma, and got in. Then I didn't have time to pray. That water was wild as a yearling colt. It took everything I could do to keep the boat from taking off in ten directions at once.

I fought with the paddle to fend us off floating logs and brush-piles. I guess I came nearer to poling it along than paddling. In the middle of all that, it came to me. . . . I didn't know his name. I twisted my head round and yelled, "Hey, Mister, what's your name?"

He looked up from his bucket, kind of startled. "Why, I'm Abe Willitts. I thought everybody in the county knowed of old Abe."

Then I really started to sweat. Everybody knew about Abe Willitts, sure enough. When I was little, Ma'd hush me up with, "Crazy Abe'll get you, if you don't be good." When his wife died, all the women looked at each other and said, "He finally killed her. I knew he would, one day." And nobody could prove them wrong, because she was buried by the time he got around to letting anybody know she was dead.

Even Pa, who wouldn't hear a bad word about anyone, had to be still when that hunter disappeared. He'd told his wife that he was going to bird-hunt down in the bottoms, and he'd intended to get Abe and his setter to help him find the birds. Nobody ever saw nor heard from him again. They looked, too. All over the place, with dogs and men. Abe claimed he never got there at all, and nobody could prove different.

So here I was in a leaky boat in the middle of a flood with a crazy man. A hog census looked mightly calm and peaceful, when I thought about it. Still, I hadn't time to worry over much, just then. Working that crazy piece of junk around the bends in the creek took all my energy. By the time we came in sight of the house, I was done in, sure enough.

Abe jumped out onto the bank, only it was the yard fence, the bank being a hundred yards behind us in the middle of the flood, and tied his rope to a fencepost. "Here we are, Boy. You just wait right here, and I'll go round and dig up my savings and be right back." His eyes slid round at me and didn't look quite sane.

"I'm too tired to move, Sir," I said. "You just get your stuff, and I'll rest. It'll take all we both can do to get us back up that creek."

Soon as he was gone around the house, I slid out of the boat and eased up the slope. It took a while, and once he looked out around the corner of the porch to see if I was still in the boat. Luckily, I'd propped up the bucket so it looked like a head leaning against the edge, and he didn't go down to check. I stayed hidden in the bushes for a while to let my heart quit thumping, then I went on.

When I peeped around the porch, he was digging hard. You could hear his shovel going "Shloop! Shloop!" in the mud, because the water had got around to that side of the house, too. He was in an almighty hurry. I scootched down and watched. I don't quite know why, but I just had to know what it was he was in such a hurry and a sweat about. He had to be living on Social Security, just like Pa and everybody else their age. I figured he couldn't have saved up enough to amount to anything.

When a shovelful of mud came out of that hole with something dark and solid on it, I perked up. It was a hunting jacket, as I could tell after it lay there a while and the rain washed off the mud. The kind with a bag in back for shot birds and shell-pockets across the front. Then Abe's hand came up with a shotgun in it and laid it on the ground.

I didn't wait to see more. All of a sudden, I figured I'd better be back at the boat—or further still—when Abe came around the corner of that house. I made it a lot quicker than I'd come and leaned back in the boat as if I'd been dozing. Then I got to thinking.

Whatever he was getting out of that hole, he'd likely send down the flood. Maybe he'd feel safe then. Maybe not. . . . The more I thought about going back up that creek with him bailing behind me, the less I liked the notion. I had a little money in my pocket. Probably about what that hunter had had. And nobody knew where I was or what I was doing.

I eased out into the bushes and crept along until I found a likely log. It was half afloat, already, so I goosed it out into the current and held onto a stub of branch, with my head close under the side so it couldn't be seen. That log and I whirled and twirled and twiddled down the creek with the rest of the stuff floating there until we lodged way down on Bobcat Ridge. I guess Abe never did know what happened to me.

He must've tried to make it back in that boat, all by himself. We'll never know, though. They didn't look for *him* as hard as they did for that hunter.

REX MILLER *is the*
author of the famed
Jack Eichord series,
featuring such novels as
Slob, Frenzy, Stone Shadow,
Slice, *and the recent* Iceman.
Miller, known for his
bulldozer style and
grim storytelling, just
completed two books in
a new crime/suspense series.
The following tale shows
Miller's lighter side—a rare
piece, indeed.

TRIGGER HAPPY
REX MILLER

The floor director cued him and he turned perfectly, turning on his mark right into the nice, shadowy two-shot, listening to the familiar theme music from *Gunfighter* surge from the studio speaker system. He gave them what they wanted. When the second dah-duh-DAH hit he made his move.

He always felt funny doing it in costume, or in civvy gear. Kid Reno was decked out in the goony-bird suit, his Elvis Suit-of-Lights he called it, the all-white outfit that Coy Champion wore on the TV show. His show biz suit.

Reno's slim profile, accentuated by the floor point-of-view shot, was moving away from the camera's perspective, which had been carefully planned so as not to catch the studio lights as he moved out of the shot.

"And two," the young woman in the master control intoned, and as her words popped into various headsets the switcher slid his pot forward, and two—also shooting upward, but cheating it so the picture wouldn't show he wasn't on a western street—caught the reverse of the shot as Kid Reno drew down and smoked an unseen adversary.

Jared Peters, just back from his third tuck job, hair sprayed to a fare-thee-well and smiling for all he was worth, announced to the small studio audience and the vast viewership at home, that it was showtime.

"Howdy, Dallas!" He articulated, in a voice rich and full and show bizzy. The applause sign blinked brightly and forty-some Texans and tourists, sounding like the Sixth Fusiliers if you were watching at home, just about broke their hands clapping.

"No, you didn't tune in *Gunfighter* by mistake!" They giggled dutifully. "That is not Coy Champion with the fast gun. And Coy, whom I have known for years and who is a sweetheart of a guy and wouldn't mind my telling this behind-the-scenes stuff, is not the guy who has the gunfight at the top of the show. The gunfighter sequence, in fact several of the sequences on the show we watch every week, were done by the guy who is our guest today on *Howdy, Dallas.*"

Reno's hands perspired, as they always did when he had to do this kind of a gig, and professionally he dried his right palm on the washcloth he always carried. In a match he'd be shaking talcum on that sucker.

He took a deep breath, popped his neck, and tried to clear his mind. It was only local television. Just something about the cameras always spooked him. No matter how many times he was on TV, or on a film set, he'd get the jitters. It just wasn't his thing.

But it was good for the promoter, good for the hobby, good for the club, good for the TV folks. It was good for Reno. Was it good for you, baby? It was good for me. Come on, man.

He was actually shivering a bit.

"The man in white happens to be a real gunfighter. The fastest gun alive, maybe. National fast-draw champ three years running, Hollywood consultant on guns and gunfighting, put your hands together for Charlie Laberino, better known as *Kid Reno!*" The winking sign brought on a thunderous applause from the tiny gallery, or so it would sound when it came amplified from a viewer's tinny living room TV speaker, and Reno ambled out into the bright light of the set, feeling Jared Peters pump his gun hand a few dozen times, blinding him with his ear-to-ear caps.

"Wanna see the fastest draw in the West?" Peters said.

"Cut to one," the headsets heard. "One's up. Stand by two. Three," the woman said urgently, "you're free to get the two-shot framed. In tighter, two. The face." Speaking her shorthand to the camera and floor personnel. "Cut to two. Two's up. One, you're free. Frame the couch shot."

"Wanna see it again?" Peters got his laugh on the old line. Reno had heard all the fast draw gags a hundred times. He made a convincing smile stay on his face.

"It's great to have you here, Charlie. Or does everybody call you Kid Reno?" Jared Peters sat down behind the desk, always thinking visual interest and momentum. Keeping the balls in the air.

"It's great to be here." He sat down. "Most folks just call me Reno."

"Old Coy gets a lot of static from the fans out there because of you, doesn't he?"

"Oh, there was some talk about wonderin' if he was really good with a gun. You know, when it was made public knowledge that I did the fast-draw stuff." Reno shrugged, trying to word things carefully as he always did. "But Champion is pretty good with a gun himself."

"Champion's no champion, though." Snickers.

"I don't think he competes."

"You guys really get into those competitions don't you?" He didn't wait for an answer. "You're in town for the national championship—right?"

"Well, not the nationals. This is—um—the South-West Fast Draw Championship. And since I don't live in Nevada anymore, they let me in, I guess."

"You live in Houston, right?"

"Yes, sir."

"What makes somebody want to be a fast draw? How do you get into it? It seems like—forgive me—such a *strange* hobby. I mean, I was pretty good with a cap gun once, but I was only nine then." The audience giggled. Reno took him through all the usual stuff. How the hobby got rolling in the Fifties, and took off around 1960, when all the shows on episodic television were quick-draw-oriented westerns.

He told him how he got started with a cheap, mail order replica. How the love of the old West and the pistolero bug had bitten him and he'd started really working at it. Perfecting his draw. Practising seven, eight hours a day sometimes. How he'd had to quit his job with State Planning. ("Estate planning?") How his wife had found it so impossible to reconcile. He tried to be honest. Keep it simple. But tell it as it was.

Peters made him get up and explain how the fast draw worked. Show the difference between fanning and thumbing. Show them the beautiful presentation model Colt he used. (Single action 32.20 on a .44 frame. Filed sear. Snap-proof DeForest mountings. Custom-sprung. Hair trigger action.) The metal-lined cutaway fast draw rig that was his own design. Then, after a spot breakaway, they got down to it.

"They say that today's gunfighters would make mincemeat out of the old gunmen of western history. How does anybody know for sure? How can this be true?"

"Obviously it can't be proved. But yes, I think it's safe to say that today's fast-draw experts would be faster than the oldtimers, just as today's athletes are stronger, faster, and in some cases—record-breakers. A lot of things account for this. For one thing the old gunmen couldn't spend seven or eight hours a day in front of a mirror or in a training room working with a timer. They had their own survival and day to day matters at hand. Also the weapons and the cartridges were not in the same league. And today you take a youngster who's been in fast draw since he was little—you can get to be mighty quick on the trigger."

"Who was the fastest gun alive—I mean of all time. Wild Bill Hickcock?"

"No," Reno said, fighting not to laugh in the man's seamless face. "Uh—in the old West I'd say John Wesley Hardin was the fastest by reputation. Of what books I've read on it. But of all time—there's no question. Milby Adams is the top gun ever lived."

"Another Texan."

"That's right."

"Milby Adams, you tell me if I'm wrong, was once a cop—wasn't he? When he won the National Fast Draw Championship?" Like all the media interviewers he had about half of it right.

"Um. I think he still is a police officer. And he won the National a whole bunch of times."

"But he no longer competes?"

"I don't believe so. But I don't really know for certain. I've never met the gentleman, but I haven't been in every tournament or match so I can't say for sure."

"Milby Adams must be—what—nearly sixty now?"

"Again, I just couldn't tell you. I think he was in his forties when he quit competing regularly."

"Well if old Milby was such a fast gun, how come he quit? Was he afraid one of you younger gunslicks were going to outgun him?"

"Oh, shoot! Not hardly. There hasn't been anybody *ever* could outdraw or outshoot Milby Adams."

They talked about Milby for a good while, which was

always the way. If the conversation wound around to the subject, everybody always wanted to know about mysterious Milby Adams, the fastest gun who ever lived. Who was this enigmatic figure who never gave interviews? This quiet, superfast gunman who was a legend in the quick-draw world. Fourteen-time winner of the Nationals. So fast he couldn't be measured on the timers.

"You can only time him by a certain type micrometer, and the only way you can actually see his draw with the naked eye is to film or tape him and then play it back in slow motion."

"Yeah," Jared Peters said, "Every year on Johnny's anniversary show they play that thing where Milby draws and busts the balloon in—what was it? One twentieth of a second or something?" He didn't bother to correct the man, who was only interested in laughing and scratching and joke-making.

Kid Reno got out of there as soon as his segment was over, and was breathing deep sighs of relief, packing up his rig, and getting ready to go to the car, when somebody told him there was a call for him waiting. Milby Adams. He laughed, knowing it would be Deke McElhenney, the crazy sumbitch. Calling to zing him. What a flake.

Reno went into a nearby office where two engineers were having a loud conversation about a "downstream keyer" whoever or whatever that was, and he picked up a phone that was on hold.

"Hello."

"Mr. Laberino?"

"Yeah."

"I just wanted to thank you for the kind, generous things you said today on that TV show. I happened to be watching. And I just wanted to say you handled yourself like a pro. You're a fine champion and make a good spokesperson for the hobby. And I wanted to tell you so." Instantly, on some level, he was sure it was not a put-on, and he was equally certain that this was the legend. Although he'd never heard the man's voice except on a brief excerpt from a TV program, he knew who it was.

"Is this . . . Mr. Adams?" His throat felt dry.

"Um hmm. Call me Milby."

"Please call me Reno. It's wonderful, heck—it's *great* to meetcha over the phone Mr.—uh, Milby. I've, you know, always hoped I'd get to talk to you. Do you pick up the show in Waco?"

"I'm here in Dallas, Reno. In fact, I've got to go right now. I had to come in and do some work for the—" it sounded like he said the drug people. "Just wanted to tell you thanks for the nice words."

Something made Reno say it. He couldn't let the chance go. He'd always been fascinated with the exploits of this man. The tournaments. His speed and accuracy were beyond legend.

"I wonder if I could impose and just ask one favor?" He made himself plunge in and say it while he had his courage screwed down tightly. "I would give anything to meet you, sir. I know you—" how to word it—he was cautious, "are a private person. Please. It would mean a lot. Could I buy you dinner or something? Just to talk with you?"

"I'm on too tight a schedule, Reno. Sorry." His heart sunk.

"Yes, sir. I understand."

"But if you get through Waco sometime, I'd be glad to have you come talk to me."

"Yes, sir. Would next week be too soon?" He couldn't believe he was hearing himself doing this. Acting like some pushy little kid begging for an autograph. *Bothering* a man. "I wouldn't take up much of your time. I know it is an intrusion on your privacy. But—I been wanting to speak with you for a long time."

"Um." The sigh was audible over the line. "All right. Better write down the address. I'm not listed." He took the address down and Milby Adams, or somebody *claiming* to be

Milby Adams, reclusive top gun of song and story, hung up.

The following Monday morning, feeling like a complete fool, but more excited than he'd been in years, Charlie "Kid Reno" Laberino, all one hundred and thirty-nine pounds of him, was standing in front of a Waco Safeway, listening to a telephone ring. What if this would prove to be a complicated hoax on the part of his fellow fast-draw nut Deke McElhenney, who was certifiable and capable of anything? He'd kill him.

"'Lo." The same voice came on the line and Reno knew. He was going to finally meet The Man.

Inside five minutes he was pulling up in front of the sprawling brick home on the outskirts of Waco, Texas, and preparing to meet the fastest gunfighter who had ever lived. Ten times faster than John Hardin on his best day. The reason he'd got into the hobby in the first place. The role model that a skinny kid had thought about while he spent all those months and years putting scars on the webbing and thumb of his right hand, and building those thick gun ridges on his left palm and right trigger finger.

"Mr. Adams," he said, when the portly man opened his front door, immediately forgetting to call him "Milby."

"Hello. Come on in." The man stepped back into the shadows and Reno stepped inside, blinking as he came in out of the bright sunlight. It was very dark in the home, which was decorated in authentic western memorabilia. And cool.

"You have a beautiful home," he said, rather inanely he thought.

"Thanks. It's comfortable. Come on. Have a seat." Somewhere along the line, maybe twenty-five years ago, there had been rumors of a wife and kids, but they'd probably gone their own way, just as his own Missus had. No woman wanted to share her man with a hobby that consumed him. And, no doubt about it, if there were two men alive who had dedicated their lives to a hobby or sport—it was these two. The two fastest guns. Together for the first time.

"I love the western items. You've really got some great things." It was a real man's room. A room decorated by a man, for a man. Indian blankets. Artifacts. Spurs. Heavy, open beams. Stone. A big, functional fireplace. A leather sofa and matching armchair. Books. Trophy heads. And guns. Guns everywhere you looked. He wanted to get up and snoop, peer in every showcase and gun rack.

"I like my home."

"I'm grateful to you for letting me impose like this, Milby. It means a lot to get to meet you. I used to read about you—" he stopped himself from saying when he was just a kid. But he couldn't stop the words. The flow broke loose like a floodgate had opened, and he asked the man a million questions. How he started? Why did he thumb instead of fan? What did he think of the Weaver, the Bianchi, the Stratton? The Krelmar hot wax load? The Arms Inc. Reloader? The b.a.t.? Plus P? Kay-loads? Wilson timers? Had he ever tried an Amarillo Gunnery cutaway? Why had he started with a buscadero rig . . . on and on with the questions.

He told him about Bucky Fuller, another real fast kid, who had switched to a heavy black load in the balloon-busting last year, and something had gone wrong and he blew his right kneecap off. He told him about the Fannits and the Fanners and the Fans and the Fandangos, and he just plain ran his mouth.

Finally it dawned on him what he was doing and he reddened with embarrassment. What a clown!

"Hey, Milby. I'm sorry, man. I just had so many things I wanted to ask. So much I've always wanted to talk to you about. It's like meeting your idol." Jeez, could he act a little more stupid?

"No problem. I'd've been the same way if I met somebody I really admired. Or would have when I was your age. When you get older—" he trailed off.

"When I was a kid—I guess I admired the oldtimers.

The frontiersman and the mountain men."

"We had a chance to get out and live in the old ways back then. I did some living rough. Liked it all right. I learned my smithing there. Old mountain man did his own gun-smithing. Crude forge and bellows operation up in the hills, and he'd turn out some of the prettiest arms and edged weapons a man ever saw."

He got up and went over to a showcase and removed an object d'art, and told Kid Reno to come over by the case. Reno felt like a devout Catholic would feel being granted a private audience with the Pope. It was almost akin to a religious experience, this feeling. This proximity to legend. Like feeling yourself brushing up against living history. He wondered what the epiphany of this religious-like experience would be.

"Isn't she a beaut?" Milby handed him the knife. It was sort of like touching Excalibur. One almost expected to be surrounded by a magical, luminous glow.

"Wow."

"Skinning knife. He made that up in the mountains. Isn't that a pretty one?" Milby took the knife from his hands. "Watch." He touched the blade lightly to the back of his arm and it was covered in small, dark hairs. "Like a razor and I've never put a hone to it."

Milby showed him his guns. It was a wonderful day. Milby Adams was nothing like he'd heard. All those crazy rumors about how he'd gone nuts and was living in an insane asylum. How he'd been fired from police force after police force for using his weapon too often. How Milby had become trigger happy. All crap.

Milby was as fine a fellow as Kid Reno could remember ever meeting. Courteous. Pleasant. Cordial to a fault. Self-effacing.

"Milby, I've got to say it. I'm so thrilled to be here, man. It's a treat. I sure do appreciate your time."

"I'm glad to meet you, Reno. I like somebody who

appreciates the old ways. I don't hold with some of the things that go on now. I liked the way it must have been in the western days, when a man could keep his life simple. You could be self-sustaining. Farm. Ranch. Learn how to provide food and clothing."

"That's a beautiful rig." He pointed to Milby's famous buscadero rig, and the man took it from the wall so Reno could inspect it.

"I skinned and tanned that hide myself."

"Gorgeous." The leather was supple like the finest kid.

"That's my work. I mounted everything you see here." He pointed proudly to the array of stuffed trophy heads around them.

"That's great."

"Here's a few of my larger pieces in the next room," Milby gestured Reno ahead of him and suddenly, as Charlie Laberino stepped past the curtains, and saw the stuffed figures, he was ice cold, and very aware of the strange, portly man behind him, still holding the large, razor-sharp skinning knife.

"Meet the wife and kids," Milby Adams said, the way a tour guide would say, "This was Roy Rogers' horse."

And the fast young gun at last learned why the number one gunfighter of all time never competed anymore. He'd found himself another hobby. Taxidermy.

ROMAN A. RANIERI *lives
in Philadelphia with his
wife Maureen. Ranieri is
a small-press regular
(especially well-known
to the readers of* Cemetery
Dance)*, AFRAID* columnist,
and New Blood *contributing
editor. The following story
demonstrates Ranieri's
emerging talent.*

THE DRIFTER
ROMAN A. RANIERI

The wooden chair groaned as Sheriff Wheeler tipped it back against the rough cement wall. He swung his legs up and set the heels of his worn cowboy boots on the edge of his desk, yawning as he gazed out the open window at the darkening Texas sky. The western horizon was a hazy, blood-red slash in the distance. The entire month of July had been sizzling hot, and it seemed that August was offering more of the same. Jagged sparks of heat lightning electrified the night air; teasing reminders of the badly needed rain that refused to fall.

Wheeler flinched and almost fell when the front door suddenly banged open. He squinted to see who was there as a dry blast of wind blew grit into his eyes. He hadn't been expecting anyone, and Ron, his deputy, wasn't due back from patrol until ten. The front legs of the chair hit the tile floor with a loud thunk as he sat upright to study the stranger now walking into his office.

The guy was a drifter. Wheeler knew that the moment he laid eyes on him. Dingy, mismatched clothes hung loosely on the man's gaunt body, and a faded green knapsack was slung over his left shoulder. Dozens of drifters had come through town over the years, they all looked the same.

"You the Sheriff?"

"Yep. What can I do for you?"

"Nothing, Sheriff," replied the stranger, lowering himself into the wooden chair facing the front of the desk. "I'm going to do something for you. I'm going to make you a hero."

Wheeler leaned forward, his eyes narrowing with concern. Something about the man triggered his lawman's sixth sense. Was this drifter just another old fool who had stayed out in the Texas sun too long, or was there something truly dangerous about him? "I'm listening."

"I'm turning myself in. I'm going to give you a full confession here and now. You're going to be a national hero for catching me."

"That so? And just what terrible crime are you planning to confess?"

"Murder, Sheriff, or to be more correct, *murders*. I've killed quite a few people in the last three years."

Wheeler remained silent for a moment as he stared at the drifter's face. The man's left eye was glass, or plastic. It gazed straight ahead, oblivious to the direction the living orb was pointing. Wavy, gray-black hair was slicked to his scalp, weighted down by a combination of sweat and road dust. A three or four day's growth of stubble covered his cheeks and chin. When he spoke, a crooked line of brown teeth were visible behind his thin, dry lips. He certainly looked like he had broken some laws in his time, but was he really a murderer? "Why don't you start by telling me your name?" said the sheriff.

"Billy Lee Tucker is my name. I'm originally from St. James Parish in Louisiana, but I ain't been back there in a long time."

"What about some of these murders you say you've committed?"

"Well, I guess the one you'd be most interested in would be Tammy Lucas. I killed her right here in Montague County about four months ago. She was my girlfriend for awhile, but I got tired of her."

"How did you kill her?"

"I strangled her with a piece of barbed wire, then I dumped her body in a ditch out along Route 59."

"You could have read about that murder in the newspapers."

"Did the newspapers say she had a yellow rose tattooed on the left cheek of her butt?" asked Tucker, grinning.

Wheeler's anger began to flare at the drifter's obvious enjoyment, but his twenty years of experience as a lawman kept him calm and detached. "Go on."

"Well, about ten months ago I picked up a black woman hitchhiking near Georgetown. She said she was running from her boyfriend; said she had got tired of him beating on her all the time. When it started to get dark, she began to talk about how hungry she was. I told her I could afford to give her a ride, but I wasn't about to spend what little money I had to feed her. So a few minutes later she says if I'll buy her something to eat, she'll give me the best blow job I'd ever had. Well, that sounded fair enough to me, so I stopped at a McDonald's and bought a couple of Big Macs and fries. After we finished eating, I pulled off onto a side road near Salado and let her pay for her dinner. She was pretty damned good at it too. If you get my meaning?" Tucker laughed.

"Then what happened?"

"As soon as she finished, I reached down under the

front seat, pulled out my hunting knife, and stabbed her."

"Why did you stab her?"

"Just for the thrill of it. It's one hell of a high—actually seeing a person die. Better than any drug I ever tried."

"You don't seem the sort who'd be bothered much by a conscience, so why are you turning yourself in?"

"For the fame, Sheriff," the drifter cackled. "I'm going to be the biggest celebrity since Charlie Manson or Ted Bundy. I'll be on all the talk shows."

"Maybe so, but you'll be paying a hell of a price for it. Texas has the death penalty, or didn't you know that?"

"Hell! Sheriff, I won't be going to no jail. All I got to do is plead insanity, then I'll just go to a mental hospital for a few years until I can convince the doctors that they cured me. After I get out, I'll start all over again."

"Got it all figured out. Eh?"

"Damned right! Now you just do your duty and lock me up so we can get the ball rolling."

Wheeler stood up and came around the desk, reaching for the handcuffs hanging from his leather gun belt. "Stand up, put your hands flat on the desk, and spread your legs," he commanded.

Tucker grinned triumphantly as he complied.

After the sheriff searched and handcuffed his unusually willing prisoner, he grabbed the man's left bicep and pulled him toward the front door.

"Hey! Where we going? The cells are back there, ain't they?" asked the drifter, jerking his head back over his shoulder.

"I'm taking you to the Rangers station over in Bowie. You're too big a catch for a small town sheriff like me."

"Oh, okay," laughed Tucker, "but I'll still make sure you get your share of the glory. Don't you worry none about that."

Wheeler helped his prisoner into the rear seat of the Ford Bronco parked in the driveway beside the Sheriff's office. A few minutes later they were heading down the long, dark ribbon of US 81.

"Hey, Sheriff? You want to hear about the man and his son I killed in California? They were on a fishing trip at Big Bear Lake and I—"

"Save it for the Rangers. I've heard enough out of you."

"Getting a little queasy, eh? This kind of thing new to you, Sheriff?" asked Tucker. There was mockery in his tone.

"You don't want me to make you shut up, do you?"

"Okay, okay. No need to get riled. I'll be quiet."

They had just passed Stoneburg when Wheeler turned left onto a narrow dirt road. The Bronco's big tires kicked up white clouds of alkali dust as a batch of tumbleweeds seemed to scurry out of their path.

"Where in hell we going now?" whined Tucker.

"I'm taking a shortcut. You just shut up till we get there."

The drifter grudgingly sat back and kept quiet. He didn't like the looks of this, not one bit.

Ten minutes later they came to a tall group of cactus and yucca plants crowded around a small water hole. Wheeler stopped and shut off the engine. The interior of the Bronco was instantly filled with the unnerving silence and blackness of the Texas flatlands.

"What is this? What in hell are we doing here?" asked Tucker, leaning forward.

Wheeler was staring out the side window at the water hole. "Damned drought's got that water hole down to about half of where it should be. I sure hope it rains soon."

"You playing some kind of game here, Sheriff? What do you think you're doing?"

Wheeler climbed out of the Bronco, opened the rear door, and reached in for the drifter.

"You better not lay a hand on me. I know my rights,"

cried Tucker, struggling as best he could with his hands cuffed behind his back. The sheriff grabbed a fistful of shirt and yanked him out, letting him fall heavily to the ground.

"This here's as far as you go," said Wheeler calmly.

"What do you mean?" asked the drifter, his real eye widening in terror. "You ain't thinking of doing something stupid here, are you?"

"I'm thinking about justice, and about the only way I can see getting it in your case."

Tucker quickly scrambled to his feet as the lawman's right hand moved toward the Colt revolver holstered on his hip. "You couldn't do that, Sheriff," he said, smiling nervously. "You're a lawman. It's your duty to arrest me. You can't just take the law into your own hands."

"The way I see it, my duty is to make sure that people like you pay for their crimes, and I just don't think that'll happen in a court of law. I think you'd get away with it, just like you said you would."

"Now wait a minute, Sheriff. You got this all wrong. I didn't really kill nobody. I just made it all up so I could be famous, that's all. I swear to God I never hurt no one," pleaded Tucker.

"You sure got all the details right about those murder cases though, didn't you? I suppose all that information came to you in a dream or something. Is that what you're going to tell me now?" asked Wheeler as he slid his gun from its holster and cocked back the hammer with his thumb.

"No! Sheriff, no! I'll tell you the truth. I've been traveling with another guy for the past year. Ottis Prince is his name. He had one of them police band radios. That's how I knew all those things about the murders. I heard the police talking about them on the radio. You've got to believe me. I didn't kill anyone, I swear to God I didn't."

"Where is Ottis Prince now?"

"I don't know for sure. We split up back in Abilene, but I know you could find him easy. All you got to do is find him and ask him about me. He'll tell you I didn't kill nobody. He was with me the whole time. I just made up this story to be famous, that's all. A lie ain't worth shooting a man over. Is it, Sheriff?" asked Tucker, tears now streaming down his cheeks.

"I was a deputy for five years. Now I've been Sheriff for fifteen," said Wheeler coldly. "I learned to tell if a person's lying by reading his face. You weren't lying when you thought you were going to get away with it, but you are now. You're scared stiff because you never figured you'd meet up with a man who'd bring true justice down on you. But you did, and here's justice."

"NOOO!"

The gun bucked in his hand, and a red splash blossomed on the front of Tucker's shirt. Wheeler stood motionlessly and stared down at the man now sprawled in the dirt. His aim was sharpshooter perfect. The bullet had torn through the drifter's heart, killing him instantly.

Wheeler holstered his gun as he went back to the Bronco, opened the tailgate, and took the folding shovel from the emergency toolbox. He walked to a spot between the two tallest cacti and dug a grave in the harsh, dry earth, then dragged Tucker's body to the edge of the hole and removed the handcuffs.

He was about to lower the body into the grave when he paused thoughtfully for a moment, then went back to the Bronco for Tucker's green knapsack and began to rummage through it. He soon found what he had expected; a long-bladed hunting knife. Wheeler took a deep breath before bending down to the task he knew he had to perform.

As a lawman, he knew if the body was ever found, the ballistics experts might be able to match the bullet to his gun. Although it was unlikely that the corpse would ever be found in such a barren region as this, it was still a risk he was unwilling to take.

A wave of nausea began to rise within him as he probed with the knife, but he managed to find the bullet and retrieve it before the sickness could overcome him.

No longer than forty minutes could have passed since he had brought Tucker here, yet to Wheeler it felt as if several hours had crept by. He sighed wearily as he surveyed the area one last time to make certain he was not leaving behind any visible trace of his visit. When he was satisfied, he stripped off his shirt and washed himself in the water hole. After dunking the shirt several times, he wrung it out and slipped it on again. In this parched climate, he knew it would be bone dry in a matter of minutes.

Wheeler climbed into the Bronco and headed back down the dirt road. Reaching the highway, he turned in the direction of Bowie. He thought it best to continue on to the Rangers station and have a friendly chat with Captain Weldon. If anyone were to question his whereabouts, Bill would unwittingly provide him with a perfect alibi.

A short time later, Wheeler parked at the curb in front of a two-story government building and walked up to the brightly-lit main entrance. To the left of the twin glass doors was a brass plaque identifying the building as the TEXAS RANGERS REGIONAL OFFICE.

He shivered as a cold blast of air blew down on him from an air-conditioning register just inside the doors. He exchanged greetings with the Rangers he knew as he made his way back to the captain's office. Bill Weldon was seated at his desk when he saw Wheeler approaching through the open office door.

"Come on in, Tom," called the captain, beckoning with his hand. "How the hell you been? You ain't been down here in over a month. This business, or a social call?"

"Just a friendly visit," answered Wheeler, shaking the captain's hand. "Thought I'd take a drive to get my mind off the heat. What's new with you?"

"Well, the Governor must have thought we didn't have enough to do. Now we're supposed to help the Immigration boys round up illegals. Damned waste of time, ain't it?

We send them back to Mexico, then as soon as they can find another way across the border, they're back here again. Can't say as I blame them for wanting to live here, but hell, we just ain't got no room for them."

"The federal government ought to beef up the Border Patrol, then maybe we could keep them on their own side of the Rio Grande."

"Yep, that might do it. But I guess it's all just part of the job. Anything new up your way?"

"The heat must be making folks short-tempered. There's been a brawl at the Redwater Saloon 'most every night lately."

"Least it gives you something to do," laughed Bill. "We had a bit of excitement around here about a week ago, but it didn't amount to nothing."

"What happened?"

"A drifter walked into the Sheriff's office down in Fruitland and told Bob that he was the worst mass murderer since Ted Bundy. You should have heard how spooked old Bob was when he called me. He told me to get my butt down there and take charge of things; said he wasn't being paid enough to handle a prisoner like that. Well, I drove right down to have a look, and guess what?"

A numbing chill clutched at the pit of Wheeler's stomach. "What?" he asked.

"It turned out to be nothing but a loco bum with a sun-fried brain," Bill laughed, slapping the desk.

"You mean it was a hoax?"

"It sure was. That crazy bastard was confessing to crimes all over the country."

"How do you know he wasn't telling the truth?"

"I did some checking. Most of the crimes had been committed only days apart, but hundreds of miles from one another. He would have needed a jet plane to move around *that* fast."

"Did you find out who he was?" asked Wheeler,

dreading the answer.

"Yep, some fellow named Tyler, or Tucker, or something like that. He had a record all right, but mainly small stuff; Drunk and Disorderly, Simple Assault, Petty Theft. He was just a nobody who wanted to be noticed."

"What happened to him?"

"Well, I tried to send him over to the State Hospital for evaluation, but they said they were overcrowded as it was and they wouldn't take him unless I had reason to believe he was violent. I held him until I had checked out his stories, then I let him go."

"You just let him walk away?" asked Wheeler incredulously.

"What else could I do, Tom? I even made up a murder that never happened, and damned if he didn't confess to *that* one too. The guy was just a crazy bum. Legally I *had* to let him go. He's somebody else's problem now."

Wheeler nodded, but said nothing. His glazed eyes stared past the Ranger toward the window.

Bill stood up. "I'm going to head over to the diner for supper. Want to come along, Tom?"

Wheeler could not answer. He gazed out at the distant flatlands, toward a water hole surrounded by cactus and yucca, toward an unmarked grave in the harsh, dry earth.

JAMES KISNER *first
came to my attention
when I read his
wonderful suspense
story—"Mother Trucker"
—in Ed Gorman's
Stalkers anthology.
I soon learned that
all of his short stories
are thought-provoking
and dark, and always
original. Kisner writes
horror novels under the
pseudonym Martin James
and under his own name.*

SWAP MEAT
JAMES KISNER

Like ink dissipating through water, a black cloud flowed across the face of the moon. Andy watched it with faint interest, then flicked his cigarette butt out into the gravel lot in front of the cheap motel. He was bored and tired even though it was only eight-thirty.

He turned to go back inside to his wife Lisa, who was probably asleep by now. Then a hand touched him on his bare shoulder. Startled, he swung around too sharply, almost losing his balance.

"Sorry, man," the stranger who had touched him said. He was tall, well-built, pushing forty, wearing a short-sleeved shirt and casual trousers. "Didn't mean to scare you."

"What do you want?" Andy asked. The light next to

the door fluttered as tiny dark insects swarmed around it, causing a kind of strobe-like effect on the man's face.

"Me and Emma are next door," he said. "Just pulled in from driving across Indiana and Ohio." He waited for a response from Andy, then continued when there was none. "I'm tired as a son of a bitch."

"Yeah, me too," Andy said impatiently, starting to push the door open.

"Bored, too," the stranger said. "Drive all day, tired as hell, should get some rest, but still we're both bored. Can't go to sleep. Isn't that right?"

Andy paused to scrutinize the stranger.

"Yeah, I guess."

"So why don't we do something about it?"

"Like what?"

"You like to play cards?"

"Some. Not too good at it. Don't like to gamble."

"No money. Just for fun."

"I don't know," Andy said, though the idea appealed to him. He wouldn't mind playing cards for a little while. "Lisa's probably . . . "

"What's going on?"

Lisa stood at the door in her robe.

"Sorry, ma'am," the stranger said. "Didn't mean to wake you."

"I wasn't asleep."

"This man's suggesting a card game—to pass the time. It's still early, you know."

Lisa looked doubtful.

"My name's Fred," the man said. "Fred Akker. Emma and me are just next door. In from Ohio. I know we're all tired and everything, but none of us can sleep, so I thought . . . "

Lisa glanced at him. Her face showed the effects of being on the road all day, but she was still attractive, especially her deep blue eyes framed by glistening, red-blonde hair. She looked at her husband, Andy, and mentally compared him to Fred, as she did when she met any other man.

Andy, she decided, was more good-looking and, of course, ten years younger. His dark hair and lean face made him more attractive than the middle-aged stranger, who was just ordinary-looking. Not ugly, or plain. Ordinary. And no one looked better in jeans than Andy did.

"Cards?" Lisa asked, yawning and looking at the man. She saw something in Fred's eyes that played with her sensibilities; it wasn't quite lust, as if he might be imagining her without the bathrobe. No, it was something more subtle, yet compelling—a kind of recklessness beneath the surface. "What game you have in mind?"

"You name it, we can play it. Bridge, poker, euchre, canasta."

They decided to play two rubbers of bridge and no more.

Emma was blonde and shapely in a distracting way. She came to Andy and Lisa's room dressed in cut-offs and a tight T-shirt over large, bra-less breasts. She wore a lot of makeup. Like Fred, she was on one side or the other of forty.

Fred had brought a six-pack of beer and a couple of wine coolers. Lisa provided a bag of corn chips, the last of the snacks she had from the car. She had put on a simple blouse and conservative shorts. Andy had donned a shirt, but otherwise looked the same.

The bidding in the first couple of hands was erratic, showing them all to be amateurs, but it was fun. Andy and Lisa won the first game. Fred and Emma won the second.

The first rubber went fast; the second dragged on as the effects of exhaustion started weighing on the players.

Finally, the last hand was played. Fred and Emma won.

"Too bad we weren't playing for money," Fred said. "We could've made a tidy sum off you guys."

"I'm not a guy," Lisa said, smirking.

"I noticed." Fred stared at her openly.

Andy caught the stare and felt a stir of anger, but decided against pursuing it. Lisa *was* nice on the eyes; he had to expect men to stare at her occasionally. Of course, Fred's wife wasn't a dog; without all that makeup she'd be really quite attractive, and, though she was older . . . He shook his head, pushing away the notion that had suddenly popped into his mind. He glanced at his watch. It was nearly midnight.

He stretched and yawned. "Guess we're all tired enough to sleep now," he said. "It's a long drive through the rest of Pennsylvania."

"It's a bitch, all right." Fred cast his eyes down and shuffled the cards. "Not interested in another rubber?"

"Can't hack it, Fred."

"Too bad. I'm still not tired. I guess—Emma?"

"What?" Her voice had a slightly raspy quality to it.

Fred kept shuffling the cards. It was getting on everyone's nerves.

"What do you think of Andy?"

Andy blushed, then looked confused.

"He's a nice guy, I guess. So?"

"So, I bet you'd like to jump in the sack with him."

Andy sputtered, words of outrage boiling up from inside him. "That's no way to . . . "

Fred glanced over at Andy with a look of pure innocence on his face. "C'mon, Andy boy, I saw you giving her the once-over. Those tits, they're incredible. Ain't that right?"

Lisa's face turned red. "Mr. Akker, if you are going to talk like that I have to ask you to . . . "

"And Lisa's nice too."

"Fred, this isn't . . . "

"Andy, listen. We like you guys. Why don't we just put it out in the open like adults? There ain't nobody—nobody at all—that don't get turned on at the idea of getting it on with somebody else than his regular woman. And most women are the same way, if they'd admit it. Right, Emma?"

Emma flashed her eyes at Andy. "I wouldn't mind."

Lisa's face was still red. She looked to her husband for a response.

But Andy was not thinking in words; his mind was filled with images Fred had put there, and he suddenly found himself with an incredibly hard erection. There was something about Fred's manner that made it difficult to disagree with him. Andy's gaze went to Emma again; she smiled and leaned forward, causing the fabric around her breasts to stretch.

Lisa reached over and clasped Andy's hand, forcing him to look at her. Her eyes were filled with questions and accusations, but she said nothing. She didn't think she had to.

Andy wouldn't look at her. He was hypnotized by the thrust of Emma's breasts. He imagined kneading them with his hands, putting his face between them, sucking at her big, jutting nipples. His desire became a low-pitched whine.

Fred smiled at Lisa and licked his lips. "It could be fun," he said. "A kind of fun like you've never had."

Lisa's mouth dropped open. "Andy?"

In the end, Lisa agreed to it. Neither she nor Andy could resist Fred's persuasive manner. It was like they were actually unable to refuse.

They would swap women—Fred taking Lisa to his room, Emma staying behind with Andy.

"This place is a dump," Fred told Lisa as they entered the room, "but the sheets are clean."

Lisa stood before the bed, frozen. She had agreed to this kinkiness too readily she realized now, without thinking about the consequences.

How would she and Andy feel later—and what about disease?

"Don't worry, Lisa dear," Fred said. "I believe in

safe sex. And your husband is safe with Emma too. She's not a fool."

Lisa stared straight ahead, barely moving her lips when she talked. "You do this all the time, don't you?"

"What?" Fred had removed his shirt, revealing a well-muscled, hairy chest.

"Talk people into—into *swapping.*" The idea of it sounded ancient, even silly. It was something people did in the sixties—not nowdays. People were more sensible today— weren't they?

"No. Honest-to-God. This is only the second time it ever happened."

"What about the first?"

"Do you want to hear about it?"

Lisa thought a moment. "No," she said.

Fred unzipped his trousers. Lisa looked away reflexively.

"Your turn," he said.

Emma had stripped and was standing at the foot of the bed, eyeing Andy with mischief and a hint of lust in her eyes.

He was naked under the covers which he had pulled up to his navel. He just kept staring at Emma. Though she was older than Lisa, she was much more attractive than he expected. He thought older women, whose faces betrayed their ages quite readily, would have older bodies as well. But Emma's body was sexual in a way a younger woman's wouldn't be—the way Lisa's wasn't, for example. Maybe it was the openness of her desire, or the ease with which she stood there naked, unashamed and unembarrassed.

He didn't expect the mere sight of Emma's flesh to start turning him on, either. He wasn't an adolescent, but there was a quality to Emma's profound nudity that tugged at the youthful urge that lurked in every man. Maybe it was the size of her breasts, or the contrast between her blonde hair and dark black pubic patch. Or the fact that she resembled all the whory women he had ever seen in cheap men's magazines when he was a kid. She didn't look like the sparkling, bright-eyed girl-next-door as epitomized by the beauties in *Playboy*; she looked like the slut-down-the-block who would do it with anyone who had a quarter. She was the embodiment of masturbatory fantasy.

He supposed he should make a move, but his conscience started bothering him. He was sure he could make it with Emma, but he had gotten the chance by sacrificing his wife's virtue and sensibilities.

Things would never be the same between them after this.

He could still stop it, though. He could just get up, retrieve his wife, and tell Fred and Emma no-thank-you. But his limbs didn't respond to that idea. In fact, he couldn't move at all.

Then Emma was on top of him, kissing him hungrily, her tongue like a live animal darting into his mouth.

Lisa had managed to strip down to her panties. Fred sat up in the bed, his erection pointing at her, while he smiled and caressed it.

"What'sa matter? Ain't you ready for Freddie?"

Lisa didn't know.

She couldn't help dwelling on what was happening next door: Her husband with another woman, a strange blonde at that, and she had sanctioned it. They both had agreed without thinking much about it, although Lisa had needed coaxing.

Now, though, the actual moment was here. She was supposed to *do* it with this complete stranger.

Yet she wasn't repulsed as she supposed she should be. Andy had always been enough for her, but now she was going to cheat on him and vice-versa.

Or was it cheating?

She walked slowly over to the bed and lay down next to Fred, averting her eyes from his erection.

He slipped a condom on.

Lisa wanted to cry out, to stop this thing now, but before she knew it, Fred was on top of her, in her, pumping, and she was responding without knowing why.

Both panting, Andy and Emma lay staring at the ceiling in the aftermath. They had done it two times in a row.

It had been years since Andy had performed twice in one night. But it had also been years since he had been that aroused.

"Nice," Emma said, without looking at him.

"Thanks, I guess."

"You know, you remind me of my husband . . . "

" . . . you remind me of my wife," Fred said.

Lisa propped herself up on one elbow and frowned at him. "What do you mean by that?"

"You're good, babe. Very, very good. Like Helen was. I ain't had it so good, since the last time with her."

"I thought your wife's name was Emma."

" . . . except, of course," Emma continued, giving him a squeeze in the appropriate spot, "you have a bigger yang."

Andy laughed mildly. He hadn't heard the term "yang" since he was in grade school. "Well, I've never had any complaints before."

"I bet not. That's a hell of a rod. The way you use it is a lot like Bill. The way you kind of twist it around when you stick it in, like putting English on a cue stick."

"I guess Fred won't be any good for you any more," he joked, feeling flattered and foolish at the same time.

"I ain't talking about Fred. I said my *husband*—Bill."

"I thought . . ."

"Everybody thinks that, of course. Bill's dead."

"So who's Fred?"

Fred's good humor, and his permanent grin, had both abruptly vanished. His hands were tucked behind his head on the pillow, his eyes locked on some point in infinity.

"Helen's dead," he said.

"Then Emma's your second wife . . . ?"

"No. Me and Emma ain't married. I never said she was my wife. Did I?"

Lisa was apprehensive. "Who is she, then?"

"Well, it's kind of a long story."

"Fred and Helen were a great couple," Emma said, her head resting on Andy's shoulder. "So were me and Bill. We were all good friends. You know, played cards together, barbecues, going out bowling sometimes—the whole friendship bit. Then one night—well, we—actually, it was me—I saw Bill out with Helen."

"So what happened?"

"Well, I called Fred, and he couldn't take it. He went to pieces. Then he started denying it, saying I was lying about it, so I had to prove it to him, and a couple of nights later, we found them together again at a cheap motel—like this one."

Her voice dropped to a whisper.

"Fred really went off then. Jesus, what a temper! I couldn't hold him back. He ran up to the door and kicked it in.

"I ran after him. I wasn't thinking about Helen—I was afraid he'd kill Bill before I got there, but when I got to the room, he had *Helen* down on the floor, beating the hell out of her while old Bill rode on top of him trying to pull him off. In a way, it was kind of a funny sight—this naked man on top of

Fred. But it was my husband."

She looked to Andy for signs he thought it humorous, saw none, and continued.

"Fred was cussing and still beating Helen and I jumped in on top of the three of them with no idea at all what I was going to do. Before you know it, there's the four us rolling around on the floor, like some kind of weird half-naked, half-dressed octopus or something, and blood was running from somebody, and we got untangled, and the four of us backed off, and just stared at each other. Then Bill got pissed, and so did Helen—and it was like Fred and *me* were the cheaters. So Fred goes over and slaps Helen so . . . "

" . . . damn hard I knocked her to the floor. Then I grabbed her neck and started choking her. . . . " Fred glanced over at Lisa.

Her face was blank, but he could sense the shock she felt.

She blinked her eyes, trying to focus on the door. It seemed so far away.

"Naturally, we couldn't let Bill go running off after him seeing Fred kill Helen. Fred would get sent up for years. I was staring at Bill, reading his thoughts, and all of a sudden, after all these years of marriage, I hated him. I hated him for cheating on me and for making Fred kill Helen who was my best friend and hated him for the fact that he was going to run to the police and get Fred in trouble—but most of all I hated him for making me *have* to hate Helen.

"In my purse, I had a little .25 I carried. Bill got it for me because I used to work the second shift at the hospital. The purse was lying on the floor where it got thrown by somebody during the fight, and it was open and the end of the gun was sticking out. I was across the room in half a shake, going for the gun, and Bill could see what I had in mind then, but . . . "

◊

" . . . she shot Bill in the head, right here." Fred laid his hand on the middle of his forehead. "Then I started thinking and the two of us made up a plan and put the gun in Helen's hand, and . . . well, we made it look like some kind of lover's fight that got out of hand." He smiled wanly. "The hell of it is the police bought it. Me and Emma had a hell of a time keeping our stories straight, but it stuck, and we got away with it. Emma said it was 'poetic justice' just like somebody on TV might talk."

"But why are you telling me this?" Lisa asked, her eyes still trained on the door.

"It's part of a lesson, Lisa, for all married people. Cheating just ain't right."

He reached for her throat.

"It was a gun just like this one," Emma said, producing a small automatic from her purse.

"Put that away," Andy said evenly.

She ignored him, hefting the gun in her hand casually, then pointing it in Andy's direction. "You ever hear of poetic justice?"

"What do you mean?"

"Adultery is what I mean, and it isn't right. Don't you know that? Don't you understand how Lisa is suffering right now because you were over here screwing me? Don't you think that's going to hurt her the rest of her life? And you—you'll always be thinking of how Fred was *inside* her—a stranger, and how you let it happen. I think it's enough that Fred and me have to carry our sins around. There's no use . . . "

She aimed.

"No!"

A dot of blood exploded in the middle of Andy's head.

◊

Emma and Fred arranged the two corpses, then stood in the doorway for one last look.

"Did she struggle much?"

"No," Fred answered. "I think she saw it coming, but she didn't know how to stop it."

"He didn't see it coming at all. He was just plain stupid right up to the end."

"They'll be better off now."

"Yeah," Emma said. "Too bad people don't think before they do things that you can't erase."

"I know it." He flicked the light off. "Ready to go?"

"Yeah."

The two of them went to Fred's car, a nondescript station wagon with a mud-smeared plate. It was nearly three in the morning, but since they had slept most of the day, they weren't very tired.

"Where to now?" Fred said, starting the engine.

"East. New Jersey. A cheap place next to a truck stop."

"We shouldn't have much trouble there."

"No." They drove slowly past the motel office. The clerk was not visible through the window, so no one actually saw them leave. Shortly, they were out on the Interstate, headed east through Pennsylvania.

They were silent for a few moments, riding through the black of night, watching the scattering of tiny black bugs in the headlights as they collided with the front of the car.

"My wife's money won't last forever," Fred said. "We'll have to go back."

"No. We can never go back. You know that."

"I know it, but I don't have to accept it."

"Besides, there are more couples out there that need to be taught, and we owe it to them. It's the only way we can make up for what happened to us."

"If only they'd say 'no,' just once," Fred said, "then it would be over."

"They never do," Emma said thoughtfully. She laid her hand over on his knee affectionately and patted it. "You know, some day I'd like to try you out."

Fred squinted at the road ahead, then his features collapsed into a frown, and he glanced down at her hand with evident distaste. Emma sighed and pulled her hand away.

"That wouldn't be right," he said simply. "You know it would be cheating."

J. N. WILLIAMSON *is
the most prolific author
in the horror genre—and
I mean that as a compli-
ment. He's also one of the
friendliest. Williamson has
published over 30 novels
and 90 short stories in an
amazingly short period of
time. His work is always
imaginative and fresh
and—as evidenced by the
following story—often
bizarre. Williamson
calls this next story
a "strange yarn." I'm
sure you will agree.*

THE OLDEST HUMAN TRICK
J.N. WILLIAMSON

"The ancients shared in nature by echoing
the violence of a windstorm or thunder squall."
—*Libra*, by Don DeLillo

1

There was nothing about the weekend weatherman
at Channel 2 that set him apart, conspicuously, from the
Saturday and Sunday fill-ins at the other local stations.

That was exactly what bothered hell out of Cale
Pittern after he'd spent nearly a year and a half at 2 with the
other weekend newspersons, Jake and Debbie, and had
endured eight minutes of Sports With Slink, sixteen minutes

every single weekend of waiting for Slink Cady, the one-season NBA flash, to stop reading off the late scores. As if he had purposely memorized every cliché from his old high school newspaper. Sixteen-hundred minutes—26 hours—of Cale Pittern's life, waiting for old "Slink" to stop rapping about "smears," "clobbers," "edges," and "rim-ripping romps," just to join Debbie, Jake, and smirking Slink in beaming at the cameras and rattling their copy sheets in accustomed farewell.

What Cale needed, he felt, was some magical, intuitive insight into the upcoming weather—preferably for the following day, Monday—that was genuinely catastrophic of nature. Some entirely unplanned freak of nature that every other weather guy, gal, or meteorologist in town had overlooked somehow. A quake, a hurricane, a truly titanic, beautiful flood that would *sweep* over women and little children as they slept—

Whatever would haul the mayor's skinny ass out of bed to make urgent phone calls to the governor, who'd have no choice then but to declare a full-scale 4-star frigging emergency, and force both pols to summon the whole National Guard!

"Who broke *that* weather story?" bigshots at the nets would demand to know—or anyway, Mr. Connelly, Channel 2's program manager. "If they'd listened to *him* in time, the *lives* they could have saved!"

Then the answer: "Pittern, Cale Pittern; weekend forecaster," the knowledgeable peons would have to answer after scurrying around, ant-like, to get the facts. "We need *Pittern Predicts* to interpret the weather trends for America!"

At last, that would end Cale's prison sentence at Channel 2, win him a promotion to weekdays (at six and eleven)—allow his escape from the terminal cuteness of pert Debbie, the pompously ponderous solemnity of read-it-from-the-wire Jake, and the sophomoric sports of the former

Purdue point guard, the only Boilermaker with less enthusiasm for defense than Rick Mount!

It'd be the Big Time for *Cale Pittern's Patterns on the 'Scope*.

One basic stumbling block obstructed sunny-today Cale's cherished fantasy: He lived in a town that never set records capable of making the wire services. Snow settled in on time every year and never topped a modest three inches of accumulation. Median temps in town could have been used as a model for middle-western normality. No tornados had been recorded locally since 1897, and an uninspired blast of wind that showed up unexpectedly in 1922 had passed after breaking a few branches in Grandma Walkerton's apple orchard.

It was late March of this year before it occurred to Cale that words were sometimes more magical than weather boards, that facts were only rounded-up on certain cable forecast shows to be employed as a means of suspensefully problematical predictions of imminent weather—and that the major nets frequently reported hurricanes that made whole regions of America sit up and shiver with fear only to "blow themselves out" before they could reach "population centers."

Instantly, the wiser Cale started questing for any sign of *potential* forecasting disaster to suit his purposes. And what he soon discovered wasn't gusting winds "capable of devastating populous regions" that might enable him to invent hypothetical "experts" to prophesy expensive destruction of "fine homes and primary industrial districts."

What he found was a report from a scarcely semi-pro seismologist whose dubious services Channel 2 went on subscribing to merely because nobody knew how to make the station computer cut him off.

Squinting with sweaty anticipation at a chart on the desk before him, Cale saw that tremors *were* possible, conceivably—"under certain conditions." That they might "theoretically" develop, and "ultimately register as high on the Richter scale as 3.5."

The proprietor of *Pittern Predicts* sat back in his chair, inched it away from the desk to reflect on his questionable find.

Three facts leaped into Cale's avaricious imagination almost at the same time:

One, "certain conditions" was not further defined. That very instant wind was ballooning the banner flying patriotically from the Channel 2 "tower"—on the third floor—and strong wind could certainly be taken as "certain conditions."

Two, earlier that day, a Sunday, when Cale had entered the station, he had automatically glanced toward the abandoned old cemetery down the street, shuddered superstitiously (as usual), and imagined for a moment that the earth moved . . . just slightly . . . beneath his feet.

Three, *nobody* could ever actually keep track of whether the successes in life were graded from a "1" down, or if 10 was the *highest* possible figure; the entire game of rating celebrities "from 1 to 10" was essentially confusing—

And one additional fact as a consequence of his ruminations:

A 3.5 on the Richter scale inevitably sounded terrifying as hell to your average Man on the Street. Just as frightening as 2.1, or 7.8! It really depended primarily on the *way* a weatherperson said it was and how *solemn* he looked while he was saying it. Hell's ringing bells, if some fatcat forecaster on one of the morning shows seemed ready to cry when he reported "a warming trend," half the nation would be certain they'd *fry* like goddam *eggs* on their way to work!

Cale became more excited. The mayor they had in town now certainly didn't know 3.5 seismological readings from Bo Derek's rear end! With a *really* super-grim delivery of "fast-breaking developments" and the corners of his mouth slipping onto the studio floor while he intoned his "warning statement" of "startling slippage of cardinal regional plates just south of the city," Cale would scare "Slink's Sports" into adverbial autism and make half the town stay up in the hope that Cale would be back on, later that night, with "vital updates!"

He spent a couple of minutes studying the morality of what he was contemplating. And the truth of the matter was, Cale Pittern did not especially want to be a hero—the part-time meteorologist who alerted a "major metropolis" to "high risks forming on the screen."

He only wanted to stay at *home* on weekends like the weekday weatherman and weatherladies, and make the super who told everybody who lived in his apartment building remember his *name*.

If I play my cards right, Cale thought while Debbie patted her perm and Jake smoothed his mustache whenever the red light wasn't on, *I'll be interviewed on* somebody's *daytime talk show!*

"To share in nature is the oldest human trick."
—*Ibid*

2

It went off without a flaw! Without a flub!

The fact that his heart was triphammering and he must have appeared terribly nervous to everybody tuned in to Channel 2 that Sunday night—so what if they were dead-last in local ratings, there were still tens of thousands of viewers!—actually seemed to make the scary things Cale was saying appear more credible. The sharp note of panic he conveyed probably said clearly to viewers, "That guy is getting *out* of town at once!" Except that Cale added thoughtfully, right before he began shuffling his papers in the proper businesslike news fashion and worked at looking dignified while Jake and Debbie shot him terrified glances that the all-seeing camera sure as hell didn't miss, that he'd "be available for further developments," clearly exhibiting the legendary courage of news people who were always willing to put their very lives on the line—just to keep the citizens up to date.

Of course, he'd be available at *home*, tucked away in bed, actually waiting for the networks to call and try to discover where he'd gotten his information.

Which would be passed along to them, Cale promised himself, during a live interview from L.A. or New York City.

Because he had been thoughtful enough not to specify that the earthquake on its way, capable of disabling half the bigger cities in the midwest from Kansas to the farthest border of Ohio, was going to happen *immediately*. The careful viewer might recall *Pittern's Patterns on the 'Scope* as stipulating a "wider time frame" of 72 hours.

Which gave the mayor, locally, and the national weather teams from cable and the nets ample time to find out what *he* knew that they didn't!

By the time he was flying either west or east with all expenses paid, Cale knew he could come up with an acceptable explanation. Along with additional warnings that might very well make him famous and win him a decent slot on *some* telecast of the nightly news!

And if it was mornings, from either coast, that was A-OK too!

There was an urgent phone call coming in from the mayor's office just as Cale headed out the front door of Channel 2. He had left word that he could be reached at home. No point in appearing to seem over-eager. This, at least, was the time when the world would come to *him!*

Cale managed a few unmelodic bars of "Over the Rainbow" by the time he began his trek across the potholed parking lot of the station and was almost to the part about bluebirds when he felt the earth shudder, and definitely move, beneath his feet.

Looking up, Cale's self-satisfied grin froze in position as if somebody had stopped the camera action. He peered back toward 2, wondering about the power of human imagination, and the grin started feeling more like a grimace. Because another tremor made him lose his balance, just slightly, and realize that he was no longer looking in the direction of his place of employment.

He was staring at the old, abandoned cemetery down the street and knew, without any need or space for doubt, that the line of movement in the earth under his feet ran unveeringly from his mid-line used Camaro to a cluster of head-stones that looked, after midnight, like a miniature version of Stonehenge.

Certain conditions were fast developing. They were, decidedly, occurring in "isolated areas," not general regions. "Isolated" in the sense that no one else was in viewing range in any direction Cale chose to look, except one.

It was the first time it had ever occurred to Cale Pittern that "viewers" was a term that was not quite restricted to the folks-at-home who helped the ratings mount. "Viewers" were also present at funerals, and burial grounds.

Three-point-five creatures who seemed gray of hue and lacking a variety of parts—three former adults and one former child—hove into view in the midst of miniature Stonehenge and what they were chanting, in unison, did not become clear to Cale until the fissure was wide enough, deep enough, for him to fall into it. *Richhhhttter,* they were saying, *Richhhttterrr.* . . .

By then he was tumbling downhill all the way.

The flag on the Channel 2 tower rippled once, and hung still.

The mayor was back asleep before any of the morning shows came on the air.

PAUL F. OLSON *is
young and multi-talented—
a winning combination.
Olson is well-known for
a number of accomplish-
ments: his wonderfully
original short stories
from* The Horror Show, *
the much-missed non-fiction
magazine* Horrorstruck, *
and his impressive debut
novel,* The Night Prophets.

FAITH AND HENRY GUSTAFSON

PAUL F. OLSON

The rain had stopped by the time they reached The Black Pike, a fact for which Henry Gustafson was very grateful. The Pike (known locally as "The Hellbender") was tricky enough to negotiate when dry. When it was muddy, as it was now from a three-day downpour, the drive became an exercise in nail-biting adventure. Toss in the extra inconveniences of darkness and rain drumming on the windshield, and Henry supposed it would be easier to pull over to the side of the road, get out, and walk.

"Whaddya think, Artie?" he said to his partner. "Call came from the old Bible camp. That's, what, maybe two-three miles more?"

Artie nodded silently and Henry turned his attention back to the twists and turns, rises and falls, of the road. The butterflies were still congregating in his belly. The first couple had arrived as soon as the call had come in. More were dropping by all the time. Right now they were having a nice little caucus. He figured that by the time he and Artie actually reached the old Singing Waters Bible Camp, his gut would be in the throes of a goddamned butterfly convention.

He wanted to talk over the situation, but knew it was useless. Artie would listen, but he wouldn't have much in the way of input. When you got right down to it, Artie was an awful lot like an old B-movie character carried out to the extreme. The tough, rugged, silent type. That was Artie to a tee.

The call had come into the Kelly's Corners Police Station at 12:37 A.M. Henry had spent the next fifteen minutes trying to raise some assistance, all to no avail. The chief was vacationing downstate. Lizzy Halprin was still on maternity leave. Bill McInnis was out east somewhere, taking a two-week course in rural law enforcement. When Henry had tried calling across the lake to Patterson Falls, the phone had rung at least thirty times without an answer. He guessed old Harv Bennedict, who had been Chief of Police over there longer than God had been making planets, was home sleeping off some Old Grand Dad. Or perhaps still out somewhere drinking it. That left the volunteer ambulance, which was supposedly on the way, maybe ten minutes behind, and the county sheriff's department, which was too far away to be much help but had told Henry to call again if he found he needed a back-up on the scene.

"Shitfire," Henry muttered, because it seemed like a good, practical thing to mutter under the circumstances. He could see the entrance to the Bible camp up ahead, and what he thought was someone waving them down with a weak flashlight. He realized a moment later that it wasn't a flash at all, just the bouncing reflection of the Blazer's headlights glinting off the mailbox at the head of the driveway.

"Ready, pard?" he asked Artie as he swung into the drive. The trees were very close here, the darkness thick. "Somebody's gotta be around," he said, mostly to himself. "I mean someone placed the call, didn't they? Sure they did. I heard 'em. I *talked* to 'em."

He pulled up in front of the administration building, feeling the tires sink hopelessly in the mud as he came to a stop. In the old days, when Henry had been a kid and they had come out here three or four times a summer for Sunday School picnics, they had called this place the Lodge. He had a fairly clear memory of the inside—an enormous open room with picture windows looking out on Conley Lake, a rough stone floor, a timber beam ceiling, the biggest fireplace he'd ever seen, before or since. On the keystone of the fireplace had been engraved *Fight the good fight of faith, lay hold on eternal life 2 Timothy 6:12*, and on the wall above had been a mounted moose head, an old, bedraggled, moth-eaten thing that the kids had predictably nicknamed Bullwinkle.

But that had been a long time ago. Henry wasn't a kid anymore, he had forgotten many of his Bible verses, and the only place you saw Bullwinkle was in reruns. The syndicate of Upper Peninsula churches that had operated Singing Waters had gone bust in the early seventies, and through some sort of court fiasco the whole shebang had been taken over by a group of Chicago idiots who had wanted to run the place as a fishing resort. That had lasted approximately an hour and a half, and the camp had sat empty, decaying, for a long, long time. Until August, as a matter of fact, just a couple of months ago, when Henry had heard that some Detroit-area business-man's association had purchased it for use as an executive's weekend retreat. That was supposed to begin next summer.

He couldn't imagine who would be there now. It was almost Halloween, for Chrissakes. But *someone* was there. Workmen, maybe, fixing the place up. Someone, somebody. Because one somebody had called the station to report that another somebody was dead.

Pulling together a dash or two of false bravado, Henry said, "Let's get going, Artie m'man," and climbed out of the Blazer. His boots immediately sank into four inches of mud, but he had larger concerns on his mind, including finding the phone caller, finding the body, and wondering how far behind the goddamned ambulance was.

There was nobody in the Lodge. That became obvious as he tried the door and found it locked, walked past the windows and shined his flashlight through the glass, picking out nothing but lots of cobwebs and ancient furniture slumbering beneath filthy dust covers. At one point, thinking he saw some stealthy movement, the butterflies flapped madly and his heart leapt almost completely out of his chest. He calmed himself, steadied his light, and chuckled weakly.

"Of course there's mice," he whispered, watching two of the little buggers scurry out of sight. "Place's been empty for years. Shit, it's prob'ly a regular Disneyland for rodents in there."

Leaving the Lodge, they tramped through the mud, past two locked storage buildings and a shack with a sign identifying it as the PX, past the collapsed roof of what had once been a picnic shelter, past the huge open-air amphitheater where long-ago campers had burned bonfires and sung hymns, to the double ring of cabins on the shore of the lake.

It would have been a lie to say the butterflies were gone completely, but Henry was nevertheless beginning to feel some hope. The longer they stayed and the more they searched without finding anyone, the greater the likelihood that the whole damn thing was a prank. It surely wouldn't be the first time. Even now he could imagine some kids, or maybe a couple of drunks using the pay phone at Worthy's Rustic Tap or the Red Rooster, laughing their asses off at the thought of cops trekking miles and miles out into the woods to search for Prince Albert in a can.

The first cabin was a ruin. Like the picnic shelter, the roof here had given way under the weight of countless old snowfalls, leaving rubble surrounded by a shell of walls. The other cabins looked all right (at least at a quick glance and in near total darkness), though most had lost their doors and windows to time and storms and vandals. Inside each one stood the stark skeletons of bunk beds, six sets to a cabin, a table, four chairs, a row of rusty lockers, and a bulletin board on which had been painted two headlines: TODAY'S CHORES on the left, TODAY'S SCRIPTURE on the right.

They went west of the cabins to the large community bathhouse. A sign above the door read KYBO. *Keep Your Bowels Open*, Henry thought. Jesus, that's a blast from the past if I ever heard one. He poked the beam of his light through the open doorway, studied the empty toilet stalls and the shower heads that now served as the anchoring points for great swoops of cobwebs, and shrugged.

His mood was improving rapidly, his step becoming lighter, his breath coming a little easier. Even Artie seemed happier. He didn't say anything, of course, but some of that perpetual tension seemed to have gone out of his broad shoulders and strong back.

The only things left to check were the old baseball diamond (it was now just a big overgrown field, dotted with sapling trees), and the lakefront dead ahead of them. They were going to come out of this okay, Henry decided. He tried, but couldn't even muster any resentment toward the kids or drunks who had done this to them. What the hell, a prank once in a while was good for the soul, it kept you on your toes.

Five minutes later, when they found the body outside the boathouse, he wished he could have held onto a few of those happy thoughts just a little longer.

"Could've saved the ambulance boys some sleep," he said when he found his voice. The last of the butterflies had been suddenly replaced by a cold leaden weight sitting three inches below the bottom of his rib cage. "This fella's past hope. What we need here's the Coroner."

He swallowed a trickle of bile that had climbed into

his throat and turned around to see what Artie thought. His mouth was open to actually ask the question—*Helluva mess, eh, pard?*—but he shut it with a snap when he saw that Artie was gone.

He sighed. That had been the way of things more and more often lately. He would get a call for a domestic or a B&E or a disturbing the peace or even a grisly smash-up out at the intersection of 41 and Kelly Road . . . he would get one of those and the butterflies would start and he would try to ignore the whispering voice that told him he wasn't cut out to be a cop, he had never been cut out for it, and that he didn't have the nuts to handle whatever the trouble *du jour* might be . . . that would happen and then Artie would be there, Artie his partner, his pard, his good buddy, and everything would be okay for a while.

There had been a time when Artie had stayed with him all the way through the calls, right up through the boring paperwork at the end. But for the last year or so, Artie had gotten him going and then split when things got hairy. It was almost as though he was saying, *I'll help you get your wheels under you, boyo, but the rest is up to you. You gotta have faith in yourself, trust yourself to pull through. You gotta learn how to handle the bad shit on your own.*

Bad shit, Henry thought. It seemed safe to say that was exactly what he had on his hands right now. He turned back to the corpse and tasted bile again. Where the hell is that ambulance? he wondered. He felt utterly, hopelessly alone and lonely. Goddammit, Artie, I hate it when you run out on me.

"The problem is," he murmured, "there's never an imaginary partner around when you need one."

The victim was male, a young and healthy guy judging from the build, but it was hard to be sure because the face was missing. There was nothing there but a pulpy mass of flayed tissue clinging to the skull, and even if there had been some slight hope of pinning down an age or even identifying the man, Henry just couldn't bring himself to examine things more closely.

It seemed his original guess had been right. The fella was some kind of workman or caretaker, probably hired by those Detroit bigwigs to start a few odds and ends repairs before the snow flew, setting the stage for the real work next spring, cleaning up, getting ready. Henry made this assessment by noting the man's dirty Joe Journeyman coveralls and muddy work boots, the tool belt he wore around his waist, the big hands toughened by rings of callouses.

He wondered briefly if the guy was local, someone from either the Corners or the Falls. Probably. It would've made sense to hire someone from the area to keep an eye on things. There were plenty of men around who did work like that for the summer folks and seasonal resorts. Shutter windows, drain pipes, shovel snow off roofs, things like that. Henry knew most of them personally. Some of them were big gents, like old Joe Journeyman here, but like the ravaged face, that was something he didn't want to dwell on very much.

He paced nervously away, down to the place where the weeds and grass of the camp property dropped off into a jumble of rocks along the shoreline. The large boathouse, whose roof had sagged dramatically in old age, was a black hulk to his left, Conley Lake an even darker patch spread out before him. It was like looking at . . . nothing . . . at nothingness. Only a faint, damp, fishy smell and the gentle lapping of water on stone confirmed that the lake was even there.

He knew there was a procedure to follow in situations like this. He racked his brain, but couldn't begin to imagine what it would be. In his eight years on the Kelly's Corners force he had seen a lot of fatalities—car, motorcycle, and snow machine wrecks mostly. Only three murders, all simple domestics that had crossed that invisible line and gotten irrevocably out of hand. In each of those three cases, George Remillet, the chief, had been there to handle things. Henry's own role had been more that of chief cook and bottle washer. Or more to the point, chief dork and body bagger. Perhaps if he'd taken George's advice and gone with Bill to that two-week course out east, he'd know what to do. Of course if he'd done that, he wouldn't be here now and this whole mess would be somebody else's problem.

He hesitated, shifting his thoughts into neutral and raising his head. From somewhere behind him, from the direction of the Lodge and the driveway and The Black Pike, he heard a noise. His initial response—*Hot damn. Them ambulance boys were slow enough, weren't they?*—changed quickly into something else: *Not the ambulance. That ain't no body buggy. Footsteps. It's the fella who called the station.* And finally from that into a thought that nearly overwhelmed him with its dark simplicity and even darker implications.

There was a murder here, you ignorant jerk-off, a goddamned murder! Who do you think that them footsteps belong to? The guy who called you? Maybe. But maybe it's Joe Journeyman's killer coming back to—

Henry swallowed and felt fear as sharp as glass sticking in his throat. There were procedures again, steps he should be taking. He groped through his mind, trying to latch onto things he had read, things George Remillet had lectured him on over the years, but all he could come up with was a simple phrase, one he'd used hundreds, maybe thousands of times, the one he used when he had a speeder pulled over out on Kelly Road or Conley Lake Drive: "Good afternoon, sir. May I see your license, registration, and proof of insurance, please?"

He didn't think a killer would be impressed with an opening line like that.

Improvising, he dropped to his knees and fumbled his service revolver from its holster. The gun had always seemed big, clunky, and inconvenient to lug around before. Now it seemed impossibly small, even dainty. *I'm trapped down here,* he thought, *trapped with my back to the water like* a bug on a wall. He tried to stay calm and trust in himself, but that was too big an order to follow, and he thought, God damn you to hell, Artie! Why can't you be *real?*

The footsteps came steadily closer, moving between the cabins now, squishing through the mud, swishing through the weeds and witch grass. He heard another sound, too, a high, thin, eerie whistle, lonely-sounding notes of a familiar-sounding song. It took him a moment to pull the memory of that song out from among the yammering terror that had seized control of his brain. A hymn, an old hymn, he thought. We used to sing it a lot. Jesus . . . that was it . . . Jesus Something.

The answer came to him in a ghostly mental chorus of children's voices

Jesus Savior, pilot meeeeeee
over liiiiiiiiiifffe's tempestuous seeeeeeaaa
and he remembered, dammit, he really remembered it.

It wasn't the camp theme song—that had been "Hail to Thee, O Singing Waters" or some hogwash like that—but every time they had come out here from town, scruffy local kids mingling with the more well-to-do (and infinitely snottier) campers who came from all over the midwest, the camp administrator, Reverend Somebody, Reverend Douglas, Reverend Davis, Reverend Dufus, had led them in a chorus of "Jesus Savior, Pilot Me" before the barbecue or the softball game or whatever it was they were there for.

Henry remembered that now as he listened to that slow, sad whistle. It was a pretty sound in a way, almost uncannily on key, but listening to it getting closer and closer sent a scurrying chill from the back of his neck all the way down to his tailbone.

Something clicked inside him, a sticky relay switch closing at last, and he lurched into action. The way he saw it, he had two options. He could follow Artie's advice, trust in himself, and play the tough guy by turning on his flashlight, aiming it at the eyes of the approaching whistler, and barking,

"Police! Hold on, or I'll blow your jewels to China!" Never having been that kind of cop, however, and finding himself constitutionally incapable of becoming one now, Henry opted for his second choice.

As quickly as he could, staying low to the ground, he moved down the shoreline to the boathouse. The door on the high side of the building was padlocked, but that didn't matter because the whole thing was off its rusted hinges, barely hanging from the hasp and lock. He slipped inside, hesitating a moment, wishing he could turn on his light and get the lay of things. Too risky, he decided. He was standing on a catwalk; he knew that much. In all likelihood it ran all the way around the building, a safe distance above the water. That was all he needed to know right now. He could hear the sound of the lake gently caressing the pilings below, and as long as he kept that sound in mind and didn't venture too far in any direction, he would be okay.

Revolver still ready, he turned back to the door and peered out. The complete darkness inside the boathouse made it appear much brighter outside. He didn't think he'd have any trouble seeing the whistler when he broke out of the cabins and came into view.

It occurred to him that he was being awfully cowardly (though as always he preferred to think of it as cautious) in the face of someone who might not even be Joe Journeyman's murderer. What if it was the man who had *called in* the murder rather than the killer himself? Henry considered that. It was possible. But it was also possible that the person who had called was miles away by now. There certainly didn't seem to be any working phones around here. And what if the murderer had also been the caller? Shit, things like that happened all the time on TV.

The bottom line was that he didn't think an innocent man would be strolling around an abandoned camp at one-thirty in the morning, whistling hymns. Only a candidate for the giggle mill, a genuine wacko, would do that.

His heart, which had actually been slowing itself to something approaching normal speed, took another staggering jolt. The whistler, still whistling, had appeared from behind the last cabin, a shadow of a shadow, almost formless. "Jesus Savior, Pilot Me" finished on a drawn-out note, like a perfect sigh, and began again.

Henry felt sweat break out on his forehead. Dartmouth, he thought wildly. The old guy's name was Reverend Dartmouth. He was from somewhere in the Eastern U.P.— Newberry, the Soo, St. Ignace—a real nut, crazy as a damned loon with some of that fundamentalist crap he spouted, strict as hell, mean to the kids, a tall guy, skinny and . . . Christ, was he really a hundred and ten years old, or did he only look that way to us kids?

The whistler's shapeless silhouette came toward the boathouse. Henry grabbed again for that elusive inner strength, missed it, and sidestepped away from the door, moving a few feet down the catwalk. Not far, he thought ashamedly, I won't go very far. I'll just slip out of sight, that's all. Maybe the guy can't see me, but God only knows what his night vision's like. He might spot me as quick as shit.

He backed into something that wasn't the catwalk railing or the boathouse wall.

His breath snagged.

His heart stuttered.

His mind registered softness, dampness, a vague sensation of radiating warmth.

He pivoted slowly, moving away from that wet embrace but simultaneously turning to face it. He had to know. Hooding the lens of his flashlight with his hand, he turned it on and stared at what was in front of him.

Four of Joe Journeyman's buddies (his mind randomly, crazily named them: Mike Mechanic, Pete Plumber, Kent Carpenter, Willie Workman) were hanging from the boathouse wall. Their shirts and jackets had been pegged over the nails upon which had once hung boater's life jackets or canoe paddles. Their faces, like Joe Journeyman's face, had been slashed and mangled beyond recognition by some object that Henry now realized must have been both heavy and wickedly sharp. Blood had flowed freely down the front of their necks to their shirts and coveralls, still wet, still warm. Henry almost choked when he understood that it was Mike Mechanic's blood he felt soaking slowly through the back of his shirt.

He was ready to turn the light off again when he noticed the legend scrawled on the wall above the victim's heads:

TODAY'S SCRIPTURE

IF THERE IS FOUND AMONG YOU A MAN
WHO DOES WHAT IS EVIL
IN THE SIGHT OF THE LORD
AND HAS GONE AND SERVED OTHER gods

YES EVIL BUSINESS YES EVIL $$

THEN YOU SHALL BRING FORTH TO YOUR GATES
THAT MAN WHO HAS DONE THIS EVIL THING
AND PUT HIM TO DEATH

DEUT 17

Deuteronomy, Henry thought wearily, finding another memory. Deuteronomy was Dartmouth's favorite book of the Bible, the book of Hebrew Laws as set forth by God and His main man, Moses. He remembered the old preacher saying once that he wished he had a book of Deuteronomy to run Singing Waters. Do this, dear little campers, do this but don't do that. You'll be blessed for one and cursed for the other.

Henry felt a wave of anger surge through him, and

he thought that perhaps his years of cowardly cophood were going to boil and explode, pushing him forward, forcing him at last to find all his hidden strength and do what was right. People didn't do things like this. You didn't kill innocent people in the name of some old collection of laws that said eating pigs was a sin but it was fine to rape a captured woman if you shaved her head and waited thirty days.

He felt some mystical connection moving toward completion deep inside his body and brain, a connection almost being made, a connection that would finally banish his fear and give him the faith he needed to charge forward without worrying about what might happen to him.

But the whistling stopped suddenly and Henry felt the two ends of that connection shrivel away in the silence. It seemed that perhaps his brain had stopped functioning and that his blood had frozen in his veins. He began to tremble, and his eyes were drawn helplessly back to that writing on the wall, the last line of which was less than an inch above the heads of the slain construction workers: *Then you shall bring forth to your gates that man who has done this evil thing and put him to death.*

"And the people shall say Amen," said a thick, slow voice behind him.

Henry screamed. The flashlight fell from his hands. He caught a quick glimpse of its beam going over the railing and cartwheeling down to the water below. Then a splash and darkness. He had a moment where his mind raced free, during which he wished for many things—that everything could have turned out differently; that the chief or Lizzy Halprin or Bill McInnis or even that old drunk Bennedict from the Falls had been available; that the ambulance had showed up when it was supposed to; that Artie was real; that he himself was more than just a no-brained, no-balled cop who needed an imaginary partner just to get him up out of his chair at the station. Any one of those things, and he might have had a chance.

His thoughts were chopped off by the sound of the boathouse door being pulled off the hasp. He saw a dark shape rising to fill the opening. Dartmouth? Oh God, oh no, he didn't think so. The old man couldn't be alive, he'd be a thousand years old by now, and he had always been so frail and skinny, while this thing was huge, towering, bulky and misshapen. It held something above its lumpy head, something he could not identify in such an instant of extreme terror but that might have been a large steel cross.

Yes, he thought, a cross . . . and it was lit . . . lit by faint light, although the boathouse and the waterfront outside were utterly dark . . . lit . . . its edges glinting like sharpened blades.

His finger twitched on the trigger of his revolver, but he didn't know what would happen if he shot, if the bullet would hit its mark, if one would be enough to kill that gargantuan thing, if he would have the time or guts to shoot again. Still he hesitated, but finally broke and turned and stumbled away along the catwalk, left hand groping for the old, wobbly railing, right shoulder bumping past the dripping corpses of Mike Mechanic, Willie Workman, and the others. He heard boards creaking beneath his weight, the pattering of rotted wood falling into the water below. He heard the sound of the railing itself, as though it were crying, weakening, about to give out.

"And the people shall say Amen," the voice said again, and then came the worst sounds of all—the dragging, thudding noise of the killer coming after him, the scythe-like whisper of that weapon slicing through the air.

Henry ran faster, tripping, barely maintaining his balance. When he reached the place where the catwalk ended at the boathouse's front wall, he stumbled in surprise on the stairway that was there. He flailed his arms, felt empty space in front and below, and almost pitched over the steps before he caught himself.

His fear was replaced by a burst of understanding—

perhaps Reverend Dartmouth would have called it an epiphany. He was being pursued by someone (some*thing*) that was left from the days of the old Bible camp. Someone (some*thing*) that had been here all these long years—here or quite nearby. Someone (some*thing*) that didn't cotton to the idea of a greedy businessman's association taking over. The same someone (some*thing*) that had stopped the Chicago idiots' fishing resort before it ever got off the ground. Was that it? Oh Jesus, *could* that be it? Henry didn't know, but he thought it very well might be.

As he descended one rickety step after another, listening to the ragged rasp of his own breath, the wild thunder in his chest, and the heavy sound of pursuit less than ten feet behind, he thought he might be facing something as large and fathomless as the spirit of the camp itself, the spirit of the place as established and embodied by a skinny old Bible beater who had loved to sing "Jesus Savior, Pilot Me" and preach from a ridiculous old legal code.

Madness. Lunacy.

Yes, it was that. But he had seen that inhuman shape. Accepting such madness and lunacy in the name of understanding, in the name of finding the strength to keep running . . . that had to be better than giving in to blind fear, didn't it? If he did that, if he surrendered so easily simply because he didn't know what he was facing, he might as well crumple into a ball right now and wait for that cross to part the top of his skull.

He reached the last step and the wooden pier at the bottom. It had been raining so much that fall that the water level had risen by inches, covering the boards. Cold water seeped into his boots as he went to the open barn-style doorway that communicated with Conley Lake. He grasped the edge of the door and swung himself around it. It was a good idea and a good try, but he missed dry ground by several feet, landed in water up to his knees, and had to scramble desperately up to the rocky shore.

The heavy thing was almost at the bottom of the stairs. The urge to stand and fight was growing strong within him, the urge to rest even stronger than that. But the thing was closer, almost upon him, and that was enough to murder all those urges and set him in flight.

It was damned funny, Henry kept thinking, the way noises carried so well in the still night air.

He had heard the thing chasing him quite clearly, and he had not allowed himself to stop running until he heard *it* stop first. That had been—what? An hour ago? Two hours? *Three?*

There had been nothing but silence after that, silence for a very long time, silence while he hunkered along the shore a quarter-mile from camp, silence while he collected his strength and what was left of his wits, wondering if he could sneak back into the camp and get the Blazer, if he'd be able to free it from the mud and escape. Silence. While he wept. While he pondered. While he tried again to make that difficult connection he had almost made several times that night already.

Eventually, as clearly as if he were standing right there, he had heard a vehicle rumbling up the camp driveway, the sound of doors slamming and the voices of Beverly Yates and Linc Wellington, the volunteer EMTs from the ambulance, calling his name.

Henry? Hey, Henry Gustafson, where the hell are you?

Other words: *We got lost, buddy* and *This place is as empty as shit, ain't it?* and *Where's this body s'posed to be?* and again, *Jesus Jumpin' Christ, Henry, where are you?*

Then more silence, not very long, followed by something short and high and horribly clipped that might have been a scream. Then a long, slow, perfectly clear whistle: *Jesus Savior, Pilot Me.*

Yes, it was funny how those sounds carried so well,

and how that thing that might have been and probably was a scream had gone straight to his heart like a big hand, grasping two loose ends and pulling them together.

He knew what he had to do. Artie had heard that scream, that sound of another human being suffering, and had come back to him, put a hand on his shoulder, and looked him straight in the eyes. Artie had told him.

"You can't hide anymore, boyo. This ain't playing at cops and robbers anymore, nabbing kids out breaking curfew. This is the real thing. You ran from the scene when you shouldn't have, you hid like a coward, you stayed here crying while them medics got taken out. Now you gotta get in there. Win or lose, you gotta try to clean this mess up. It don't matter that you're scared. It don't matter that you don't know how it's all gonna end. You just gotta do it. You're a cop, boyo, like it or not. That's what cops do."

Henry's mouth had dropped open in amazement. "Artie . . . I don't believe it. Artie, Jesus Christ, you're *talking!*"

But Artie had shaken his head solemnly, and after a moment Henry had understood. It ain't Artie talking, he thought, it's me. Good Sweet Lord, it's actually me. It's me who felt that person's pain, me who's going to react to it. It's me who knows what's going on. It's me who knows what needs to be done.

He thought about what he had seen back in camp and wondered how much of it had been real. Some of it? All of it? A huge creature that killed in the name of God? Was that possible? And if it was, then how could he ever hope to stop it?

He shook his head and sighed, knowing that didn't matter anymore. What waited in that camp was a mystery light years beyond him, but the connection, so long in the making, had been completed. The wires were hot and tingling. He had what he'd always been missing before. The ability to trust in himself and not worry about the outcome. The ability to do what was right.

He smiled. He couldn't exactly say that he'd be going into battle with God on his side. Images of scrawled scripture, misshapen beasts, and sharpened steel crosses made it impossible to think that. But something, something from within, would be there next to him, something good, something right, or at least something very simple and pure. He couldn't quite touch it, but he didn't doubt it either. When your back was to the wall and the screws were to your balls and you finally found what you'd been lacking . . . well, the power that came from that had to mean something, and you couldn't just turn away from it.

He stood up from his hiding place in the weeds and rocks, slapped his service revolver briskly from hand to hand, and drew his shoulders back. Artie was standing in front of him, tall and strong, but Henry shook his head firmly.

"Not anymore, pard. Get out of here. This is my job. I'm a cop. It's what cops do."

He thought a smile crossed Artie's rugged features in the moment before he disappeared for good.

Henry sighed. The sound of that ageless hymn reached him across the gulf of darkness, the notes perfect and clear. Tempestuous seas all right, Henry thought. Second Timothy, chapter six, verse twelve.

His lips parted and he found the notes of his own whistling song. He took one step, and then another, and a third, his shadow huge and strong as he advanced through the black of night into the even darker heart of the eternal mystery.

NANCY A. COLLINS *is the Bram Stoker award winning author of* Sunglasses After Dark, Tempter, *and the forthcoming* In The Blood. *Although most of her short fiction is shocking and graphic, the following tale is a subtle slice of southern pie. Attached to this story was a cover letter, in which Collins asked, "Who says small towns are normal?" Who says, indeed?*

HOW IT WAS WITH THE KRAITS
NANCY A. COLLINS

They're tearing down the old Krait house today. I reckon half the town will turn out to watch the bulldozer knock it down. Not that most folks here still remember anything about the Kraits, but in a place like Seven Devils you got to get your thrills where you can.

There was a time, back before the Second World War, when the town centered on the Kraits and their comings and goings. That was because Old Man Krait owned it, right down to the last pair of raggedy underwear on the skinniest cropper's ass. I can still see him in my mind, clear as day, although I wasn't more than five or six when he died.

He was a long drink of water with wide shoulders and a face like an angry owl's. He'd suffered some kind of illness as a child and wore a funny-looking shoe with a heel as thick as my pa's workboot. I remember how he used to clomp down Railroad Street—which was Main Street back then—clutching that cane of his, and my pa and the other men-folk would take off their hats to bid him good day. I don't recollect him saying anything back. My mama, bless her soul, once slapped the bejesus out of me for asking why Old Man Krait wore such a funny shoe while he was still within ear-shot. I was only three or four and didn't know nothing about mortgages and the difference between bank presidents and dirt farmers.

While Old Man Krait might not have been much to look at, he had himself a pretty wife. Eugenia Krait was a fine-looking woman, no two ways about it, and Old Man Krait married her before she was out of school. She was fifteen and he was fifty, so you *know* tongues wagged about *that*.

It was five years before they had themselves a kid. Jasper Krait and me was born in 1920; that's how I can keep most of what went on straight.

Jasper wasn't a well baby. He had the colic and cried all the time. I reckon Old Man Krait was too set in his ways to put up with having a little baby in his house. My mama found out from some of their help that Old Man Krait had his son's bottles doctored with cognac so he wouldn't cry.

When Jasper started to walk and get into things, Old Man Krait's way of handling it was to send his wife and child off to visit her kinfolks in Biloxi. For three years. Sometimes he'd take the train to spend holidays with them, but usually *she* would come to *him*. Without the boy, of course.

Then in 1925 Old Man Krait up and died while taking supper at his home. The day of the funeral everyone in Choctaw County, if not the whole of Southeast Arkansas, turned out on Railroad Street to watch the fancy hearse with etched glass and black plumed horses make its way to the Baptist church. My pa even put me up on his shoulders so's I could get a better look. Hell, it was almost as good as the time the circus came to town!

Everyone figured Eugenia would up and marry again right quick, what with her being beautiful, young, and rich to boot. But she never did. And she stayed put in Seven Devils, even though her folks were in Mississippi.

Turned out she learned a lot from Old Man Krait in the ten years they was married. The gal had a head for business, as Choctaw County soon discovered when she took over running her husband's bank. But although she was good at driving hard bargains, the one thing Widow Krait was bad at was raising her son.

My mama was a tender-hearted woman by nature, and she felt sorry for Jasper, what with him losing his daddy and all; so she decided to invite him to my birthday party.

The day of the party there comes this knock on our back door. When mama answered it she found one of Widow Krait's niggers standing there holding a big box wrapped in a fancy ribbon. The nigger told mama that Widow Krait regretted that Jasper would be unable to attend my birthday party, but wanted me to have a present anyway.

The box was a wooden case full of painted tin soldiers laid out on a velvet lining. They were the finest toys I'd ever seen—much less owned. Since I couldn't have cared less if Jasper Krait came to my birthday party, I couldn't understand why my mama got her nose so far out of joint. She wanted to send the toy soldiers back, but I kicked up such a fuss she let me keep them. However, she made me put them in the closet so's the kids too poor to bring nothing but oranges or pecans wouldn't feel shamed. My mama was good that way. Afterwards, I overheard her tellin' my pa that it'd be a cold day in July before she'd extend another kindness to the Kraits.

I started first grade in '26 and went to the old three-room schoolhouse that used to stand where they got the Burger Bar now. That's where I met up with Heck Jones, the Wilberforce Twins, Freddie Nayland, and the gal I ended up marrying. If Jasper Krait ever saw the inside of that school,

I never heard tell about it. Hell, far as I know, he never set foot in a *real* school at all. His mama hired some fancy-pants tutor from the college over at Monticello to teach Jasper at home. The tutor came in on the train early each morning and left late every afternoon. I don't recall ever hearing his name.

The Widow Krait was still visiting her folks in Biloxi every summer and during Christmas. Her usual custom was to leave Seven Devils just before Decoration Day and stay gone until the first week of September. But for some reason, no one knows why, Widow Krait came home in July, 1928, and never went to Biloxi again.

It wasn't long after that the rumor started that Widow Krait had bought a little nigger boy as a "companion" for Jasper. Not that anyone was surprised, mind you. By that time Jasper was already on his way to being, well, Jasper. He was the kind of young'un you'd have to hang a hambone on just to get the dog to play with him.

Every so often me and the gang would catch a glimpse of Jasper and his pet nigger playing in the Krait's fenced-in backyard, but we couldn't have cared less. The gang didn't have much use for sissies, and you couldn't get much sissier than Jasper Krait. Why, his ma used to dress him up in Little Lord Fauntleroy outfits, just like Mary Pickford! Hell, any self-respecting boy would have gone to church nekkid rather than be seen dressed like that! As it was, the only time folks in Seven Devils got an unobstructed view of Jasper was during Sunday services, and even then the Kraits had a pew all to themselves.

Things pretty much kept on like that until '32. That was the year the Widow Krait got herself a beau.

She'd been having business dealings with some fella out of Memphis, who came down on the train to get her to sign some papers. Once he got a good look at her, he stayed a week. It was all proper, of course. He stayed at the Railroad Arms, which was a right nice hotel back in them days. No one was surprised, truth to tell. Eugenia Krait was still young and had her looks, and the fella from Memphis was real handsome and polite. Not a thing like Old Man Krait.

The fella from Memphis started paying more and more calls on Widow Krait, and it was plain to see she enjoyed his company. My pa commented on how it'd do Jasper good to have a man around and once his ma remarried she wouldn't spend so much time fussing over the boy. Mr. Svenson, the barber, nearly took off Pa's earlobe agreeing with him.

When the *Choctaw County Squib*'s social page announced that the Widow Krait was planning to take a trip to Memphis *without* Jasper, all Seven Devils was abuzz with the news. To the best of anyone's memory, it would be the first time since Old Man Krait's death that mother and child had been separated.

Widow Krait was to take the train to Memphis early that Friday and return by Sunday evening. She never made it past the depot.

Just as the porters were smashing her baggage, Jasper's pet nigger rode up on a mule. Seems Jasper fell out of the hayloft in the barn in back of the house and busted his collarbone. Widow Krait went straight home to look after her boy.

Turned out Jasper smashed a sight more than his collarbone; his right knee was hurt so bad the doctors couldn't mend it properly. He ended up with a permanent limp and had to use his daddy's cane to go up and down stairs.

When the doctors told her that her son would be a cripple, Widow Krait had the old barn destroyed. No one saw the fella from Memphis again, although someone said he'd gone on to open a chain of dry goods stores.

To tell the truth, Jasper Krait was pretty much a non-person as far as the citizens of Seven Devils were concerned. I had my own interests and entertainments and Jasper never once figured in them. Come the Second World War, his trick knee kept him out of the draft. I ended up in the Infantry and saw action in France. In '42 I married my gal,

Nadine, while home on leave. I didn't see her again until '46.

During that time Jasper was workin' in his mama's bank. Or was *supposed* to be. He'd picked up a taste for gambling and spent more time than not in Hot Springs, playing the ponies. When the track was shut, he'd hop a train down to New Orleans and waste his time in the casinos on River Road.

In '44, while I was gone fighting the war, there was some kind of hoo-ha over at the bank. My Nadine was working as a teller at the time, which is how I come to know about it. Seems that when the banking authorities came in and audited the books there were some—'irregularities.' Things got settled—exactly how I don't know—but the upshot was that Jasper got "laid off" and put on an allowance. He never did a lick of work from there on in.

When I got home in '46, the last thing on my mind was the Kraits. I had me a wife I hadn't seen in four years, a three-year-old boy I was a stranger to, and a G.I. loan. But when I got back to Seven Devils I found the whole county gossiping about Jasper Krait having himself a girlfriend.

Her name was Bessie Lynn Haig and she wasn't exactly what you'd call glamorous. I'm not saying she was ugly, mind you. The girl was as plain as butcher-paper, that's all. Bessie Lynn was the organist at the Baptist church and the Lord only knows how she and Jasper ever got together. But as homely as she was, she seemed to exert a good influence on Jasper.

He stopped drinking and gambling and took to bathing regular and actually doing things like telling folks "howdy" when he saw them on the street. The change was monumental.

One Sunday in '47, Reverend Cakebread got up in front of the congregation and said that it was his pleasure to announce that Jasper and Bessie Lynn would be tying the knot in a month's time.

On the day of the wedding everybody in town turned

out to see what had once seemed as likely as men on the moon: Jasper Krait marrying a decent, god-fearing woman. Bessie Lynn was dressed up in a fancy bridal gown that almost made her look pretty. The men-folk took Jasper out by the privy behind the church for some last-minute "fortitude" for his nerves. I was one of them, and as we stood around smoking roll-yer-owns, sipping white lightnin' out of fruit jars, and cracking wedding-night jokes, it was like Jasper had always been part of the group.

I felt happy for Jasper, in my way. I was enjoying being a husband and a daddy after all the killing I'd seen and done over in Europe; and I wanted other folks to know being part of a family heals all wounds, if you have a mind to let it.

I forgot that families have a way of creating wounds, too.

When Jasper's pet nigger showed up on the mule, I saw the happiness drain from Jasper's face like someone had pulled a plug in the back of his head.

It was the Widow Krait. She'd fallen down the stairs.

Jasper went straight home and never made it back to the church that day.

After the first thirty minutes Bessie Lynn was anxious. After an hour had gone by she got mad. By the time the third hour rolled around, she was crying. I couldn't take no more and left not long after. I can still see poor, plain Bessie Lynn standing in the vestibule, boo-hooing into her bouquet. It was not a pretty sight.

Bessie Lynn was too ashamed to show her face in Choctaw County after that, so she went to live with a maiden aunt somewhere in the Ozarks. No one ever saw her again.

I guess that's when Jasper really started in drinking. He'd always been one for the bottle, but once Bessie Lynn was gone he ended up being the town drunk.

In '53, Sheriff Campbell retired and, seeing how I was one of the few white men left under thirty who'd seen military service living inside the town limits, I ended up with the badge.

Mostly my job consisted of making sure Rial's Package Store wasn't selling to minors and hosing off the highway after wrecks. It wasn't like they show it on television; no car chases or bank robberies or nothing exciting like that.

I tell you, being the Law for twelve years opened my eyes to a lot of things. Most of them not so good. I ended up knowing more about my neighbors than either them or me wanted. It was one thing to gossip about Mordecai Simpkins's drunken rages, but another to lock him up for putting his baby's eye out with a coathanger.

I guess it was—what? 1960?—when it happened. It was a nice spring day and Heck Jones gets a knock on his door. He's kind of surprised to see Jasper Krait standing there, pretty-as-you-please, even though the Kraits were his neighbors. Heck sees Jasper's got a stack of records—them hi-fi long-players—under his arm.

"Afternoon, Heck," says Jasper, as if he come calling every day.

"Afternoon, Jasper. What can I do you for?" Heck was nonplussed by Jasper stopping by unannounced and smelling like the Jack Daniels plant, but he was curious to find out what the richest man in town was doing on his front stoop.

"Well, Heck, I was hopin' you'd do me the favor of keepin' these here record albums for me while I go outta town."

Heck thought that was mighty peculiar at the time, seeing how the passenger trains didn't stop at the depot no more and he knew Jasper didn't have no driver's license, but he let it pass.

"You going outta town? Where to?"

Jasper looked nervous and shrugged. "Just outta town, that's all. Look, you gonna keep these records for me or not?"

"Sure, I'd be happy to oblige, Jasper. But why can't

you leave 'em home?"

He commenced to sweating and for a moment Heck was afraid Jasper was gonna puke all over his wife's tulip bed. "I just can't. That's all." He started to get this belligerent look on his face, like a mule that's decided it don't want to move, that was a watered-down version of what Old Man Krait used to give folks who were late paying their notes on account of their crops got washed away. So Heck ended up taking in Jasper Krait's records.

Later on, I found out Jasper made similar spur-of-the-moment visits on his other neighbors that day, asking each of them the "favor" of boarding a particular cherished object of his while he was "outta town;" he left his paperback book collection with Mamie Pasternak, his prize shotgun with Carlton Tufts, his good Sunday-go-to-meeting suit with Sam Wilberforce, and his fishing rod and tackle with Freddie Nayland.

The next night the Krait house caught fire.

I'd just come in from a hard day of plowing the south forty when the call came in. The volunteer fire department was already on the scene, the old hook and ladder pulled up on the Krait's front lawn. Reverend Thurman, who took over the Baptist church after Brother Cakebread passed on, was standing there in his braces and oilcloth coat, an axe in one hand and soot on his face, as if he'd just come back from freeing souls in Hell.

"How is it, Reverend?"

"Not too bad. The back porch got burnt up real good, but we got the worst of it."

"Anyone hurt?"

"See for yourself."

Just then Heck Jones and Sam Wilberforce come out the front door, carrying the Widow Krait between them. She was in her sixties and getting on the frail side, but she still had her dignity. And she weren't bad-looking, as old ladies go.

"What kept y'all so long?" fumed Brother Thurman.

"She wouldn't come out 'til she put on her housecoat and got her teeth in, Reverend. Said she refused to stand in front of every soul in Choctaw County in nothing but her flimsies and her bare gums," Sam explained.

I could tell Reverend Thurman wanted to let fly with a few choice words on the vanity of Eve, but the look the Widow Krait shot him made him shut his mouth before he got started.

Jasper showed up the next day, asking the neighbors what had happened to his mama. When Heck Jones told him she was over at St. Mary's in Dermott, being checked out for smoke inhalation, Jasper looked more surprised than relieved.

Everyone knew it was arson. Hell, even Granny Simple—who was blind in one eye, deaf as a post, and hadn't had her wits about her since Hoover was in office—could see *that*. Someone turned up a bunch of oily rags and an empty can of gasoline under the floorboards in Jasper's pet nigger's shack and there wasn't much I could do except arrest him.

Now, I ain't a niggerlover, but I ain't proud of what I done. I knew that nigger didn't do it—or if he had, it was on orders—but I arrested him anyway. I still feel bad about that, but I had a few more years to go on paying my note and my oldest was fixing to go off to Fayetteville and major in business. There wasn't much of a trial and Jasper's pet nigger got sent to Cummins for seven years. When the state troopers came to take him, he looked kind of relieved. I got the impression he was happy to go anywhere, so long as it was away from the Kraits.

After that, things quieted down some. It was easier for folks to believe that Jasper's pet nigger, full of Martin Luther King and cheap shine, got it into his head to burn down the Kraits' house, than for them to think about the truth.

Widow Krait hired a mess of carpenters to fix up the house and got shed of everything that got smoke or water damage. Most of the time Jasper laid low, drinking even harder than before. My own mama, bless her, passed on that winter, so I was more preoccupied than usual.

Then, about a year after the fire, I get this call before Nadine left the house for Sunday school. It was the Kraits' nigger maid, Amberola. Seems she found Widow Krait unconscious at the foot of the stairs. I told her to stay put and called Doc McFadden then phoned the ambulance service over in Desha County.

Turned out the Widow Krait took herself one hell of a bad spill. She came to for a spell while Doc McFadden was checking her over and asked to see Jasper.

I found him sleeping it off in his bedroom. When I told him his ma was hurt and asking for him, he looked real funny—like he's swallowed his chaw—then puked all over his bed.

Doc McFadden rode with her to St. Mary's over in Desha County, since Choctaw didn't have a hospital back then. He told me later that she'd busted her hip, collarbone, and a couple of ribs, and that it was a testament to God's mercy she'd lived to tell about it.

She was in the hospital for a long time. Most of the women-folk in Choctaw County paid her a visit while she was stuck in bed. My Nadine took her some *Upper Rooms* and a couple of crossword puzzles. She said that the Widow Krait was quite gracious, even with her hip in a plaster cast, but acted like she was the queen of England granting an audience. Nadine said that seeing her that way helped her understand Widow Krait. She didn't like her any better, mind you, but it made things clearer, at least woman-to-woman wise.

It was six months before the Widow Krait came back to Seven Devils. She couldn't do for herself too well, thanks to that busted hip, so Amberola pushed her in a wheelchair whenever she had to visit the bank. An electrician came in from Pine Bluff and installed a special elevator seat so's she could get up and down the stairs on her own.

Funny how the Kraits seemed to run to cripples: first the Old Man, then Jasper, and finally Widow Krait.

Doc McFadden and me knew a lot of things that most folks hereabout wished we didn't. Things like that happen when you're the only doctor and the only law in a town this size. So it was only fittin' he'd call me that night.

"Jimbo? You set down to dinner yet?"

"Just gettin' ready to, Doc. What is it?"

"It's the Kraits. You better get on over here. I'll be calling Dewar's Funeral Home next."

I felt my guts cinch up. The last thing I wanted to do was go and look at Eugenia Krait's corpse, but I got in the truck and drove over anyway.

I was a tad surprised to see the Widow Krait sitting in her front parlor, Amberola hovering over her like a huge shadow. She glanced up when I entered the house then quickly looked away.

Doc McFadden took my elbow and started leading me to the stairs. "Come on up. It's Jasper."

The only son and heir of Josiah Krait was sprawled across the bed, dressed in a pair of dirty boxer shorts and socks that didn't match. There were a couple of empty Jack Daniels bottles on the nightstand and a beat-up dime novel with a picture of a woman being tortured by Nazis laying face-up on the floor. Jasper was colder'n a wet mackerel in January.

"Shit, he's dead, alright. What was it—did he die in his sleep?"

Doc shrugged. "Can't rightly tell. I wouldn't be surprised if it turns out he drank himself to death. Anything's possible." He looked at me when he said that and I knew what he was getting at.

Anything's possible.

Amberola looked at me like I was a mealie in the cornbread when I entered the parlor. She'd been with the Widow Krait since before the Old Man died, and I knew she wouldn't have me upsetting her mistress, but I had my job to do, nigger maid or no.

I cleared my throat and held my hat close to my chest with both hands, gripping the brim like a steering wheel. The Widow Krait looked up and frowned for a second, as if trying to place me.

"Sheriff Turner," she said, her voice tired but far from weak.

"Yes, ma'am."

"Is he dead?"

I gripped my hat tighter. Lord, I hated that part of my job more than hosing off the highway. "Yes'm. I'm afraid so."

She nodded her head and sighed to herself but didn't offer to say anything else.

"Uh, Miz Krait—when was the last time you saw your son? Alive, I mean. I hate to be asking you these questions, ma'am, at a time like this . . ."

"I understand, Sheriff. It's your job. I know what it's like when something has to be done." She looked up at me again, and I could see her eyes were as clear and blue as a summer sky. "I reckon the last time I saw Jasper was last night. He brought me some hot cocoa and we sat and drank it in the sitting room. Yes, that was the last time, I'm pretty certain of it. When he didn't show up for dinner this evening, I had Amberola go up and fetch him. It wasn't that uncommon for him to stay in his room most of the day, on account of his . . . condition, but he usually came down for supper. That's when Amberola found him. . . ."

"Yes, sir. I found him like that." Amberola folded her meaty arms as if daring me to try and wrassle any more information out of her.

I left them sitting in the front parlor, the Widow Krait looking as delicate as a china doll. But I knew the porcelain was hiding a cold steel core.

When Doc McFadden pumped Jasper's stomach he

HOW IT WAS WITH THE KRAITS

found a Moon Pie, some cocoa, and enough whisky and painkillers to kill a team of mules. Doc recognized the painkillers as being those he'd prescribed Widow Krait for her hip. I asked him if he thought Jasper had committed suicide.

"Ain't saying no such thing, one way or another. Could have been accidental. Jasper had arthritis in that bum knee of his. Maybe he dosed himself with his mama's pain pills. That, on top of his drinking, would have done the trick. Anything's possible. As it is, I still owe the bank for my car."

Jasper's death was listed as heart failure and a day later he was cremated. Reverend Thurman was scandalized that the Widow Krait had her son stuck in an urn instead of buried, like the Good Lord intended. It just didn't seem *Baptist*.

Jasper's ashes hadn't cooled on the mantlepiece before Eugenia moved to Florida, taking Amberola with her. I don't know if she took Jasper's urn, though. If she ever came back to Seven Devils, I never heard of it. Talk has it she lived in a retirement community near Boca Raton and became a mean hand at shuffleboard.

Over the years the gossip surrounding the Kraits slacked off. And once the state banking authorities took over running things in '64, people didn't have any real reason to think about 'em. The Krait house, once the biggest and finest home in all Choctaw County, fell into disrepair.

A couple of years ago word got out that Eugenia Krait had died. A niece in Biloxi ended up inheriting the estate and she drove up from Mississippi last summer to look things over. I reckon she didn't like what she found, since they're tearing the place down.

I guess I'll go and watch 'em bulldoze the house. I'm the only one left who remembers how it was with the Kraits, now that Doc McFadden's retired and moved to Arizona, and Heck, Reverend Thurman, and even my Nadine, bless her, gone.

I can't help but wonder what it was like for them in that big, fine, lonely house. Spending all that time together, needing each other so bad love and hate became one and the same thing.

I'd *like* to think he was the one who put the pain-killers in the hot cocoa, and that she switched the cups when he wasn't looking.

Anything's possible.

WILLIAM F. NOLAN *is a
legend in the horror/suspense
genres. Best known as the
co-creator of the* Logan's Run
*series, Nolan's short stories—
tales such as "Ceremony,"
"The Yard," "My Name is
Dolly," and "Stoner"—are
his strongest work.
A multi-talented man
(he is the only person I know
who draws as well as he
writes), Nolan is also one
of the nicest writers alive.*

BABE'S LAUGHTER
WILLIAM F. NOLAN

She was in the motel shower when she thought of the Hitchcock scene with the knife. That was a very scary movie, and the shower scene terrified her. She couldn't sleep for two nights after seeing that movie, and she didn't take a shower with the door closed for a month. But she got embarrassed thinking that her father could see her naked and that made her start shutting the door again.

Her father's dying was why she was here, in this motel. His dying at the Franklin Hospital in Oak Park, where he'd been for the last month, failing fast, getting thinner and weaker. His face looked like a death's head when she came to visit him from Kansas City. They'd lived in the same house in K.C. for fourteen years after her mother died, and then he'd been forced to go to Chicago for advanced treatment for the cancer. The shitty damn cancer! Ate him up inside, just hollowed him out until he was nothing but a shell. No hair left. Cheeks sagging, sunken. Coughing up blood near the end. She would see him weekends, when she had time off from her job, stay in Chicago at a motel, then fly back to K.C. Expensive, but you don't count dollars when someone you love is dying. He had his insurance, so that end of it was taken care of at least.

This was the last weekend she'd spend in Chicago. She hated the town. It smelled of death. Of cancer. They'd asked her, at the hospital, what she wanted done with the body. (That's all he was now—the body.) And she told them to cremate him. Fire purifies. The grave rots you. Food for the worms.

She hated graves.

He'd been holding her hand when he died. Tight. Real, real tight—as if death couldn't take him if he held tight to her. But he died anyway. With a little gasp and a gargling sound deep in his throat. They'd warned her he wouldn't last through the night.

Once it was over she'd accepted his death, rejoiced in it, actually, for his sake; no one wants to go on living looking and feeling the way he did toward the end. No one.

Then, in the shower, she thought about the girl in the Hitchcock movie dying under the spray, with the blood from the knife wounds running down the drain, and she felt suddenly vulnerable. Her skin tingled and little waves of apprehension rippled through her.

She carried a knife in her purse. From her Girl Scout days. But of course she'd never killed anyone in a shower with it.

Getting out, folding herself into the big white terry cloth robe, she felt dizzy. Kind of giddy. Not sad. Not how she thought she'd feel when his death was real and not something coming at them. She was lightheaded, the way she got when she drank three Manhattans in a row. Giddy and lightheaded.

She brushed her hair, using hard firm strokes. Then she got dressed. Tight green skirt. White blouse with ruffled lace at the neck. Kind of old-fashioned, but she liked the effect against her pale skin. Black stockings. High heels.

Sitting in front of the dresser she found, to her surprise, that she felt wonderful. My God! Not sad at all. Liberated and wonderful. The dark weight of her father's illness had been lifted from her shoulders. He was gone now, and she could do anything.

Anything.

She put on her makeup, carefully applying just the right amount of eye shadow and making sure her lipstick was perfect. But, shit, she didn't need to be perfect anymore. Nothing about her needed to be perfect.

On the way out to her rented car she killed the motel manager.

For no particular reason—except that maybe he looked something like the doctor who'd first told her that her father had terminal cancer. There *was* a definite resemblance. In the cheekbones and along the jawline.

She'd cut his throat.

She still felt lightheaded when she got into her car. It was good doing just what she felt like doing for a change after holding back all these years—being the perfect daughter. (Being perfect is a real bitch.) His blood, the motel manager's, was on her coat and blouse. Mostly on her coat. Didn't matter.

Nothing mattered.

Which was kind of wonderful.

The car smelled of cancer. The smell from the hospital, from her father's skeletal body. Sour and intense.

She rolled down all the windows before she started the engine. To air out the car.

Then she drove away from the motel. The night air was cold against her skin.

She wondered what the police would say about the motel manager. But who cared? Who gave a flying fuck *what* the police said or thought or did?

It was a long drive to the bar-restaurant—from Oak Park to the Loop. On Michigan Avenue, a place called Charlie's. Dave would be waiting for her there. She'd called him from the motel and suggested they get together for a late drink. Old Davy boy. His hair had been thinning last time she'd seen him. He was probably bald by now.

She and Dave had a few heavy dates the summer she spent her vacation in Chicago. He'd wanted to take her to bed, but she hadn't gone to bed with him. Or anyone else. Her father didn't like her seeing men.

Maybe she'd go to bed with Dave tonight. Maybe she'd let him do all the things to her that her father warned her against. The nasty things.

Maybe she would.

Charlie's was crowded, which surprised her. Somehow, she had expected to walk through the door and see Dave sitting alone in a corner booth, and they'd just stare hotly across the empty room at each other. But it wasn't like that at all. It was a Saturday night, and the place was filled with smoke and loud voices and a mass of people who flowed around her as she looked for Dave.

He was on a stool at the bar. And mostly bald, like she'd figured. In some kind of shiny polyester suit that looked crummy on him. He'd grown a beard since she'd seen him. To make up for the hair loss on top; lots of men do that. (How would a beard feel between her legs?)

"Hello, Dave," she said, slipping out of her coat.

"Hi, Babe." (He always called her that and she'd hated it, his not using her name. Tonight she didn't mind.)

He gave her a tight hug and a kiss on the cheek.

"I got a table for us," he said. "Near the back."

"Sure," she said.

"Great to see you," he told her when they were seated. "Been a while."

"Six years this summer," she said. And ordered a Manhattan, no ice. He asked for a gin and tonic.

He looked steadily into her face. "I'm curious."

"About what?"

"About why you called me tonight."

"My father died a few hours ago. At the hospital in Oak Park. Of lung cancer. I thought I'd like some company."

"Jesus!" he said softly. "I'm sorry, Babe."

Their drinks arrived. She raised her glass.

"Here's to better times," she said.

"Jesus," Dave repeated softly. "I should hope."

"I guess you think I ought to be in mourning," she said.

"No . . . oh, no. It was just . . . I mean, if my old man ever—"

"Didn't anyone ever die of cancer in your family?"

"Uh, sure. An aunt in Cincy. Aunt Martha. She was my Mom's sister. She did. About a year ago."

"It hits every family," she said. "My father got it from smoking too much. Four packs a day. I never smoked. He didn't like to see girls smoking."

"And you always did just what Daddy told you to do," said Dave.

"How do you know that?"

"He didn't want you to see me. You said so in the letter I got from you after that summer. Said you didn't want to get him all upset, so we'd better knock it off. Tell you the truth, I never expected to hear from you again."

"Well . . . you did. And here I am."

He was staring at her in the hazed dimness of the bar.

"The front of your blouse," Dave said. "That . . . dark stain."

"It's dried blood," she found herself admitting.

(Why the hell not?) "There's more on my coat. A lot more."

And then she couldn't help herself, just couldn't, because of the way his face looked. (Like her father used to look when she'd tell him about some awful thing she'd been thinking about.) She didn't want to, it wasn't appropriate, but she couldn't stop herself.

From laughing.

From howling with laughter.

She just couldn't.

RICK HAUTALA *is*
best known for the classics
Night Stone *and* Little Brothers,
but his recent books Winter
Wake *and* Dead Voices *have*
gained much attention.
A resident of Maine, Hautala
only recently turned to the
short story form, with tales
appearing in Stalkers,
Cemetery Dance, *and*
The Overlook Connection.
Keep an eye on this guy.

HOTEL HELL
RICK HAUTALA

"Would you *please* stop talking?" Phil Vernon said to the two detectives. Squinting his eyes, he concentrated on the small circle of yellow light that hovered in the darkness above the bed between him and the blood-splattered wall. "I *must* have *absolute* silence if I'm going to pick up on anything." Barely aware of his own breathing, he focused his attention on the circle of light, willing it to brighten and resolve.

Without comment, the two detectives walked over to the single bed in the hotel room and looked down at it. The sheets, in a tangle on the floor, and the ratty mattress cover were stained with brick red splotches of dried blood and shriveled chunks of flesh. The larger splash of dried blood on the wall looked like a large, inky flower. Both detectives wrinkled their noses at the lingering stench of death in the room. The body had been removed earlier that morning after festering in the August heat for three days.

"You wanna know what I think?" Fred, the older of the two detectives said. "I think we're wastin' our fuckin' time on this. It's so friggin' obvious it was a whacko-suicide case." He folded his arms across his chest and leaned against the wall. His eyes reflected his impatience as he shook his head with frustration.

Jack, the other detective, got down on his hands and knees and shined his flashlight under the bed. Wide puddles of dried blood had mixed with gray clots of dust. Wrinkling his nose, he looked over his shoulder at his partner and said, "This isn't exactly my idea of a fun time, either; but there's something about this whole thing that stinks—stinks *bad.*"

"Yeah, but they already carted it down to the morgue," Fred said, laughing as he hooked his thumb over his shoulder.

"Real funny," Jack said. "But as long as Lieutenant Fisher says this *obvious* suicide case isn't shut up tight, then it's our ball game."

The entire time the detectives were talking, ignoring his request for quiet, Vernon watched as the hazy circle of yellow light dimmed and then finally winked out. He had the unnerving feeling that he had seen that circle of light before, but he couldn't quite place it. Was it on a case similar to this? Or, sometime in the past, had he had a precise premonition of this hotel room and the murder—not suicide—that had taken place here.

Whatever it was, he was positive the idle chatter of the detectives had made the illusion disappear.

Sighing with frustration, Vernon went over to the window and peeked around the edge of curtain at the heat-hazed skyline of Bangor, Maine. The direct sunlight stung his eyes fiercely, so he drifted back over toward the closet door. All the while, he was trying to contact the murderer and his victim telepathically. By his own admission, Philip Vernon was the best psychic detective in the United States . . . possibly the best in the world. He couldn't help but chuckle at the misguided conversation of the detectives.

—*As if this was a suicide!* he thought bitterly.

The moment he had entered this room in the seedy hotel on Union Street, even with his eyes wide open and his mind unfocused, he could sense the sharp panic and pain of the victim. Right away, he knew her name was Estelle Phillips, no matter what was on the obviously phony IDs in her purse. He also knew *exactly* how she had died. She had picked up her third "john" of the evening shortly before ten o'clock on Friday evening. After making fierce, violent love, still naked and bathed with sweat, her customer had reached down to the floor beside the bed and picked up her fishnet stockings. Covering her mouth with one hand, he had looped the thin fabric around her neck twice and then pulled back slowly, inexorably, silently enjoying the terrified glaze that came into her eyes as the air in her lungs went stale and the life drained out of her. In the close silence of the room—at least whenever the two blabbering detectives shut up—Vernon could still hear the faint echo of her choking gasps as her windpipe closed off and her lungs collapsed inward.

But then why all the blood on the wall, mattress, and floor? Vernon wondered as he studied the back of the detective who was looking under the bed. He wasn't entirely clear on what had happened once Estelle was dead. Had the "john" abused her lifeless body? Maybe he had taken out a knife and carved her up. Maybe he had done something even worse....

"It's incredible how we piss away our time on low-life creeps like this," Fred said. He hawkered deep in his throat but refrained from spitting onto the hotel floor. "That fuck-head did the world a favor when he blew his brains out. One less hemorrhoid on society's ass."

Jack ignored his partner's comment as he swung his

flashlight back and forth under the bed, scanning the floor. He didn't expect to find anything that might have been missed earlier. The lab techs were pretty damned thorough. Still, he might find a scuff mark from a shoe heel, a fingernail clipping, or something else that would help him get rid of this feeling he had that they had missed something. The stench of dried blood—and worse—started getting to him, so he pulled back, stood up, and took a deep breath to clear his mind.

Vernon cleared his throat before speaking, but neither detective bothered to look at him.

"The only *fuck-head* here, as you so elegantly put it, is you for not seeing what's so bleeding obvious! This was no suicide, and the dead person sure as hell was *not* a man! The girl was a hooker, and she was murdered—strangled, all right? Can I state it any clearer than that?" He shook his head with disgust. "Damn! It's a wonder you boys can find your way to the police station without a map."

"I say we head on back to the station," Fred said. "This place has been photographed and dusted and raked over with the proverbial fine-toothed comb. There ain't nothing more to find."

"I suppose so," Jack said, still gagging from the stench that lingered in the room. He covered his nose with his hand and took a deep breath as he looked around. From the blood splotch on the wall, his gaze swung over the bed, past the bureau to the exit, then to the closet door, the bathroom door, to the drawn window shade, and back to the blood stain on the floor. Not even for an instant did he make eye contact with Vernon, who stood in the center of the room, watching both of them in amazement.

"There's something here, though," Jack said, scratching behind his ear. His voice was almost a whisper. "I can ... can *feel* it, It's like a . . . a—" He shook his head and finished, "Shit! I don't know."

"A *hunch* perhaps?" Fred said. He didn't even try not to betray his opinion of detectives who placed any faith in hunches.

"I can't *believe* you can't sense *anything* about what happened," Vernon said, knowing that the off-handed reference to hunches was a direct slam at him and his abilities. "Or is it simply that the two of you don't believe me when I tell you what I feel—what I *know* happened in this room?"

"I always get the creeps in a room where someone's snuffed it," Fred said. " 'Specially when it's been a suicide."

"I just can't *believe* you guys!" Vernon shouted. "The killer signs into the hotel under the name 'John Smith.' He pays, up front, in cash, for five days and leaves specific instructions at the desk that he doesn't want the chambermaid to clean his room or change his sheets and towels. Now, assuming he wasn't in town on business, in which case he would have charged the room to his company and probably wouldn't have chosen such a flea-ridden hole like this, that right away should make you suspicious. So anyway, sometime during the weekend—I guarantee you it was late Friday night—he picks up this whore downtown, brings her up to the room and after having a bit of fun, has some *serious* fun. He strangles her with her pantyhose. Once she's dead, he stuffs her inside the closet and leaves her there until he has a chance to get her out of here unobserved. He dumps her body and a bundle of her clothes off the bridge into the Kenduskeag River where, if you bother to do a bit of trolling, you just might find what's left of her."

"There ain't nothing else we're gonna find. Are we outta here?" Fred asked.

Stroking his chin, Jack nodded and said, "Yeah—I guess so."

"Will you fellas just hold on a minute?" Vernon said. "I need to spend a bit of concentrated time here, all right? Otherwise, I'll never get all of the details. The psychic vibrations of the hooker's death agonies are so strong, I can't get a clear impression of who her killer was."

Feeling mild surprise that neither detective started

razzing him about "picking up vibes," Vernon walked slowly toward the closed closet door. If he touched the doorknob, which the killer must have touched, he just might get a sharper sense of who he was. Slitting his eyes, he focused his mind. A faint tingling began at the base of his skull and spread up the back of his head. The psychic space of the room filled with a hushed expectancy, like a thunder storm, lurking just over the horizon. There was an unnerving sense of familiarity to the room, but Vernon ascribed that to the psychic impressions he got which often made other people's thoughts and feelings startlingly more real than his own.

Before leaving the room, Jack moved over to the window and with a quick motion pulled the curtains aside. Vernon yelped with surprise when the sudden burst of sunlight entered the room. He started toward the window to close the curtains again but stopped in the middle of the room when Jack drew them back over the window.

"Wait just a second, all right?" Jack said. "I can't get rid of the feeling that we're . . . we're missing something here . . . something so obvious." He placed his hands on his hips and stared blankly around the room. "Let's run it through just once more, okay?"

Fred folded his arms across his chest and sighed heavily. "You're wasting your time and mine, pal," he said, wrinkling his nose as he sniffed the rancid air in the room.

"So," Jack began, rubbing his hands together, "after signing the hotel register as 'John Smith,' this guy pays for the room up front for five days."

"In cash," Fred added.

"Christ! I just *told* you that!" Vernon snapped, angered at the way these two men were ignoring him.

"And now he has a 'John Doe' tag on his toe down at the city morgue unless—or until—his fingerprints get ID'd."

"The tag no doubt reads '*Jane* Doe'," Vernon said. "And I already told you her name is—or was—Estelle Phillips. And she fucking-A *didn't* commit suicide! She was murdered! All right?" He shook his head with disgust. "What in the *Christ* are you two talking about? The only *man* involved here is the man who killed *her!* Get it?"

"And no one on the hotel staff took any notice of him, right?" Jack continued. "This guy is practically invisible. He's just some lonely asshole who comes out of nowhere and takes a room for five days."

"You've got it," Fred replied.

"So far, so good," Vernon said sarcastically. "Then he hires a prostitute, fucks her, then strangles her with her panty hose, and dumps her body into the river. Christ on a cross, you guys are like blind men!"

"Come on. Let's get the fuck out of here," Fred said. "Tell you what—I'll buy you a beer at Pedro's."

"Yeah—yeah," Jack said, still not moving. "It's just that I can't shake this feeling . . . " He let his voice drop as he looked around the room again, his eyes darting from dark corner to dark corner.

Vernon's anger rose in a sharp spike. Throughout his career as a psychic detective, he'd had to deal with plenty of skepticism and outright hostility, but *these* two men were beyond belief, ignoring him as if he wasn't even there. Vernon started toward them just as they turned to leave. He held his hand up as a signal for them to stop.

"Yeah," he said, more mildly as he let his hand drop to his side. "Maybe it'd be better if the two of you waited down in the lobby. Give me ten minutes here alone, and I'll tell you the killer's name, address, and Social Security number. If I'm lucky, maybe I'll even get an idea where he went from here."

"Shut that door, will you?" Fred said, nodding in the direction of the closet.

Frowning deeply, Vernon glanced over his shoulder at the closet door. He hadn't touched it, and he could clearly see that the closet door was still shut tight. He hadn't had to open it to know that's where the killer had stuffed Estelle's body.

"The closet door's already closed," Vernon said with exasperation. He wondered if Fred was having trouble seeing in the dimly-lit room. As if to prove his point, he reached out for the doorknob. He grunted with surprise when his hand passed through the tarnished brass door knob. The illusion was so strong, for a moment he couldn't tell which was real and which wasn't, his hand or the door.

"Okay, I get it," Vernon said, realizing he was seeing a psychic impression of the door as it had been when the killer left Estelle's body there. "You had the door removed for evidence, right? Taken to the lab to be checked for finger-prints and blood stains, huh?" He glanced around the room again, wondering what else these two lame-brained detectives couldn't see. Surely, the bed and the bureau were there, and the blood stains on the wall and floor, but what else was apparent only to his inward-turning eyes?

Maybe that's why he wasn't getting a clearer impression of the killer—there was too much psychic turbulence in the room. It frustrated him that he could only receive distinct impressions of what Estelle had experienced as she died. He could hear her weakening grunts of resistance, the grating squeak of the bedsprings as the man held her down and twisted the panty hose tighter and tighter. He could feel the icy terror in her mind as her pulse rate shot up and spinning lights flashed across her retina. He could hear her dwindling internal scream as she was sucked down . . . down into the eternal black gulf.

But he could feel nothing of what the killer had thought and felt as he viciously twisted the life out of Estelle. Maybe because that's what the killer *had* felt—a cold, abso-lute, limitless *Nothing!*

Fred opened the door to leave. Jack started after him; but just as he passed by Vernon, he stopped short. Slapping his hands against his upper arms and rubbing them vigorously, he shivered wildly.

"Jesus H.," he muttered, his eyes widening with fear.

"That's so *weird.*"

"Huh?"

"Just now, right here in the middle of the room," Jack said, shivering again. "There's this—like, cold spot here."

"Yeah, sure," Fred said as he walked out into the hallway. He moved out of sight but then stuck his head back into the room when his partner didn't follow. "You comin' or not?"

"Yeah, I'm coming," Jack said. He shook his head as though just waking up. "It just feels so . . . so strange."

"There's nothing *strange* about it!" Vernon yelled. "There was a *murder* here! A young woman was *killed!* The psychic residue is as thick as morning fog. You can't touch it or carry it down to the crime lab to analyze, but it's here just as surely as you and I are here!"

"Come on, man," Fred said. "I can already taste how good that beer's gonna go down."

Before Jack could take a step, the hallway echoed with the sound of the elevator door opening. He heard Fred call out a greeting to Lieutenant Fisher, and then both men entered the room.

"Well, I guess you boys can take a break on this one," Fisher said, smiling widely. "The fingerprints checked out. We've got a positive ID on the stiff."

"And her name's Estelle Phillips, right?" Vernon said.

"No shit," Fred said. He cast a smile at his partner as he slapped his fist into his open hand.

"Yup," Fisher continued. "The case is ruled a suicide and is now officially closed."

"What the fuck—?" Vernon shouted when Fisher didn't even glance at him. He was about to say more, but just then a pulsating warmth washed over his shoulders from behind. At first he thought the curtain was still open, and sunlight was spilling into the room; then he realized he was standing with his back to the bed, not the window. Before he could turn and look, the heat quickly rose until it was burning hot. In frustrating slow-motion, Vernon turned and saw that the pulsating circle of yellow light had returned. It was hovering at eye-level, just above the bed.

"What the—" he sputtered, staring wide-eyed as the circle gradually expanded. The temperature in the room started to rise. Before long, Vernon could see nothing of the bed or the splotch of blood on the wall.

"Yeah," Fisher said, nodding. He put his finger under his collar and tie, pulling to loosen it a bit. "You may have even heard of him."

Vernon couldn't tear his eyes away from the steadily expanding circle of light. The center was changing subtly. At its core, the light seethed with ripples of darker red and orange, like raging thunderheads underlit by a fiery sunset. The circle of light seemed to telescope backward. Within seconds, the hotel room dissolved into a long, bright tunnel. Fisher's voice still rang in Vernon's ears, but it seemed to be coming from miles away, warbling with a curious Doppler effect.

"Actually, he was quite famous in his own way," Fisher's distant voice continued. "His name was Philip Vernon."

"Oh, yeah, sure," one of the detectives said. His voice was so distorted, Vernon couldn't tell if it was Fred or Jack. "He was that guy who billed himself as a . . . a—what do you call 'em?"

"Psychic detective," another warbling voice said. "He went all around the country using his supposed psychic abilities to help police solve crimes. But wait a second. There's more."

The conversation barely penetrated the cresting waves of fear that were sweeping through Vernon. The blazing tunnel continued to stretch outward, disappearing into a fiery core that seemed to be sucking Vernon into it. Mounding folds of glowing red and orange condensed into shapes that looked like gnarled hands, reaching outward from the mael-strom of light.

"Yeah—" a voice even further away said. "Earlier this afternoon, we got a call at the station. Some kids playing down by the river found the body of a woman washed up on shore. She had a couple of priors, so it was pretty easy to get a make on her. Name was Estelle Phillips. A hooker. But guess whose wallet was tangled up in the bunch of clothes we found a couple of hundred yards upstream?"

"You don't say."

"Uh-huh. We did a quick lab check on the skin we found under her fingernails, and it looks like a pretty good match with Vernon's. She must've put up quite a struggle. What it looks like to me is, after he dumped her into the river, he must've realized his wallet was missing and might turn up in the wrong place, so he came back here and blew his brains out all over the wall."

Vernon wanted to shout, wanted to scream that it wasn't him, but his thoughts and words were drowned out by the steadily rising roar of flames that belched out of the tunnel of light. Huge hands clawed at him, pulling him forward. He tried to shake loose, but the pull was inexorable. He looked down at his feet and stared in horror as they slid helplessly across the hotel room floor. Pure, stark terror flooded his mind when he realized his body was dissolving, being crushed by the reaching hands, consumed by the raging inferno. Nothing could stop his rising panic and pain; it only increased in a wild crescendo.

The voice came again, no more than a hissing whis-per from the edge of reality. "So once we get more detailed lab work done, I'd say it's pretty much an open and shut case of murder/suicide."

No! I'm not dead! Vernon's mind screamed, whin-ing higher and higher. *I can't be dead! I can't be dead!*

A monstrous roar from the center of the tunnel blended into guttural laughter that filled Vernon's mind. He dissolved in the blazing lances of flame, and still the bestial laughter rose louder and louder until it and pain were all he knew.

ED GORMAN *writes
mystery, crime, horror
(as Daniel Ransom) and
western novels—all excep-
tionally well. He is also
well-known as the editor
of such projects as:*
The Black Lizard
Anthologies of Crime Fiction,
Stalkers, *and* Mystery Scene
*magazine. All of Gorman's
work is marked by razor-
sharp prose, a grim sensitiv-
ity, and deep compassion, but
his Jack Dwyer mysteries are
his best. Try* Cry of Shadows
and The Autumn Dead
*and you'll be a Gorman
fan for life. Dean R. Koontz
said of him: "If Ed Gorman's
name doesn't eventually
become as famous as that of
Lawrence Sanders, it's an
unjust world." I agree
wholeheartedly.*

DARK WHISPERS
ED GORMAN

The store had one of those bells that tinkled when you walked in. It also had one of those owners who never looked happy to see teenagers, especially unfamiliar teenagers.

Gabe Malley came in, nodded, and started looking around. The place intimidated him. It was big and sunny and obviously everything sold here was expensive. It was unlike the dingy shops in Gabe's neighborhood.

"Help you?" the man said. He was short and bald and wore the sort of apron a shoe repairman might. He also wore a red necktie which told you instantly that he wasn't just some employee. He was the owner.

"Just looking, I guess."

"For anything in particular?"

Gabe shrugged. "TV set, I guess."

The man looked Gabe over. Gabe was a tall, lean kid with brown hair, neat if a little long, and an appealing but not handsome face. He had dark, sad eyes and the few girls at school who paid him much attention always wondered what had put the sadness in those eyes. "Your parents send you or something?"

"Uh, yeah. My Dad." Of course, Gabe's Dad had been dead the past four years.

The man eased up a little. He took a roll of Tums from somewhere in his apron and flicked one into his mouth with his thumb.

"TV set for your bedroom or something like that?" the man said.

"Uh, yeah. For my bedroom. Kind of a birthday present." For his bedroom, right. Mom slept in the only bedroom, he always slept on the fold-out couch in the living room.

"How old you going to be?"

"Fifteen." Gabe shrugged, as if turning fifteen was not exactly a major accomplishment. Of course it would have been for his sister Karen. She hadn't made fifteen at all.

"Got a daughter your age," the man said. There was warmth in his voice now. Gabe felt bad about lying to the guy.

The front door bell rang again. A middle-aged couple came in. "We're looking for a home entertainment center—tv, stereo, tape deck, everything," the woman said. She sounded excited.

"Be with you in a minute, kid," the store owner said, and turned his complete attention to the couple.

For the next ten minutes, Gabe looked around. The store was laid out in three sections: TVs, stereo and tape gear, and home video equipment.

Gabe spent most of the time examining the TVs. Or pretending to. He was really checking out the home video stuff but he didn't want the owner to notice this.

Not that the owner was paying any attention. He was practically going down on the middle-aged couple. They had made him positively ecstatic—positively keening—by asking him about the most expensive Zenith home entertainment center the man had ever put on the floor.

Gabe took this opportunity to wander into the rear of the store. Beyond a partition, he saw a small office-like area with two desks and phones; a work bench with three picture tubes on it and the smell of burning solder in the air; and the alarm system. Over the past two weeks—ever since he'd decided what he was going to do—he'd studied the various kinds of alarm systems he'd found out about at the public library. The most modern kind was the digital key pad system which would be, in the parlance of computer hacks, difficult to "defeat." In fact, a downright bitch. Then there were the two dominant older systems that were still much in use today, the door switcher mechanisms which were deceptively easy to "defeat" but which a guy could screw up and get himself busted over, and the photo cell mechanisms. Glancing around the rear area, he checked first at the back door. And saw what he was looking for. The TV store was secured by a photo cell system.

His work done back here, he wandered up front again. The store owner was now downright evangelical about the pluses of the Zenith home entertainment center. If Christ were alive today, this was no doubt the one He'd choose for His own condo.

Gabe didn't notice the camera till last. It was partially hidden, for one thing, behind a much larger and more formidable camera, one that looked as if it would do everything except maybe wash your car for you.

The little black camera, the tiny one that looked as if it would sit comfortably right in Gabe's hand, was exactly what he'd been hunting for.

Not that he made a move toward it.

Not that he even let his eyes linger very long on it.

For now, it was enough to know that he'd found what he was looking for. And that it was sitting right there.

Waiting for him.

He walked to the front of the shop. Only when he put his hand on the doorknob did the owner seem to notice that Gabe was leaving. "Didn't find anything, huh?"

Gabe shrugged. "Maybe I'll stop back."

"Sure, kid," the owner said. He winked at Gabe. "You have a happy birthday."

Then he was caught up again in the ecstasy of selling the big Zenith rig.

On the bus home, Gabe stared out the window as the good neighborhood of venerable brick apartment buildings and fashionable glass-and-steel high rises gave way to his own neighborhood, the drab and crumbling inner city outpost that was the last bastion against the onslaught of not only blacks but now Vietnamese and Central American refugees as well. Most of the cars parked along the curb resembled hulking animals dying out rusty deaths. Most of the old people and junkies and winos and garden variety crazies shambling along the streets also resembled dying animals. This was his neighborhood. His mom was up to three dead-bolts on the apartment door at night and she kept talking about getting a gun. Ever since Karen had died, his mom had become a trembling old lady.

When he stepped off the bus, he caught a glimpse of the silver Mercedes just darting down an alley.

Gabe checked his watch. Almost five.

The silver Mercedes would just now be starting its nightly rounds.

Cocksucker.

"Honey?"

"Uh-huh." Gabe knew what was going to come next:

*You mind if I don't feel like cooking tonight, if I just heat like
a TV-dinner in the microwave?*

"You mind if I don't feel like cooking tonight, if I just
heat like a TV-dinner in the microwave?"

"That's fine, Ma."

"You sure?"

"I'm sure."

She stuck her head out of the bathroom. White
vampire toothpaste foamed around her mouth. She was in her
white slip. She was very pretty in a fragile way. She was only
thirty-four. She should date. Gabe always told her that, how
the neighborhood kids always told him what a fox he had for
an old lady, and what a waste it was that she didn't date. She
always said she'd think about it.

"You sure?" she said again with the toothpaste
foaming around her mouth.

He smiled at her. She was cute just the way Karen
had been cute.

He thought of the silver Mercedes again.

Cocksucker.

He did his homework. That was one thing about
Gabe. He was determined to someday get out of this neighborhood. Karen had always been so proud of him. She didn't care
that some of her friends thought her little brother was kind of
a geek, so lonely and unto himself and always poring over
science fiction paperbacks and being real tongue-tied and
embarrassed whenever they teased him about taking them
out and things like that. When he was nine, he'd told her that
he would someday be a writer and make a lot of money like
Stephen King and then he'd buy Mom and her this huge big
mansion to live in. They'd have a swimming pool and neat cars
and Karen would no longer be ashamed to have her friends
over. Even by neighborhood standards, their apartment was
a pit.

He did his homework.

He sat in the living room with the TV on low playing some old black and white sitcom, and studying about how General Lee in the Civil War had marched 10,000 of his men across the Potomac River, and how the average age of the soldiers had been twelve and how most of them had to fight without shoes or blankets to keep them warm at night, and how many of them died from disease and starvation rather than wounds.

He tried to imagine what it would be like to be a twelve-year-old soldier, fighting and dying.

At first, it was unimaginable, almost a silly concept when you thought about it.

But then he thought of the silver Mercedes.

Maybe being a twelve-year-old soldier was hard to imagine.

But being a fifteen-year-old soldier wasn't.

In the bathroom, he washed up and put on clean clothes—a black shirt and jeans—and then he went into his mother's room.

She whimpered. Every night. That was the only word for it. Whimpering. Ever since Karen had died. She dragged through her waitress job every day and then came home and was in bed within an hour or so. Sleeping. Whimpering.

Now she lay somewhere between sleep and waking, some troubled purgatory in which her loss of Karen was worse than ever.

Over and over she said Karen's name, dark whispers in the dark room that smelled of cheap perfume and cigarette smoke.

He went over to her and sat on the edge of the bed and took her hand and held it.

The older he got, the more she was his daughter than his mother.

He leaned over and kissed her damp forehead. She stirred slightly, starting to come awake and then falling with a childlike sigh deeper into sleep once more.

No point in waking her.

He let himself out, leaving a vague note about where he was going, careful to lock the front door behind him.

Ghosts and phantoms rode the city bus, the urban old and the urban poor with night jobs and desperate meaningless errands. In the weary yellow bus light, eye sockets were blank and reaching hands seemed to be bone with no flesh, and mouths that yawned emitted screams that only other ghosts and phantoms could hear, like those whistles only dogs are attuned to. If you looked closely at the faces of the passengers, you could see evidence of diseases, leprosy perhaps. Or so it seemed to Gabe.

The driver listened to a scratchy portable radio that bass-thumped rock and roll on a golden oldie station. He had Elvis Presley sideburns so no wonder he didn't want to hear Heart or Prince or any of the singers Gabe liked.

Gabe got off a block from the TV store where he'd been this afternoon.

Five minutes later, he was in the alley behind the TV shop, using a burglary tool he'd fashioned himself in shop at school.

Seven minutes later, he opened the back door. The stench of burning solder was still in the air.

Moonlight through the front window created deep shadows.

He stood in the doorframe. He would not move inside yet. He had to defeat the photo cell system.

He located the transmitter and then the receiver. Both were hung at angles on opposite walls. A stupid thief would barge right in, walk straight through the invisible beam, and have the police nailing his ass to the wall inside of ten minutes.

Gabe, who was not really a thief let alone a stupid one, got down on his hands and knees and crawled under the angle of the invisible beam. Because the beam was so narrow, he didn't have to dog-walk far.

Then he stood up and walked without any sense of panic to the front of the store, plucked the small hand-held camera from its display shelf, and then got down on his hands and knees to crawl back under the beam once more.

Gabe was the only passenger. He sat far in the back. A fat woman with her hat at a cute angle drove the bus. He'd noticed that she'd had a small flower tattoo on the top of her right hand. As he was dropping his tokens in the coin, she'd given the camera a long, curious stare.

Now, as Gabe sat in the back of the bus, he felt the powerful bus engine throb beneath him. The whole floor vibrated with its power. The air smelled of diesel fuel. For some reason, it was a smell Gabe actually sort of liked.

The driver let him off on a busy street corner. Two apartment buildings shot straight up into the black night. At their front doors limos and Porsches dropped off people who appeared to be, in equal parts, elegant and impatient. They flung greetings to their respective black doormen—who were all got up in what looked to be light opera military costumes—and then they flung themselves inside the bright fortresses of their apartment buildings. You could see them waiting for an elevator in the brilliant interior light. They looked like beautiful creatures in display windows.

Gabe went in back of the first apartment building to an oak tree that sat next to the long row of dumpsters. On the June air, the smell of garbage was sweet and sour simultaneously.

Clutching his camera, Gabe shot up the tree with the skill of a gymnast. He went all the way to the top. By the time he reached the leafy branch that angled out over the alley, his face and arm pits were sticky with sweat.

He crawled out on the branch and sat there for a few minutes, letting his sweat dry in the breeze, and watching the fifth floor condo window directly across from him.

He had come here every night for the past three nights. To this tree. Out on this branch. Waiting for the night he'd have the camera and could get the videotape he needed.

They did the same thing every night. And in the same way. Gabe considered this kind of weird, actually. Why would a man have a mistress if sex was going to get just as predictable as it presumably was with his wife?

There they were now, in the window.

Same old stuff.

Sleek gray-haired guy stripped down to red bikini briefs, bit of a pot jiggling as he crossed the room.

Voluptuous—maybe too voluptuous—bottle blonde also stripped down to matching red bikini briefs, wonderful sumptuous breasts swaying slightly as she walked over to him.

All this seen through sheer curtains. The same kind of gauzy look skin magazines liked to use with their nude layouts.

Guy and woman come together with porno film urgency.

And here's where it always got kind of kinky.

In the middle of this desperate standing-up embrace in the bedroom, the woman puts her left leg up on the bed. She stretches her leg as far as it will go.

And then the guy slips into her.

Standing right up in the middle of the bedroom floor.

Neither one of them taking off their bikini briefs.

And both of them really starting to hump away, holding on to each other's buttocks as they grind into each other.

It never takes long, of course. Not at this rate.

The guy gets off in under three minutes every night. And then always does the same thing.

After he's done coming, he pulls his penis from her and holds it straight out like it's something that should be admired, the makings of a museum tour maybe.

And then she drops to her knees and does him.

God, she really goes at it.

She's so good she somehow gets him up again and then lets him come in her mouth.

When he's blasted away for the second time, he turns to face the big oval bed and then does this swan dive flat out across the waiting sheets.

She jumps up and straddles him and starts giving him this really long back rub.

Then there isn't much for the camera.

He's already slipped into her. They've humped each other remorselessly. He's come twice. She's gobbled the knob. And now she's giving him a back-rub.

Talk about anticlimactic.

Gabe shut off the camera and started down the tree. Getting down was always spookier than getting up. He had this fear of getting entangled and pitching over backwards. Broken back. Crippled for life. That kind of thing.

He got down with no problem.

The underground parking garage was next. Going down the tunnel leading to the garage, the temperature felt as if it had dropped ten degrees.

He smelled car oil and dead exhaust fumes and gasoline. All these odors coming from a variety of new cars that ran to Lincolns and BMWs.

He had no trouble finding the silver Mercedes sedan. He got a wide shot first, so you could easily identify the garage itself. Then he got a close-up of the car, including the personalized plate that read: SEXY. That was obviously how the guy saw himself. Sexy.

What a fucking ego, the cocksucker.

One last thing to do now. Go around to the front of the building and get a nice shot of the lobby area with the name of the building clear across the top of the frame.

When Gabe whipped out the camera from behind

his back, the doorman gave him this funny look and actually started lunging toward him. That's why Gabe had saved this for last. Because he knew he'd probably have to haul ass.

He got the shot he wanted and started running down the street, the doorman shouting after him.

Gabe caught the last bus of the night. After making its last stop, this bus would go to the city barns where it would be cleaned up and gassed up for the next day.

This time Gabe sat up front. This time the driver was a skinny woman instead of a fat one.

"Nice camera," she said. "I've got a granddaughter now so I'm savin' up for one of those. A lot less hassle than film."

"Yeah," Gabe said. "Yeah."

When he got off the bus, she said to him, "Don't do anything I wouldn't do." She smiled. "With the camera, I mean."

He didn't know exactly what to make of her remark, so he just said "Yeah" again.

Gabe finished up near midnight, the manilla envelope neatly addressed, the video tape tucked safely inside. He put three strips of tape around the envelope for extra safety.

He sat and stared at it.

God, was the guy in the silver Mercedes going to be pissed when his wife told him what she'd received in the mail. After Karen died from the cocaine she'd taken, all Gabe could think to do was find the guy who'd sold it to her. That's how he'd learned about Morrow, the cocksucker in the silver Mercedes. That's how Morrow could afford such a car. Preying on teenagers like Karen.

He tried not to think of how she'd looked there at the last, the eyes glazed, the spittle silver on her small pink mouth, her body jerking almost angrily. In terror, he'd called an ambulance but by the time it arrived, it was too late. Karen lay in his arms jerking and crying and clinging to him even though her eyes seemed not to recognize him at all. Then she was very still and he knew she was dead and then he could not cry at all. He was just cold and empty and the siren came loud and close and in the bedroom his mother began sobbing then. She did not quit sobbing for long days afterward.

Gabe's first thought had been to kill Morrow. But he knew he'd get caught. Somehow, someway, he'd screw up and get caught. And then what would happen to Mom? She had nobody except Gabe.

So Gabe started asking more questions about Morrow. What kind of guy was he? What did he do for kicks? And eventually he found out what a real shrew of a wife the guy had and the mistress Morrow kept in this condo.

Thanks to the videotape Gabe had taken tonight, the wife was about to find out about the mistress. All about the mistress.

He heard the whimpering, then.

The mewling sounds his mother made in her lonely, desperate sleep.

Gabe got up and went into her room and sat on the edge of the bed and held her hand tenderly and looked down on her sleeping.

He wiped away the sweat from her forehead.

He listened to her dark whispers in the dark room.
Karen. Karen. Karen.

It was true, he thought, and for some reason now he felt very lonely: she wasn't as much his mother any more as she was his daughter.

He kissed her on the forehead and went back to the living room.

He sat up till dawn drinking coffee and then he took the package to the mailbox.

RICHARD LAYMON *writes*
graphic, gut-wrenching
fiction that makes people
squirm with disgust and
giggle wildly—often at the
same time. His first novel,
The Cellar, *is a cult classic,*
and his most recent release,
Funland, *is a rollarcoaster*
of terror. Despite his
literary style, Laymon is
a friendly family man,
seemingly unaffected
by the attention heaped
upon his work. Look for
his forthcoming novels,
The Stake *(St. Martins)*
and Alarms *(Ziesing).*

SAVING GRACE
RICHARD LAYMON

At the top of the hill, Jim stopped his bike, planted a foot on the pavement and twisted around. Mike was far back, red-faced and huffing, fat bouncing as he pumped his way up the slope.

While he waited for his friend, Jim took off his shirt. He wiped his sweaty face with it, then stuffed it into the basket on the rack behind his seat.

"It's all downhill from here," he said.

Mike rolled to a halt beside him. He draped himself over the handlebars, gasping. "Shit on a stick," he muttered. Sweat dripped off his nose and chin. "Gonna have a heart attack."

"Beans. Nobody fifteen has a heart attack."

"Oh yeah?"

"Just think how neat it'll be at the lake."

"If we ever get there. You and your great ideas. I bet there won't even *be* any babes there."

"You'll see." Yesterday, when trying to talk Mike into a bike trip to Indian Lake, he'd told all about the girls who'd been there last Saturday when he picnicked on the shore with his family. "There were some real yucks," he'd said, "but some were fantastic. This one, she had on a white suit you could see right through. You could see *everything*. Everything! And some had on these bikinis you wouldn't believe. It was just incredible. We'll take our binoculars, you know?" Mike had listened, nodding, his lips pursed, and readily agreed to make the twelve mile trip.

"Man," Mike said, "if you're wrong . . . "

"Trust me. Your eyes are gonna fall out."

"They better."

"Let's get going." A shove at the pavement started Jim's bike rolling. He pedalled a few times, picking up speed. Then the road slanted downward through the dense forest. He coasted faster and faster, sighing as the summer air rushed against him. It was better than standing in front of a big fan, the way it blew his hair and buffeted his face and rubbed his arms and chest and belly and sides. It felt really wonderful against the heat of his armpits. It felt best where it slid up inside a leghole of his swimming trunks, cool on his hot groin.

With a glance back at Mike, he saw a car come over the crest of the hill. "Watch out behind you!" he called.

Mike looked around, then steered toward the edge of the road. The car swung out and crossed the center line a bit, giving him a wide berth. As it sped down, Jim eased his bike over. The car stayed far to the side. It shot past him, and quickly returned to its own lane before disappearing around a curve to the right.

"Did you see that babe?" Mike called.

Jim looked over his shoulder. "Huh?"

"The gal driving. Hope *she's* on her way to the lake."

"Hot stuff?"

"Didn't you . . . look out!"

Jim snapped his head forward. Just in time to see a black van straight in front of him. Parked. Its rear jutting into the road. He braked and swerved to the left. Missed it. But his bike was skidding sideways, tires sliding out, dropping him toward the pavement. He shot his foot down, swung his other leg clear and hopped a couple of times as the bike flew out from under him. From the feel of things, he knew that dismounting hadn't solved his problem. A twister suddenly seemed to grab him. It whirled him, whipped him down, tumbled him.

He lay there.

Mike came to a stop and grimaced down at him. "Are you okay?"

"Shit fuck damn hell."

"Should've watched where you were going."

Groaning, Jim sat up. The side of his left knee was filthy, scuffed and bloody. So was a patch of his left forearm, just below the elbow. He tried to brush some of the grit out of the wounds, and winced. I'll wash up when we get to the lake, he thought. He struggled to his feet and limped to his bike.

His shirt and towel were still in the basket. His lunch bag and binoculars had fallen out.

"Oh, man," he muttered, picking up the binoculars. He pulled them out of the case, glanced at the lenses.

"They okay?"

"Yeah, I guess so." He stuffed them back into the case. "Asshole. Why didn't he pull *all* the way off the road?"

"Well, there's a ditch."

"The bastard." He hobbled close to the van and kicked its side.

"Jeez! Don't! What if someone's in there?"

That hadn't occurred to Jim. With a grimace, he

hurried over to his bike. Mike was already starting off. "Hey, wait up." He jammed his binoculars and lunch back into the basket and lifted his bike by the handlebars. Giving the van a nervous glance, he planted a foot on the lower pedal, gave himself a push and swung up his other leg.

And heard a high-pitched shriek.

It seemed to come from somewhere nearby in the woods.

Mike stopped and looked back at him. "Jeez!"

Jim rolled past him, then steered to the roadside in front of the van and braced a foot against the pavement. He stared into the thick, shadowy woods.

Mike glided over and stopped. "It was a scream, wasn't it?"

"Sure was."

"A gal."

"Yeah. But I don't know."

"Don't know what?" Mike asked.

"You know girls. They scream all the time just for the fun of it. I mean, it doesn't mean she's in trouble, or anything. She might've just been messing around."

"Yeah, or she saw a spider."

They stopped talking and listened. Jim heard a soft breeze stirring the treetops, birds squawking and twittering, insects buzzing.

Then, *"Please!"*

"God," he muttered, "maybe she *is* in trouble."

Mike's eyes widened. "Maybe she's *screwing.*"

Jim felt his heartbeat quicken. "Yeah," he said. "I bet that's it." He dismounted and lowered the kick stand. "Let's check it out."

"Are you kidding?"

"No I'm not kidding. Besides, what if she *is* in trouble?" He plucked his binoculars out of the basket, removed them from the case, and slipped the strap over his head.

"Oh man, oh man," Mike muttered, propping up his bike. He took out his own binoculars.

Jim led the way, Mike close behind him as he made his way to the bottom of the shallow ditch and climbed its other side. He entered the shadows of the forest. He walked slowly, weaving around bushes and trees, setting his feet down as softly as possible, cringing at the quiet sounds of leaves and twigs crunching under his shoes.

Flies buzzed around the scrapes on his knee and arm. Mosquitos settled on him. He wished he were wearing more clothes. But this was neat, in a way. Exciting. Creeping through the woods like an Indian, nearly naked.

What if there really *is* a gal getting screwed?

It'd be like a dream coming true, getting to watch something like that.

As long as we don't get spotted.

What if the guy sees us and comes after us?

God, he'd kill us.

Jim stopped and looked around at Mike.

"What?" Mike whispered.

"Maybe we'd better not."

"Oh, man."

"I mean, what if we get caught?"

As if stabbed with pain, Mike bared his upper teeth. The expression pushed his cheeks so high that they seemed to squeeze his eyes shut. "We've gotta at least take a peek," he whispered. "This is our big chance."

Jim nodded. He knew Mike was right. They'd seen naked women in movies and skin magazines, but never in the flesh. If he should turn back now, he would want to kick himself later.

Probably won't see much, anyway, he thought as he turned away from Mike and began walking deeper into the forest.

Probably won't even be able to find her.

Less than a minute later, he glimpsed movement

beyond some trees far to the right. His heart gave a lurch. Halting, he pointed.

"Yeah," Mike whispered.

They made their way slowly in that direction. Jim couldn't see much. The trees were too close together, offering only glimpses of someone through the tiny spaces between their trunks. Soon, however, he began to hear a rustle of dead leaves and twigs. There were also a few muffled moans and squeals.

Crouching low, he crept up to a tree that he hoped might be near enough so he could get a good view. He squatted, one hand on its trunk. Mike came up behind him. He felt Mike's knees push against his back.

Hearing a soft intake of air, he realized that Mike was already looking.

Jim eased his face past the side of the trunk.

And gasped.

And felt his bowels shrivel.

The girl in the clearing ahead was naked, just as he'd hoped. She was slim and beautiful, probably no older than eighteen. Sunlight slanting down through the trees made her hair shine golden, her damp skin gleam. She was sweaty, dripping. She had a dusky tan except for where a skimpy bikini must've hidden her skin from the sun. Her breasts were creamy mounds. The darker flesh of her nipples jutted. Lowering his eyes, Jim gazed at sunlit hair so fine and meager that he could see right through it, see the soft edges of the split between her legs.

This was so much better than he'd ever hoped.

But so much worse.

Worse because the girl was suspended from a tree branch by a rope looped around her neck, because she was writhing and weeping, because her mouth was stuffed with cloth to stifle her noises and the man behind her was doing something that must be hurting her terribly.

As Jim watched, stunned and breathless, the man

stepped around to the front. He was not very old, maybe twenty. He was very handsome. He was grinning. He was naked except for his socks and sneakers. He had a huge boner. He had a hunting knife in one hand, pliers in the other.

He turned toward the girl. Crouching slightly, he put his face against one of her breasts. She jerked her head from side to side, a wild look in her eyes. She made whimpery noises through the gag. She tried to kick him, but lost her balance. The rope yanked at her neck. Her eyes bulged. She made choking sounds. Then she found her footing and shut her eyes.

The guy moved his face to her other breast. The one he'd left behind was no longer creamy. It had a reddish hue. Above the nipple was a curving row of dents—teeth marks.

When he sank to his knees, both her breasts looked that way.

His face pushed against her groin.

Though the girl twisted and squirmed and shook her head, she didn't try to kick him away. Nor did she reach for him. Obviously, her hands were bound behind her back.

He tilted his head back. Then he reached up with the pliers.

He shut their jaws on her right nipple.

As the girl let out a muffled shriek, Jim leaped up and ran, raced at the man, swinging his binoculars by their strap.

The guy looked over his shoulder.

Started to turn around.

But he was on his knees. Not quick enough.

The binoculars smashed against the side of his face. His head jumped as if he wanted another quick look at the girl's crotch. Her knee pumped up. Jim heard teeth crash together. He leaped out of the way. The man flopped backward and slammed the ground. His head struck with a quiet thump. He had landed with both knees up. Now, one slowly sank sideways. The other leg straightened out, his sneaker sliding in between the girl's bare feet. She stomped on his ankle and he let out a groggy groan.

He groaned again when Mike stomped on the wrist of his right hand. Bending over, Mike took the knife away. The pliers, Jim noticed, had already fallen from the other hand.

The man raised his head off the ground.

"Get him again," Mike gasped.

Jim twirled the binoculars by their strap. Faster and faster. Then he whipped his arm down and crashed the binoculars against the man's temple. The head jerked sideways, sweat and spit spraying.

He lay motionless.

"Out like a light," Mike said.

Jim and Mike both faced the girl. She had tears in her eyes. Her chest was heaving as she sucked air through her nose. Jim glanced at her rising, falling breasts. Saw their redness, the marks left by the bastard's teeth. Her right nipple was bright red and looked as if it were swelling up because of what the pliers had done.

He felt no desire. He felt only weak and shaky and nauseous.

"You'll be all right," he told the girl. Stepping over the man's legs, he pulled the cloth from her mouth. Red, lace panties, moist with her saliva. As he tossed aside the wadded garment, the girl gasped air through her mouth. "We'll get you down," he said.

Mike, using the assailant's knife, cut through the rope above her head.

She slumped forward. Jim caught her. He wrapped his arms around her and held her up. Her face rested against the side of his neck. He felt her slick, hot skin against his bare chest. The soft push of her breasts. And something warm running down the backs of his hands.

Mike stepped behind the girl. He winced. "God, the guy cut her."

Moments later, her arms went around Jim. She clung to him, gasping and sobbing. Mike raised the severed ropes for Jim to see, then tossed them down.

"You'll be all right," Jim whispered.

And realized that, in spite of his shock and revulsion, he was starting to get hard. The feel of the naked girl was just too much. Embarrassed, afraid she might notice his arousal, he eased her away.

"Maybe you'd better sit down."

She sniffed, nodded, wiped her eyes.

Holding onto her upper arms, Jim guided her sideways. He watched her head turn as she tried to look past him at the man.

"It's all right. He's out cold."

"He . . . he might wake up."

"Don't worry," Mike told her. "We'll take care of him."

She started to sag. Jim lowered her gently. When her knees met the ground, he released her. She hunched over and braced herself up with straight arms.

He saw her back.

It was slick with blood.

Mike stepped up beside her. He'd found a T-shirt. He wadded it and patted the bloody mess. When he lifted the rag, Jim saw a design carved into the girl's skin.

"My God," he murmured.

"A face," Mike whispered.

"It's a *skull*. It's a goddamn *skull*."

As he stared at the skull, its lines of blood thickened and began to trickle down the slopes of her back.

"We oughta kill the bastard," Mike said.

"I'll kill him," said the girl.

"Just take it easy. Mike, why don't you pull down that rope and tie him up? I'll take care of the girl."

Mike lowered the bloody cloth to her back, then hurried away. Jim gently mopped the cuts. Sidestepping, he rubbed the crimson mounds of her buttocks, then the backs of her legs. He returned to the skull, blotted it, and left the rag there. "I'll get your clothes."

She stayed on her hands and knees, her head drooping.

The man was still sprawled flat, motionless.

Mike, face to the tree, was busy working at the knot that bound the rope to its trunk.

The girl's clothes were scattered on the ground. Jim picked up the damp ball of her panties. Pulling them open, he found that their sides had been severed. The man must've cut them off her. He dropped them and spotted a red bra nearby. Sliced apart the way it was, it would be of no more use than her panties.

Her skirt and blouse were not far from the bra. Jim went to them. The short, denim skirt appeared to be all right. The plaid blouse was pretty much intact, though one sleeve hung loose from its shoulder and all its buttons were gone.

He glanced around, but couldn't find her shoes and socks.

The T-shirt used to clean her back, Jim realized, must belong to the man. A pair of jeans were neatly folded on top of a boulder near the edge of the clearing. No shirt. Just jeans.

"Want to help me tie him up?" Mike asked, dragging the rope down from the limb.

"Okay. Just a second." He returned to the girl. She raised her head and watched him approach. Crouching, he set down the skirt and blouse in front of her. "Here, you can put these on."

"Thanks."

"Your other stuff's wrecked."

She reached out a shaky hand and lifted the blouse. Then she pushed herself back and settled onto her haunches. She seemed much calmer now. She rubbed her face with the blouse.

"How are you feeling?"

"I guess I'll live. Thanks to you and your friend."

"Jim," he said. "I'm Jim. That's Mike over there." He nodded toward Mike, who had already managed to roll the man over. Knife clamped between his teeth, he was straddling the guy's rump and tying one of the hands.

"I'm Grace," the girl said. "I owe you two my life, I really do." She gave him a sweet, trembling smile. "Could you help me with this?" She held the blouse toward him.

He took it, and tried not to look at her breasts as he slid a sleeve up her outstretched arm. He remembered how they'd felt, pushing against his chest. He wondered how they would feel in his hands.

Don't even think about it, he warned himself. After what she's been through . . .

Embarrassed, he leaned forward and pulled the blouse across her back. He held it while she struggled to get her other arm in.

"Thanks."

"That's all right. I'd better go and help Mike."

She nodded.

Jim stood up and hurried over to his friend.

Now, both wrists were bound together behind the man's back. Knife in hand, Mike was climbing off.

"Looks like you've got him taken care of."

"Yeah. But what about his feet? We don't want him running off."

"I don't know."

"What are we gonna do with him?"

"I wonder if that was his van."

"Probably."

Jim turned around. Grace was on her feet, bent over and stepping into her skirt. She straightened, pulling it up her legs. Jim caught a last glimpse of her downy pubic hair before the denim ruined his view.

"That van by the road, is it his?"

"Yeah." Grace raised the zipper and fastened the button at her waist. Then she came toward them, walking a little stiffly, making no attempt to close her blouse. She halted in front of Mike. "I'm Grace," she said, and held out her hand.

"Nice to meet you. I'm Mike." He blushed fiercely as he shook her hand.

"You two saved my life."

Mike shrugged. "Glad we did."

"We're trying to figure out what to do with him," Jim said. "If that's his van, I guess we should try to get him into it. We could drive him into town and turn him over to the cops."

She stared down at the man, and said nothing.

"Or we could stay here with him," Mike suggested, "and she could go for the cops."

"I'll stay," Grace said. "You guys go for help."

"Are you kidding?" Mike blurted.

"Yeah, you don't want to do that. He's bound to wake up."

"I'll be okay. He's tied. Just leave me the knife."

"But we're on bikes," Mike pointed out. "It'd take us a long time to reach town."

"We could take the guy's van," Jim said, though he thought it was crazy to let Grace stay behind. "Maybe just one of us should go."

"Meaning me," Mike said, looking a little sour. "You're the one with the learner's permit."

"This is an emergency. The cops aren't gonna worry about whether you've got a driver's license."

"Why don't you just take your bikes?" Grace suggested. "I don't think anybody oughta use the van. When the cops come, they'll want to search it for evidence. It shouldn't be . . . you know, tampered with. I think he's had other girls in there besides just me."

"Really?" Mike sounded surprised.

"Yeah. There were some clothes in the back. And I

saw stains. I think he's one of those guys who goes around
. . . getting a lot of people."

"A serial killer?" Jim asked.

"Yeah, something like that."

"Geez," Mike said.

"How'd he get you?" Jim asked.

She pressed her lips together hard. She looked as if
she were struggling not to cry. After a few moments, she said,
"He just grabbed me." Her voice sounded way too high.
"I was going to my car." She sniffed. "He came up behind me
and . . . gave me a jab. With his knife? And he said, 'Come
with me. I wanta show you something.' And he made me go to
his van. And he pushed me in. He didn't even know me.
I never did anything to him."

Jim's throat had gone tight while he listened and
watched her painful struggle to communicate. Now, he reached
out and put a hand on her shoulder. She sniffed. She wiped
her nose.

"I've never been so . . . scared. And then . . . "
Her breath hitched. "The things he did to me."

The way she looked at Jim, the way she leaned
toward him, he knew she needed to be held. He took her into
his arms. The back of her blouse felt sodden and sticky.
She squeezed herself against him. He wished her blouse were
open wider so her breasts would be bare against him like
last time.

Mike was watching. Frowning. "Come on. We'd better
do something about this guy."

"Why don't you go for the cops?" Jim told him. "I'll
stay with Grace."

"Thanks but no thanks."

"You should both go," Grace said. "I'll be okay here."

"We can't leave you alone with him."

"Yes, you can." Easing out of his arms, she wiped
her eyes. "Go. I mean it."

He suddenly realized why she wanted them both to

leave. A thick weight seemed to sink inside his stomach. "You're gonna *do* something to him."

"No, I'm not. Just go. Please."

"So you can kill him." It made Jim hurt, talking to her this way. He wanted to hold her, to kiss her, not to stand here accusing her. "You'll kill him. Then you'll probably take his van and leave."

"Oh, man," Mike said. "You're right."

"You saw what he did to me. *Some* of what he did." Her face was red, twisted with agony, tears spilling down her cheeks. "He would've . . . My God, don't you think he deserves whatever he gets?"

"Yeah, but . . . you can't just murder him in cold blood."

"That's *just* what he was gonna do to me. Once he got done torturing me. And raping me. And I bet I'm not the first. I bet he's done it to a lot of girls."

"I don't know about killing him," Mike said.

"You guys don't have to watch. Just go. I'll wait till you're gone."

"We'd still *know*," Jim said.

"So would you," Mike told her. "Right now, you want to make him pay for what he did. But what about later? If you kill him, you'll have to live with it for the rest of your life."

"I'll always have to live with what he did to me," she said. She took a deep, shaky breath. "As long as he isn't dead, I'll be . . . afraid he might come after me again."

"He won't be able to," Jim said. "They'll never let a guy like him out of prison."

"Yeah, sure."

"What if they can't prove any murders on him?" Mike said. "He might get . . . I don't know, ten or twenty years for what he did with Grace. And they give time off for good behavior."

"That's right," Grace said. "He could get out in five or ten years, and then what'd happen? Even if he doesn't come after me, he might get someone else."

"She's got a point."

"And it'd be *our* fault." She was no longer crying. She seemed completely focused on changing Jim's mind. "If they let him out or he escapes or something and kills somebody, we'll be to blame. We've got a chance, right now, to get rid of him. Nobody will ever know but us. And he'll never, never be able to hurt anyone again."

"It'd be murder," Jim said.

"*I don't care!*" She suddenly lurched sideways, grabbed the knife from Mike, and threw herself at the tied, motionless man. His body shook as she dropped onto his rump. She raised the knife high.

"No!"

Even as the knife slashed down, Jim slammed her to the ground with a flying tackle. She rolled and squirmed under him. "Get off me!" she gasped. "Leave me alone!" He caught her wrists and pinned them down.

"Let go of the knife!"

"God, Jim," Mike blurted from behind.

"We can't *let* her!"

She stopped struggling. She stared up into Jim's eyes. "Let me do what I want," she said, "and you can have me. You both can."

"What?" Jim gasped.

"You want to. I know you do."

"Oh, my God," Mike said.

Breathless, Jim gazed down at her. He was sitting across her hips. Her blouse hung open, showing her breasts. He could feel her heat through his trunks and her denim skirt. He thought about how she was wearing no panties. He started to get hard.

"I mean it. I like you both. We can make love right here. Right now. If you'll let me keep the knife and . . . take care of him."

"Oh, man," Mike murmured.

"Kiss me, Jim. Kiss my breasts."

"Geez. Go for it."

He released her left hand—the one without the knife. Gently, he caressed her breast. He thought he had never touched anything so smooth, so wonderful. Grace moaned softly. "Am I hurting you?"

"No. No."

He fingered the crescent of dents made by the man's teeth.

And flinched with surprise as Grace's hand rubbed his penis through the trunks. No girl had ever touched him there before.

She's only doing this so I'll let her kill the guy.

So what? Let her.

It'll be the same as if I killed him with my own hands.

He's the price.

He's a monster, anyway.

Grace's hand slipped inside his trunks. Her fingers curled around him, glided slowly up and down. He shuddered. He felt as if he might explode.

"No!" he shouted. He grabbed her wrist, forced her hand away and pinned it to the ground. "We can't. We can't do this. It'd be wrong."

"Please," Grace said.

"No."

"Don't be an idiot," Mike said. "When'll we ever get another chance like this?"

"It doesn't matter! We can't just murder the guy. I don't care what he's done, we can't just murder him. We'll take him to the cops. This is something for the law, not for us. If we kill him, we wouldn't be any better than he is."

"Shit," Mike muttered.

Releasing Grace's left hand, he reached across her body and tried to take the knife from her right hand.

She held on tightly. "You don't know what you're doing," she said. "Please."

"I'm sorry." He pried Grace's fingers away from the handle. He picked up the knife, then scrambled off her and got to his feet.

Mike, frowning, shook his head. "Man, we could've . . . "

"It wouldn't have been any good."

"Oh, yeah, right. *Look* at her."

Grace lay on her back, braced up with her elbows, looking from Jim to Mike. Her blouse was wide open. Her skirt was rumpled high around her hips. Her knees were up, and spread apart. "Please," she said. "If we don't kill him . . . I don't know what I'll do. I'll always be afraid. I don't want to always be afraid. Why can't you understand that?"

"I do understand. I'm sorry. I really am. God, how I'd love to . . . but I'm not a murderer. I don't want you or Mike to be murderers, either."

"It'd be kind of like self-defense," Mike said. "You know?"

"He's *tied up*, for godsake. And out cold."

"We could untie him."

"Oh, that's a neat idea. Come on, let's get going. It'd be nice if we can get him to the cops before he wakes up."

"What're we gonna do, carry him?"

"Drag him, I don't know." Jim walked over to the man's folded jeans. He picked them up. As he searched the pockets, he watched Grace struggle to her feet. She straightened her skirt. She closed the front of her blouse and held it shut. She stared at him. She looked betrayed.

Jim found the car keys and a wallet.

Curious, he flipped open the wallet. The driver's license identified the man as Owen Philbert Shimley. "Shimley," Jim said.

The man on the ground moaned as if awakened by the sound of his name.

"Oh shit," Mike said.

"Maybe it's better this way," Jim said. "He can walk

under his own steam."

Mike, looking alarmed, snatched up the length of rope he'd cut away after binding Shimley's hands. He quickly made a slip knot in one end, dropped to his knees, and pulled the loop down over the man's head. A tug sent the knot skidding until it stopped against the back of his neck.

Jim let the jeans fall. He had no pockets, so he tucked the key case and wallet under the elastic waistband of his trunks. They seemed secure there. Knife clenched in his right hand, he hurried over to Mike.

Mike, standing behind the man's feet, held the rope taut.

"Get up, Shimley," Jim ordered.

Face pushing against the ground, he struggled to his knees. A tug at the rope yanked him backward, choking. Upright on his knees, he glared at Jim. Then at Grace. She hunched over and seemed to shrink as he looked at her.

Jim ducked, picked up his binoculars, and dropped their strap over his head. "On your feet," he said.

Shimley stood up.

"We're taking you in," Jim said. "Don't try any funny stuff, or you'll be sorry." Boy, did that sound trite and dumb.

But the man didn't make any remark about it. He nodded his head.

"Let's go."

"I want my pants."

"Fuck you," Mike said.

Shimley glanced around at him.

"Come on!"

Shimley started walking.

Grace stayed behind him, stayed with Mike.

She hates me, Jim thought.

But this is for the best. We're doing the right thing.

He walked backward, watching Shimley. The man really looked pitiful stumbling along with his head down, his shoulders slumped, his limp penis wagging.

Big, tough monster.

But not so tough now.

With a roar, Shimley charged. The rope clamped his neck like a choke collar. His head jerked. His face went scarlet. But he didn't stop coming.

"Shit!" Mike yelled. Either he'd lost hold of the rope or . . .

Jim thrust his knife straight forward at Shimley's chest.

The man lurched to a halt inches from its tip. He hunched over. He bared his teeth. He growled.

"Don't move!" Jim shouted in his face.

"Abracadabra, motherfucker." Shimley's arms came around from behind him. He dangled a knotted tangle of ropes in front of Jim's eyes.

Mike and Grace hit him at the same instant.

Mike slamming against Shimley's back.

Grace tackling him low.

They hit him hard, smashing him forward.

Jim's knife plunged into his chest.

Shimley crashed into him. As he went down backward, he knew he'd killed the man, after all.

Then his head struck something.

Jim awoke with a horrible, raging headache.

He sat up, and saw that his feet were bound together with rope.

Then he saw Mike's head. It was near enough to touch. It was upside down. A big red ball with teeth and open eyes. Some spinal column, jutting from ragged stump of neck, pointed at the sky.

Then he saw Grace. She had a rope around her neck. She was hanging from the limb of the tree. Her feet didn't quite touch the ground. Her tongue was sticking out. From just below her neck all the way down to her knees, she was raw and pulpy and strange. Skinless.

Shimley stepped out from behind the tree.

He was red all over. And grinning.

His left hand was pressed tight against his ribcage. His right hand held the bloody knife.

He walked toward Jim.

"Too bad you slept through the fun, asshole."

Jim lurched forward and started to vomit on his thighs.

He was still vomiting when Shimley kicked him in the forehead.

Dazed, he dropped backward and hit the ground.

"But you didn't miss *all* of it. Get a load of this."

Jim bucked as the knife punched deep into his belly.

WILLIAM RELLING JR. *is a part-time teacher, full-time St. Louis Cardinals fan, unsuccessful softball coach, and one of the funniest men I know. He's also a wonderful writer. His novels include* Brujo, New Moon, *and* Silent Moon. *If you haven't read Relling, pick up a copy of his short story collection,* The Infinite Man, *from Scream Press. Relling's short stories are often humorous, always successful. He enjoys a unique perspective on our world; a perspective which he shares with his readers through his work.*

THE PHANTOM OF THE FREEWAY

WILLIAM RELLING JR.

(A Cautionary Fable)

(I)

To paraphrase William Shakespeare: Some are born monsters, some achieve monstrousness, and some have monstrousness thrust upon them.

(II)

The Phantom of the Freeway wasn't born a monster. He was, for the first thirty-four years of his life, a man named John Colba. He lived in Los Angeles, California, in an area of the San Fernando Valley known as Reseda. He had a wife named Trudy and a daughter named Jessica, both of whom he loved dearly. The only thing remotely unusual about him was his job—which, if you think about it, wasn't all that unusual for someone who lived in Los Angeles, where so many movies and television shows are made.

John Colba piloted automobiles for a living; piloted them very fast and very skillfully. Consequently, he worked for many of the movie and television production companies in Hollywood as a stunt driver. He worked as often as he wished, because his reputation was such that his employers believed that behind the wheel of any vehicle, he was magic.

The key word here is *magic*.

(III)

This is how John Colba became a monster:

He, his wife, and his daughter were returning home one Thursday night from a baseball game at Dodger Stadium. They were traveling west on the Ventura Freeway and had just passed the interchange where the San Diego Freeway crosses the Ventura. As Los Angelenos know, that particular interchange is one of the busier trafficways on the entire planet, regardless of the time of day.

Whenever he drove in public, John Colba was especially careful, as professional drivers are. They're careful because they know that the majority of people who drive are poorly-trained amateurs. The most cautious amateur driver can still make an occasional mistake which, unfortunately, may prove fatal. The least cautious of them are dangerous assholes.

John Colba's skill was no protection from a man named Temple who was driving a yellow Mercedes 300 SEL. Already Temple had narrowly missed collisions with two other drivers as he abruptly slid in front of them in order to reach the exit ramp that dumped from the southbound San Diego Freeway onto the westbound Ventura. Had he been paying more attention to his driving—rather than paying attention to the young woman with whom he was having aural sex on his cellular telephone—he might not have snaked unthinkingly into the lane already occupied by the Colbas' Dodge Caravan.

Far too often bad things happen to human beings simply because of someone else's thoughtlessness or selfishness or stupidity. How much better would all of our lives be if we would think—for only a moment—before we act. The consequences of our behavior can be so devastating, even when the thoughtless, selfish, or stupid act is quite small. As small as cutting someone off on the road.

Because John Colba reacted reflexively: braking hard as he whipped the wheel of his mini-van to the right to avoid rear-ending Temple's Mercedes. Reacting by reflex— and remembering too late the dark, looming shape of the gasoline tanker truck that had been pacing the Caravan on the passenger's side for the last mile or so. While Temple drove on, unheeding and unawares.

(IV)

The collision caused an explosion that threw a massive fireball several hundred feet into the air. The flames—and the black mushroom of smoke that accompanied the flames— could be seen for miles.

Eleven people were killed at the scene: three passengers of an automobile that was behind the tanker truck; four more who were in an RV that was trailing the Colbas' Caravan; a motorcyclist who was heading east on the freeway and had been decapitated by a piece of flying metal debris; the driver of the tanker; and Trudy Colba and her daughter Jessica.

It took hours for the freeway to be cleared of wreckage and the bodies taken away, so that traffic could begin moving again. The concrete surface of the freeway above which the tanker truck had exploded was seared to the color of charcoal.

When at last rescuers were able to pull John Colba from the smoking ruin that had been his mini-van—when they were able to get close enough to withstand the awful, intense heat—they thought at first that he was dead. The skin of his entire body was so charred that he did not remotely resemble anything human.

But he was breathing. His heart was beating, and his eyes were open and alight with inconceivable agony. He should have been dead. But he was not.

(V)

The law enforcement officer in charge of investigating the accident was a detective-lieutenant named Kincaid, from the Van Nuys division of the Los Angeles Police Department. After leaving the scene of the accident, Lt. Kincaid drove to Sherman Oaks Community Hospital. John Colba had been rushed to the hospital's burn unit.

A doctor there appraised Kincaid of John Colba's condition. The man had suffered third-degree burns over 96% of his body. His epidermis was virtually gone.

"We human beings are nothing more than big sacks of guts and fluid and muscle and bone," the doctor told Lt. Kincaid. "Our skin is the sack that holds everything together. It also protects what's inside from infection. Rupture it, burn it away, and . . ."

"Is there any chance he'll live, Doctor?" Kincaid asked.

The doctor shook his head solemnly. "There isn't a snowball's chance in hell that Mr. Colba will survive the night," he replied.

(VI)

John Colba was placed in a special room near the

hospital's intensive care unit. The room was hermetically sealed and germ-free, as sterile an environment as the hospital could provide. He lay on a slab of stainless steel, his ravaged body wrapped in a cocoon made of a recently-invented, lightweight polymer of plastic designed to imitate the function of human skin. Tubes ran into his body, feeding him oxygen and water and blood, as well as nutrients and pain-killing drugs. Wires connected him to machines that measured his heartbeat and respiration and brain activity.

Lt. Kincaid observed John Colba through a viewing port mounted in the door to the room. Kincaid looked at the man on the slab and thought about how death would be a blessed release for John Colba. He thought about the man's dead wife and daughter. He also thought about the son of a bitch in the Mercedes who, witnesses said, had been the cause of the accident. But who would never be caught because no one had been able to see clearly his car's license plate number.

Without even knowing the driver of the Mercedes, Kincaid hated him. The detective wished that something, *anything*, could be done to fix the inconsiderate, irresponsible motherfuckers who did unspeakable things like this to innocent people like John Colba. He wished very, very hard.

(VII)

Shortly after 3:00 AM an alarm went off in the nurses' station of the intensive care unit. The alarm was connected to the monitors that were recording changes in John Colba's vital signs. The two nurses who were occupying the station at the time looked immediately at the video screen which provided them a view of John Colba's room. What they saw caused them to gape in surprise.

They dashed from the station to the room and ran inside, not bothering to change into sterile gowns. And they discovered that what the video monitor had told them was true.

The stainless steel bed was empty. The wires and tubes had been disconnected and thrown aside. John Colba was nowhere in the room.

A quickly-organized search of the hospital grounds turned up nothing. John Colba, a man who should not have been able to move, who should not have been *alive* much less been able to get up and walk away, had disappeared.

(VIII)

That same morning, an hour before dawn, two curious thefts occurred at a movie studio in Burbank. The first theft was of a costume: a kind of jumpsuit made of thin, supple, skin-tight, jet-black leather; a pair of boots; and a motorcycle helmet, also black, with a visor made of smoked plastic.

The second was of a car: a modified Ferrari 348, the same color as the missing costume. The car was being used in a sci-fi movie about road gangs that terrorized the highways of the future. Hence its unusual modifications.

At first, no one considered the two thefts related.

(IX)

Three nights later, the Phantom of the Freeway appeared on the roadways of Los Angeles County for the first time.

It was on a Sunday evening, a little after 10:00 PM, along a stretch of the Glendale Freeway just north of the suburb of Eagle Rock. Two teenaged boys from Tujunga were drag-racing each other in separate cars. They were heading south on the freeway, their contest having begun in La Canada near the juncture of the Glendale Freeway and Verdugo Boulevard. Though traffic at the time was light, neither of the teenagers was paying any mind to their fellow motorists. One of whom, an elderly woman from nearby Pasadena behind the wheel of a fifteen year old Ford Maverick, had been run off onto the shoulder of the road by the two speeding scofflaws.

Later, the little old lady from Pasadena testified to law enforcement authorities as to what happened after she had braked her car to a screeching halt, and the cloud of dust and gravel raised by her frantic stop had settled. What she saw was this:

A black-colored wraith that came swooping down from the overpass entrance ramp at Mountain Street. The wraith seemed to detach itself from the very fabric of night that surrounded it. As it reached the bottom of the entrance ramp and rolled onto the freeway, the wraith resolved itself into the shape of an automobile. Its headlights swung upward, opening like a pair of eyes.

Subsequently it was estimated that when the Phantom of the Freeway caught up with the two teenagers from Tujunga, the boys were traveling at a speed in excess of 95 miles per hour. But the Phantom's Ferrari moved up on them so quickly that they may as well have been standing still.

The Phantom had closed to within a thousand yards of the first boy's car, when there opened a small port covering the snout of a hidden laser-cannon mounted in the Ferrari's front end. A thin, scarlet beam of concentrated light speared from the laser-cannon, slicing into the back of the first boy's car. When the laser-light burst through the car's gasoline tank, the vehicle exploded.

An instant later, the Phantom of the Freeway blew up the second boy's car in a similar fashion. Then with a spurt of almost-unbelievable acceleration, the Ferrari shot away, melting into the night.

(X)

Within a fortnight, the Phantom of the Freeway had made two dozen reported appearances all over Los Angeles County. The sleek, black Ferrari had been sighted as far east as the Glendora Ridge Motorway, and as far west as Topanga Canyon Road near Malibu.

Though primarily the Phantom haunted the freeways: Foothill, Glendale, Golden State, Harbor, Hollywood, Long Beach, Marina, Pasadena, San Bernardino, San Diego, Santa Ana, Santa Monica, Ventura. He appeared as if from nowhere, wreaking his terrible retribution on the careless and the selfish and the inconsiderate. Then he vanished as suddenly and mysteriously as he had come into sight.

By then, of course, a public outcry had arisen for the Phantom's capture. It wasn't all that difficult for a task force made up of officers from the Los Angeles Police Department, the LA County Sheriff's Department, and the California Highway Patrol to deduce the true identity of the Phantom of the Freeway. They concluded early on that he was a man named John Colba. Who, tragically, seemed to have only one thing to live for. To be an Avenging Angel.

But the task force also learned early on that knowing who the Phantom was and knowing how to *catch* him were two different things.

(XI)

On the Thursday afternoon five weeks to the day after John Colba's wife and daughter were killed, Lt. Kincaid walked into the office of the CHP captain who was heading the Phantom of the Freeway task force. The captain's name was Hippler. His office was in the county courthouse building in downtown Los Angeles, the space having been donated by the Sheriff's Department. Lt. Kincaid was the ranking officer representing the LAPD on the task force, the chief liaison between his department and the other two law enforcement agencies involved.

Captain Hippler was sitting behind his desk as Kincaid walked in. The Captain motioned Kincaid to a seat on the other side of the desk, then said to the detective in a challenging tone of voice, "Well?"

Kincaid said, "I've got a plan. I've got an idea how we can get the Phantom to come to us."

Hippler sighed a sigh of weary skepticism. So far, the Phantom of the Freeway had been responsible for the deaths of thirty-one bad drivers on the streets and highways of Los Angeles County. Nothing that the task force had done to try and stop him had met with the remotest success. Pursuit cars, helicopters, stakeouts—all had been employed futilely. The Phantom was too fast, too elusive, too clever. He might— and did—strike anywhere within the 465 square mile area of Los Angeles. Even if Captain Hippler had the authority to borrow every officer from every other duty he or she might have, there wasn't enough manpower in the LAPD, the CHP, and the Sheriff's Department combined to keep watch over all the roads in L. A. County all of the time.

"All right," Hippler growled resignedly to Kincaid. "What the hell. Let's hear what you got."

Kincaid began to describe the trap that he had devised.

As he spoke, he noticed that the look of sour fatigue seemed gradually to fade from Captain Hippler's face. Kincaid could read the other man's expression as clearly as if he were reading a newspaper. Hippler was reacting visibly, showing his realization that Kincaid's plan—if correctly executed—would indeed work.

Kincaid concluded outlining his plan. He sat on the edge of his chair, waiting.

Hippler rubbed his chin thoughtfully. He locked his eyes onto Kincaid's. Then he leaned across the desk, extending the hand for Lt. Kincaid to shake. "How long will it take to get everything set up?" Hippler asked.

"I'll need twenty-four hours," answered Kincaid.

Hippler smiled grimly. "Then let's do it," he said. "Tomorrow night."

◊

(XII)

Twelve hours later, a little after 4:00 AM on Friday morning, Lt. Kincaid lay in his bed wide awake.

He lived alone in a sparsely-decorated studio apartment in Sherman Oaks. The apartment was a five-minute drive from the Van Nuys station where he worked. He lived alone because his wife had divorced him a few years before, and he had never remarried.

For all intents, Lt. Kincaid's job was his life. He believed firmly—some would have said rigidly—in doing what was right. He believed that anybody who broke the law was a criminal who must be arrested, tried, and sentenced to whatever punishment he or she might deserve.

Which was why he lay awake now.

A pair of thoughts nagged at Kincaid. The first had to do with something that Captain Hippler had said to him as he was on his way out of the office that afternoon. Almost in passing, Hippler had told Kincaid about a curious blip in the crime statistics for Los Angeles County during the past month. Hippler showed him a computer printout of the statistics. Kincaid read the printout.

What Hippler had wanted to bring to Kincaid's attention was this: Since the initial appearance of the Phantom of the Freeway a month before, it appeared that drivers in Los Angeles were behaving demonstrably better. In the past four weeks the number of citations for traffic violations across the board—compared to the number of violations recorded in the previous month—had dropped by one-third. There was a similar drop-off in the number of reported traffic accidents. Fewer people were speeding, cutting each other off, hitting each other, illegally changing lanes, failing to stop for pedestrians.

"Haven't you noticed it?" Hippler asked Kincaid. "Even on surface streets, nobody's gunning through yellow lights any more or triple-parking or any of that shit. It's funny, but doesn't it seem like everybody's being a lot more careful on the road? And a helluva lot more polite?"

Kincaid admitted that he hadn't noticed. Even though he had.

The reason why he'd told Hippler that he hadn't noticed was because of the second thought that nagged at him—and had been nagging at him for weeks. Each night for the past month as he lay in bed, Kincaid had recalled the moment when he'd stood at the door to John Colba's hospital room and wished hard that something could be done about the bastards who caused horrible things to happen to people like Colba and his family. The recollection nagged at him, because he realized that the Phantom of the Freeway was granting his wish. He had begun to wonder if he himself weren't responsible, somehow, for the Phantom's existence.

It wasn't until after sunrise that Kincaid was able to fall asleep. After convincing himself finally that the important thing was that the Phantom of the Freeway was a murderer who must be caught and punished. Everything else was irrelevant. What mattered, Kincaid told himself, was the Phantom's capture. Which was going to be happening in eighteen hours.

Kincaid slept poorly. He awoke at noon. He spent the rest of the day restlessly counting the hours until nightfall and trying not to think about John Colba at all.

(XIII)

The trap was set at midnight.

The bait was a purple 1975 Gremlin traveling south on the San Diego Freeway. The car had turned onto the San Diego from the eastbound Ventura—the same junction where, five weeks before, the Phantom of the Freeway had been born. Behind the wheel of the Gremlin was a disguised CHP trooper named Kajikawa.

Along the stretch between the Ventura Freeway and Mulholland Drive, Trooper Kajikawa did all that he could to attract the Phantom's attention. He disregarded the speed limit; he tailgated; he sideswiped; he switched lanes without signaling; he whipped in and out between the other vehicles that shared the freeway with him; he drove selfishly, heedlessly, without regard for anyone else on the road. As if he were in one great big fucking hurry to get nowhere fast.

And it worked.

As he crested the rise at Mulholland and began his descent into the Los Angeles basin, Kajikawa glanced into his rear-view mirror. He saw the Phantom's black Ferrari swooping down toward the freeway from the entrance ramp at Mulholland. Kajikawa reached for the microphone of the two-way radio beneath the Gremlin's dashboard. He switched on the microphone and said into it cooly, "He's coming after me."

On the receiving end of Kajikawa's radio transmission was Lt. Kincaid.

Kincaid was six-and-a-half miles away. He was positioned behind a barricade that blocked off the western end of the curving, eighth-of-a-mile long tunnel where the Santa Monica Freeway dumped onto the Pacific Coast Highway. Standing beside him was Captain Hippler. With them were two dozen law enforcement officers. All of the officers were heavily armed.

Kincaid hoisted the walkie-talkie he was holding and acknowledged Trooper Kajikawa's message. He nodded tersely to Captain Hippler. The captain turned to the group of officers that surrounded him and Kincaid and called to them to get ready.

Kincaid's walkie-talkie crackled again. Contacting him this time was an officer who was aboard an LAPD helicopter flying over the junction of the Santa Monica and San Diego Freeways. The officer reported that Kajikawa's Gremlin was behaving according to plan. The Gremlin had bolted onto the ramp that connected the southbound San Diego with the westbound Santa Monica. The Phantom's Ferrari was giving chase. And closing.

Kincaid switched the walkie-talkie in his hand to an open channel.

However, just as he was about to speak, he hesitated for a moment. A small frown of uncertainty creased his forehead and curled his lips downward.

Captain Hippler was still beside him. "Is something the matter?" Hippler asked with concern.

Kincaid looked to Hippler and shook his head. "Everything's fine," he said as he lifted the walkie-talkie and pressed the transmit switch. He took a deep breath. "Now," he commanded into the mouthpiece. His voice was chill and firm.

The trap was sprung.

Every ramp leading on to and off of the westbound Santa Monica Freeway from the junction of the San Diego Freeway to the tunnel had been blocked an hour earlier by police vehicles. As the Gremlin and the Ferrari sped toward the ocean, from behind them they were joined by nine squad cars—three each from the law enforcement agencies participating in the task force—that had been lying in wait just east of the San Diego overpass. Everything was going according to Kincaid's plan. Except for the Gremlin, the Ferrari, and the nine pursuit cars, the westbound Santa Monica Freeway was deserted of traffic.

It was five minutes past midnight.

Kincaid was listening to the helicopter officer's report of the chase. The other officers surrounding him were silent, so they could hear the walkie-talkie as well.

"The Gremlin's peeling off," said the radio over a hiss of static. "He's pulling to the shoulder of the freeway just before the Cloverfield exit. The Ferrari's still coming your way. I got him clocked at . . . one hundred ten MPH . . ."

From behind him, Kincaid heard the ratchet of a

shotgun being cocked.

"Coming up on 14th Street," the radio hissed. "Pursuit cars aren't gaining any ground . . . "

Kincaid frowned again. Because he suddenly had become aware of another voice. Inside him.

A voice that whispered: *This isn't right.*

Kincaid forced the voice to be still.

"Approaching the Lincoln exit," hissed the radio. "He's still accelerating . . . one *twenty* . . . "

All at once the men behind the barricade could hear the distant wail of approaching sirens. The wail grew steadily louder. But it could not drown out the soft voice that was still whispering in Lt. Kincaid's mind: *This is wrong.*

He should get away. He should be free.

"You say something?" Captain Hippler muttered to Kincaid.

Kincaid shook his head fiercely.

The radio crackled. "He coming up on the tunnel . . . Jesus Christ, *he's not slowing down* . . . "

It was then that the men behind the barricade could hear, above the wailing sirens, the roar of a mighty engine. The sound was echoing off the walls of the tunnel like rolling thunder. Growing louder. And louder still.

And then:

Captain Hippler shouted: "Everybody *move!*"

They scattered, scrambling away from the barricade. Kincaid leaped over the guardrail that separated the westbound and eastbound lanes. He fell to the pavement atop the walkie-talkie, smothering it beneath him, just as the radio voice was crying out, "He's in the tunnel! I've lost him! He's out of sight—"

And the unbidden voice inside of Kincaid whispered: *Please let him get away . . .*

The voice was drowned out by the banshee scream of an agonized machine pushing itself to its very limit. Coming from the tunnel. Coming.

And then, just like that, it was gone.

The motor-roar vanished.

It was replaced by a stillness so deep and encompassing as to be unreal. For a moment Kincaid thought that he had suddenly, inexplicably gone deaf.

Until he heard Captain Hippler's hushed voice from the darkness somewhere nearby. "What the fuck . . . ?"

Kincaid raised himself slowly. He stood, staring toward the mouth of the silent tunnel—as all of the men who had been behind the barricade were doing. They watched the tunnel expectantly. And they waited.

And waited.

And waited.

Until the walkie-talkie at Kincaid's feet hissed, "What the hell's going *on* down there?"

Kincaid bent over to pick up the walkie-talkie. He raised it to his lips. "Didn't he come back out your end?"

"Who?"

"The Phantom!"

"What the fuck are you talking about—?"

Kincaid switched off the walkie-talkie and dropped it to his side. He was still looking toward the tunnel. He told himself that he should have known better than to ask if the Phantom had turned around and gone out of the tunnel the way he'd come in. Because Kincaid already knew that the Phantom was gone.

(XIV)

They searched the tunnel for hours, checking every square inch. They found no secret exits, no hidden ramps. And no Phantom of the Freeway.

Kincaid stood fifty yards from the mouth of the tunnel watching the other men. Beside him stood Captain Hippler, who had left the searching party to join him. "What happened to him, Lieutenant?" Hippler whispered. His voice was hushed with disbelief. "Where the hell did he *go?*"

"I don't know," Kincaid said.

He thought that Hippler—and all of the other men who had been searching the tunnel—looked like children who were afraid of what-it-was that hid in the closet waiting to come out when the lights went down. Hippler was gazing at the tunnel with wide eyes.

Then he turned to Kincaid and asked hesitantly, "He's gone, isn't he, Lieutenant? That's what we wanted, right? If we couldn't catch him . . . ?"

Kincaid turned away from the captain to look toward the black maw of the tunnel once more. He didn't want Hippler to see his face. He didn't want the other man to read in his expression what he had decided was the right thing to do.

"I guess the Phantom's gone," Hippler said flatly but with little satisfaction. "For good, I hope."

Kincaid grunted.

"That *is* what we wanted, isn't it, Lieutenant?" said Hippler.

"Yeah," Kincaid lied. He was aware that he was concealing a small, dark look of triumph and expectation. "That's what we wanted all right. He's gone."

But he'll be back, Kincaid said to himself.

And he smiled.

ANDREW VACHSS *is known world-wide as an attorney specializing in matters concerning children and youth. His novels* Flood, Strega, Blue Belle, Hard Candy, *and* Blossom *are controversial, grim, and brutally honest. The following tale is actually two stories wrapped around each other—look close. Vachss comments: "Demystification of legend is a legitimate goal of horror writers: we had* Multiple Personality Disorder *(and its etiology: child abuse) before we knew what to call it, so we came up with* Werewolves.*"*

LYNCH LAW
ANDREW VACHSS

May, 1959

The predator slouched against the soft leather seat, eyes half-closed. Parked near the edge of a drive-in hamburger joint on a thick summer night, listening to the frightened voices swirl like fog around his open windows. The little weasels were whining about a story they thought only their pitiful little town knew. But the predator knew better—he heard the same story everywhere he traveled: some ancient black madman living in the swamp out past the abandoned factories and mill works; a monster with the strength of a dozen men, escaped from a chain gang years ago and never brought to justice. And he waited out there every night, living on human flesh. You don't give Fear a Christian name in the

Bible Belt, so they called him "The Nigger." Those who claimed to have seen him said he had a hideous scarred face and only one hand—the other stump ended in a hooked spike.

The Nigger only lived to make people die.

A stupid myth—the predator had used it before.

And this time, he couldn't miss. Last Saturday night, two of the town's bright little stars hadn't returned from their date. They found them the next morning on the edge of the swamp. Both heads hacked off—not cleanly. The boy's wallet had been torn open and his mouth stuffed with dollar bills. The girl's body was naked except for her underpants, but the investigators couldn't tell who took her that far.

The kids knew. Everybody had known about Rob and Sally for quite a while. Rob talked a lot because it was his first and Sally didn't care if he did because it wasn't. Or so people said.

The church people got hard around the eyes when they heard the stories. Punishment for sin was one thing, but God wouldn't pick a nigger to do his work.

Frightened wisps of talk floated past the predator's window:

"It was a tramp—some hobo who got thrown off the train. Probably camping out there when he saw them . . . "

"He didn't take the money."

"An escaped convict . . . run off from the prison farm."

"It was the Nigger . . . had to be the Nigger!"

"There *is* no goddamned Nigger out there."

"Lots of folks saw him."

"Yeah, well, whatever it is, I'm not going out there again without a gun."

"I suppose you'd go even with a gun, huh?"

"I might . . . "

The predator listened carefully. He was a good listener. Patient, doing his work. Teenagers gathered around his new Coupe de Ville, sat on the hood, lit their cigarettes with the lighter from his dashboard. The predator blended in easily—a professional stranger with soft ways about him. He was twenty-four years old—could look seventeen or thirty, depending on what he needed.

The predator added nothing to the conversation unless someone pushed him. His smile never got near his eyes.

That was his way—stand close, but apart. A wolf watching the campfire. He remembered one night in Chicago. A crap game behind a car wash where he'd been working to build up a stake after they let him out the last time. He faded the shooter all night long, never touching the dice. But finally they passed cubes to him, telling him he had to roll. He refused again. Politely. One of the men patiently explained to him that the odds were always a little bit against the shooter so it wasn't fair to hang back like he was. The predator listened to the explanation, no expression on his young face. He knew all about the odds. But he didn't touch the dice. They crowded in around him, telling him to roll or walk . . . and leave his winnings behind. With a frozen face and a crackling thunderstorm in his chest he grabbed the dice and threw eight straight passes. He walked away from the car wash with four hundred dollars of their rent money. Miserable slugs didn't know how lucky they'd been—if he'd had a gun instead of the straight-edged razor in his jacket pocket . . .

An old man who had been in the game caught up with the predator at the end of the alley.

"I hope you learned something, son," he said.

The predator looked at the old man. "I'm not your fucking son."

The old man knew it was the truth.

But this was way south of Chicago. And young people never knew the truth. He got Joanne's phone number from one of the grinning boys at the drive-in. He knew why they were smiling—any number they gave up so easily had to be a girl they hadn't gotten to. The kind he wanted.

Three nights later, they were coming back from the movies. Driving in the Cadillac an old woman had bought for him in Phoenix. There had been a newsreel about the lynching of Mack Charles Parker in nearby Mississippi. A mob had stormed the jail where Parker had been waiting trial for rape—his body had never been found. Joanne had been horrified. She kept saying, "It's not right—he didn't do it."

The predator knew she would have sacrificed the black bastard in a minute if he had. Knowing things—that's how you got on in this world. Patience. He drove out past the old factories, watching the quick pulse throb in her neck.

"Where're you going?"

"I thought we'd park the car and talk for a bit. I can't handle the drive-in and all those silly kids."

Joanne responded to the implied threat to her sophistication. "Anything's better than that," she agreed.

The predator parked near the edge of the swamp, fitting his car inside the sulfurous mist. He left the engine running—windows up, air conditioner on. Started his work in the dead-quiet night.

"I can't believe those punks were really serious about some nigger living out here and slicing people up . . . you can tell when a kid's never left home."

"Well," she said, "they really are pretty immature. I never go out with any of the boys around here any more, not since I got back from college . . . "

"Christ, you can't see a thing out there, huh?"

"This is the first time I've ever been out here. None of the town boys come out here now. You know, ever since . . . "

The predator lit a cigarette, watching her face over his cupped hands. "Doesn't bother *you*, right?"

The old factories shifting on their rotten foundations made a moaning sound that seemed to blossom from the ground around the car. A tiny red light appeared in the distance. The predator glanced at the glowing tip of his cigarette—just a reflection in the windshield. He smiled his smile.

Joanne shuddered in the chill of the air conditioner. "I know a much better place, out by the lake. It's really beautiful in the summer . . . "

"Ah, let's stay here. Besides, I thought you liked niggers, the way you were carrying on in the movies and all . . . "

The predator pumped the gas pedal, listening to the engine roar against the swamp-sounds. The Caddy rocked in its place, a frightened beast chained by the predator's foot.

"No," the girl said. "I don't want to stay here. I don't . . . please . . . "

"Come on, what's the big deal? Wouldn't you like to have some big black gorilla get hold of you? You might like it."

Joanne opened her mouth, trying for indignation, but nothing came out. The predator reached for her with his right hand, flicking away the hem of her full skirt, shoving his hand roughly between her legs. He grabbed the soft flesh of her inner thigh, pulling her around to face him, holding tight.

"It's getting pretty stuffy in here; I think I'll just open this window and . . . "

"No!"

"What's your problem?" he whispered, still holding her, "I've got this." The predator pulled a shiny little automatic from under the dash, holding it up so she could see it gleam in the darkness.

"Please . . . please. I want to go home . . . "

"I got something to do first," he told her, watching the dice bounce on the blanket and thinking "natural" in his mind. It was a word he liked.

Joanne's head whipped back and forth on her neck, no longer feeling the pain in her thigh. "No, no, no . . . no, please, take me home . . . I'm so afraid . . . god, please!"

The predator twisted his hand, making her see his face. The swamp-sounds tightened around the car, but the predator was calm within himself. The key was knowing when to move—picking your time. He made her look until she understood.

"Take me home and I'll do whatever you want," Joanne said, her voice quiet now.

"Sure. With Mommy and Daddy watching, huh? You must think I'm a fucking idiot."

"No! I think you're wonderful . . . so strong. My parents are up north on vacation . . . we'd be all alone. Please?"

The predator's teeth flashed. He had known all about the vacation before he'd called Joanne.

"I don't believe you," he said. "How do I know you wouldn't just run in the house and call the cops?"

"Oh, I wouldn't. I never would. Just take me home . . . to my house . . . and . . . "

"You do something for me first. Just so I'm sure."

"Wh . . . what?"

The predator took his left hand off the wheel. He stepped on the gas, hearing the engine scream as he unzipped his slacks. He backed off the engine, letting the car idle down. "Show me," he told her.

Joanne reached uncertainly toward him and his *slap!* was a whipcrack in the quiet night.

"Not with your hand."

"No! I can't . . . I never . . . "

The predator took his hand from her thigh and moved it to the back of her neck. He slowly forced her head down and held her against him, the pistol in his left hand tapping a steady rhythm against the driver's window. When he was sure she was going to do the right thing, he took his hand away from her neck and let it rest across the top of the seat.

When she finished he jerked her back by the short hair at the base of her neck.

She looked at the predator, her eyes milky, unreadable.

"Do you believe me now?"

He nodded, waiting.

"I love you," Joanne told him. "I swear I do. Take me home now. Please . . . hurry! We have to leave, honey . . . I will, oh . . . anything! Just take me home."

The predator stomped the gas, shoving the Caddy into gear—it fishtailed on the soft ground, clawing for a grip. The predator expertly flicked the wheel, guiding the big car out of the dying swamp. He released the girl, shoving her against the passenger door.

The predator drove straight to her house. He didn't need directions. When they pulled up, he pushed her out her side of the car, following close behind, never taking his hand off her.

An hour later the predator remembered he'd left his pistol in plain view inside the car, but the doors were locked, so he went back to what he was doing. He kept asking Joanne, "Isn't this better?" and she didn't know what he meant but knew enough to say "Yes" every time.

It was still dark when the predator left the house. He was going to the furnished room he'd rented and sleep until the next night. Then he'd finish with Joanne and move on, doing his work.

He walked around to the driver's door, keys in hand, like walking out of that alley in Chicago.

A heavy, hook-twisted steel spike was dangling from the door handle, swaying gently in the night breeze. Its thick base was crusted with flesh, torn off bloody at the root.

DAVID B. SILVA's *prose*
is silky smooth, his style
subtle and soft, but
the results are often
deafening. Best known
as the former editor of
The Horror Show,
Silva's novels include
Child of Darkness *and*
Come Thirteen, *and his*
short stories are considered
among the strongest in the
genre. Silva is writing
full-time these days—
a great reason to
stand up and cheer.

BLEED RED, BLEED WHITE

DAVID B. SILVA

"You make me sound like an old man," Joseph said. He had been pacing the hotel room, gazing out at the city lights against the black-curtained backdrop of the night. But now, with the phone in one hand and the receiver in the other, he sat on the edge of the bed, unhappy with the tone of his wife's voice. She was in an unusually sour mood tonight.

"You *are* an old man, Joseph Milano."

"Ah, baloney. You save that for your father, Evelyn. I'm not so old as you make me out to be."

"Older," she said stubbornly.

"What is it, Evelyn? Huh? The roses in the garden, they dropping their pedals or something? The aphids back? Is that how come you can't speak with a little civility tonight?"

There was an uneasy silence at the other end of the line. Joseph took in a deep breath, feeling tired and a little bit guilty. It had suddenly occurred to him where her sourness had come from. She was scared. Not for herself, but for him.

"Hey, you don't worry. Things . . . they have a way of working themselves out." That wasn't always true, he knew. Things didn't always work out, not for everyone. But there was no easy way of reassuring her that he would be returning tomorrow. Sometimes—though never in his own experience, thank the Blessed Mary—a hit could turn horribly ugly. You never knew how things were going to play out. All you could do was trust the aces would end up in the hand you were holding, because bluffing in this business was its own form of suicide.

"I'll be home by dinner," he said evenly. "You'll see."

"What time's your flight coming in?"

"Uh, I'm not sure. Hold on a second, let me check." He returned the phone to the nightstand and draped the receiver over his shoulder, freeing both hands. The airline tickets were in his jacket, the left inside pocket. He dug them out, along with his reading glasses. "Looks like a one o'clock flight out. I should be landing some time around four and be home by five. That won't be so bad, now will it, Evelyn?"

"You'll be careful tomorrow, won't you?"

"I'll be careful."

"Promise me?"

"I give you my word," he said, rubbing the weariness from his eyes. "Nothing stupid will happen. I won't let it."

She was silent once again, and this time he waited patiently until she was ready to speak. "How about the bleeding?" she asked cautiously. "Has it started yet?"

Of course that was it, he realized. The thing that had been on her mind all along. He glanced down at the white shirt he was wearing. It was a new shirt. She had bought it for him on sale at Mervyn's over the weekend, and since it hadn't been ironed, the creases from where it had been folded were still quite unmistakable. There was no blood yet.

"No," he said. "Not yet."

"Maybe this time you'll be spared, you suppose?"

"Maybe," he said, though it lacked conviction. He stared a moment longer at the area above and to the inside of his left shirt pocket, half-expecting to see the first bright-red pattern of a blood stain as it took shape. He had seen such a pattern before—in fact, many times before—and he expected to see it again tonight. But no, it hadn't started yet, and for that he had mixed feelings. In its own perverse way, it was reassuring to know exactly where tomorrow's bullets would be striking their target.

"I love you, Joe."

"I'll call you from the airport when I get in."

After he hung up, he sat on the edge of the bed, lost in thought. Late last night as he had been packing, he had promised her this would be the last time. It was a promise he had made to her before, and never kept. This time, however, he honestly believed tomorrow was going to be his last two-step with the devil. When you get a feeling in your gut like that, you trust it. And that had been his feeling. He had already two-stepped with the devil a little longer than he should have, and he knew sooner or later this business of murder would turn on him if he didn't get out of it.

So this one is it, huh, Joe? Then you take that sweet missus of yours on a long trip around the world and retire somewhere in Florida where the sun shines all year round and the life is a good life?

That was it exactly.

He had pulled the file folder out of his briefcase before calling Evelyn and now he spread its contents across the bed, where he could study them one last time. There was a photograph of the target, a woman by the name of Marian Dolores Salerno. Thirty-eight years old, a *spallone* who had been skimming off the top from the Ruggiero Family. There was an old Sicilian proverb that went like this: He who has money and friends, has justice by the ass. In the case of Miss Salerno, she had just lost her friends, and tomorrow morning her justice was going to belong to someone else.

Porca miseria.

He tossed the photograph aside, and wandered into the bathroom to wash up. The early flight out of San Francisco had been delayed twice and even though he had arrived in town ahead of schedule, it had been a long day.

A business envelope had been waiting for him at the front desk of the hotel when he checked it. It contained a key, and a note typed on an old cloth ribbon typewriter with a clogged "o." The note read:

The Greyhounds are running.
Bet on Street Wise, Number Two in the Third Race.

After he had had a chance to settle into his room, he took a walk down Sutter Avenue and eventually ended up at the Greyhound Depot on 23rd Street. The key, which he had placed back in the envelope, belonged to a baggage locker standing in a dark corner of the building. He had found the file folder inside the locker, along with some background information and Miss Salerno's itinerary for the following day. Paperclipped to the file folder, he had found another note, this one written in longhand. It had read:

Happy Birthday 2 U. Have one on me.
A free round at Jamie's Downtown.

Jamie's was the name of a coffee shop at the corner of 23rd and Downtown. He had eaten there once before, six or seven years ago, when he had been in town on a similar job, and he remembered the food as being heavy. The spaghetti had left him with an uncomfortable, bloated feeling that had stayed with him overnight and most of the next day. This time, however—even though he was hungry—he sat at a table near the back of the place and ordered a cup of coffee to keep him going and that was all.

By the time the coffee arrived, he had removed a 9 X 12 manila envelope from the underside of the table. It had been held there by two strips of masking tape, one of which had broken free and was sagging badly. So it had been a good thing he hadn't arrived late. The envelope contained a map of the city with Miss Salerno's route highlighted in yellow, and a set of specific instructions. He looked them over while finishing his coffee, left a dollar on the table, and stepped out onto the street again.

It had been nearly four o'clock by then. Several minutes earlier, the sun had sunk below the peak of surrounding skyscrapers and the downtown area had become a checkerboard of shadows, evenly divided by the pattern of streets and avenues running east and west. He walked along 23rd Street, over to Independence Avenue and from there to Powell Street. It was near the corner of Independence and Powell where Marian Dolores Salerno would be taking her final bows tomorrow. There would be no encores.

A Rexall Drug sat on the southeast corner of the intersection, next to a vacant business building with its windows painted over. Across the street, on the northeast corner, a Woolworth's shared a shaft of afternoon sunlight with a used bookstore called the Book Place, and next to that, Himmel's Jewelry, which was where Miss Salerno was expected to arrive the following morning.

Joseph leaned against the corner of the Rexall Drug, watching the flow of people move through the intersection, buried in their own private thoughts, places to go, people to see, completely insensitive to the fact that someone would be dying here soon. In a city this size, it was easy not to think of such things, he supposed. They happened all too often, all too near. No, there were more important things to think about. After all, life did go on.

He watched the traffic pattern, made note that no cops had come by during the fifteen minutes he stood there, and finally—satisfied that he had seen all he needed to see—he left for one final stop before heading back to the hotel.

His last stop had been at a place called the Mail Box,

where he picked up a package he had mailed to himself a week earlier. The package was under the name of Wilford Haddleton, and inside, there was a gun that had been stolen from a police evidence locker. It was a Coonan .357 Magnum Model B: compact, solid, flat, smooth walnut stock, seven-shot magazine, accurate and reliable. He had used one before, and it had been the most accurate and comfortable handgun he had ever handled.

A craftsman is only as good as his tools.

No better, no worse, Joseph thought.

He had splashed water over his face, and now he found himself looking through his splayed fingers at his reflection in the bathroom mirror. Evelyn had been truthful when she had said he was an old man. It was hard to face up to it, but yes, time had somehow caught up with him. The mirror didn't lie about such things, did it? His eyes, which were slate-gray, had always been displeasingly cold, but recently he had begun to notice a cloudy film around the edges of his sight, and it had become apparent that even the fact he had never needed glasses was now meaningless.

Okay, so you're an old man, Joey. So who gives a damn, huh? No one stays young forever. No one.

He used a washcloth from the rack hanging on the wall at the end of the counter to dry his face. It wasn't being old that bothered him. Old happened. There was nothing you could do about it, only watch in the mirror as it stole bits and pieces of the way you remembered yourself. No, the bother that had been shadowing him all day had come from some-where else.

He straightened up—feeling a muscle in his lower back strain slightly, then loosen—and realized the bleeding had finally begun. A small circular indentation, the size of a dime, had appeared in the center of his forehead. He watched several drops of blood collect at the bottom of the impres-sion, then trickle thinly down his forehead and over the ridge of his nose.

He had bled the first time, nearly twenty-five years ago. It had been the night before a hit on an enforcer for the Cantalano Family. He remembered how uneasy he had felt, how he hadn't been able to watch the episode of *The Fugitive* on television because he couldn't concentrate. Something inside him that night had felt as if it were about to explode. In a way, he supposed, that was exactly what happened. Something had exploded and blood had started pouring out from an invisible hole in his midsection. The sight alone was enough to stagger him, and though he had wiped the blood away time and time again, it hadn't stopped.

He had bled all that night, and all the next day until the moment he stepped up on the sidewalk and fired three shots into the midsection of his target. The man was blown backwards through a window display, and landed in a pool of glass fragments and blood. And Joseph's bleeding had abruptly ended.

Evelyn had called it a stigmata back then. Maybe that explained it. Not in religious terms, certainly. But perhaps in other terms. Perhaps by the very nature of what he did for his living.

It hadn't happened again until the night before his next hit, and even now, as he was standing before the bathroom mirror, Joseph realized he had never been completely comfortable with a hit until the bleeding had started.

He stared at the blood trickling down his forehead, and knew now precisely where the first shot would strike tomorrow. It would be a quick death, he realized. Nearly instantaneous, and quite likely painless. The second shot, he gathered as he watched a blood stain begin to form on his shirt, would strike Salerno in the left side of her chest, just above the heart. And that would be all the insurance he would need.

He ran the washcloth under the faucet, and wiped away the first trickle of blood. There were Band-Aids in his travel case, under his razor. He had searched out a large round one which covered the indentation in his forehead, and had just dropped the wrapper into the waste basket when someone knocked at the door of his hotel room.

"What?"

"Room Service. You ordered dinner, sir."

"Hold on." He applied the last Band-Aid strip and buttoned up his shirt. It was a small blood stain—he had caught it in time—but it was still noticeable. On the way to the door, he stopped at the bed and slipped on his jacket. He wouldn't bleed dangerously over night, but he would bleed enough to put a scare into someone who wasn't used to it.

The next morning, he woke up in time to watch the sun rise. It rose over a line of faraway buildings instead of a distant horizon of mountains as he would have preferred. Still, it was quite beautiful, the soft blue and orange colors. He watched it from his bed until the full circle of the sun had finally broken free of the skyline, then he climbed out from beneath the covers and headed for the bathroom.

He had slept fitfully during the night, as fitfully as he had ever slept in a strange hotel room. Of course he was never completely comfortable at night unless Evelyn was sleeping next to him. Her body was often cool, and sometimes in the morning she would make mumbling noises that could almost make him forget the ugly side of his life. *This* morning, however, was strictly business. Besides, the bleeding had continued throughout the night and Evelyn would have been troubled by the sight of all that blood if she had been here with him. It had left stains on the pillowcase and both the bedsheets, top and bottom.

When he had climbed out of bed, he had stared back at the pillow, and for one shuttering second he thought he had seen the face of Christ in the blood. He had been aware, even then, that another person might have seen a much different face or perhaps no face at all. After all, you see what you want to see, he supposed. Still, at that moment, there was no question in his mind that it had, in fact, been the face of Christ. If Evelyn had been here, she would have seen the same face. Then, in all likelihood, she would have tried to convince him to change his mind about the hit, and that—as maybe only he understood—would have been the death of him.

So okay, he told himself. It was best she wasn't here this morning.

In the bathroom, he moistened the washcloth under the faucet and wiped the dried blood from both wounds. The bandages had fallen off during the night and were now most likely buried somewhere at the bottom of the bed beneath the rumple of sheets and blankets.

The shot to his forehead was perhaps as clean and perfect a shot as he had ever seen. Miss Salerno should be thankful for that. Her death was going to be quick, and for the most part, painless. He covered the wound with another circular Band-Aid. For the wound in his chest, he used a gauze pad and several strips of white medical tape. That would be enough to absorb the blood until the hit, and then it wouldn't matter anymore.

The bleeding will have stopped by then, he thought. *Once and for all.*

By the time he closed the door to his hotel room and started down the corridor to the elevators it was approaching nine o'clock. He had changed his suit to a navy tweed, and carried a briefcase in one hand, a duffel bag in the other. His white shirt from the previous night, and the stained bed linens were rolled up inside the bag. Something would have to be done with them somewhere along this morning's route.

In the back of his mind, he had decided to dispose of them in the dumpster in the alley behind Jamie's. However, to his convenience, a maid had left a laundry cart in the corridor, unattended. He stopped long enough to empty the bag of its bloodstained linens, then moved merrily on to the elevator, where he left behind the empty duffel bag as he exited.

It had been nearly five years since he had last been in this particular city. The downtown section had changed little from the way he remembered it, and yesterday's walk had been all he needed to reacquaint him with the layout. He walked along Sutter Avenue, looking every bit the successful executive, perhaps a few minutes late for a morning meeting. The air was humid, unlike the previous day, and he could feel his shirt sticking to the small of his back, where the Coonan .357 was holstered.

The clock on the Bank of America Building read nine-thirty by the time he arrived at the Rexall. He had stopped at a corner newsstand and picked up a newspaper on the way. Now, as he placed the briefcase on the sidewalk beside him and leaned back against the building, he pulled out the paper and scanned the headlines.

He had never been as patient a man as he should have been. The waiting—even when it was for only a short time as was the case here—gave him too much time to think, and thinking made for mistakes. He had once read a story called "The Small Assassin" and remembered reading months later that its author, a man by the name of Bradbury, had a sign above his desk that said: DON'T THINK. DON'T TRY. JUST DO. Joseph liked the idea behind the sign even more than he had liked the story (which hadn't been about assassination at all, at least not the way he had always thought of assassination.)

Don't think about it, he reminded himself now. *When the time comes, just do it.*

The pedestrian traffic had begun to thin. Most of the downtown workers were finally pulling their chairs up to their desks, he supposed. He watched a young mother and her child cross Powell and hurry along the sidewalk in the direction of Independence. Then he turned his attention back to the Woolworth's across the street, and watched as a Yellow Cab pulled up to the curb.

Time to earn your keep, Joey.

Remember, just do it.

Marian Dolores Salerno, a long-legged woman—wearing a khaki blazer over a white, mandarin-collared blouse and ice blue pants—stepped out of the cab and onto the sidewalk. She looked briefly in his direction, not noticing him, then leaned in through the passenger-side window to pay the cabbie.

Joseph folded the paper and dropped it absently to the sidewalk next to his briefcase. *One hit to the head,* he told himself calmly. *And one to the chest, maybe a quarter of an inch to the left of the heart.* He felt something damp against his forehead, and realized blood had started to seep from beneath the Band-Aid. There was nothing to do about that now. It wouldn't be bleeding much longer anyway.

In his mind's eye, he had already played through this scene a number of times. He would get to within five feet of her before she would turn and look at him. There would be a moment of recognition—her face would twist into a crossed expression of surprise and horror. He would only need the two shots. They would do the job quite nicely. Then there would be some screams from passers-by, and a moment of confusion, and he would calmly disappear down the street before anyone was sure of exactly what had taken place.

He had played it out this way in his mind, but that was not the way it happened.

Marian Dolores Salerno *did* turn and look at him, and there *was* a moment of recognition when her face twisted into a crossed expression of both surprise and horror. But all that happened much too early. Joseph was still in the middle of the intersection, some forty feet away, when she looked up and saw him and immediately began to back away from the cab. In that instant, she had realized who he was and what he was there to do, and she wasn't going to make it easy for him.

Joseph froze for the beat of a second, exposed and—

not unlike Miss Salerno herself—a little surprised. He had placed himself in a position of do or die, he supposed. His right hand swept instinctively under the tail of his suit jacket and brought the Coonan out from under cover.

He would have gone into an immediate crouch, but a man in a business suit crossed between the two of them, and he had to back off while another precious second was lost.

Too long, he told himself. *This is taking much too long.*

By the time he was able to set and fire his first shot, it was not the shot he would have preferred. He pulled it to the right, where it ricocheted off the roof of the Yellow Cab and sailed off down the street, eventually burrowing into the brick fascia of an old movie house.

His second shot fared better, though not much better. He took aim and squeezed the trigger as Salerno had turned to run. The slug slammed into the back of her right arm, high, near the shoulder blade. She flinched and her arm went visibly limp. But she managed to keep moving somehow.

He had taken aim for a third shot before suddenly realizing it wasn't going to happen. Salerno was safely under the cover of the jewelry store now, and a man in a nearby blue Buick had begun to hit his horn.

Joseph lowered the gun. The intersection was perfectly still for a moment, and then heads began appearing from behind parked cars and newspaper stands and out of business doorways. He tucked the Coonan back into its holster, where it was out of sight. The blood had been pounding in his temples, and even now he realized he was going to have a whopper of a headache when this was over.

He glanced at the driver of the blue Buick. The man took his hand off the horn, and ducked down across the car seat, safely out of sight.

That's good, Joseph thought. *You stay right there. It'll be safer for you. In fact, it'll be safer for both of us.*

He crossed Powell Street, trying not to appear

hurried, though that was exactly the case. Behind him, he heard a child crying and the soft murmur of a gathering crowd. He glanced briefly over his shoulder, and realized Salerno was emerging from the doorway of the jewelry store. Hit, yes. Bleeding, yes. But not seriously hurt. That was something he would have to deal with some other time.

And there was something else he would have to deal with.

He didn't fully realize it until nearly fifteen minutes later, after he had waved down a cab at Forty-Second and Montgomery. But the bleeding . . . his *own* bleeding . . . it hadn't stopped. A bright crimson pattern had spread across the front of his shirt, like one of those tie-dye jobs from the sixties, and even as he was staring at it, the pattern was continuing to spread.

It was supposed to have stopped by now. But it hadn't. And he wondered bleakly if he was going to bleed to death in the back seat of the cab on the way to the airport. Now that would be irony, wouldn't it?

The flight home arrived on time, surprisingly enough.

He hadn't bled to death as he had feared he might. But he had stopped at the airport gift shop to pick up additional Band-Aids and gauze and tape. Three times already, he had had to change the bandages. The wound in his chest seemed to be bleeding the worst, though they were both bleeding more than he had ever imagined possible.

Outside the airport restroom where he had changed his bandages the third time, there was a bank of pay phones, six altogether. Only one was available, near the middle of the crowd, and he stepped into it to call his wife as he had promised he would.

Ever since the failed hit, he had been riding an emotional rollercoaster of sorts. The old adrenalin had kicked in almost immediately and had pumped through his veins for five or ten minutes afterwards, leaving him jittery and restless. It was around the time he had flagged down the cab, though, that something a bit like a shot of novocaine had swept through his system and left him both numb and slightly disoriented. The dull sensation had remained with him through-out his flight, but now—as he was waiting for Evelyn to pick up the phone—it was beginning to wear off and he was thinking clearly again.

He had missed the hit.

For the first time in his life, he had missed the hit.

The phone rang again at the other end, and finally she picked it up.

"Evelyn?"

"Joe, you're at the airport already?"

"Yes," he said, looking down at his jacket, which he hadn't meant to leave open. The crimson stain had stopped expanding some time ago. Still it covered the front of his shirt from the left pocket down to near his belt line. With his free hand, he buttoned the jacket again. "I'll catch a cab and be there in about forty-five minutes."

"Are you all right?" she asked. "You sound . . . rushed."

He stared at his reflection in the chromed faceplate of the phone, seeing a man he very nearly didn't recognize. "No, I'm fine. The flight was a little hectic is all."

"It's over then?"

He closed his eyes. *No, I don't think so,* he thought. *I missed the hit, dear, and now I'm bleeding like a* porca. The hand holding the receiver was trembling slightly, and he found it necessary to add his other hand to steady it.

"As over as it will ever be," he said evenly.

"I love you, Joe."

He loved her, too. Though he couldn't always say so.

"I'll be home in a few minutes. We can talk about seeing the world from one of those cruise ships. That sound nice to you?"

"It sounds wonderful."

"Then that's what we'll do," he said softly.

After he hung up, he checked the bandages and was pleased to find them doing the job. It was cooler in this part of the country, and maybe that was helping. Or maybe . . . maybe the bleeding was finally starting to slow.

Wouldn't that be a blessing? he thought; and he went off to find a cab.

It would have been a blessing if it had been true, but it wasn't. By the time the cab had dropped him off in front of his house, he could feel the blood seeping out from beneath the bandages on his chest. Evelyn was going to be shocked when she saw him. There was no getting around that.

He opened the front door and was struck immediately by the smell of something baking in the oven. Lasagna, he guessed. He could smell the Italian sausage, the sweet aroma of basil, even the mozzarella.

"Evelyn?"

The first thing he was going to do was change out of his bloodstained shirt, take a long shower, and wash the blood away. On the way home from the airport, he had decided the bleeding probably hadn't stopped because he had missed his mark this morning. And it probably wasn't going to stop until he corrected that little problem. Somehow, in the course of the next couple of days, he was going to have to find a way of finishing the Salerno job. Otherwise, as crazy as it sounded, he might actually find himself bleeding to death.

"Evelyn?"

He checked in the kitchen, found there was indeed lasagna in the oven—less than five minutes away from being ready, according to the timer—then moved through the dining room into the living room and returned again to the foot of the stairs at the entry.

"Lasagna, Evelyn. How in the world did the good Lord ever find it in His heart to bless me with such a thoughtful woman, huh?"

He had started up the stairs to the second floor, thinking how nice it was going to be to get a shower and sit down to a warm dinner. For the moment at least, he was happy to put aside this morning's screw-up. He wouldn't be able to keep it there for long, he knew, but maybe long enough to fill his belly and clear his head. That was all the time he would need, he hoped. Maybe then the situation wouldn't look as bleak as he now feared it did.

Maybe.

"Hello, Joe."

The voice, which was a man's voice, came from the landing at the top of the stairs. Joseph looked up in time to see the man step smoothly out of the shadows. There was a gun in his hand. A .38, Joseph thought, though he couldn't be sure.

"Who the hell are you?" he asked. "What are you doing in my home?"

"You know why I'm here, Joe."

Christ, yes, he supposed he did. He felt a chill creep up his spine. "I'll fix the Salerno thing. There's no need to worry about it."

"No one's worried. It's already been taken care of."

"It was *my* hit."

"You're an old man, Joe. You didn't come through and now you're not needed anymore."

"I would have handled it."

"Like a true *combinato*, yeah?"

"Yes," Joseph said.

"A man of honor does what he's asked to do."

"You don't tell *me* that. I *know* that. I was living it when your mama was still cleaning the crap out of your—"

He had taken another step up, knowing that no matter what he did his life was very nearly over now. It had crossed his mind to ask about Evelyn, but it had also crossed his mind that he didn't want to hear the answer. This was a dirty business to which he had given his life. It was a little late now for wanting to wash his hands of it.

"Sorry, Joe."

A drop of blood trickled free from beneath the Band-Aid on his forehead and ran down across the bridge of his nose. He reached up to wipe it away, but the first shot went off before his hand could get there. He saw a flash from the barrel of the gun, but never heard the sound. The bullet struck a perfect bulls-eye in the heart of the Band-Aid he had affixed at the airport. Then a second shot, fired before his head had had a chance to pitch backwards, hit him squarely in the chest, just to the left and a little above his shirt pocket.

He tumbled backwards down the stairs.

At the bottom, he lay on his back against the cool tile, arms splayed, legs crossed. It was a curious sight. Not because of the way he had landed, which had been awkward and a little unnatural, but because both shots had been clean and effective, and yet neither wound was bleeding.

RAMSEY CAMPBELL *is one of the field's most polished stylists. A winner of both the British and World Fantasy Awards, Campbell sold his first short story to August Derleth in 1962 while still a teenager. His first collection,* The Inhabitant of the Lake and Other Less Welcome Tenants *appeared from Arkham House two years later. Since that promising beginning, Campbell has established himself as a bestselling novelist* (The Parasite, Obsession), *short story author* (Demons By Daylight, Scared Stiff), *and editor* (New Terrors, Fine Frights). *His current novel is* Midnight Sun *(MacDonald). The following section is a chilling and suspenseful excerpt from Ramsey's forthcoming (late 1991) crime/terror novel,* The Count of Eleven.

THE COUNT
OF ELEVEN
RAMSEY CAMPBELL

Jack had just reached the edge of the village, where each side of the road bore a 30 on a pole, when a sports car red as a traffic light caught up with him. The driver, a flat-capped man with a puffy face, appeared to be mouthing at Jack. Was he drunk or mad? The car veered around the van as Jack slowed to the limit, and he realized from a snatch of music which the sports car left behind that the driver had been singing along with a car radio. It was too easy to call people mad; most folk—maybe everyone—must seem that way sometimes, especially when nobody was there to see them.

At the end of half a mile of semi-detached houses interrupted by a petrol station he turned right where the road forked. A humpbacked bridge led him to a steep road called The Rock, on which garden paths were carved out of the hillside which a row of houses climbed. Two blond children stood at a garden gate and watched a horse cantering up and down a field across the road. At the top Jack steered left at a crossroads and drove between scattered cottages until he reached a signpost indicating a walk over the brow of the hill. He urged the van up the steepest road yet and parked by a stile at the edge of a wood.

Two crows flapped croaking out of a tree as he walked around the van, and a transistor radio so muffled he could hear only the percussion of a rock song was playing in one of the houses on the slope he'd just conquered, but those were the sole signs of life. His timing seemed perfect. The locals were all in their houses, and in any case nobody would remark a vehicle which had been left at the start of the walk. He unlocked the rear doors of the van and wheeled the pram out, then he headed back towards the crossroads.

He had to dig his heels into the road all the way down the slope. The pram or its contents seemed more eager than ever to arrive at their destination. Pushing them uphill again might give him some trouble, except that now he felt ready for anything. But he wasn't ready to be hailed as he pushed the pram alongside the cottages at the foot of the slope. "Has the little man been up on the hill?" a woman was calling to him.

Jack turned, jerking the pram to a stop. She was in her seventies, wearing tweeds and muddy boots and leaning on an eccentric stick with which she thumped the tarmac as she bore down on him. "Sorry, who?" Jack stammered.

"The wee fellow. Been out for some air, has he?"

Jack was struggling to cope with his growing hilarity, wondering whether she was referring to some legend of fairies on the hill or accusing him of having exposed himself, when she halted in the middle of the road. "You men," she said, shaking her head. "You wouldn't know which end to put the nappy on if we didn't tell you which."

"Oh, you mean the baby," Jack said, rocking the pram as he used to rock Laura's to put her to sleep. "It's a girl, that's why I didn't know who you meant. I'd better keep moving in case she wakes."

He took one step, and the woman came thumping three-legged after him. "Don't cover up the poor mite like that. Here, let me show you how she ought to be."

"She's fine. That's how my wife has her in the pram. That's how she likes it herself," Jack said, walking and pushing, cursing the woman's rude rustic health that was letting her catch up with him. "And the doctor approves."

"I've never had to call a doctor in my life, and that's because I was always out in the fresh air. It's cruel to deny light and air to a child on a day like this."

She was still gaining on him. He imagined trying to outrun her, dashing away with the pram while she sprinted after him, waving her stick. That's me, Mr. Unobtrusive, he thought wildly as she said, "Can't I at least see her little face?"

"Believe me, you don't want to come face to face with this baby." He wasn't sure which of him might have said that, his old self or his new, but at once he knew what to say aloud. "She doesn't like being wakened by strangers. If you waken her she'll scream all the way home."

"Good heavens, I've had longer than you to learn how not to waken babies. I've put a good few to sleep in my time. I'm a nurse."

She was about to grab the pram, Jack thought. She would lift the cover, and then . . . At that moment he heard a car approaching swiftly up a side road just ahead of him. If the driver didn't see the old woman in the roadway . . . But she retreated to the corner of the junction and leaned on her stick, ready to take up the chase again as soon as the car passed.

Jack wheeled the pram past the junction while she was trapped by the car. "If it's all the same to you I won't take the risk," he called across the wake of fumes. "I'd have to answer to her mother when I got home."

If that didn't satisfy the woman it at least confirmed her opinion of him. "You men," she said, digging her stick into the triangle of verge at the junction as though she was thinking of launching herself after him, then contented herself with a parting shot. "What's her name?"

Jack took a long breath and released it through his nostrils. "Bernie," he said.

She didn't think much of that, and shook her head as she plodded down the side road. Jack watched her out of sight before he set off for the crossroads. He could already see his destination, a house standing by itself several hundred yards beyond the shimmering cross of tarmac. "Let's hope we won't need to wake you up, Bernie," he said.

The house was a steep-roofed block of red brick, almost featureless except for a satellite dish protruding from beneath the gutter like a toadstool from a tree. The large square garden was surrounded by a six-foot privet hedge. At first Jack thought the metallic gleam within the hedge was an illusion caused by the quivering of the air above the tarmac. He was almost at the gate before he realized that the inside of the hedge was reinforced with barbed wire. The plaque on the gate, which he'd assumed showed the name of the house, proved on closer acquaintance to say NO TRESPASSING. He pushed the pram across the gateway and stopped with one hand on the latch.

A wiry man dressed in slacks and sandals was lying on a striped recliner beside the cobbled path to the front door. One arm lay across his eyes, the other held a tumbler half full of what Jack deduced was gin and tonic balanced on his bushy chest. As Jack unlatched the gate the man raised his head and shaded his eyes to squint unwelcomingly at him. "Mr. Arrod?" Jack said.

"Nobody else here, so I must be."

"Stephen Arrod?"

"I've said so." He peered past Jack and saw the

pram. "Ah. No thank you," he said at once.

"Excuse me, what do you think you're saying no to?"

"Whatever. Newspaper, household goods, free samples. I want none of it, whatever it is."

"It's nothing like any of those."

"You aren't telling me you've got something for me to repair in there."

"In a way I suppose I have," Jack said, and pushed the pram through the gateway.

"You're a beggar, aren't you."

Jack assumed Arrod meant that to express some kind of grudging admiration; at least, he did until he turned from closing the gate and saw Arrod staring at the pram. "No trespassing means no beggars," Arrod said. "And if you think your brat can soften my heart you're out of luck."

"I'm not here to beg, Mr. Arrod."

"I don't want you here at all. You're interrupting my cocktail hour. And I especially don't allow brats on my property. I've taken enough pains to keep them out."

He was referring to the barbed wire, Jack thought, shivering. The shiver was at least partly of fear on Arrod's behalf. He pushed the pram towards Arrod, and felt the contents stir as the wheels trundled over the cobbles. "You'd be doing yourself a favor by listening to me," he said.

"I don't do favors for anyone. Incidentally, before you leave, how the devil do you know my name?"

"It was on the letter I sent you."

"What letter?"

"One like this," Jack said, reaching beneath the cover of the pram.

"Don't bother. Whatever it is, I don't want to know. The only thing I want to see is you out of the gate."

"Please, Mr. Arrod. For your own sake," Jack said, unfolding the letter.

"What the devil's my sake got to do with you?" Arrod swung his legs off the recliner and dumped the tumbler on the lawn, where it toppled over, spilling gin and ice cubes. "It's yourself you should be worrying about," he snarled. "Worry about what'll happen to you if you aren't gone before I call the police."

As Arrod shoved himself off the recliner Jack ran the pram along the path and used it to block the front door. "No need for that, Mr. Arrod. I haven't harmed you."

Arrod's face darkened so instantly it put Jack in mind of a special effect in a film. He lurched at Jack and trod on an ice cube. His sandaled foot slipped from beneath him, and Jack watched him sprawl backwards on the recliner, which gave way, depositing him on the ground with all his limbs flung out. Swallowing his mirth, Jack went towards him, the letter fluttering in his hand as a wind trembled the hedge. "Here, let me—"

Arrod screamed with rage and tried to heave himself to his feet, only to sprawl again. "Don't you come near me or it won't be the police who fetch you, it'll be an ambulance," he shouted. He managed to get his knees under him, and as he staggered upright he saw the letter Jack was holding. For a moment Jack thought the writhing of his face was a distortion caused by heat in the air. "It was you who sent me that, was it?" Arrod said.

"One like it."

"And what do you think happened to it?"

"I'm hoping you'll tell me."

"Shall I give you a hint? Shall I tell you what to do with the one you've got there? If you're so hard up, use it to wipe your brat's arse."

As he finished speaking he rushed at the pram and ripped back the cover. Jack imagined him doing that to a pram with a sleeping baby in it, and felt a grin tighten over his teeth. Arrod stared into the pram and turned to Jack, still staring. "What the blazes is this for?"

"I wish you hadn't done that, Mr. Arrod."

Arrod swung back to the pram and reached in.

"Who are these, my fellow victims?"

He had picked up the letters and was reading the names and addresses on the envelopes. Up to that moment Jack had intended to give him a choice, but now— "Put them down," he said through his teeth, and strode forwards. "They're none of your business."

Arrod dropped a handful of envelopes into the pram. Still peering at them, he seized the blowlamp from beside them and heaved it up with one hand. Apparently he meant to use it as a shield or weapon, but it's weight took him unawares. He let go of the the handle with an outraged cry as it bruised his fingers, and then he gave a howl which hurt Jack's ears. He'd dropped the blowlamp on one sandaled foot.

As the blowlamp rolled onto the grass Arrod hopped backwards wildly as if he could somehow outdistance the pain. He appeared to have no idea where he meant to go, except perhaps away from Jack. He didn't stop until he had backed into a corner of the hedge, where he began to struggle and jerk.

The wire fence must be electrified, Jack thought. Arrod's eyes bulged as he flung himself back and forth; even the hair on his head was quivering. Jack lifted the blowlamp with both hands and advanced on him. By now his jerking had grown so violent that in the midst of his uncontrollable hilarity Jack pitied him. He raised the blowlamp as high as his arms would reach and brought the tank down with all his strength on Arrod's skull.

He was afraid that a single blow wouldn't suffice, especially when Arrod stared at him with a mixture of disbelief and reproach as the dull knell of the impact contin- ued to sound in the tank. Perhaps that lasted only a second or two, but it seemed much longer. Then Arrod's eyes rolled up to show the whites, an effect Jack had thought was purely a cliché manufactured by films, and his head and torso slumped into the hedge.

His hair continued to quiver, and so did the top of

the hedge, in a wind. The fence wasn't electrified after all. The belt of Arrod's slacks had caught on the barbed wire; his jerking had been a desperate attempt to free himself. Jack had never seen such panic. At least he would be putting the man out of his misery, he thought, now that Arrod had read the envelopes and left him no choice. He put down the blowlamp and made sure that nobody was in sight; he jumped several times to see over the hedge. Then he stood upwind of Arrod and lit the gas with his lighter, and covered his nose and mouth with his free hand, and closed his eyes until he could see only the flame.

TOM ELLIOTT *is the
author of* The Dwelling
and the former publisher of
AFRAID: The Newsletter
for the Horror Professional.
*Elliott's main weapons
are a wonderful sense of
humor and a morbid
imagination, and the two
blend perfectly in the
following story—one of
the most original tales
you'll ever read.*

COLORADO GOTHIC
TOM ELLIOTT

I was down at Harley's Grain & Feed, warming my hands on the space heater on the counter, waiting for George Barton to finish jewing Harley down a nickel on a hundred-weight of cracked corn. Barton loved to haggle; rumor had it he made his wife charge him for sex just so he could talk her into giving it away. The feeling was just coming back into my fingers when I saw it.

At first I thought that Barton was growing a goiter on the back of his neck. That's what I thought it was: a misplaced goiter. A discolored, fleshy protuberance on the back of his neck. I watched in silence as it hung there, covering the back of his worn shirt collar, pulsating slightly.

Harley and George haggled on, oblivious to my

stare. Harley tired first, as he often does, and turned to get the hundred-weight while Barton slapped the countertop, chortling at besting Harley in the manly art of negotiation.

When Harley bent over to pick up the feed sack, I saw that he had one, too. Lighter colored than Barton's, but larger. It pulsated with the same rhythm.

Harley heaved the feed-sack up on the counter, and Barton was reaching for his wallet when the two of them froze; they turned as one and stared back at me.

Barton cleared his throat. "What's matter with *you*, Dearborn? You look like somebody just goosed you."

Harley chuckled at that, absently scratching the lump on his neck. The sound his fingers made against it reminded me of petting a cat on a dry day: that almost subliminal sound of a hundred tiny static discharges. Neither Harley nor Barton seemed aware of it.

I put on a grin and shrugged my shoulders. "Just had a chill, I guess," I said. I stood there with that stupid grin on my face until they returned to their business, then quietly made an exit.

Outside, the air was icy steel, that bitter bleak cold that sometimes hits the Colorado Rockies in February and makes you wish you lived in the Okeefenokee Swamp, or along the banks of the Amazon. A cold no amount of weather-stripping or insulation can keep out of the house. Normally that kind of cold makes for a dry spell, but looking up, I saw great, dark clouds dragging their snow-fat bellies over the mountains to the north. If it snows in this cold, I thought, it'll be a killer.

Barton came out of Harley's, the feed sack resting easily on his shoulder. From where I stood, it hid the fleshy lump George had somehow grown, but whether he'd done that purposely, I don't know.

He nodded at me, seemed about to say something, then apparently thought better of it, because he dropped the sack into the back of his battered, fenderless pickup and climbed into the cab.

As he was pulling out, he stopped the truck with a jerk and rolled down his window. "You joining the league this winter, Dearborn?"

I shook my head. "I'm not sure."

Barton made a *tsking* noise. "Harley's already polishing up his bowling ball. Me, I think I'm gonna get a new one." He eyed me speculatively. "Be a shame not to have you on the team."

"I'll have to think about it."

"Sure," he said. "But you oughta join. Ain't much else to do up here in winters. Man could go bug-fucked locked up in his house all winter."

"I'll keep that in mind, George."

He nodded curtly, then smiled, rubbing lightly at his lump. "See ya around, Dearborn." He rolled up his window and pulled out of the parking lot.

I stood there a long moment, watching his pickup disappear down Highway 285, until I remembered that I was supposed to pick up a few staples Janey wanted from the Pic N Sav.

The girl at the checkout stand had one, too.

It was smaller, rose-colored, almost pretty. She caught me staring at it and smiled self-consciously. Her hand rose to tug at her ponytail.

"Does it look all right?" she asked.

"What?"

She colored slightly. "I had a chestnut rinse put in down at the Hair Apparent yesterday, Mr. Dearborn. Do you like it?"

"Oh! Yes," I said quickly, and she smiled.

"That'll be eleven dollars and thirty-three cents," she said.

I paid her, and carried my groceries outside, but before I got to the truck I found myself dumping the bag and its contents into a litter can. When I got home, I told Janey I forgot to pick up the groceries.

She harrumphed, the way she does when I've forgotten to screw my head on right, and glanced out the window.

"I bet it's going to snow a nasty one tonight, Bill," she said. "Might take two days to plow the road between here and Bester, and me without any flour. I guess you'll have to have your gravy on stale store-bought instead of biscuits in the morning."

I agreed with her, shamefaced, and she went into the kitchen to finish making dinner. She didn't even notice how the 24-carat gold choker I'd given her for her birthday was starting to cut into the growing lump of flesh at the nape of her neck.

I couldn't sleep that night. Outside, the gathering clouds began dumping their burdens of snow on the valley while inside, I spent the passing hours fingering the back of my neck for any sign that I was growing a lump, as well. As far as I could tell, the skin was the same as it'd always been; through it I could feel the bumps of my spinal column. Janey snored softly beside me, and tentatively I touched the bloated sack of skin just below her hairline. It was hot, feverish, repulsive, like touching the swollen face of a corpse.

And this close, I could smell it. A fruity smell, like cantaloupes just starting to go bad in the refrigerator bin. The gold choker had nearly disappeared into the flesh, and I pressed down lightly on it to find the clasp. As I did, Janey moaned in her sleep, and I froze, wondering what I would say if she woke up. But her moan soon died and when she began snoring again, I carefully undid the clasp and pulled the choker from the valley it had made in her flesh. The ring it left was bloodless, white, and for nearly an hour it remained there, but when the alarm clock went off at 5:30, the white ring had disappeared.

But not the growth.

It had grown larger.

Janey was silent as she went about making breakfast. She put my plate in front of me and after pouring coffee for us both, she sat down.

"Aren't you going to eat?" she said, nodding at my plate.

I blew on the coffee. "Not real hungry this morning. Maybe I'm coming down with something."

She nodded, then looked thoughtful. "Have you seen my choker?"

I nearly spat out a mouthful of coffee. "What?" I sputtered.

"My choker, the one you gave me for my birthday. I was wearing it yesterday. I thought I had it on when I went to bed. But when I woke up this morning, it was gone."

I thought about lighting a cigarette, but didn't because I was afraid my hands might tremble. "Did you check the bed?"

She snorted. "Yes, Bill, I checked the bed. And under it. I've looked everywhere." Her expression grew pained. "I really *loved* that choker, Bill. It was the nicest gift you ever gave me."

I couldn't think of anything to say; I certainly wasn't going to tell her the choker was coiled up in my pants pocket.

I shrugged. "How's the weather?"

Janey pulled aside the kitchen curtains and scowled. "Still snowing solid as a wall. Is it going to let up today?"

I reached around and turned on the radio, but instead of KDZW, it blasted nothing but static.

"Storm must've knocked out power over north of town," I said, and turned the radio off.

I stood up and pulled on my parka. "Guess I'd better feed the livestock. Sounds like they're getting anxious." Outside, I could hear the cattle lowing in the storm like ghosts trapped between dimensions. I looked at Janey. "What you doing today?"

"Oh," she said, taking the breakfast plates to the sink, "I thought I might watch Donahue and my soaps, then, just before you come back in, spray a little Pledge behind my ears so you'll think I've been working."

I smiled at our old joke, and Janey offered her lips to kiss, but as I lowered my head I caught sight of her lump, and I hesitated.

Janey pulled back. "Bill, is something wrong?"

I gave her lips a peck. "No," I said. "Just worried about the storm."

"Uh-huh," she said uncertainly. After a moment, she returned to the sink to wash the dishes. I went outside.

That day passed slowly; it was impossible to tell the time because the storm reigned supreme, blotting out the sun. I'd hit my watch on the watering tank a few days previous; and it was stopped forever at 11:17. I'm not even sure why I was still wearing it.

I spent a few hours making sure the livestock were all in the corral, then reluctantly headed back to the house.

Janey was in our bedroom, sitting in front of her mother's antique vanity. She had her head turned and was obviously examining the lump of flesh on her neck, which had grown to nearly football size while I'd been feeding the animals.

She glanced around hurriedly when she saw me in the mirror. Her stare was blank.

"What's wrong?" I asked her.

She shook her head, and the lump jiggled gelidly. "Nothing's wrong, Bill. What makes you think anything's wrong?"

"What's that thing on your neck?"

"What thing?" As she spoke, her fingers brushed the growth gently, lovingly.

"Goddammit, Janey!" I shouted, "You *know* what I'm talking about!" I stomped over to her and grabbed the growth roughly. I felt it squirm beneath my fingers.

"*Don't*," she said, twisting away from me. "That hurts."

I let go; the growth retained the bruise-shape of my fingers for several seconds. "What's *happening* to you, Janey? What *is* that thing?"

She began brushing her hair. "I don't know *what* thing you're talking about, William Dearborn. You always get crabby when the weather's like this, you know. Well, I'm not going to let you take it out on me, not this time. You just go watch television or something until you cool down."

"Are you trying to tell me there's nothing wrong with your neck?"

"I'm telling you exactly that."

"If there's nothing on your neck," I said craftily, "then what was that I just grabbed?"

"You grabbed my *neck*, Bill."

"That thing on your neck has always been there, I suppose."

"There you go with this 'thing' again." She turned on the stool toward me, furious. "What's gotten into you?"

"What's gotten into *you* might be a better question!"

She snorted and threw up her hands in exasperation. "Go! Watch television! I refuse to argue with you!"

So I went into the living room and watched television, or, I should say, I turned it on and sat in front of it; I can't say what was on. Perhaps visual static, what the TV people call snow. I knew I was supposed to be doing something, but I didn't know what it was.

By bedtime I still had not come up with any reasonable explanation for the growths, and Janey climbed stonily in beside me, then reached out and flicked off the light. I put my hand on her shoulder, but she rolled over, her shoulder sliding out of my grasp. I sighed, rolled over, and went to sleep.

◊

The next day, the growth on Janey's neck was so large it was actually forcing her head down. From the front she looked like she might be praying; her chin nearly touched her throat.

"Are you going to tell me now that there's nothing wrong with your neck?"

"Oh, Bill, don't start up with me again." When she spoke, her voice was distant, as if heard through a long, metallic pipe.

By afternoon the growth had begun to show features, just some random bumps and hollows, really, but I could tell what it was becoming. Especially because Janey's head was beginning to sink into her throat.

I tried asking her about it, but apparently she could no longer talk, or at least no longer wished to. The eyes on her shrinking head just stared back at me balefully.

That night, I bunked on the couch, and listened to the storm howl in the darkness.

In the morning the growth sat firmly and resolutely atop Janey's throat; her real face was now nothing but discolored bruises on her throat—a horizontal one for her lips, an oblong one for her nose, and two dark depressions for her eyes.

The growth regarded me with cautious, alien eyes. "Honestly, Bill," the growth's mouth said, "How long are you going to keep this up? You've had your moods before, but never this long. It's been three *days*."

"I'm sorry, dear," I told the growth. "I guess this damn weather has really got my fur up."

The growth smiled at me forgivingly. "I think the storm's letting up; I heard Fergy's snow-plow out on the highway earlier. You ought to go into town and take care of that shopping you forgot."

"Yeah," I agreed. "Just let me finish my coffee."

"Anytime," the growth said.

◊

Fergy had indeed been by with the snow-plow; he'd had a job of it, if the snow banks on either side of the highway were any indication. The sign saying "The Elks #32 Welcomes You to Bester—Where the Rockies Kiss the Sky! Pop. 342" was nearly buried; only the twin stubs of the sawed-off telephone poles sticking out of the snow drifts proved the sign still existed.

At the Pic N Sav I loaded the grocery cart quickly, checking off Janey's list, then headed for the checkout stand. The same girl was running the register; on her throat were four finger-sized bruises: two horizontal, a vertical in between, then below that, another horizontal. The growth sat on her neck.

"That'll be eleven dollars and thirty-three cents," the growth said with a smile.

I paid her and headed out for my truck; this time I didn't throw the groceries away. The next stop was the feed store.

Harley's growth smiled at me as I walked in. "Better knock the snow off your boots, Bill," it said affably. "The floor's enough of a mess already."

I obediently kicked off chunks of dirty snow, then opened the door and kicked the chunks into the parking lot.

"Some coffee?" Harley's growth asked me, but I shook my head and continued to examine the side wall, the one Harley used to display the latest in saws and axes.

I knew from long experience with cattle that for my purposes, a fine-toothed saw would work best. Something that cleans itself as you work, because gristle and fat tend to clog the teeth rather quickly.

I found what I was looking for and carried it over to the counter.

Harley's growth examined it, then eyed me speculatively. "Look's like the Missus is making you work for a living."

I must have looked confused, because Harley's growth nodded at the saw, then glanced out the big window in the front of the store. "Every time it snows, the wife always finds projects for me to do around the house. Drives me buggy. Seems a fella can't even enjoy a day off ever' now and then."

"Oh," I said. "Yeah. Gotta fix a bad leg on the dining room table."

"Women," Harley's growth said in commiseration.

"Can't live with 'em," I said.

"Can't live without 'em," Harley's growth finished.

I paid for the saw and went home.

Janey's growth came off much easier than I expected; the saw was worth every penny I'd paid; it sank through Janey's neck like a hot knife through unripened cheese. When I was finished, I dropped the growth in a gunny sack, tossed it in the back of the truck, and headed for town. Only 340 to go.

It took me another three and a half days to do everyone else in Bester. Not that I had any trouble; in a small town like ours everybody knows everybody, and doors are never locked. Mary Thayer's growth looked up at me as I sawed, and its eyes glimmered with tears, but I'd already cut through the windpipe, so really, it couldn't say anything.

We didn't have a police force; hell, Bester didn't even have a post office (a wall with a few boxes in it at Harley's served us just fine). We were snowed in, and the only person with communication with the outside was Fergy, who worked part-time for the county plowing and salting the roads whenever necessary. I got to him by dinnertime, on the third day, while he and his wife were just sitting down to pot roast. I'd already worked out a routine for couples: I'd smack one with a ball-peen hammer that had been rattling around under the seat of my truck since time immemorial, then I'd saw off the other's head.

With Fergy and his wife taken care of, my work was

finished. I'd done Harley first for a specific reason: he had mounds of empty gunny sacks.

Three hundred and forty-one head-sized growths make one heck of a heap, and when I tossed in Fergy's and his wife's, they both rolled down and nearly dropped over the side, and I cursed myself for not thinking of putting on the stock racks before I'd begun.

But some rummaging behind the seat revealed a moth-eaten tarp, and I lashed that over the heap. It wouldn't hold for long, but it didn't need to. Fergy's was only a half-mile from Bud's Texaco.

At Bud's I backed the pickup into the mechanic's bay and cleared off the long workbench. It took me nearly ten minutes to find the keys to the compressor room (they were in Bud's overall pocket), and another five to figure out how to start it. Then, while the compressor filled the pressure tank, I began unloading the pickup. It might have gone faster, but the heads all insisted on watching me as I worked, their gimlet eyes swiveling to follow me as I crossed from the pickup bed to the bench and then back again. Gave me the willies.

I originally thought I'd be able to set them side-by-side, but three-hundred-plus severed heads take up more space than you'd imagine, and I had to squeeze them in tight, and even then I wound up making two rows. The seldom-used workbench was fuzzy with accumulated dust and oil and grease, and it bothered me that the gook was getting into the neck tissues of all the heads, but I guess it was a little late to worry about that sort of thing.

Just as I was setting George Barton's head on the bench the compressor kicked off, signaling a full pressure tank. Good. Up in the cab of the pickup I had about five dozen short lengths of airhose, and a heavy terminal block bristling with air nipples; it took nearly another hour to hook all the hoses up to the block.

Finally, I was done. The main air hose ran from the

pressure tank to the terminal block, where 20 smaller hoses carried air pressure up into the open windpipes of all those severed heads. I knelt by the terminal block and eyed the hose coming out of Barton's neck; when I was sure I had the right valve, I gave it a twist, and was rewarded with a satisfying hiss. I stepped over to the bench and put my ear next to Barton's lips to make sure the hiss wasn't coming from one of the other heads nearby.

Barton tried to bite me.

I stepped back a bit and gave him a cuff against his ear, and he nearly toppled over, but the head next to him—Harley's—stopped the roll. The sound of the two skulls smacking together reminded me of the sound a bowling ball makes as it comes up that chute in the floor and hits another. Barton's eyes teared up a little from the concussion.

"Why is this happening?" I asked him.

Instead of answering my question, Barton glanced at the tangle of air hoses around my feet. "I hope you didn't pay retail for those," he said.

"The hoses?"

Barton tried to nod, but of course that was a little impossible. "Yeah," he said finally.

"I didn't pay for these. I just took 'em."

Barton made his *tsking* noise, made all the more stern by the constant hiss of air between his teeth.

"Look, Barton," I said, "I'd love to price air hoses and such with you all day, but I've got other things to do. So you'd better answer my question."

Barton stared at me for a moment, probably calculating just how far he could push me. I stared back and it was he who lowered his eyes first. I felt a small tingle of triumph.

"I don't know," Barton said, and grinned.

"You're lying."

"Am I?"

"Don't try to be clever, Barton," I said. "You're in a hell of a fix here. If you want my help, you'll cooperate."

"You got me there," Barton admitted. "What do you want to know?"

"You heard my question the first time."

"Well, you're gonna have to tell me again. My memory ain't so good these days."

I sighed. "'Why is this happening?'"

"Oh, yeah. Well, my guess is that you went crazy and slaughtered everybody in town, and now you're trying to talk to the severed heads." Barton winked at me. "They'll say you're off your nut, you know."

"What about the growths?"

"What growths?"

This was going to take longer than I'd imagined. Not only that, but I was getting angry; that 'off your nut' crack had stung. I jerked the hose out of Barton's throat and stuck it into Harley's.

"Are you going to be Goofus, or are you going to be Gallant?"

"What the hell are you talking about?" Harley asked. The air hose made a tiny farting noise against the wet flesh in his throat, and he gave me a hurt look.

"You know," I explained, "Goofus is the bad boy, never does what he's told. Gallant's the good boy, the one who follows orders."

"Better put me down as Goofus, I s'pose."

I punched Harley in the forehead and the hose fell out of his windpipe; it lay hissing on the dirty garage floor. "Have it your way," I told him.

I spoke to every one of them in turn, and every one of them pretended not to know what I was talking about. Hester Smith, the librarian, wouldn't answer me at all; she kept harping about some book she says I checked out last year that was now way overdue.

After I'd wasted my time trying to get some answers from the heads, I got an idea. I went over to the terminal block and turned all the valves on; the steady hiss of air increased in volume, and then the twenty that were hooked up to air began to sing.

They started on "Tuxedo Junction" and then had a go at "Winter Wonderland." They were pretty good, for a bunch of severed heads.

I reached through the pickup window and laid heavy on the horn for about thirty seconds. That stopped them, mid-chorus, and when I let up on the horn they were all staring at me warily.

"Look," I said loudly. "If you don't want to cooperate, that's fine. You can sing songs until hell freezes over for all I care." I paused, studying each face in turn. My wife's head looked a little sad, and I thought maybe she was ready to crack, so I turned all the valves off but hers.

"I'll talk," she said before I'd had a chance to say anything. "I'll talk—but not here." She rolled her eyes to indicate that she didn't want to say anything in the company of all the other heads.

"Sorry, Janey," I said. "I don't see how you can talk without the air hose."

She smiled indulgently. "Doesn't Harley sell those little air tanks?"

"Yeah . . ."

"Well, silly, why don't you get one and hook the air hose thingy to me. That way, we can go anywhere you want. Someplace where we can *talk*," she added significantly.

I grabbed her head and hopped in the pickup. At Harley's I found the oxygen bottles and after a few minutes had her hooked up.

"Ahhh," she said. "You might want to wrap some duct tape around my neck, to make sure the hose doesn't fall out."

"Good idea," I said, and went back inside.

While I was looking for the duct tape, I had another idea. I imagined that Janey was getting cold; she didn't have a hat, and getting her blood circulating might be a little difficult, what with her body being a few miles away from her head. I rummaged through Harley's office until I found what I was looking for, then went back to the pickup.

"What's that for?"

I unzipped Harley's bowling-ball bag. "Thought you might be getting cold."

Janey's head smiled. "You're so thoughtful, Bill. Yes, I am a bit chilly."

I picked her up and set her down carefully so she could look out of the bag and see me. I wrapped the oxygen bottle in an old towel and shoved it in behind her.

"Well—?" I said when I was finished.

"Perfect," she said. "Bill, would you mind some advice?"

"Sure. What is it?"

"We'd better get out of town. This snow won't last forever, and by now I bet the Sheriff's Office down in Pine Bluff is getting curious about us."

I nodded. "Thanks, Janey. But right now, my main concern is finding out why all this is happening. Why did everybody in town grow a new head? And why not me?"

"That's easy, Bill. Nobody grew a new head. This is all in your imagination. You just slipped over the edge and killed a town full of innocent people."

"That's bullshit. I'd never do something like that."

"Okay. Have it your way, Bill. You always do."

"Let's just suppose for a minute that you're right. Why would I kill my friends?"

"Who knows why some people go crazy? You just snapped, Bill. Maybe it was my fault."

"Your fault?"

"Yes. Maybe if I'd been a little more aware, a little more sensitive, I could have helped you—"

"Wait a minute!" I interrupted. "You're just telling me what I want to hear!"

Janey's head smiled. "See? Doesn't that prove my point?"

"How do I know you're not just saying what I want to hear to put me off-base?"

"Why would I do that?"

"You tell me."

"I can't tell you anything you don't already know, Bill."

I started the pickup and jammed it into gear. "Then you know where we're headed."

Janey smiled again. "You're so romantic, Bill. We haven't been to Denver since our honeymoon."

That shook me, but I already had a plan forming, and I couldn't let her little tricks change my mind.

I stopped off at the sporting goods store and picked up another half-dozen bowling ball bags. Another stop at Bud's Texaco, and then I was on my way. A few places where the road hadn't been snow-plowed were hairy, but by sundown I was halfway to Denver.

I've been here in this apartment building for a week now, and the waiting is making me nervous. Ironically, though I'm here to stop the spread of the growths, they're my only company, and even though when I give them air they do their best to confound me, it still beats sitting around with nobody to talk to. I sometimes have to turn off Harley and Barton's air, though: they *love* to argue. Any topic will do.

Most of the time, though, they sing for me. I even sing along, when I know the words. I'm developing a nice baritone. At least that's what Janey says.

Today, I was feeling a bit low, beginning to wonder if I'd made the right decision coming here to the big city. Truth is, I was ready to give up, until the girl in the apartment next to me knocked on the door to borrow some flour.

"You a bowling ball salesman or something?" she said as I led her through the living room to the kitchen.

"Yeah," I said. "How much flour do you think you'll need?"

"The recipe just calls for a cup."

My hands were shaking as I measured it out. After all this time with no human contact, I was afraid to look at her.

"Thanks," she said on the way back to the door. "You're a life-saver."

I nodded.

"Say," she said suddenly, "I'm having a party tonight. Just some other people from the apartments. Would you like to come?"

"Sure," I said, and she smiled.

"It's a date then. Seven o'clock, okay?"

I nodded, unable to trust my voice. She stepped out into the hallway.

And gave me a perfect view of the discolored mole at the nape of her neck. It pulsated rhythmically.

I locked my door, unzipped all the bags, and switched on the oxygen tanks. They were all in particularly fine spirits, and together we did a rousing *a capella* version of "It Had To Be You."